OBSESSION

By

Monica Burns

Erotic Historical Romance

New Concepts   Georgia

Be sure to check out our website for the very best in fiction at fantastic prices!

When you visit our webpage, you can:
* Read excerpts of currently available books
* View cover art of upcoming books and current releases
* Find out more about the talented artists who capture the magic of the writer's imagination on the covers
* Order books from our backlist
* Find out the latest NCP and author news--including any upcoming book signings by your favorite NCP author
* Read author bios and reviews of our books
* Get NCP submission guidelines
* And so much more!

We offer a 20% discount on all new Trade Paperback releases ordered from our website!

Be sure to visit our webpage to find the best deals in e-books and paperbacks! To find out about our new releases as soon as they are available, please be sure to sign up for our newsletter (http://www.newconceptspublishing.com/newsletter.htm) or join our reader group (http://groups.yahoo.com/group/new_concepts_pub/join)!

The newsletter is available by double opt in only and our customer information is *never* shared!

Visit our webpage at:
www.newconceptspublishing.com

Obsession is an original publication of NCP. This work has never before appeared in book form. This work is a novel. Any similarity to actual persons or events is purely coincidental.

New Concepts Publishing, Inc.
5202 Humphreys Rd.
Lake Park, GA 31636

ISBN 1-58608-844-0
© 2006 Monica Burns
Cover art (c) copyright 2006 Eliza Black

All rights reserved, which includes the right to reproduce this book or portions thereof in any form whatsoever except as provided by the U.S. Copyright Law.

If you purchased this book without a cover you should be aware this book is stolen property.

NCP books are available at special quantity discounts for bulk purchases for sales promotions, premiums, fund raising, or educational use. For details, write, email, or phone New Concepts Publishing, Inc., 5202 Humphreys Rd., Lake Park, GA 31636; Ph. 229-257-0367, Fax 229-219-1097; orders@newconceptspublishing.com.

First NCP Trade Paperback Printing: October 2006

Chapter 1

London, 1888

The inside of Chantrel's was quiet as a tomb as Sebastian Rockwood, Earl of Melton stepped through the establishment's front door. Popular among men of the peerage, the exclusive brothel was known for its unique offerings. The sole proprietor of her establishment, Chantrel, trained her girls to speak and act like women of nobility, except in the bedroom. There, her pupils performed with an enthusiasm that was often lacking in the lives of most noblemen.

Sebastian handed his top hat and cane to the footman on duty as he asked to see the owner. As the servant hurried off, he turned to survey the empty parlor opening off the foyer. Why would the brothel be so quiet at this time of night? The man next to him cleared his throat.

"Bad business this, if what Caleb says is true," said Devin Morehouse, Viscount Westbrook.

With a sharp nod of agreement at his friend's observation, Sebastian frowned. The occasional mistress easily addressed his sexual needs, so his knowledge of Chantrel's was by reputation only. In fact, the only reason he'd even agreed to visit the place tonight was to keep his younger brother from doing something rash.

Earlier this afternoon, in typical Rockwood fashion, Caleb had stormed into Sebastian's office like a man possessed. Unlike his siblings, controlling his emotions was a skill Sebastian had learned a long time ago. He could only wish his siblings would do the same.

It had taken him more than a quarter of an hour to learn that Caleb's ladylove had been missing for more than a day. From what little information his brother had provided him, the girl had uncovered evidence of brothels kidnapping innocent young women and selling them against their will.

"I doubt the girl is here," he murmured. "But I truly believe Caleb would have torn this place apart if I hadn't agreed to come this evening.

"Unlike his older brother's controlled and methodical approach, of course." Wry amusement threaded his friend's words. Sebastian arched his eyebrow in response to the jibe.

"There's a great deal to be said for exercising restraint in all matters."

Looking around, he studied his surroundings closely. The silence in the brothel wasn't just unusual, it made him uneasy. Something about this place set his teeth on edge, and for the first time since Caleb had burst into his study, he realized his brother's worst fears might well be true. It was quite possible his brother's ladylove was in grave danger. Leaning toward his friend, Sebastian tipped his head in the direction of the blue and gold salon adjacent to the foyer.

"I'm beginning to wonder if we're even in a brothel given the selection is decidedly nonexistent."

"I agree," Devin nodded. "Usually a fellow can expect at least one or two ladies available for the unexpected customer. Is it possible the murder in Whitechapel yesterday is affecting business?"

Sebastian considered the possibility. Although the murder of the Nichols woman had been more brutal than most slayings, he wasn't sure the incident would have been enough to threaten the daily business of a well-known brothel like Chantrel's. If this were any other house of ill repute, he might think business was bad, but this wasn't just any brothel. The exclusivity of it set the house apart from any other of its kind. There had to be another reason why the parlor was empty.

He shrugged as the sound of a door opening made him turn his head. A statuesque woman passed through the doorway. Sailing into the foyer, she presented the picture of a figurehead on a sailing ship. Swathed in red taffeta and gold fringe trim, the gown brazenly proclaimed her for the madame she was with its decadent sleeves and low cut bodice. The taffeta, draped artfully over her bustle, rustled softly as she moved toward them.

Madame Chantrel greeted them with a smile and a look of speculation in her eyes. "Lord Melton, you honor me with your presence. What may I do for you this evening?"

Sebastian bent over the hand she extended to him, his lips brushing the air over Chantrel's knuckles. "My friend and I were hoping for some special entertainment this evening. Naturally, I thought of you and your ability to offer us something unusual ... different."

As he straightened, he watched the woman's face. Hesitation and avarice flitted across her features. Avarice won out as her eyes narrowed slightly. The hesitation was enough to increase his concerns. Damnation, if Caleb were correct, it would not be easy finding the girl or proving the brothel was involved in selling women against their will.

"Actually, my lord, we have a most unusual form of

entertainment tonight." Chantrel smoothed the tight fitting material swathed around her waist. "My guests this evening are my most frequent patrons, but there is always room for fine gentlemen such as the two of you. I think you both might find it amusing. Won't you come this way?"

With a practiced sweep of her hand and the skill of any noblewoman, Chantrel ushered them into a large salon. Red and gold couches, divans and chairs littered the room, serving as seating for the twenty or more men lounging about. Dark cherry walls, trimmed with gold molding, gave the room a heavy, decadent air.

Studying the room's occupants, Sebastian only recognized two or three men. The others were strangers to him. To his disgust, he noticed the Marquess of Templeton standing in one corner of the room. A notorious gambler and womanizer, the man's luck was exceeded only by his bad temper.

The last time Sebastian had met the man, it had been across the card table. It had been a pleasurable experience--beating the man at cards--but he realized he'd also made an enemy. Templeton hated to lose.

"Templeton," he muttered to Devin who stood at his side. "If he's here, we can expect something perverted."

The brothel owner had excused herself and moved to stand at the foot of a small dais shrouded by a burgundy velvet curtain. Clapping her hands, the woman smiled at her patrons.

"Gentlemen, my lords, if you please. I'm delighted you could join us this evening as we have something highly unusual and special for your enjoyment." The woman turned and nodded her head at a tall, slender man standing at a nearby door who immediately tugged on a gold rope. A smile on her face, Chantrel turned back to the men in the room. "Tonight, I'd like to offer up for auction a delectable flower, ripe for the picking."

As the brothel owner spoke, the curtain behind her slowly parted to reveal a woman seated on a gilded chair of immense proportions. A flowing, white silk chemise barely covered the woman's lush body. To his surprise, Sebastian's groin responded to the sight immediately.

Seated in the chair with her legs slanted to one side, her figure was luxuriant, exotic and tempting. The delicate chemise, deliberately cut to reveal a long expanse of leg, hinted of more treasures beneath. Even from a distance, the woman's enticing legs looked soft as silk.

Red color heightened the fullness of her mouth, and it tugged at him, filling his head with images of her pleasuring him with those delectable lips. Lustrous locks the color of uncut wheat tumbled down over creamy shoulders in soft curls. The thought of entwining his hand in her hair, while his other hand traced the sensuous curve of her thigh, was more than just a pleasurable thought. It excited him. The prospect of being the first to introduce this siren to the decadent and erotic delights of sex was intoxicating. The thought made his cock stir like an unruly beast. He swallowed hard. What the devil was wrong with him? He'd come here in search of Caleb's ladylove, not to contemplate buying a woman. Despite reminding himself of his reasons for being in the brothel, it was impossible not to notice the succulent shape of her breasts.

Barely hidden by the transparency of her white chemise, her breasts were full, and his palm itched to cup them. The thought of suckling on those dusky peaks produced a knot in his throat, which he immediately tried to swallow. Damnation, he was hard as rock. It had been a long time since he'd been this aroused simply from looking at a woman.

Determined to regain control of his senses and libido, he focused his attention on the woman's face. She reminded him of someone, but he couldn't recall whom. Could this be Caleb's woman? Mentally, he shook his head. No, his brother had described his sweetheart as having dark hair.

His gaze returned to the woman's red, sensuous lips and the way they parted in such an inviting manner. The thought of tasting the sweetness of her mouth tightened the muscles in his groin. Just as quickly as the image flittered through his head, he knew the girl was far from willing. The seductive pout she wore was an illusion.

Revulsion, not enticement, gleamed in her wide green eyes. The repugnance in her gaze had to be the reason for her rapid breathing. Yet she didn't try to escape. She simply sat on the dais' throne with a mixture of panic, disgust and a blazing anger glowing in her luminous eyes.

"Who'll start the bidding for one night with this rare creature, gentleman? Who will be the first to introduce her to the art of lovemaking? Do I hear a starting bid of one hundred pounds?"

"A hundred pounds," a stout gentleman shouted.

"Two hundred," another voice called out.

"Good God," Devin growled beneath his breath. "Caleb was right about the auctions. Now what in the hell do we do?"

Sebastian's stomach knotted with disgust. The disgust in Devin's voice matched his own inner turmoil. Thank God, he'd convinced Caleb to let him investigate the matter. The moment this auction had started, his brother would have begun tearing the place apart without any thought to his safety or the girl's.

Somehow, he needed to discover whether Chantrel had already auctioned off the girl or if she was even in the brothel. Either way, they needed information before they did anything. If the girl was still here, she could easily be spirited away. Should Chantrel suspect someone was about to expose her illegal, yet lucrative, side business, she would remove any incriminating evidence.

Chantrel wouldn't be the first madame to hold a woman prisoner and sell her to the highest bidder. However, the laws had changed, and this type of crime carried a stiff penalty. Was Chantrel involved with other brothels in this scheme or was she practicing this unsavory business alone? And the woman? His gaze returned to the tempting vision in white. What was her story?

"Five hundred pounds." Lust and something else filled Lord Templeton's voice. Sebastian turned his head to study the man's salacious expression. The marquess licked his lips in a lascivious manner. Sebastian had never cared for the man, and now he understood why. There was something malevolent about Templeton.

Beside him, Devin shook his head in disgust as the bidding continued. "I've seen enough. I'm leaving."

Sebastian didn't answer as Templeton raised the stakes one more time over another bidder. The way the bidding was going, the Marquess would soon add another filly to his debauched stable of women. His gaze returned to woman on the dais. Something about her tugged at him--prevented him from leaving. How could he possibly leave here without saving her from a fate worse than death?

Templeton's reputation for sordid sexual acts was well known. The image of her at the Marquess' mercy twisted his insides. He was certain he'd feel this way if it was any other woman on the dais. The voice to the contrary was quickly silenced.

"A thousand pounds." The Marquess' bid drew a gasp from the men, and the room went silent.

"One thousand pounds, gentlemen. I have one thousand pounds to Lord Templeton. Do I have any other bidders? One thousand going once, twice--"

"Two thousand."

Sebastian couldn't believe his ears. He'd actually placed a bid on the woman. Had he lost his mind? The back of his neck tingled with the weight of censorious eyes. He didn't have to turn around to know what his friend thought about his behavior. If anyone was astounded, it was he.

Tightening his mouth, he slid a glance toward Templeton. The man was livid. So he'd managed to unbalance the marquess. He smiled, savoring the pleasurable sensation. Chantrel, extremely pleased by this new competition, smiled broadly at Sebastian.

"Two thousand pounds to Lord Melton, do I hear any other bids? Going once, going twice--"

"Three thousand," Templeton snarled.

"Five." Sebastian didn't hesitate. Silence filled the room, and he slowly turned his head toward the marquess. The other man's face was beet red with fury. Sebastian studied him in silence, taking care to keep his own features impassive. Templeton shook his head at Chantrel.

"I have five thousand, do I hear more? Going once, going twice, sold to Lord Melton for five thousand pounds."

The room erupted into a loud frenzy of conversation. At his side, Devin hissed. "For God's sake, Sebastian. Do you realize what you've just done?"

"*Yes*."

Devin stared at him in open mouth astonishment, but Sebastian turned away to watch Chantrel approach. Steeling himself for the matter at hand, he bowed as she stopped in front of him.

"My lord, you surprise me. I expected Helen to enchant everyone, but for you to pay so much for her, I never would have guessed it."

Studying Chantrel's jaded features he frowned. Something about her reminded him of a well-fed cat expecting to indulge in consuming the mouse once it finished playing with the creature. Forcing himself to smile, he bowed. "Might we discuss our business arrangement in private?"

"But of course, my lord." The woman laughed, her eyes gleaming with calculation. With a grim smile, he followed her out of the salon. As they walked down a narrow hallway, the train of her gown forced him to stay at least three feet behind her. Entering a private office, he took a seat as Chantrel skirted a large oak desk to sit before him. The room's lack of ornamentation reminded him this was the seedier side of the business.

"Now then, my lord, shall we discuss the matter of payment?"

"Of course, I believe the bid was five thousand?"

"Yes, my lord, and I know you'll find it money well spent."

"I'm sure." He nodded with derision. "Naturally, you'll allow me to pay another thousand to take the creature off your hands permanently."

The brothel owner started violently, her eyes narrowing. "I'm not sure I understand, my lord. The auction was for one night with Helen and nothing more."

"Of course, but no doubt you're an astute businesswoman, Chantrel. I'm sure you'll agree that for an additional one thousand pounds, you'll give--Helen did you say--into my care permanently. I'd hate to see you lose any money over such a lucrative transaction as this."

"I don't see how I could possibly lose any money, my lord."

"Don't you? I'm certain a business such as yours relies heavily on the discretion of its clientele when it comes to special events." Sebastian flicked an imaginary piece of lint from the black broadcloth of his jacket before sending the woman a hard look. "It would be a tragedy if one of your patrons disclosed unsavory information to the authorities."

He looked up to see the woman glaring at him, but there was a hint of fear in her eyes as well. When she didn't respond, he pulled a wallet from inside his jacket. Removing a calling card, he leaned forward and picked up the fountain pen on Chantrel's desk. With fluid strokes, he wrote his marker on the back of the card and slid it across the desktop toward her.

"Have Helen and all her possessions placed in my carriage immediately." He rose to his feet and headed toward the door.

"It appears you leave me with little choice, my lord." Chantrel snapped.

Ignoring the woman's bitterness he left the office, the door closing quietly behind him. He moved down the corridor to the front hall at a furious pace. He was acting completely out of character tonight. What was he thinking to buy a woman like a prize mare? Reaching the foyer, he snapped his fingers at a nearby footman and demanded his overcoat. As the servant scurried away, Devin emerged from the salon, his face grim.

"So have you settled your account?" Devin sent him a look of disgusted disappointment.

"Yes." Sebastian nodded. He chafed at the expression on his friend's face. It wasn't as if he intended to bed his expensive purchase. Although the tantalizing thought had definitely presented itself.

"What the hell were you thinking to bid on the woman like that?"

"I couldn't bloody well let Templeton have her, could I?" Sebastian shot a glare in the direction of his friend. Retrieving his favorite watch from his vest pocket, he examined the face of the timepiece then snapped it closed.

"But what happens to her after tonight? In case you didn't hear Chantrel, the auction was for only one night with the woman." Ignoring his friend's grim disapproval, Sebastian accepted his hat, cane and gloves from the footman. "The auction might have been for one night, but I bought her freedom."

His friend stared at him with his mouth agape. Somehow, Devin's stupor rankled deeper than he thought possible. Did people really think him devoid of compassion? Simply because he was meticulous and methodical didn't mean he couldn't feel sympathy for those in need. In all good conscience, he couldn't have just left the woman for Templeton.

Angry, he scowled at his friend and the footman who was curiously watching their exchange. His behavior in the past hour had been irrational and impulsive--the exact opposite to his usual manner. It was infuriating.

"And now that you've bought her freedom, what to you intend to do with her? You can't just throw her out onto the street," Devin snapped.

"Damn it, man, I might prefer to live my life without the galling encumbrances of a wife, but I'm not completely without sympathy for the woman's situation." He tugged his white evening gloves on in a deliberate fashion and kept his eyes averted. "Now if you'll excuse me, I must see to my prize. Although heaven knows what I've gotten myself into."

The last part of his statement he muttered beneath his breath as he strode out the front entrance of the brothel and down the steps to pace the sidewalk as he waited on his carriage. Damnation. What had he been thinking when he'd bid on the woman?

Templeton. He'd been thinking about how pleasurable it would be to steal the man's prize out from under his nose. And it was quite understandable why the Marquess had wanted the woman. Images of a voluptuous thigh and full breasts teased his thoughts. God almighty. Had he really bought the woman out of pity or was it because he wanted to rut with her. His body tensed at the erotic images darting through his head. Suppressing a groan, he tried to think about where he could send the woman. A place where she'd have the opportunity to make a respectable living.

The sound of his shoes scraping against the stone walkway grated on him, much in the way the entire day had. Attending to the woman's needs was the first order of business, then he had to formulate some type of plan to see if Chantrel was holding Caleb's ladylove hostage. Heaving a sigh, he frowned as the face of the woman he'd just bought filled his head. There was something very familiar about her. Where had he seen her before? He shrugged with exasperation. It would come to him eventually.

His pacing ceased at the sound of carriage wheels rumbling over cobblestone. What had happened to the self-control he prided himself on? The rest of the Rockwoods were habitual in their irrational behavior, but not him. Not since childhood, had he succumbed to such illogical or unexpected deportment. Behind him, he heard Devin leaving the establishment. The memory of his friend's censure still stung as the man stopped at his side.

"Sebastian, I apologize for doubting your intentions. You did right by the woman."

"Perhaps," he replied gruffly without looking at his friend. "Then again, perhaps not. We both know what sort of man I am, Devin. I've never had much patience with women, and I'm too old to start now."

"Good God, Sebastian." Devin laughed. "You're only thirty. Hardly a doddering old man."

Far from feeling humorous about his present situation, he opened the door of his carriage as it halted in front of him.

"Then why the hell do I feel so Goddamn old?" He choked out with restrained frustration. "I'm not equipped to deal with a female guaranteed to wilt at the sound of my voice."

Without waiting for an answer, he climbed into the vehicle and threw himself onto the padded leather seat. Across from him sat his high-priced acquisition. He barely cast a glance in her direction before staring out the window. What in the blue blazes was he going to do with her?

He sighed wearily and closed his eyes. With the addition of the woman to his household, his schedule would be in shambles tomorrow. He'd somehow have to see to her clothing, determine what skills she possessed and then seek possible employment for her. Why the devil hadn't he just contacted the police? Then the woman would be someone else's problem. The answer irritated him. He didn't want her to be someone else's problem. For some strange reason, he wanted to protect her.

Furious with himself, he clenched his jaw. It was quite simple, he was mad with lust. The woman had teased his senses and he'd had no choice but to buy her. But now he was in his right mind again. He swung his gaze back to the woman opposite him. A veil obscured her features, and it made her even more enticing.

She hadn't moved since he'd climbed into the carriage. Come to think of it, she'd not even uttered a sound. What was wrong with her? Something inside him stirred. He wanted to see that succulent figure of hers again. See those wide green eyes. See if she truly was worth the five thousand--no, six thousand pounds he'd paid. After all, forbidden fruit always stimulated the senses.

"Lift your veil," he said in a tight voice. She didn't move. Sebastian bit the inside of his cheek. The woman wasn't going to make things easy for him, was she? Didn't she realize he was trying to help her? "Damn it, woman. I want to see what my money bought me."

Still she didn't stir. She could have been a statue if not for the soft flutter of her veil as she breathed. Outside, the clouds parted and moonlight suddenly streamed through the carriage window. The cape she wore had fallen open to reveal her voluptuous curves, and he sucked in a sharp breath as the glow of the moon poured over her.

Up close, her body was every bit as sensuous as he'd imagined. His gaze lingered on the rose-colored tips of her breasts. They were stiff beneath the sheer fabric, and his fingers itched to touch her. Would those delicious nipples taste hot against his tongue? Tasting her right now would give him more pleasure than he'd had in a long time. Far too long. It had been months since he'd parted with his last mistress. That's why this woman had captured his interest. She intrigued him. Tempted him. Christ Jesus, how she tempted him.

Just the sight of her wearing next to nothing made him rock hard. His gaze dropped to the dark triangle of hair peeking through the sheer white fabric of her chemise, just at the apex of her thighs. The thought of filling her with his cock made his mouth go dry. He wanted her. He couldn't remember the last time he'd wanted a woman as badly as he wanted this one. Mesmerized by the erotic visions flashing through his head, his hand stretched out toward her.

His fingertips lightly brushed across one nipple, before he came to his senses. Bloody hell, he'd lost his mind. He'd rescued her from Templeton to spare her just this sort of unwelcome attention. Now he was acting no better than the Marquess. Aggravation made him grit his teeth. With a jerk, he reached up to pull the veil away from her face. A cloud passed over the moon, casting her features into the shadows. When moonlight drifted through the window once more, he stared at the face he'd witnessed earlier. Society would never deem her a classic beauty, but there was something compelling and familiar about her large, almond-shaped eyes. Where the devil had he seen her before? Outrage glistened in the deep green of her eyes, and he waved his hand in a gesture of exasperation.

"I'm not going to eat you, woman." Although that was exactly what he wanted to do. He wanted to slide his mouth over every inch her, suckle her nipples until she cried out with pleasure, stroke that tender nub between her folds and he wanted to taste her hot cream. He wanted to taste her on his tongue, the heat of her, the bite of her desire.

He watched her, looking for a response, but she didn't even

wince at his harsh tone. Frustration evident in her green eyes, a single tear escaped to trickle down a pale cheek. Bloody hell, she was going to cry. The last thing he needed was a woman bawling in his carriage. The memory of the auction made him heave a sigh. He supposed it was to be expected.

She reminded him of his sisters when they were upset. How many times had he wiped tears off Louisa's cheek, in particular? The baby in the family, Louisa was always trailing after him like a puppy. High-spirited, incorrigible and loyal was a good way to describe his youngest sister. But even when Louisa or one of his other sisters cried, he wanted to leave the room until they stopped wailing. It was damned uncomfortable listening to them sob.

Aggravated, he abruptly stretched out his hand to wipe the tear away. Fury and frustration flared in the woman's eyes, but she didn't flinch or turn away from him. The expression in her eyes made him frown. If she didn't want him to wipe her tears away, why didn't she-- Damnation. She'd been drugged. Chantrel had used sweet vitriol or some other narcotic to immobilize her prize. The moment he figured out how to rescue Caleb's beloved, he'd bring the brothel madame to her knees and her business along with her.

Flinging himself back against the black leather seat, he folded his arms. He was struck by the fact that her eyes told him more than he ever thought possible. Outrage remained, but hope flickered in the beautiful eyes fixed on his face.

"Damn!" Out of habit, he pulled his watch from his white vest and flipped it open. The feel of the gold pocket watch against the pads of his fingers always soothed him. Noting the time, he tucked it back into his pocket. "It appears Chantrel's drug has rendered you immobile and speechless. Can you possibly blink your eyes?"

Relief lit her gaze and he saw her eyelids blink once. Satisfied they were finally getting somewhere, he nodded sharply. "Excellent. One blink is yes, two is no. Understood?"

Another blink of her eyelids answered his question. His mouth curled in a slight smile. "You're quick. I like that."

Irritation flared in her gaze, and he grinned. "I must admit, I don't think I've ever been in such a fortunate position before. That is--being in the company of a woman who doesn't talk, for whatever reason."

He chuckled at the daggers her eyes threw his way. Raising his hands in a surrendering gesture, he shook his head. "Fair enough, I'll restrict my comments until you've regained use of your tongue."

Contempt darkened her gaze and the moonlight reflected the gold sparks glinting in her eyes. The look she gave him would have been lethal if it had been a weapon. It didn't matter. He enjoyed watching the entrancing sparks of outrage illuminating her eyes. Sweet mother of God, he'd truly lost his senses. Maudlin rubbish is what it really was. He needed to remain focused on the business at hand

"Is your name really Helen?" He paused. The affirmative response allowed him to proceed. "Do you have family?"

The fear in her eyes permeated the carriage as she blinked once. He frowned. "Mother? All right, Father?"

Once more, she blinked twice. Her agitation increased, and he saw her lips twitch as if she was desperately fighting the drug that controlled her. A garbled sound tumbled from her lips. "Eh ... erd"

"What? I don't understand."

Panic flickered in her eyes as she silently pleaded with him to comprehend. He sighed. It would be some time before she was coherent. With a comforting gesture, he leaned forward and squeezed her hand.

"It's all right. The drug should wear off by morning. We'll sort everything out then."

The coach jerked to a halt and Sebastian climbed out of the vehicle. The lights of Melton House were a soft glow on the side of the carriage as he leaned back inside and lifted Helen into his arms. As he strode up the steps into the town home, he tried to ignore the way her body warmed his in all the wrong places. The sooner he found a safe haven for her, the better. If he waited too long, his prized control might easily slip with this woman. And that was unacceptable.

Chapter 2

Helen stirred beneath a warm blanket. A fierce thumping pounded her head with vengeance, and she moaned. Raising a hand to her throbbing brow, she forced herself to sit up. Eyes squeezed shut against the pain; she gently massaged her aching temples.

"Oh, Miss! You're awake at last."

Her eyes flew open to see a young girl at the foot of the bed. Confused, she blinked. Where was she? Strange, jumbled images flooded her head, and she moaned again. Dear lord, but her head hurt. No wonder, given the horrible nightmares she'd suffered throughout the night.

"Where am I?" Her voiced sounded so hoarse. It was almost a croak.

"Melton House, Miss. His Lordship asked that you be shown to the library by nine this morning."

Melton. Where had she heard that name before? Last night. She'd heard it last night when Madame Chantrel--Oh, dear God, it hadn't been a nightmare. She really had been bought and sold. *He'd* bought her. Of all the images mixed up in her head, his face was the only one that wasn't a blur. Tall and broad shouldered, he had stood out amidst the small crowd of men last night. Those black eyes of his, blazing with fire in the darkness. It had been as if he wanted to devour her.

She inhaled a sharp breath. He'd touched her. One hand resting against her throat, a tremor ran through her. His thumb had brushed across her nipple. Teasing what little senses she possessed at the time. She swallowed hard. Why had he bought her? What did he want from her? She exhaled a small sound of self-disgust. That was a ridiculous question to ask herself. The man had bought her in a brothel, just because he seemed in no hurry to take what he'd paid for didn't change his intentions.

"Come along now, Miss, his lordship don't like to be kept waiting." The petite maid clucked as she urged Helen to her feet.

"Lord Melton ... is this his house?"

"That it is, Miss. The man has his hands full with all of his sisters living here with him. It's good that his brothers have their own livings over near Bond Street."

"Is there a Lady Melton?" The moment she asked the question, she winced. If the man was married, it was doubtful he'd bring in a stray from a brothel auction.

"Oh, heavens no, Miss. His lordship doesn't have the patience for women. He says he'll never marry." Busy shaking out a yellow silk gown draped over a folding screen, the maid laughed. "Although it's a pity. Quite the handsome one he is. And those eyes, mercy me, they're enough to make a girl melt right where she stands."

Helen bit her lip. The maid was right. The man's eyes were hypnotic. In the carriage last night, his eyes had caressed her the way a lover might. His gaze had explored every visible part of her body, until the blaze in his eyes had threatened to consume her. Then, as if he'd suddenly realized he'd revealed too much, he'd retreated behind a mask of indifference. The mask had slipped only when he'd expressed amusement at her inability to voice her protests.

"The earl is a real stickler for time, Miss, so I'll go get your breakfast while you freshen up. I've brought you one of Miss Louisa's gowns. I'm sure it will fit you since the two of you are about the same size."

"Miss Louisa?" Helen used the heel of her palm to apply pressure to the spot just above the bridge of her nose. Lord, but her head throbbed like a church bell.

"Yes, Miss. She's the youngest of the Rockwoods. And the most mischievous of the lot. His Lordship's had a devil of a time with her over the last year." The maid looked at a small watch pinned to her bodice. "Lord, love me. I'll be hearing his Lordship holler if I don't have you downstairs in less than an hour. Go on now, freshen up and I'll be back shortly with your breakfast."

Helen slid out of bed as the girl darted from the room. For the first time since waking, she took in her surroundings. She liked the simplicity of the bedroom. White gauze draped softly from the bed's canopy, its filmy lightness echoed in the window's curtains. Next to the dressing screen stood a washstand, while a dressing table with a mirror reflected her image back at her.

She grimaced at her tousled hair. Brushing out the knots would take time. To the right of the bed was a small fireplace with a marble mantle. Except for a small clock, the mantle was devoid of any ornamentation. The sight of the timepiece reminded her of how nervous the maid had been about being on time. Clearly, the earl ran a precise household. Her mouth tightened with pessimism. A man of time usually meant a man devoted to rules. She had no use for men and their rules. It was the reason she'd fled Mayfield with Edward.

"Oh my God! Edward." Her stomach gave a sickening lurch. Sinking onto the mattress, she pressed the back of her hand to her mouth as bile rose in her throat. How could she have forgotten her brother until now? Where was he? Had the earl sent for him? She needed to know Edward was safe. With a movement born of fear, she sprang to her feet and hurried to the washstand.

The cool water chilled her as it splashed over her skin. It was a vivid reminder of her fear. In short order, she performed her ministrations and proceeded to pull on the pantaloons and the bustle petticoat provided. The yellow silk dress rustled quietly as she pulled the gown over her head.

Despite the softness of the gown's fabric, it scraped painfully across her skin. Swallowing the urge to cry out, she clenched her teeth as she waited for the fire to subside into a familiar raw throb. The whip marks were more than a week old, but they were still tender. This time the crop had bit deep into old scars. Cuts that had barely healed from the last time. A quiet knock on the door made her jump, her pain forgotten. Had he come for her?

The anticipation skimming through her body shocked her. Dear lord, perhaps her uncle had been right about her all along. Turning her head, she watched the door open to reveal a young woman close to her in age. The girl, her dark brown hair gathered up on top of her head in a style that flattered her heart-shaped face, tilted her head as she smiled mischievously.

"Good morning. I see my dress fits you quite nicely."

Helen glanced down at the dress she wore, then back to her visitor. "Are you Louisa?"

"Well, I was last night when I got home. But when Sebastian learns I'm here and not at the family estate in Scotland, I won't be surprised to hear him call me something quite different." With a merry laugh, the girl moved forward. "Turn around and I'll do up the rest of those buttons for you."

Helen took a quick step backward, remembering her wounds. The young woman misinterpreted the vacillation. "Come along now, you can't do it by yourself."

Without waiting for a response, Louisa stepped forward and spun her around. An audible gasp echoed over Helen's shoulder, causing her to stiffen. Because the whip marks were still so tender, she'd forgone wearing the corset the maid had left her. From the other girl's shocked outburst, the ugly wounds had to be clearly visible through the thin chemise covering her back.

"Who did this to you?" Louisa exclaimed with suppressed fury.

The question didn't surprise her. Not looking at the young woman, Helen shook her head. She had no desire to explain the circumstances she and Edward had left. Uncle Warren had contacts among members of London's society. The slightest slip of information might lead him to where she was.

"It is of little consequence," she said with stoicism.

"Little consequence," the girl behind her bit out. "I think you should have your head examined. These marks are barely healed. Have you had a doctor look at these?"

"There's no need." Helen reached behind her to continue buttoning the dress. A gentle hand squeezed hers as Louisa pushed her hands aside and resumed closing the back of the gown. Determined to avoid any further questions, Helen fingered the yellow silk skirt of her dress. "Thank you for the loan of your dress; it's very generous of you."

Louisa did not reply immediately. When she did, her voice reflected a compassion Helen had longed for ten in the past twelve years.

"I'm pleased we're about the same size. Anyway, it gave me the excuse to meet you. Everyone is in a dither over your mysterious arrival last night. Polly, my maid, was all agog about how romantic it was."

"It was far from romantic, I assure you." Heat burned her neck and cheeks as she remembered Lord Melton carrying her into the house.

Even rendered powerless by drugs, her nerve endings had tingled from the man's touch. A frisson slid across her breasts at the memory of his thumb brushing across one nipple. Swallowing hard, she glanced at the clock on the fireplace mantle. It was almost nine. She could not afford to irritate the earl. It was quite unlikely Madame Chantrel would have released Edward as well as herself, and she would need the earl's help in rescuing her brother.

"Oh dear, I'm sorry. I'm being nosy again. Sebastian dislikes it enormously when I pry into someone else's affairs," Louisa said as she moved around to eye Helen with a gleam of speculation in her warm, hazel eyes. "Still, I must say, my brother's behavior is extremely unusual. I can't remember the last time he even looked at a woman, let alone brought one home. But then, Sebastian has always worked hard to bury the romantic side of him."

Helen breathed an inward sigh of relief. She didn't know which to be grateful for, her rescue or the earl's discretion. Another knock echoed in the room, and the maid entered with a breakfast tray. The smell of eggs and kippers drifted into the room, immediately making her feel queasy. The last thing she wanted to do now was eat. It would be impossible to do so until she knew Edward was safe and unharmed. Without hesitating, she walked toward the door.

"Where on earth are you going?" Louisa stopped Helen with a gentle tug of her arm. "You haven't even eaten yet."

"I'm sorry, but I must speak with his Lordship."

"Of course, but Sebastian can wait."

Helen shook her head firmly. "His Lordship might be willing to wait, but I cannot."

"As you wish," Louisa replied, eyebrows arched in curiosity. "But I must warn you, Sebastian is not someone you want to face on an empty stomach."

The sincerity in Louisa's voice made her hesitate. The earl was most certainly intimidating, but she'd faced far more daunting inquisitions from her uncle than anything the Earl of Melton could inflict on her. Edward's visage entered her mind's eye once more, and she responded with a firm shake of her head.

"No, I must speak with his Lordship now."

"Very well," Louisa nodded with a perplexed smile. "Beth, will you show--Good Heavens, I don't even know your name."

"Helen. Helen Rivenall."

"Well, Helen," Louisa said with a smile. "Since I can't convince you to eat breakfast, Beth here will show you to the library."

Helen nodded her gratitude and followed the maid out of the room. Behind her, Louisa called out. "Remember, his bark is worse than his bite."

The puckish remark almost made her laugh. Despite her worry for Edward, she found herself liking the earl's sister. Not that it mattered, she wouldn't be here long enough to grow attached to anyone. Following Beth down the hallway, Helen enjoyed a brief moment of pleasure at the sound of her dress whispering against the carpet.

The gown was lovelier than anything she'd worn before. Far more so than the two dresses she owned, which were threadbare and marked with darning. She'd learned a long time ago never to ask for anything new from her uncle. Her requests always resulted in his lecturing her about how ungrateful she was for the home and food he provided her out of the goodness of his heart.

The lectures never failed to include his denouncement of her as a Delilah filled with vanity and conceit. So she'd made do with the hand-me-downs she received from one or two ladies from church. They were infinitely preferable to Uncle Warren's tirades.

With the petite maid in the lead, they turned the corner of the hallway and moved down an impressive staircase. Melton House had a completely different air from Mayfield. The creamy colored walls were a refreshing change from the dark, dreary wood that lined the interior of Uncle Warren's house.

Even the ancestral portraits on the walls were of a different quality. She paused in front of an older man's portrait. It was their expressions. That was what made these paintings so unlike the portraits at Mayfield. The subjects didn't stare down at her with stern, critical eyes. Out of the corner of her eye, she saw Beth had reached the foot of the stairs, and she moved quickly to catch up with the girl. If the earl was as rigid as her uncle was, she had no wish to be late for their appointment.

* * * *

Sebastian leaned back in his chair, rubbing his chin as his gaze touched on his mother's portrait above the fireplace. A pang lanced its way through him as he remembered the sound of his mother's laughter. If only he hadn't--he buried the memory deep in his head as he glanced down at the newspaper he still held in his hand.

Frowning, he read the sensational headline *Horror in the East End*. The brutal murder of the Nichols woman in Whitechapel was fodder for the scandal sheets to increase sales. They fed off this type of tragedy. Still, the woman's murder had been viciously carried out, it might be best to be cautious under the circumstances.

Louisa would have to be told not to go anywhere without an armed escort. Although the murdered woman had been a prostitute in an area far removed from Mayfair, he wasn't about to take chances with any of the women in his care. And that included Helen Rivenall.

The thought of the woman made him close his eyes for a moment. Last night had been one of the most uncomfortable evenings he had in a long while. Wild and erotic images of Helen entwined in his arms and riding him with wanton abandon had tortured him all night long. With a groan, he leaned forward to rest his elbows on the library table and clutched at his head.

He was a master at self-control. How was it that one woman could drive him to such distraction without having spoken one word to him? It was the most frustrating experience he'd encountered in a very long time. Focus. He needed to focus on where he could send her. No, he didn't want to send her anywhere. He wasn't ready to give her up just yet.

Disgusted with the direction of his thoughts, he gritted his teeth and turned his attention to the mail lying on the table. Opening the envelope from the dressmaker, he grimaced at the total. Louisa had gone shopping again. He needed to give serious consideration to finding her a husband or he'd be in debtor's prison before he was forty. With a sigh, he set the bill aside for his secretary to handle. The familiar handwriting on the card in front of him tightened his stomach in a knot. Aunt Matilda.

Certain of the envelope's contents, he reluctantly opened it. As he scanned the letter, he winced. His aunt and his sisters were returning to London sooner than expected. He thought he had another two months before she barreled through the front door intent on seeing him married off to one of the women in the Marlborough Set or even one of the American heiresses so popular with the Prince of Wales.

Tossing the letter down onto the tabletop, he slouched backward in his chair. There had to be some way to keep his aunt from hounding him on the subject of marriage. Of all the women he'd ever met, she was the most logical and serene of creatures. She'd understand his reasons for not marrying. He shook his head. She'd understand, but it wouldn't stop her from badgering him with potential brides.

He could always run to the continent for a lengthy stay. No, that wouldn't work. There'd be no one to ensure that his siblings didn't get into trouble during his absence. And knowing Aunt Matilda, she'd have a bride waiting for him at the dock the moment he returned. He frowned.

If there was any woman in the world who could manipulate him, it was Aunt Matilda. She could do so without him even recognizing it until it was too late. Whatever he intended to do to ward off her matchmaking schemes, he needed to do it quickly. The soft click of the library door opening jerked his head up.

She was here.

Inhaling a deep breath, he watched her as she moved across the floor. The dress she wore accented her curvaceous figure and full breasts. The memory of a dusky rose nipple made him dig his fingers into the arms of his chair. He had one of two choices. He could find somewhere else for Helen to live or he needed to find himself a mistress--quickly. One or the other. No, that wasn't quite true. He had a third choice--he just didn't think it was a sane one.

Content to watch her from a distance, he watched the amazement flitting across her face as she studied the books lining the walls. Preoccupied with shelves stocked with all manner of literature, she walked toward the fireplace as she continued surveying the room.

She'd never seen so many books. Uncle Warren had books, but not this many. Hastily, she banished all thoughts of her paternal relative. Thinking about the man only made things seem worse. Huge, leather chairs faced a massive fireplace, while books were stacked on nearby tables. A clock on the mantle ticked off the minutes quietly, while the portrait of a beautiful, raven-haired woman hung over the fireplace. With the exception of the woman's portrait, the room declared itself a male haven. Engrossed in her observations, she jumped when a deep voice echoed in the library.

"Since you're walking, I can assume the sweet vitriol has worn off, or are you still unable to speak?"

There was just the mere hint of amusement underlying the words. Helen's gaze swung toward a worktable situated less than three feet from her. Behind it sat the man who had bought her the night before. She froze as stared into a familiar pair of eyes that gleamed like polished onyx.

His thick chestnut hair was slightly ruffled, and it threw his otherwise immaculate appearance off balance. It made him seem more approachable. So much so, that she almost moved forward to smooth the tousled locks with her fingers. The unexpected and alarming notion made her swallow nervously.

A pocket watch in one hand, he took a quick glance at it before snapping it shut in a sharp movement and tucking it back into his waistcoat. He studied her for a long moment, his square jaw tightly set. When he stood, she inhaled a sharp breath. He was even taller than she remembered.

Her own height exceeded normal standards, but this man towered over her by at least a foot, if not more. The breadth of his shoulders reminded her how easily he'd carried her last night. The cut of his dark blue coat and tailored trousers expressed a meticulous attention to detail, and he was clean-shaven. It sent the message that he disdained the current fashion for extended sideburns or a mustache. Everything about him said he was his own man and answered to no one. He was obviously aware of her stare, and a hot flush warmed her skin as he arched an inquisitive eyebrow at her.

"Perhaps the drug is still affecting your tongue." Again, there was that note of amusement in his deep voice. It skimmed across her skin with a delicious tingle. Troubled by the sensation, she avoided his intent look.

"I am fully capable of speech this morning, my lord."

"Excellent. Last night our conversation was a bit one-sided, but I did manage to learn that your given name is Helen, but I want to know your full name." He rounded the table and walked toward her. Instinct immediately forced her back a step. She watched his eyes narrow at her retreat. He noticed everything. She would have to remember that.

"Rivenall, my lord, Helen Rivenall." Then in a rush, she spread her hands in a pleading gesture. "My lord, I must know what you've done about Edward."

Frowning, the man shook his head in confusion. "Who the devil is Edward?"

"My brother. I was hoping you'd secured his freedom as well."

"How could I do anything for someone I didn't know existed?" Irritation edged his deep voice. His response reminded her of Edward's reaction whenever he'd somehow failed to do something important. Inhaling a sharp breath, she shook her head.

"But I told you last night--in the carriage. I said Edward's name. It's one of the few things I do remember."

"Madame, if what you said was your brother's name, then I'll eat my hat. Your response was a muddled sound at best." Indignation made his answer sharper, cutting through the tension that hovered in the air between them.

"Oh dear, Lord." Her hands clutched at the yellow silk of her gown as she tried to think. Turning away from the earl, she paced the floor. The police, she could go to the police. No. They would help her rescue Edward, but when they learned she wasn't her brother's legal guardian, they would send word to Uncle Warren. *That* was unacceptable. She would *never* go back to Mayfield.

"I can't leave him there," she murmured to herself. "I have to go back for him."

"That's one thing you won't do." The harsh note in his voice drew her up short, and she turned to face him.

"I refuse to leave my brother in the hands of that woman," she snapped.

"Your freedom cost me six thousand pounds, and I'll be damned if I let you near that woman's establishment again."

"Six thousand pounds?" Helen stared up at him in shock.

"Quite." The singular response told her how put out he was over the price of her freedom. How could she ever repay him? She had nothing to offer him, except--swallowing hard, she chose to focus only on Edward. Her brother's safe return was all that mattered.

"Please! I can't leave my brother there. He's not quite twelve and I promised ... I promised to take care of him."

"Perhaps you should have been more careful in the selection of your friends." The hard note in his voice angered her. Who was he to judge? He knew nothing about her or her circumstances.

"Friends," she spat with vehemence. "That woman wasn't my *friend*. She *lied* to me. She promised me employment and that Edward could stay with me."

His black eyes narrowed as he studied her in silence for a long moment. "It seems I have little choice then but to see to the boy's rescue."

Relieved by his agreement to help her, she heaved a sigh. Not only had he saved her, but he had agreed to save Edward.

"Naturally, I'll require your agreement to my proposition before I do so." The moment he flung the coolly worded statement into the air, she stiffened.

Proposition? What a fool she was. Of course, there'd be a price to pay for Edward's freedom, as well as hers. Her eyes met his and a shiver skated down her spine as she studied the dark, angular planes of his face.

There was an aura about him that intrigued her and sent the blood pounding through her veins. It wasn't an unpleasant sensation. In fact, she found the frisson in the room almost exhilarating. Too exhilarating. She needed to get as far away from this man as possible. He was far too dangerous. Whatever his proposition was she'd refused.

No. She couldn't even think about refusing him. Edward's life was at stake. Sacrificing her principles was a small price to pay for her brother's safe return. If serving this man as his mistress would save Edward, then so be it. The memory of his intimate touch sent another shiver down her spine. Something told her it would be quite pleasurable to be this man's lover. Shaken by the thought, she swallowed hard and composed her features into what she could only hope was a cool and serene mask.

"If becoming your mistress is the price of my brother's safe return, I'll do so gladly."

"Good *God*, woman. If I'd wanted a mistress, I certainly wouldn't have visited a brothel for one."

The furious explosion enveloped her, and she flinched. Had she misjudged him? The resentment in his eyes said he believed her guilty of doing so. Dear Lord, she'd insulted the man, and he was infuriated. Would he change his mind and refuse to help her? Frightened that he might do so, she took a quick step forward and touched his arm. Beneath her fingertips, his muscles grew rock hard.

"Forgive me, my lord. I meant no offense," she pleaded.

Her eyes met his, as he seemed to weigh her words. The intensity of his look darkened then burned its way through her. The maid had been right. The man could melt you with the heat of his gaze. Every part of her body was on fire as she struggled to maintain her composure. Unable to help herself, her gaze focused on his firm lips, and she swallowed the knot rising in her throat. The sudden image of that sensual mouth lacing with hers stole her breath. This man wasn't just dangerous--he threatened every one of her sensibilities.

She tried to ignore the way her heart hammered inside her chest, as she flicked her tongue out to wet her dry lips. The action made a muscle in his cheek twitch, and he grasped her chin with long, tapered fingers. His touch made her suck in a sharp breath of air. Then as if he could read her thoughts, he kissed her.

The firmness of his mouth against hers pulled a sigh of pleasure from her. Spice and a hint of tobacco tickled her nose. The sensual maleness of the scent was intoxicating. She'd never realized how wonderful a man could smell. The hardness of his mouth against hers sent heat coiling through her limbs. It spread below her belly until she was warm in places only she had ever touched. In a deep fog, she acknowledged that it would be immensely pleasurable to have him touch her so intimately.

His lips nipped against hers, and she gasped. As she did so, his tongue slid across her teeth to mate with hers. The wicked finesse of his kiss teased her taste buds with just a hint of hazelnut coffee. As his tongue tantalized hers with a slow, seductive swirl, he fed the fire growing inside her until her skin burned.

Leaning into him, her fingers spiked through his hair as she kissed him back. With complete abandon, her tongue danced with his--teasing him into a state of arousal unlike anything he'd experienced in recent memory. Damn. He wanted to take her right here and now. Bury himself deep inside her until she cried out from the intense pleasure of his possession. The thought of it increased the tension in his groin, and he released a groan.

Unable to help himself, his fingers slid down the side of her neck toward her breast as he cupped the nape of her neck with one hand. Shock plowed through him as his thumb brushed over a stiff nipple. Christ Jesus, she wasn't wearing a corset. The knowledge made his cock tugged painfully at his groin as his thumb brushed over a rigid peak. Her response was a soft moan of pleasure. The sound sent his senses reeling. Control. He needed to regain command of his faculties before he did something completely rash. But her warm, lush body was making it almost impossible to think straight. He wanted to explore every inch of her.

Heart pounding, he stroked her again, his hand caressing her breast as he did so. She was full and lush in his palm. Were her breasts as silky and sweet tasting as her lips? Gently he circled the rigid peak with his thumb. Another moan escaped her, swallowed in the heat of his kiss.

The pressure of his mouth against hers deepened as his hot

tongue dueled with hers, and it flooded her body with a hunger she'd never experienced before. Heaven help her, he tasted so good. This extraordinary, languid sensation uncurling deep inside her felt wonderful. No--not just wonderful. It left her breathless and craving more. She didn't want him to stop. The sudden sound of Uncle Warren's voice echoed in her head.

'You're a Delilah, girl. A curse to any God-fearing man. The devil made you in the form of a temptress to try and win more souls from the Almighty.'

Fear and shame twisted through her. How could she? How could she want to go on kissing him? She barely knew the man. Wicked, that's what she was, wicked. But oh how good being wicked felt. The sweetness of it pricked her with fear. Almost as if he'd read her thoughts, he shoved her away from him in a sharp movement. With what little willpower she still had, she suppressed the urge to offer up a protest.

"Bloody hell," he growled as he put distance between them.

In seconds, his long stride carried him to one of the library's large windows. She lightly touched her swollen lips, her ragged breath cooling her fingertips. With his back to her, she could see his muscles flexed with tension as they stretched the material of his dark blue jacket snugly across his shoulders. Clearing his throat, he did not look at her. It was as if he couldn't bear to do so, and she winced at the notion.

"Miss Rivenall. It's not my habit to--" he cleared his throat again and fell silent as he stared out the window.

Helen didn't know how to respond to his clipped words. Guilt charged through her. Somehow, she'd encouraged him, given him the idea that she would welcome his advances. The blame lay at her feet. She'd done nothing to stop him. Could Uncle Warren be right? Perhaps she was a wanton. Fire stung her cheeks at the thought.

Furious with herself for allowing her uncle's words to make her doubt herself, she swallowed hard. She wasn't a wanton. Uncle Warren had found any occasion to find fault with her. He'd even used an innocent kiss to condemn her as being immoral. That day so long ago in the orchard, William had simply been trying to catch her as she stumbled over a hole in the ground. Instead, they'd both fallen onto the grassy meadow. Uncle Warren had heard their laughter and followed the sound, but it was the sight of William kissing her as they lay where they had fallen that had spurred his unending wrath. No. Her uncle was wrong.

William had been a dear friend. Someone she might have grown to love over time if Uncle Warren had not forbidden them to see each other again. A wanton was eager for the kisses of any man, and she had never been like that. If she had been, she would have been as eager for her Cousin Albert's touch as she was for the earl's. The thought of her cousin curled a wave of nausea through her. No. Her uncle had to be wrong. She couldn't possibly be the wanton he claimed her to be, or was she?

The quiet in the room whispered around her, and she snuck a glance in the earl's direction. He'd turned to face her, and the grim look on his face was bewildering. It seemed as if he were in the midst of a deep and dark inner struggle. What manner of man was he? She'd never met anyone like him. Intrigued once more, she straightened and broke the silence.

"It would seem that we both have committed unintentional offenses this morning, my lord. Shall we start over?"

With a tentative smile, she stretched out her hand to him. Although his dark frown didn't disappear, he begrudgingly accepted her peace offering. Stepping away from the window, he moved forward to accept her hand and brushed his mouth over the tips of her fingers. An instant later, he released his hold on her as though he'd touched a flame. The silence between them was fraught with tension as he retreated to his worktable. Absently, his long fingers rifled through a stack of papers on top of the mahogany furniture. Watching him in silence, she studied the ruggedness of his handsome profile. Everything about this man whispered danger and intrigue. Worse, it excited her. She jumped as his deep voice teased her senses.

It would seem, Miss Rivenall that we are in need of each other's assistance. You need me to secure your brother's freedom, and I--I need your assistance in convincing my aunt that I am no longer in the marriage market."

Helen looked at him in astonishment. "I beg your pardon?"

"Although I am quite content with my life the way it is," he said tersely. "My aunt has taken it upon herself to find me a wife. Therefore, to avoid any undesirable entanglements, I require your assistance in acting as my betrothed for a short period of time.

Her mouth agape, she stared at him for a moment before she laughed. "You cannot possibly be serious. I have no social skills to speak of other than those I learned as a child."

"I take it you're not up to the task then." The cool rejoinder mocked her as his sensual mouth curled into a devilish smile. Her laughter died abruptly. There was something dangerously wicked in his smile. Something that coaxed her mind into considering all the sinful possibilities she might find in this man's arms.

"I am more than capable of the task, my lord," she snapped. "I only wish I knew where to find my--"

She swallowed the rest of her sentence. Dear God. If she told him about her grandfather, he might insist on finding him. And when he or someone else discovered she wasn't Edward's guardian, they'd send them--no, she wouldn't go back to Mayfield.

"You have family in town?" He arched an arrogant brow as she averted her gaze.

"Edward and I have each other."

"That doesn't really answer the question," he said with a penetrating look. When she didn't make any effort to reply, he conceded her right to keep her own counsel with a slight tip of his head. "Tell me how you came to be in Chantrel's company."

"Edward and I had just arrived in London. Our funds were limited and I wasn't sure what to do. The woman seemed like an angel sent from heaven when she approached us in the railway station. If I'd realized the employment she was offering was …" She averted her gaze as she swallowed the knot in her throat.

"Who are you running from, Helen?" His soft question made her start violently.

Her eyes jerked back to meet a piercing black gaze, and she bit her lip. Could she trust him? She wanted too. There was something about him that invoked a desire to trust him. No. It was too much of a risk. She'd trusted Madame Chantrel, and that had ended in near disaster.

"I'm running from no one, my lord."

"I see," he murmured in a disbelieving tone. Folding his arms across his chest, he frowned. "Exactly what type of work did Chantrel promise you?"

"She said she needed a bedchamber maid for one of her clients, and that the woman she was expecting didn't arrive on the train from Gloucester.

"And when you realized the type of business Chantrel ran," he said as he frowned darkly. "Did you agree to her conditions of employment?"

"Of course, not," she snapped. "I wasn't desperate enough to lower myself in that manner."

"And yet you weren't afraid to offer yourself to me." The silky note in his voice stroked her across the small distance between them.

She shivered at his statement. He was right, she'd been more than willing to sacrifice her principles with him. But that was for Edward's sake, not because she desired the earl. Liar. Giving herself up to this man's touch to save her brother would have been far too pleasurable. Straightening her back, she set her chin at a proud angle and steadily met his assessing gaze

"I'm my brother's keeper. I will do whatever necessary to protect him," she said in a quiet voice.

Emotion flashed in his dark eyes at her words. The intensity of it burned through her before his expression became shuttered. The tension in him was almost a tangible object as he turned away from her. "Tell me what you did when Chantrel explained what was expected of you."

"I tried to leave, but she separated us and locked me in a room. She didn't give me anything to eat or drink for almost an entire day. Then when I did receive food, I was too hungry and thirsty to even consider the possibility that it was drugged."

Helen took a deep breath as she recalled those long, horrible hours in the brothel. Fear had never left her, but her foremost fear had been for her brother and his safety. She'd spent hours blaming herself and regretting her decision to leave Mayfield with Edward in tow. Logic had never been one of her strong suits, and there had been little to no logic applied to her hasty departure from her uncle's house.

"Did you see any other young women in the brothel that looked out of place? Perhaps just like you?" He asked gently.

She flinched at the question. Most of the women she'd seen at Madame Chantrel's establishment appeared resigned to their position, but there had been a young woman who had appeared no more willing to be in the brothel than Helen. About the same age as herself, the young woman had called out to her as she'd been carried downstairs for the auction, but the only thing she could remember was Chantrel roughly shoving the girl back into a room.

"One woman did try to speak to me." She said with a nod as she stared at a spot on the wall. "I could tell she was just as frightened as I was."

"I know this must be difficult for you, Miss Rivenall, but this is quite important. Can you tell me what the woman looked like?

Despite his soft words, there was a fierce intensity to his tone. Looking at him, she noted he stood ramrod straight with his arms locked behind him. His features revealed nothing, but she could see the tension in him. A tightly coiled spring could not have been more taut. Why would he be curious about the woman she'd seen?

"She was about my height with dark hair and she had the loveliest violet eyes."

Her words pulled a muffled curse from his lips. Jerking his watch out of his waistcoat pocket, he flipped open the timepiece in a sharp movement. After a brief glance at the watch face, he snapped it closed and jammed it back into his vest.

"I believe it's time I secured your brother's freedom," he said in a crisp tone. "When I return, I shall outline my expectations for your role as my fiancée. Naturally, I will see to it that you're amply rewarded."

"But I haven't agreed to help you with this absurd plan of yours," Helen exclaimed.

"I think we both know your options are limited given the circumstances." The earl narrowed his eyes as he sent her a hard look down his regal nose. It was a look meant to intimidate. Reluctantly, she admitted it was working. When she remained silent, he nodded his approval. "Excellent. I will return shortly."

The satisfaction in his voice made her bristle. He might have forced her hand into helping him, but she had no intention of remaining behind while he rescued her brother. Determination shot tension through her limbs.

"I'm going with you."

"Absolutely not," he growled with irritation. "The area is far from safe."

"My brother doesn't know you, and although he wouldn't admit it, he's quite apt to be afraid. It's highly unlikely he will trust you unless he sees me."

"Perhaps I didn't make myself clear, Miss Rivenall. Two nights ago, a woman was butchered in the area near Chantrel's establishment. While you're in my care, I'll do whatever is necessary to keep you safe, and that includes forbidding you to accompany me this morning."

There was a grim note in the earl's voice as he referred to the murder. It was enough to make her hesitate, and she shuddered. As terrible as the murder might have been, she couldn't allow it to stop her from going with him. What would he do if she defied him? Would he hit her as Uncle Warren was often apt to do? She gulped back a sliver of fear. None of that mattered. Edward was her only concern at the moment.

"Then I shall remain in your carriage while you go in to retrieve Edward. But I will go with you."

Anger darkened his face, but she refused to cower from him. Her chin set at a stubborn tilt, she forced herself not to flinch as his furious, dark gaze bored into hers. This was a man who didn't like to be thwarted, but she had little choice. For all his youthful swaggering, her brother would be frightened. It was her fault they were in this horrid mess, and she wouldn't allow him to experience fear any longer than necessary.

It was this thought alone that enabled her to remain defiant in spite of the earl's intimidating expression. When he realized she refused to give way in the matter, he expelled a loud whoosh of air to illustrate his disgust.

"As you wish, Miss Rivenall. But if you so much as step foot out of the carriage, I will extract a measure of punishment the likes of which you've never seen."

"Thank you." Her quiet gratitude made him release another snort of disgust. His gaze skimmed over her figure in a critical fashion, and his jaw tightened with annoyance.

"Have you eaten this morning? You're looking rather peaked. Is it the lack of nourishment or are you feeling the strain of defying me."

Helen glared up at him. "You, my lord, could use some lessons in good manners."

"So I've been told many times." The barest hint of amusement flickered in his dark gaze before it was snuffed out. "I'll see to the carriage. If you're not ready to depart in ten minutes, I shall leave without you."

Without giving her the opportunity to respond, he walked around her and left the library. The moment the door closed loudly behind him, Helen rested her forehead in the palm of her hand. How in the world had she managed to get herself into such a mess?

"You were a fool to bring Edward with you, Helen Rivenall." Her statement echoed off the library walls. Would it have made any difference? The earl would have forced her hand with this ridiculous plan of his. Deeply in his debt, she really had little choice but to agree to his demands.

She swallowed the knot of fear rising in her throat. Occasionally, she would hear tales of the Marlborough Set, but she'd never moved about in society of any form. Uncle Warren had viewed anything related to society as frivolous. Despite initial protests from several ladies in the local parish, he'd intentionally neglected her social training. Instead, he had decided to focus on her moral character. Each and every day started and ended with him subjugating them to stern morality lectures. Repeatedly, he'd threatened dire consequences if she and Edward didn't heed the lessons he taught.

She contemplated her recent mistakes in detail. No doubt, Uncle Warren would enjoy pointing out each of her transgressions over the past week with zealous fervor and furious outrage. A shiver shot down her spine, and she rubbed her arms to ease the chill bumps on her skin. There had never been a time when her uncle had relaxed his rules and morals to offer her or Edward love and affection. Then there had been the problem of

Cousin Albert.

From childhood, he'd tormented her. The man had always found a way to put her in a bad light with Uncle Warren. But in the last year, Albert's idea of torment had taken on a new form of devilment. He had taken every opportunity to grope her in a disgusting manner. She had known better than to bring up the matter with Uncle Warren. He would simply have accused her of being the instigator of Albert's attentions. Just as he'd accused her of teasing William until he'd kissed her.

She considered the thought. Had she somehow given William or her cousin the idea that she would welcome their attentions? No, she shook her head slightly. She'd done nothing to encourage William or Albert. The only difference was that she'd welcomed William's touch. But Albert's attempts to touch her sickened her. In fact, she'd even slapped Albert the last time he'd tried to kiss her. In retaliation, her cousin had run to his father declaring she was acting in a sinful manner.

Uncle Warren had been furious and extracted his usual punishment. The pain had been excruciating, but the wounds were healing. The beating had convinced her she could no longer remain under her uncle's roof. She'd done nothing to deserve such treatment. Although Edward had never suffered such harsh punishment from their uncle, her departure could have made the man angry enough to change his habits. She'd had little choice but to bring Edward with her when she fled Mayfield in the middle of the night.

Even if she had told Uncle Warren about Albert's advances, he would still blame her for tempting his son. The man would never understand that the idea of Albert's touch revolted her. *But you certainly didn't mind the earl kissing you. In fact, you enjoyed it quite a bit.*

She sucked in a sharp breath as the memory of his touch warmed her body once more. No, she hadn't minded at all when the earl had kissed. She had liked it far more than even William's gentle touch. Every inch of her had screamed out a demand for more of the earl's touch. A rush of heat flooded her senses as she closed her eyes and imagined his hand stroking her between her thighs.

She'd discovered it could be quite pleasurable to touch herself in that manner, but something told her she would find it infinitely more so if the hand touching her so intimately belonged to the earl. The image of the earl pleasuring her, his fingers touching her until she shuddered with longing, sent a hot wave washing over her body and a rush of warmth settled in her nether regions. Swallowing hard, she struggled with the wicked images dancing through her head.

If Uncle Warren were here and could read her sinful thoughts, he would rail at her for harboring such wicked sentiments. His punishment would be swift, but it wouldn't be enough to stop this need she had to feel the earl's mouth on hers again. To have his hand caress her breast and nipple. To lie in his--inhaling sharply at the direction of her thoughts, she shook her head. If she didn't take care, she truly would become the wanton her uncle declared her to be.

Chapter 3

Habit made Sebastian pull his watch from his vest pocket as the library door slammed shut behind him. Noting the time, he snapped the timepiece closed and shoved it back into his waistcoat. With a glance back at the door behind him, he gritted his teeth. Damn the woman. Her staunch refusal to do as he commanded was a perfect example of why a woman in his life would only complicate matters. Monitoring the activities of his sisters was enough trouble. He didn't need to add to his woes.

But then again, he had no one to blame for his present situation except himself. He expelled a grunt of disgust at his behavior over the past twenty-four hours. Since yesterday morning, he'd agreed to help his brother find a Missing woman, witnessed a brothel auction, bought a woman and to make matters worse, he'd kissed her. Touched her. Worse yet, he wanted to go on touching her until he was embedded inside her and felt the ripples of her orgasm over his cock.

He groaned. The woman was under his protection and yet he'd not been able to keep his hands off of her. Worst of all, his behavior was completely irrational. He'd not been this out of control since his mother's death. What sin had he committed to deserve such as beleaguered fate? More importantly, what had happened to his calm, peaceful, orderly existence in the space of a single day?

Now there was the matter of the boy. No doubt, he'd need to buy the child's freedom as well. If things continued in this manner, he'd be penniless before the end of month. Then there was the issue of his brother's ladylove. Helen's description of the woman she'd seen was almost identical to Caleb's description.

"Damn it to hell! Madison." His loud curse brought a tall, distinguished looking man out of the breakfast room. He gestured the butler toward him with a sharp wave of his hand. Not much shorter than Sebastian, the servant approached at a quick walk and bowed his head.

"Yes, my lord?"

"Have the carriage ordered, and see to it that Jones is driving. I also want two of the strongest groomsmen on the back of the coach. Make sure they're armed."

"Very good, my lord." The butler nodded as he started to turn away.

"One more thing, Madison. This business in Whitechapel bothers me. I don't think this devil's done killing. None of the women in the household, including staff, are to go anywhere unescorted. Every safety measure is to be taken."

"Yes, my lord. I'll see to it."

As the butler walked away, he caught a flash of movement out of the corner of his eye. Turning toward the stairs, he stood thunderstruck at the sight of Louisa descending the staircase. When in the hell had the youngest of the Rockwood litter gotten home? Aunt Matilda's letter had said that she and his sisters weren't due to leave the ancestral home in Scotland for another four weeks. Christ Jesus, had his aunt posted her letter to him and then changed her mind to come even earlier? He suppressed a groan.

"What the devil are you doing here? Why aren't you in Scotland?"

Amusement lit his sister's face. "It's lovely to see you too, and in such excellent spirits. If you must know, I returned early because I promised Lady Morehouse that I'd assist her with the benefit for the orphans of St.. Paul's church."

"Bloody hell, Louisa. This is damned inconvenient." His anger echoed in the foyer, and he winced at the amused curiosity on his sister's heart-shaped face. He hadn't raised his voice to Louisa in years.

"Whatever is wrong with you?" His sister's hazel eyes narrowed to peer at him with artful shrewdness.

"I had a late night."

"I see," she said in a puckish tone. "Would that be because of Helen?"

"How the devil do you know about Miss Rivenall?"

Glancing over her shoulder, Louisa shook out a wrinkle in the short train falling from her small bustle. He saw right through her pretense of nonchalance and gritted his teeth as she turned back toward him.

"Well the servants are all agog about the romantic way you swept up the stairs with the woman late last night. Polly described how the poor dear had been drugged and had nothing on but a decadent gown of sheer material covered with a poor excuse for a cape. Fortunately, she's the same size as me, and I told Polly to give her one of my dresses."

"Thank you," he muttered grudgingly.

That explained Helen's miraculous transformation into a lady this morning. Despite his desire to control his reactions, he realized he much preferred to see her the way she'd looked last night. Sensual, alluring and ready to occupy his bed. He tightened his jaw as he saw his youngest sister's expression of amusement.

"When I visited her this morning I found her charming and quite lovely." A mischievous smile curved his sister's lips. "Of course, she'll need more clothes, unless you've sent for her belongings."

Damn, Louisa was far too observant. He shook his head. "She has nothing."

Sympathy played out across Louisa's face, and for a moment, it seemed as though she wanted to share something with him. She shrugged. "Well, I'll see to it that she has several more of my dresses to wear until we can arrange something. Of course, you do owe me for this small gift."

"Louisa." He stressed her name with a veiled threat.

She wagged her finger at him. "Oh, no you don't, Sebastian Rockwood! There's a mystery here, and I want to know what it is."

"No, there's not," he grunted. "There's nothing to tell."

Determination set her jaw in a tight line. The stubborn look reminded him that she was a Rockwood. And a Rockwood never took no for an answer. "I think there is, and if you don't tell me what it is, you'll be sorry. Just think what Aunt Matilda will say when she finds out about your Miss Rivenall."

The last sentence was offered up in a mockery of innocence. Why the little hussy was blatantly blackmailing him. Youngest sister or not, she needed to learn her place just like Helen Rivenall. Straightening to his full height, he assumed his most unforgiving expression. "If you tell Aunt Matilda anything you little minx, I'll see to it that you'll spend the rest of the year and some of the next in Scotland."

Louisa laughed. "We both know that would be more of a holiday for me than a punishment. You might as well tell me where you met your Miss Rivenall."

He averted his eyes from Louisa's probing gaze. That was the last thing he wanted to do. He had no wish to sully her ears with a tale of where he'd been last night. Louisa was far too worldly for her own good, and he wanted to shelter her from some things.

Deliberately, he bought time by moving to study the latest acquisition of his ever-expanding art collection. Sebastian tilted his head to stare at one of the women in the artwork. Was it his imagination, or did the woman have Helen's full, sensual mouth. A warm tempting mouth that tasted like the sweetest honey. He turned away from the painting. This obsession with the delectable Helen Rivenall was becoming troublesome. His gaze met Louisa's challenging one.

"Well, Sebastian, are you going to tell me where you met Helen?"

"I can't answer that."

"Hmm, all right, I'll let that pass for the moment. If you won't tell me where, tell me why."

"She was in trouble," he said fiercely.

"Well, that's a first," Louisa exclaimed in a provocative tone. "Since when do you act rashly? Percy and Caleb are the ones who're always rushing in to save fair maidens, not you. It's unheard of."

The incredulous tone of her voice wasn't just irritating--it was insulting. Why was it so unbelievable he might come to a woman's rescue? After all, Helen had definitely been in need of rescuing.

"That's a harsh and unjust observation, Louisa." He stiffened at her light laugh.

"I never thought I'd see the day when you'd act like Sir Lancelot. Heavens, after all the women you've cut it's unbelievable. One can only imagine what nefarious purpose you have in mind in bringing her to Melton House."

"Enough! I grow weary of this inquisition," he growled.

"Yes, I suppose you do, but you've still not explained why Miss Rivenall is our guest."

"Miss Rivenall is here because I needed a woman." He cringed. Where in the hell was his brain today? Normally, he wasn't nearly this half-witted.

"*What?*" The expressions on Louisa's face ran the gamut of horror, dismay, confusion and finally indignation. "Do you mean to tell me you rescued the poor woman, simply to have your way with her?"

"No," he grounded out, well aware that his sister wasn't far from guessing the truth. He did want to have his way with Helen. He wanted the woman with a ferocity he'd not experienced in quite some time. Angry at the revelation, he glared at his sister. "She was in trouble. I thought that if I helped her, she might be able to help me as well."

"Well, that's illuminating," she said "I know as much now as I did before. You're making no sense, Sebastian, something that's *highly* unusual for you."

The stark observation nipped at him as a young pup would his heels. Depending on how one looked at it, the greatest fault or strength his baby sister possessed was a dogged determination. If he didn't explain everything, she would hound him until the end of the world. Sebastian closed his eyes as he pressed his fingers to the bridge of his nose and groaned.

"If I tell you, do you swear not to share this with anyone else. Not even the family?"

"Of course," she said. "I swear it."

"Do you swear it by the sword and blood of Angus Stewart?" He dropped his hand and sent her a hard look.

At the sharp question, Louisa grew still, her eyes rounding with surprise and not a small fraction of trepidation. The family oath he'd called for was one a Rockwood only used in extreme circumstances, harking back to their mother's Scottish ancestry. It was not to be taken lightly, and Louisa knew it. Nodding slowly, a look of solemn commitment swept across her face.

"I swear by the sword and blood of Angus Stewart not to reveal what you're about to tell me."

He heaved a sigh, satisfied she wouldn't break his trust or the oath. In some small fashion it was a relief to tell someone the entire story.

"I rescued Helen from a rather disreputable situation, and in exchange she's agreed to help me."

"Exactly *where* were you when you rescued her?"

"Helen was lured into a house of ill repute where they auctioned her off to the highest bidder. Me," he muttered the last bit of his explanation.

"You bought her?" Louisa stared at him with horror. "How could you do something so reprehensible!"

"Because if I hadn't done so, someone else would have," he said harshly.

A glimmer of understanding swept the horror from her face as she smiled. "Oh, Sebastian, that's positively heroic. You truly are a romantic at heart. It's just like a fairytale."

He suppressed a groan at the elated look on her face. The girl was a miniature copy of Aunt Matilda when it came to matchmaking. Like his aunt, the youngest Rockwood took every opportunity to find him a wife.

"Get the notion out of your head, Louisa."

"Whatever notion are you referring too?" Her innocent response didn't fool him. The minx was already hatching some plot in that pretty head of hers. She pinned him with her hazel eyes. "So, what task have you set for your Helen?"

"She's not my Miss Rivenall," he bit out as Louisa arched her brow at him. Gritting his teeth, he remembered Helen's initial resistance to his plan. If he was going to rescue her brother, the woman would damn well help him keep Aunt Matilda from meddling in his personal affairs. "You know how determined Aunt Matilda is to see all of us ... situated comfortably."

"Yes, and I know how resistant to the idea you've been, but

how--" Louisa gasped then burst into laughter. "You're going to try and convince Aunt Matilda that you've found a wife!"

"I am. I'm certain that once I've given the woman a few lessons in social etiquette, she'll do quite nicely when she meets our aunt." Hands clasped behind his back, he sent his sister a superior look.

"What! You can't possibly be serious." Louisa's response reminded him of Helen's earlier declaration. Why couldn't he be serious about this plan. It was the perfect solution to his problems with Aunt Matilda.

"I'm quite serious, thank you."

Peals of laughter poured out of his sister. "Oh, Sebastian, you are a dear, but you might as well send Aunt Matilda a note explaining you intend to deceive her if you believe you can teach Miss Rivenall the ways of society."

"I'm well acquainted with what the peerage expects of its members," he said with umbrage.

"Perhaps the expectations of your sex, but certainly not those of the matrons who'll be watching her closely. Have you even thought about how to introduce her?" She paused, taking in his bewildered state. "I can see you haven't. Really, Sebastian, you rescue the poor woman from hell, but you've no qualms about tossing her to the lions. How will you explain her living here under your roof?"

He frowned at the question. Bloody hell, this was growing far too complicated. "Since you're home, you can act as chaperone."

"That will barely pass the rules of respectability, but when have we Rockwoods ever worried about respectability. Still Helen should be consulted about the situation."

"I've already consulted her on the matter. When I return with her brother--"

"Her brother! Oh sweet heaven, is he being held prisoner as well?"

"Damn it, Louisa. Stop asking so many questions. As for chaperones, the boy will serve as one just like you. That should satisfy society's fire-breathing dragons."

His sister impulsively threw her arms around his neck and kissed his cheek. "I'm so proud of you, Sebastian. I know how much you dislike uncontrolled displays of emotion, and yet you have the most noble and generous of hearts."

The words wrapped around his chest in a warm squeeze. Louisa had always been his champion, but he wasn't certain he deserved the credit she was affording him. He might have bought Helen's freedom, but in exchange, he was expecting something in return. He wasn't worthy of his sister's obvious adoration. The thought twisted his lips into a grimace. With a gentle, yet firm, grip, he pushed Louisa away from him.

"Now that we've settled the matter of chaperones, perhaps you'll let me go see to the boy's welfare."

"Of course, but there's one other thing you're forgetting." Louisa's look of adoration was now an expression of wicked amusement.

"*What?*" he bit out between clenched teeth.

"Who exactly is going to tutor the poor woman?"

"Since you seem to think me incompetent in society matters, you can act as her teacher."

"Me?" Louisa's hand rested at the base of her throat, her eyes glittering with devilish amusement.

"Yes you, minx." He glowered at her, despite the urge to laugh. Louisa had always been able to make him laugh even when he was furious with her.

"As you wish, but I shall eventually call in my marker."

He narrowed his gaze at his sister's smug look. About to retort, he heard the library door opening. Instantly, his body reacted as he turned his head to look at Helen. It was as if he were standing next to a bonfire. Despite an attempt to control his thoughts, he couldn't block out the image of her mouth beneath his. He wanted to kiss her again. Frowning, he suppressed a grunt of irritation. Where the devil was his hard-earned discipline? He watched his sister sweep across the floor and grasp Helen's hands.

"Let me have a look at you. No bite marks, no scratches?" Louisa chuckled. "Well, it looks like you managed to survive Sebastian's foul mood."

His hands itched to paddle his youngest sister for her irreverent teasing. Jaw clenched, he glared at Louisa only to see her grin with smug satisfaction. It was definite now. He'd committed some mortal sin, and God was demanding atonement from him in the form of this torment.

Outside the house, he heard the carriage pull to a halt. Walking to the foyer's accessory rack, he tugged on his grey gloves and retrieved his bowler hat. Ignoring Helen, he focused his attention on his youngest sister.

"Louisa, a woman was brutally murdered in the Whitechapel area the other night. I doubt there's anything to worry about, but you're not to go anywhere without an armed escort is that understood." He sent her a stern look and was grateful when she simply nodded her agreement.

"Miss Rivenall, the carriage is here." Not waiting for Helen's response, he charged through the front door of Melton House.

As he plunged into the bright sunlight, he offered up a small prayer that Louisa would prevent Helen from coming with him. Behind him, his sister protested loudly. Excellent. Exactly as he'd hoped. Louisa couldn't help herself when it came to meddling. For once, he was happy to let her interfere. Anything to thwart Helen's plans to join him. His satisfaction was short-lived as the musical note of her voice floated over his shoulder.

"I'm beginning to think, my lord, that you are more in need of lessons in civility than I. You seem sadly lacking in the wherewithal to let a lady precede you into a carriage."

The sharp reprimand made him frown. He knew she was right. His treatment of her was abysmal, but old habits were difficult to change. The past twenty-four hours were precisely why he had refused to marry. Having a woman in the house only upset the order of his life.

Without a word, he turned and extended his hand to assist her into the coach. The moment his fingers touched hers, desire punched through him with an almost tangible force. Damn it, he wanted to hold her again. Feel her warmth seeping through his clothes to warm him. Hell, even better if there was nothing between them at all. The provocative image of Helen naked beneath him tightened his groin as his arousal tugged at him with relentless pressure. He released her hand as quickly as he could.

As he followed her into the carriage, things went from bad to worse. In the confines of the vehicle, her lavender scent wasn't simply enticing. It was maddening. Even worse, he was now hard as nails, and with those large luminous green eyes staring at him so intently it made his cock all the more unruly. Watching her, it was impossible not to envision all the ways they could pleasure one another. Something flared in her eyes, and just as she jerked her gaze away, he could have sworn he saw awareness there. Inhaling a deep breath, he tried to diminish the crushing need to touch her. Difficult to do, considering the taste of her was still on his lips.

Focus. He needed to focus. He stared out the window, forcing himself to contemplate the matter at hand. When Helen had begged him to rescue her brother, the note of alarm in her voice made him believe she knew the boy was in terrible danger. Did she realize Chantrel's darker clientele would enjoy nothing more than to have access to the boy? Perhaps it was simply a fear the brothel owner would abuse the lad out of spite. Either way, he could only hope he was able to rescue the boy before something terrible happened.

Helen's brother wasn't the only problem he had on his hands. The moment Caleb learned someone had possibly seen his sweetheart inside Chantrel's there would be no stopping him from storming the place. But before he could allow his brother anywhere near the brothel, he needed to develop a plan of attack. It was the only way to keep Caleb from doing something rash. The situation called for cool reasoning and controlled emotions, not the Rockwood propensity for irrational behavior.

Although he wanted to call in the police, he knew it would make Caleb's woman harder to find. The minute Chantrel sensed danger, she'd cover her tracks well, possibly even harming the girl. No, they needed to find a way to rescue Caleb's sweetheart *before* they notified the police. It was the only alternative. The thought wasn't a pleasant one, given the size of Chantrel's footmen. There was a reason why the men were large and burly. Brothels often had to deal with unruly customers, and in Chantrel's case, preventing the escape of women unwilling to accept the fate awaiting them.

Heaving a sigh, he turned his head and saw Helen studying him. The curiosity in her eyes made him quirk an eyebrow upward, but he remained silent.

"Must we perpetrate this fraud on your aunt? Surely you can find some other way to convince her you have no wish to marry."

"You've not met my Aunt Matilda," he said with wry amusement. "If the woman had been born a man, she'd be Prime Minister right now and not Salisbury. She has a talent for manipulating people into doing exactly what she wants before they're even aware of it."

"You obviously admire her very much."

"I do," he replied quietly as he glanced out the window. Aunt Matilda had been the only one to understand the depth of his grief when his mother died. His mother could never be replaced, but his aunt occupied a special place in his heart. "She is a remarkable woman, and I feel certain she will find you most . . . suitable."

"But you know nothing about me, where I come from, who I--"

If she hadn't broken off so abruptly, he never would have guessed she had something to hide. Her ability to conceal her emotions was excellent. The cool composure of her features revealed nothing as she turned away from him. What was going on in that lovely head of hers? There was much he could deduce about her so far. Loyalty and family were important to her.

The determined insistence that she accompany him to rescue her brother had proven that. Courage she held in abundance. Given her recent experience at Chantrel's, her willingness to go back for her brother vouched for her ability to face terrible odds.

Still, there was a mysterious quality about her. She was a puzzle. Despite any information as to her past, he was convinced she was running from someone or something. But who? And why? And then there was this niggling sense of having seen her before.

"I pride myself on being a good judge of character, Helen. If you're as quick a student as I think you'll be, you will make quite an impression on my aunt."

"And if I fail?" The tentative edge in her voice reminded him of Louisa's comment. Throwing her to the lions was what his sister had said.

"You won't," he said with confidence. "Louisa has insisted on being your instructor. In truth, it's for the best. I would only ensure your failure."

"Do you not follow society's rules?"

Sebastian pulled out his watch to check the time. After a quick glance at the timepiece, he tucked it back into his waistcoat pocket. "I follow my own rules, which generally are at odds with society. I'm not known in the Marlborough Set for my social polish."

"So I've witnessed."

The humor in her voice made him jerk his gaze to her face. Although her expression was neutral, amusement sparkled in her green eyes. There was no judgment in her expression or that brilliant gaze of hers. It was almost as if she was giving him permission to be himself with her. Once again his thoughts darted off on a wild tangent as he envisioned his mouth caressing her neck while his fingers stroked that sensitive spot between her legs. The heady image was intoxicating.

His mouth went dry at the thought. What the devil was wrong with him? He was well accustomed to physical pleasures and had always found it easy to restrain his desire. At least until now. His jaw tightened. Keeping his distance from her was critical if he wanted to avoid any involvement with the woman. Although, parts of him begged for the opportunity to become engrossed with her. Uncomfortable with his feelings and thoughts, Sebastian pulled out his watch again. As he snapped it open, she turned her head toward him.

"Are you late for an appointment?"

"What? No." The question bewildered him. "Why do you think I have an appointment?"

"Because that's the second time you've looked at your watch since we left."

"Harrumph," he grunted. She was far too observant. The watch helped him remain in control of his life--his destiny. Aware of her eyes on him, he returned the watch to his vest without looking at the timepiece.

Uneasy silence settled between them once more, and Sebastian could feel her tension reverberating off him. Why did this woman affect him so? He had no wish for involvement of any sort. Besides, women had a way of driving a man to deadly distraction as his father had proven so well. His mother's death had driven his father to drink his way to an early death. The proclivity for irrational behavior was a plague on all the Rockwoods. He was not immune to it, as the guilt he carried inside reminded him daily. Nonetheless, he'd learned to apply logic instead of emotion when making decisions. The task had been far from easy.

He'd worked long and hard to achieve a measure of control and order in his life. The disruption of that ordered existence was something he could not allow, no matter how lovely or enticing the temptation. Wrapping his attraction for Helen up in a ball, he buried it deep inside him. He would curb his base instincts and emotional reactions. After Aunt Matilda returned home to Scotland, he'd reward Helen handsomely. He would treat their relationship like that of an employer and employee.

The carriage rocked to a halt, and with one look at her face, his resolve immediately wavered at the consternation he saw on her features. Eyes wide with worry, she met his gaze in silence. He wanted to reassure her, but couldn't find the words to do so. Instead, he tightened his lips and cleared his throat. "Do not leave the carriage."

Anger flashed in her eyes, but she nodded her head in an abrupt fashion. Ignoring her irritation Sebastian exited the vehicle. With a quick stride, he climbed the steps to Madame Chantrel's establishment and pounded on the faded red door. When no one answered immediately, he gritted his teeth with exasperation. Was there no one available to answer the bloody door? In that brief flash of anger, he found himself eye to eye with Lord Templeton standing in the open doorway of the brothel. A nasty smile curled the man's lips as he studied Sebastian.

"Ah, Melton," he sneered. "You're up early this morning."

Sebastian ignored the bitter sarcasm and nodded an abrupt greeting. "Templeton."

"What brings you back to Chantrel's so early--ah, the lovely Helen." The marquess fixed his gaze on the carriage, an odd glint in his gray eyes. Sebastian glanced over his shoulder to see Helen retreat into the shadows of the coach interior. "Don't tell me you're disappointed with your purchase, Melton. It's not every day one finds such a treasure in the cesspools of London's brothels."

Turning to face the man once more, he smiled grimly. "Given that my knowledge is limited in such matters, I gladly yield to your expertise on this and other perverse subjects."

"One man's perversion is another man's pleasure," the marquess replied in a nonchalant tone. "In fact, if you've finished with the woman, I'm happy to buy her from you. Even soiled, I still find her enchanting."

Discipline gave him the wherewithal to keep from hitting the man. Instead, he arched an eyebrow in disdain. "Surely you jest, Templeton. That would mean I would have to lower myself to your standards, something I'm not willing to do."

"You weren't so discriminating with your standards last night, Melton." "Actually I was. I saved the woman from enduring the boredom of your company." His cold response made Templeton's eyes darkened with anger.

"A word of advice, Melton, I'd clip the wings on your soiled dove. It would be a pity to see the lovely Helen carved up as brutally as that Nichols woman was in Whitechapel the other night." With a ruthless smile, the marquess brushed past him and strode down the steps.

As he watched the man walk down the street, the cold warning sluiced through Sebastian like ice. Crime wasn't unusual in the Whitechapel district, but as Templeton had pointed out, the Nichols woman had died from viciously inflicted stab wounds. If the murderer chose to continue with his murderous killing spree, it seemed likely he'd target other prostitutes. And that meant Caleb's ladylove could be in far more danger than just a brothel auction. What better place to find a light skirt than in a brothel?

The creak of the door closing behind him made him spin around. One hand pressed against the wood, he stopped the barrier from swinging shut. With the strength of his arm, he pushed it open, and stared down at an old woman.

"Inform Madame Chantrel that Lord Melton is here to see her."

"But milord, she's still asleep at this hour of the morning!"

"Then perhaps you might help me find a young lad named Edward."

The woman smiled broadly. "Aye, a good lad that one is. Pity though that the mistress don't care for him none."

"Would it be possible for me to see him?" Sebastian held up a gold coin. Hunger brightened the woman's eyes at the offering. Shaking her head, the woman glanced furtively over her shoulder.

"The Missus would have me head, milord. I dare not risk it."

"Well, take it anyway." He pressed the coin in the old woman's hand. "Now then, inform Madame Chantrel that I'm here. If she isn't downstairs in five minutes to speak with me, then I'll see to it that this establishment will close within the day."

The servant studied him carefully as Sebastian removed his gloves with precise motions, slapping them into his hat with irritation. When she didn't move, he sent her a fierce look. Without further prodding the woman scurried up the steps, leaving him to survey his surroundings. In the dim light of day, the brothel looked dirty and unkempt. Daylight presented a completely different character to the foyer. Blood red designs, dingy with age, flocked the wallpaper. Its well-worn appearance matched the floor's threadbare rugs and runners. The gilded molding and other wood trim was cracked and peeling slightly. It was a disreputable house at best.

Time stretched on and glanced at his watch. Just as he replaced it back in his waistcoat, a sharp voice from the top of the stairs greeted him.

"I wonder at your audacity in returning here, my lord." Chantrel stormed down the red-carpeted stairs, her pink wrapper barely covering her nude body. "And according to my maid, you return with more threats."

When she reached the foot of the steps, he offered her an abrupt bow. "You're a businesswoman, Madame, and while I appreciate the great value of tradesmen, I do not appreciate being cheated."

"Cheated," she exclaimed with outrage. "I object to your insults, my lord. I gave you Helen free and clear."

"But you did not give me all of her possessions."

Hesitation flitted across the woman's puffy features. Sebastian marveled how any man would find the woman attractive. Candlelight did much to enhance her features, but in the light of day, she looked as sordid as some of her more lascivious clientele.

"I don't understand, my lord."

"Don't you?" He narrowed his eyes at her. "Then let me make myself quite clear. Last night I ordered you to place Helen and *all* her possessions in my carriage. While Helen was placed in my vehicle, her brother was not."

"Surely you're not insisting that I relinquish the boy as well. I took both of them in, fed them, cared for them. I should have some recompense for my trouble."

"And is it your policy to entice your protégés with promises of decent jobs, only to drug them and sell them to the highest bidders?"

"I don't know what you're talking about," Chantrel snapped. "I don't have to drug any of my girls. They're here because they want to be."

"Then perhaps I should see to it that Helen explains to the authorities how she was promised decent employment by you and found herself drugged and auctioned off," he said in an icy voice. "Now then, produce the boy, or I'm certain your business will suffer a permanent loss of profit within the hour."

Sebastian smiled coldly as the woman gave him a venomous look. Without another word, she spun on her heel and retreated to the back of the house. She was gone for only a moment and, when she returned, she was dragging a young boy by the ear. No longer a lady of the manor, the brothel owner hissed like a cornered snake. "Here! Take the whelp and may he rot in hell along with that useless tart you bought. I doubt she's even capable of warming your bed at night."

The muscle in his jaw twitched violently. It was the first time he'd ever had the urge to hit a woman. His fists clenched with anger, he stepped toward her. "Be grateful I'm a gentleman, madame, or I would have your head for that remark."

With a quick movement, he pulled the boy from her pinched grasp. The lad did not resist as Sebastian guided him to the front door. When they reached the threshold, Chantrel called out to him.

"My lord, you've made yourself a dangerous enemy today. Be on your guard at all times. I've powerful friends in many places."

Sebastian did not pause as he propelled the boy out of the brothel. He wasn't about to give the woman any satisfaction by responding to her words. They were empty threats. And idle warnings were the least of his worries at the moment.

Chapter 4

From the moment she'd recognized the man speaking with the earl, she'd hidden in the darkness of the carriage. The conversation between the two men had been difficult to hear, but she'd heard the earl address the man as Lord Templeton. He was the same man who Lord Melton had out bid last night at the auction. She wasn't certain why, but something about Lord Templeton frightened her. Perhaps it was his gray eyes she found so disturbing. Steely and fathomless, they were bereft of emotion.

The sound of the carriage door opening made her jump violently in her seat, as daylight exposed her hiding place in the shadows of the carriage's interior. A cry of relief escaped her as Edward climbed into the coach. As he sank down on the seat beside her, she scooped him into her arms holding him tight as the earl sat opposite them.

The earl tapped the roof of the carriage signaling the driver to move on, while Edward squirmed in her embrace, before breaking away from her. "I'm all right, Helen, really I am. There's no need to squeeze me so tight."

"Are you certain you're all right? I've been so worried." Brushing his hair away from his face, she scanned his features closely. The boy patted her hand and smiled.

"I'm fine, Helen. Truly I am." He turned to face the earl. "Might I know your name, sir? I owe you a deep debt of gratitude."

The maturity in Edward's voice was surprising. She studied him for a moment. Was his experience in Madame Chantrel's the reason for this new found confidence, or had she simply not wanted to acknowledge he was no longer a boy but a young man?

"Lord Melton at your service, Master Rivenall." He nodded his greeting to Edward. Her eyes locked with the earl's, and she inhaled a quick breath. Was that look in his eyes compassion? The emotion vanished. Impossible. And yet he had taken pity on her, freeing her from Chantrel's yoke. Freeing Edward. Why would he do such a thing if he were not a man capable of feeling compassion?

It puzzled her. He had rescued her and Edward from a horrible fate, but in exchange, he expected her to take part in a deception that met his own needs. Compassion and control. He was a contradiction in terms. Her personal experience with the man left her with no choice but to believe he only had one purpose in mind. Controlling his life and those in his sphere. And he wanted to control her, as well.

A chill sped down her back at the thought. Would he try to control her in the same way Uncle Warren always had? Icy fear tightening her skin with tension, it pulled at her wounds until the sting of it made her bite the inside of her cheek. The lashes stung as potently now as when Uncle Warren had brandished his riding crop against her back.

She swallowed her trepidation. The earl had given her no reason to think he would harm her. If anything, he'd gone out of his way to protect her. No, she wasn't afraid of him. Apprehensive was a better word. His kiss had unsettled her more than she wanted to admit.

Even more disturbing was how much she'd enjoyed the wanton sensations his touch had ignited inside her. Now he'd rescued her brother and her obligation to him had increased.

"Your kindness in rescuing my brother places me deeply in your debt, my lord." She glanced down at Edward, choosing her words carefully. "This business proposition you mentioned earlier. I'll do my best to assist you in the venture."

The muscle in the earl's cheek twitched slightly as he met her steady gaze. Banked embers glowed in his dark eyes and her heart skipped a beat at the flash of emotion in his gaze. He was looking at her in the same way he had in the library. Just before he'd kissed her.

The memory of that kiss sent heat skimming across her skin. It aroused the need to feel his mouth against hers again. To enjoy the pleasure of his touch against her breast. Fire burned her cheeks at the thought, and she ducked her head to avoid his gaze.

What was it about this man that stirred such wild emotions in her? Being in his company made it almost impossible to think. The idea of spending even more time with him had her wavering between fear and hope that he'd kiss her again.

"My lord, I hope you have no intention of compromising my sister in exchange for my freedom." Edward's thin voice of disapproval filled the carriage.

"*Edward.*"

"I beg your pardon." The earl choked on his exclamation as he scowled furiously at the two of them.

It was clear he found her brother's remark deeply offensive, and she was certain he'd never been accused of such disreputable behavior in the past. Any other time she would have laughed at his spluttering outrage, but at the moment, she was too angry with Edward to find anything about the situation amusing. She glared at her brother.

"Edward Rivenall, His Lordship has been nothing but--" She hesitated for a fraction of a second as she remembered the pleasure of his kiss, before plunging onward. "... a gentleman in every sense of the word. If it were not for him, things would have been much worse for both of us."

A frisson tingled over her skin as she made the mistake of looking into the earl's eyes. Had her hesitation reminded him of their kiss? The flash of fire in his gaze confirmed her unspoken question. Yes, he remembered. Was that one of the reasons he'd reacted so strongly to her brother's question? Did he regret having kissed her? To her amazement, she realized she had no regrets about the incident. She jerked her gaze away.

"Edward," she said in a low voice. "You will apologize."

Embarrassment reddened her brother's face, and he nodded toward the earl. "I apologize, my lord."

"Apology accepted," the earl cleared his throat as he regained his composure.

"However," Edward continued, "You must understand that I'm my sister's protector, and I have her reputation to consider."

This time it was Helen who sputtered with indignation. What on earth had possessed Edward to say such a thing? Protector indeed. The moment they were alone, she'd see to it that he never attempted to act as her keeper again.

"I understand completely, Master Rivenall. These are dangerous times we live in, and allowing a woman as lovely as your sister to venture out into the city without an escort is quite foolhardy."

Startled, her cheeks grew warm at the compliment. He thought she was lovely. She'd never thought of herself as even pretty. Once a long time ago, Uncle Warren had caught her looking in the mirror. His irate reaction had ensured she rarely ever viewed herself in a looking glass. Her gaze flew toward the earl, and the amusement she saw glowing in his eyes made her stiffen. What did he find so humorous?

"You're quite right, my lord," said Edward. "I did try to convince Helen of that fact when we left Uncle Warren's house."

"I can understand your dilemma. She's quite strong willed."

Again there was that dry note of amusement. Strong-willed? The man was simply put out that she'd defied him and insisted on coming with him to fetch Edward. He arched an eyebrow at her, as she scowled at him.

"Yes, she is quite stubborn, my lord. But she does have several other wonderful qualities as well."

Exasperated, Helen jerked her gaze back to her brother. "That's quite enough out of you, young man. His Lordship doesn't need to hear any of your outlandish tales."

"On the contrary, Miss Rivenall. Your brother's offer to elaborate on your extraordinary qualities intrigues me." The penetrating look he directed at her accelerated her heartbeat. Only when he redirected his gaze to her brother did the tension in her muscles ease. "But I suppose there will be plenty of time for Master Rivenall to elaborate on your finer qualities since you're to be my guests at Melton House."

Edward immediately shook his head in disagreement. "That's most kind of you, my lord. However, I'm afraid we cannot accept your offer. Helen and I must find our grandfather, and right away." Acute interest flashed across the earl's face at her brother's words.

"Your grandfather?"

"His Lordship has been most generous already, Edward. We do not want to trouble him unduly with our problems." She pressed her fingers into her brother's arm sharply. A pair of green eyes that matched hers glittered up at her with exasperation.

"But Helen--"

"If I can be of assistance in some way, I would be happy to do so."

The deep timbre of his voice washed over her like a gentle wave as she looked at him. Despite their short acquaintance, she was already beginning to recognize how he used his voice to get his way. The seductive tone gave one a sense of security. But were they really safe? She wanted to believe they were, but she couldn't risk it. Curiosity darkened his mesmerizing eyes, and for some reason it unnerved her. She returned her gaze to Edward.

"Thank you, my lord, but we will solve this particular problem on our own," she said firmly.

Edward seemed ready to protest, but Helen stared him down until he heaved an angry sigh and looked out the window. He didn't remain silent for long. As if remembering something, he turned back to her.

"Helen, what is this business proposition you've agreed to help Lord Melton with?"

She opened her mouth then shut it. Exactly what was she supposed to tell Edward about her agreement with the earl. There was nothing unlawful about the arrangement, but it was far from honorable. Turning her head toward the earl, she silently pleaded with him to say something. For a split second she was certain he wasn't going to offer up any explanations. As a slow smile curled his lips, he arched an eyebrow in her direction. Oh the rogue! He enjoyed seeing her flounder about as she tried to think of an explanation.

"Master Rivenall, may I speak to you as one man to another?"

The serious tone of the earl's voice made her catch her breath. The man was up to something. Edward sat up straight beside her as he nodded.

"Of course, my lord. I prefer it."

"I'm sure you can understand me when I say how annoying it is when people interfere in our personal affairs, wouldn't you agree?"

"Most certainly." Edward scowled as he sent her a sideways glance.

"Especially when they're people we happen to care for a great deal."

Heaving a disgusted sigh, the boy nodded. "That makes it even harder, because you know you don't want to hurt their feelings."

"Exactly." He sent her brother a conspiratorial smile. "Unfortunately for me, my Aunt Matilda--who I have great affection for--is determined to see me married, even though I have no desire to do so."

"But what does any of this have to do with Helen?" She watched her brother frown in puzzlement.

"Your sister has graciously agreed to help me convince my aunt that there's no need to parade a long line of prospective brides in front of me."

"I don't understand. Are you going to tell your aunt that Helen is your betrothed?"

The earl hesitated for a brief minute before he shook his head. "Nothing quite so definite. But I shall make certain that my aunt believes I am giving serious thought to the state of matrimony."

"I see," the boy said quietly. "So Helen is really only pretending to be your sweetheart."

The statement made her inhale a quick breath as she looked at the man seated across from her. A strange light flickered in his eyes as he met her gaze before he returned his attention to the boy at her side.

"Precisely, and I know I can count on your discretion when my aunt arrives for her visit."

"Most assuredly, my lord." Edward sent the man a sharp nod. The seriousness with which her brother was contemplating this matter made her wonder if she should feel irritated or amused by the entire conversation. Suddenly, she caught the suspicious glint in his green eyes as he narrowed his gaze on the earl. "And have you made arrangements for a chaperone while we are staying in your home?"

The earl smiled. "My sister, Louisa, lives with me and will be an adequate chaperone for your sister. Not to mention your guardian services as well."

"Hmmm." Edward seemed to be weighing the matter with great seriousness. Any thought of amusement she'd had disappeared at her brother's expression. First, the earl thought to emphasize he master of her fate, and now Edward was under the same misapprehension.

"I've heard quite enough." Helen snapped. She sent the earl a cutting glance before switching her gaze to her brother.

"I am more than capable of making a decision on my own, Edward Rivenall." She watched him flinch at her fierce tone, and she turned her anger on the earl. "As for you, my lord. I have agreed to your proposition simply because I'm in your debt. However, please remember I am *not* and never *will be* your property. Is that understood?"

Edward looked completely cowed at this point, but Helen noted the earl seemed bored. In fact, she would have thought him filled with ennui except for the fiery glint in his eyes. Good, he was angry. It was important to lay the foundation for their business arrangement. She refused to let any man control her again. More importantly, she knew she could trust no one to take care of her or Edward. The only person she could rely on was herself. Not even the earl's assistance was a guarantee of safety.

Silence drifted through the carriage. It was a thick, emotional drain on her senses, almost tangible. When the carriage rolled to a stop, the earl flung the coach door open with repressed violence. As he did so, the handle cracked the side of the vehicle like gunfire. Climbing out, he waited just outside the door, his face like a stone carving. Edward followed and stood on the sidewalk as Helen slid across the seat toward the open carriage door. With an abrupt gesture, the earl offered his hand to her. Heat washed over her skin the moment his large hand captured her fingers. Quivering slightly, a strange sensation curled in the pit of her stomach as he bent his head toward her, his lips a hair's breadth away from her ear lobe.

"You're right about one thing, Helen. You are deeply indebted to me." Despite his whisper, the anger in his voice thundered in her ear. Obviously, her declaration of independence didn't please him. Aware of Edward's presence, she resisted giving the man a tart response and satisfied herself with glaring at his departing back as he strode up the steps to Melton House. One arm about her brother's shoulders, Helen urged Edward to follow the earl.

The moment they entered the impressive entryway, her

brother's small gasp of awe made her look more closely at the massive foyer. For the first time, she noted the elaborate gilding on the room's molding and doorframes. Buttress arches poured out of the walls to meet and form a star in the center of the high ceiling. It was a room whispering of more riches to come. Helen shivered as she remembered Uncle Warren. He would call this house a den of decadence and evil simply for its rich beauty. She ignored how the thought of her uncle sent a trickle of fear scraping down her spine.

Uncle Warren had to be wrong about his assessment of the nobility. The earl was far from decadent and evil. He'd rescued her and now Edward. There was goodness in the man, no matter how much he wanted to control everything around him. She didn't want to believe the earl had rescued her simply to save himself from a meddling relative.

No, her uncle had to be wrong. If she were to believe everything her uncle told her, then she would have to believe that she truly was the sinful wanton Uncle Warren had always declared her to be. Over the years, the constant barrage of admonitions and lack of affection had taught her to rely on no one but herself, but even that was hard to do. No matter how hard she tried not to let Uncle Warren's hateful words affect her, it was impossible to shut his voice out completely. His rants had even made her doubt herself.

The earl thought she was stubborn, but if the man only knew how difficult it was for her not to run from confrontation. Uncle Warren had taught her that standing up for one's self always resulted in punishment. And yet the earl had done nothing to make her think he would harm her. Louisa was right. The man's bark was worse than his bite. The sudden, sharp sound of his commanding voice made her jump.

"Madison," the earl called out.

The abrupt cry brought a tall man out of a back hallway at a quick pace. The distinguished looking man nodded at the earl. "Yes, my lord?"

"We have another guest staying with us. Apprise Mrs. Stoner of the situation."

From the top of the stairs, Louisa's laughter-filled voice floated down to them. "I see your ill-temper hasn't improved, despite your obvious success in rescuing Helen's brother."

Helen glanced at the earl, curious as to his reaction at the good-natured teasing. As expected, the man glared at his sister before turning back to the butler. "See to our guests, Madison. I'll be in the library, and the first person who disturbs me is fair game for a tongue-lashing they'll never forget."

The earl wheeled about on his heel, his gaze brushing over Helen. The look on his face startled her. Frustration, anger and another emotion raged on his handsome features. He looked almost as though he were in pain. It was an expression of vulnerability.

Impossible, how could this commanding man be vulnerable? But it was there in his face. She recognized the seething turmoil. She'd experienced the same emotion every time Uncle Warren found fault with her. Her heart ached for him. She knew what it was like to be alone with no one to offer you comfort.

She wanted to reach out to him, soothe the pain from his brow. The need to ease his suffering intensified with each breath she took. Afraid she would give in to the desire to touch him, she took a quick step back. Their gazes locked, and she saw his eyes narrow at her abrupt movement.

"Bloody hell. There's no need to look so terrified, woman. I ate a substantial breakfast this morning," he growled as he strode past her toward a closed door. Louisa, having just reached the bottom of the steps, shook her head as her brother disappeared from the foyer, the loud crash of a door slamming shut behind him.

"Pay him no mind. He's like a horse with a burr under his saddle. He'll come around soon enough." Moving toward Helen and her brother, she smiled. "You must be Edward."

In a courtly gesture, Edward bowed toward Louisa. "Yes, my lady."

"Heavens, but you'll break some hearts in a few years." Mischief in her hazel eyes, the earl's sister laughed. Turning to Helen, she smiled. "As for you, my dear, we have some shopping to do. Why don't you help Edward settle in, then join me in the salon so we can get started?"

Grateful for an opportunity to speak with her brother alone, Helen nodded her agreement. Together she and Edward followed Madison up the stairs. From the foot of the steps, Louisa's voice made the small party come to a halt.

"Madison, I almost forgot. Would you see to it that Master Rivenall's measurements are taken so I might give them to the tailor when Helen and I go out?"

"Yes, Lady Louisa," the butler murmured politely before continuing up the staircase to the second floor. As they hurried to keep up with the butler's long strides, Helen noticed their footsteps led them in the opposite direction of her room. When the butler halted, he opened an oak door and bowed politely.

"This will be your room, Master Rivenall. Mrs. Stoner, the housekeeper, will send one of the maids up with water and towels for your bath. I shall have the clothing trunks in the attic searched for something suitable for you to wear, Master Rivenall. Once you've had your bath, I'll return to take your measurements."

With another bow, the butler left the room. What must the man think of them? First she and now Edward had appeared unannounced in the earl's house wearing nothing but the clothes on their back. A small laugh made her turn just in time to see Edward flop backwards onto the bed. Following him into the room, she closed the door behind her.

"Edward, behave yourself," she snapped.

He grimaced at her before glancing down at the thick mattress he sat on. "I'm sorry, Helen, but this bed is so soft. Nothing at all like the hard mattresses Uncle Warren made us use."

Reluctant to quell his enthusiasm, she smiled. "It is lovely, isn't it?"

"Yes, but even Uncle Warren's beds were more comfortable than the floor where Madame Chantrel made me sleep." There was just a hint of anger in her brother's voice, and Helen crossed the floor to sit on the bed beside him.

"Edward, can you ever forgive me?" she gently brushed a lock of hair off his forehead as she spoke. "I had no idea what the woman really intended when I accepted her help. If I'd known--"

She blinked back tears at the memory of Chantrel's men forcibly dragging her away from Edward. A smaller hand slipped into hers.

"I don't blame you, Helen. It wasn't your fault." The blanket statement of forgiveness didn't ease her conscience as she swallowed her tears.

"She didn't hurt you, did she?"

"No." The sharp anger in his voice troubled her. Gently, she touched his shoulder.

"Did ... no one ... no one else hurt you, did they?"

Edward shook his head, a bitter expression on his face. "No."

Something in his voice created a thin layer of ice over her skin, chilling her to the bone. She hesitated. Should she persist in questioning him further? Before she could make a decision, he turned to her with an inquisitive look.

"Helen, why didn't you want the earl to know about grandfather?"

Startled, she sprang to her feet and moved to one of the windows, eager to avoid Edward's inquisitive gaze. Dark green curtains framed the wide glass, and her hand clutched the heavy material just above a gold sash that held the drape open. Why didn't she want the earl to know about her mother's family?

How could she answer Edward?

How could she explain her need to feel in control of her own life? Not subjected to the dictates of Uncle Warren, Lord Melton or any man. A part of her wanted to trust the earl, but she couldn't. His obsession with rules told her how orderly he wanted his existence to be. She could hardly trust a man who needed to control others. Her life at Mayfield had taught her all to well what that meant. There was no forgiveness for breaking a rule, only punishment.

The wounds on her back tingled at the memory of all the beatings she'd endured for breaking this rule or that. No, she needed to make Edward understand that finding their grandfather was something they had to do on their own. If their maternal grandfather rejected them, she didn't want the earl to feel sorry for them.

Pity was the last thing she wanted, especially from the earl. Nor did she want him to feel obligated to notify Uncle Warren as to their whereabouts. She'd sooner be dead than return to Mayfield. She focused her gaze on the street below.

Busy with traffic, the cobblestone avenue presented a charming picture, but she knew firsthand how dark it was behind that picturesque image. What was it Sebastian had told his sister? There had been a brutal murder and it wasn't safe outside. Suddenly, she dragged in a sharp breath. When had she taken to thinking of the earl as Sebastian?

"Well, are you going to answer me? Why don't you want the Earl to help us find grandfather?" At Edward's plaintive demand, she pushed aside her thoughts with relief as she turned to face him.

"His Lordship has helped us enough already, Edward. I can't ask him to help us find someone we're not even sure exists, let alone knowing whether or not we're wanted."

"But if he helps us, we'll have the answer to that question."

"And what if Grandfather is dead? Worse yet--what if everything Uncle Warren said is true? What if Grandfather doesn't want us? If we let the earl help us and the worst happens, Lord Melton might feel obligated to take care of us or he might even send us back to Uncle Warren. I'll not risk that. I won't go back to Mayfield."

"But Helen, I don't think His Lordship is the type of man who would do something like that. He seems like a man of honor."

"I have no wish to be in this man's debt anymore than I already am. And I'm certainly not willing to jeopardize our future on a man I don't know. " Or trust she finished silently.

"Don't you like the earl, Helen?"

She frowned. "I'm very grateful for His Lordship's rescue of us and his giving us shelter. However, I don't know him well enough to say whether or not I like him."

"Well, I think he likes you," Edward said with a grin.

"You're imagining things." Helen scoffed at the idea. But deep inside a small voice teased her with the thought Edward might be right. Why was the earl helping them? Surely, the man could find some other way to stop his aunt's matchmaking schemes without entering into this elaborate deception. She had no answers to the question, which made her uneasy.

"I'm of no more interest to His Lordship than an ant."

"Then why does he look at you so funny?"

Helen sighed with exasperation at her brother's persistent questioning. "Probably because he's so annoyed with me for disrupting his schedule."

"Schedule?"

"Yes, His Lordship maintains a very precise and orderly existence from what I've gathered. Unfortunately, I've managed to upset his timetable a great deal today. So you see--his Lordship isn't the least bit interested in me."

A knock on the door prevented Edward from asking any more unsettling questions as he bade the visitor to enter. Beth came through the door followed by two burly footmen carrying buckets of steaming water. The expression of disgust on Edward's face made Helen laugh.

"I'll leave you to your bath, and don't you dare try to get out of it." With another smile, she left the room. Relieved she no longer had to answer her brother's probing questions, she made her way back to the main stairs. The serene quiet of the hallway soothed her nerves. It was such a stark contrast to the menacing corridors of Mayfield. Despite their problems, she reassured herself she'd done the right thing in leaving their uncle's home. She was so thankful Edward was safe. If something had happened to him, she never would have forgiven herself. But his safety meant her obligation to Lord Melton had increased. Would helping him deceive his aunt be sufficient repayment for the debt she owed him?

If only she knew where to find her grandfather. Her mother had rarely spoken of him, and when she did so, it was with tears in her eyes. From what little she remembered as a child and the facts Uncle Warren had occasionally let slip, their grandfather lived in London. There was little to go on except for her mother's maiden name of Worthington and the fact that her grandfather was a peer of the realm.

Perhaps helping the earl would help her to find her grandfather.

If she were discreet, discovering her grandfather's whereabouts might not be too difficult after all. The more challenging aspect of her problem would be securing an audience with her grandfather without revealing who she was. She had no wish to expose herself or Edward to any more pain. As to what they would do if Uncle Warren were correct, she refused to dwell on that thought. Surely her grandfather could not be so embittered as to refuse acknowledgment of his grandchildren.

Her foot touched the marble floor of the foyer at the same moment a door to her right opened. Automatically turning her head toward the sound, she tensed at the sight of the earl's tall figure in the library doorway.

"You, in here, now." The harsh command scraped over her skin like abrasive soap.

"If you wish to speak with me, my lord, you'll request my presence, not command it." Not only was he a rake and autocrat, he lacked manners as well. What made him think he could order her around like a servant? Antagonism stiffening her limbs, she stalked away from him toward the salon.

"Helen ... please." The obvious effort it took him to speak politely made her bite back a smile. So there might be a gentleman behind that abrupt façade after all. She turned around to face him. Narrowing her eyes, she deliberately waited for a long moment. The sight of his clenched jaw made her realize she could only push him so far. The man needed time to learn manners, just as she needed time to learn how to move about in society. A needle of trepidation pricked her at the idea of mingling with people superior to her in station and birth. Was she capable of matching wits with the Marlborough Set as she'd heard them called? She pushed the thought away as she walked toward him.

He stepped aside so she could pass through the doorway, but it was impossible not to brush against him as she walked into the library. The delicious scent of spice and leather wafted beneath her nose. It was a tempting aroma, and she quivered at the pleasure the smell gave her. Once she reached the middle of the room, she turned to face him. His features were unreadable as he closed the door with a quiet snap.

She wasn't quite sure what to make of his closed expression. Was he still angry? The man was such an imposing figure. It was difficult to keep her hands from trembling in his presence, so she clasped them in front of her as he moved toward her. The breath she'd been holding eased past her lips as he stopped a short distance from her.

"I'm not good with words, Helen. However, if I'm to convince my aunt to end her meddling in my personal affairs, we must make our relationship believable."

"I see, and how do you propose we do that?" Warily she studied him.

"You indicated earlier that I needed to learn how to act when in the company of a lady." He ran a hand through his chestnut hair. The movement ruffled the thick waves, giving him a rakish air as he pulled at the collar and tie at his neck. "You were right. All of my sisters have tried to reform me, but failed."

"All of your sisters?" Helen asked with curiosity.

He swung his gaze toward her, his mouth twisted in a half smile. "I have two other sisters besides Louisa."

"Well if your sisters have failed to teach you manners, I doubt there's anyone else more capable of instructing you." She sent him a skeptical glance as she arched her eyebrows.

Indecision furrowed his forehead and darkened his features. It was an expression of uneasiness. Again, he showed a vulnerability that tugged at her heart. Her steady gaze seemed to unnerve him. Clasping his hands behind his back, he tightened his jaw and looked away from her.

"What about you?"

"*Me?*" Helen gaped at him in astonishment. "If your sisters have been unable to instruct you in this area, whatever makes you think I could succeed?"

"Because you're different."

"Lord Melton, I'm not sure I understand."

"My name is Sebastian. Say my name." His voice was a low growl as he stepped toward her. Instinct ordered her to flee, but she held her ground.

"For a man who just asked me to instruct him in appropriate behavior with a lady, I am fairly certain that such familiarity is highly improper, my lord."

In one long stride, he towered over her. "Propriety be damned. I want to hear you say my name."

Not sure what to think, she stared up at him. Was now a good time to defy him again? Was he testing her? She remembered all the times Uncle Warren had made her tremble and cower before him. But Uncle Warren wasn't here, Lord Melton was. She tightened her mouth into a firm line of anger.

"If this is the way you act with ladies in society, then it's no wonder your sisters have failed. Your arrogance and tyrannical behavior are enough to dishearten even the most loyal of siblings. As for me, my lord, your dictatorial conduct neither impresses nor sways me to do anything but leave you to contemplate your fate. Whatever that may be."

Head high, Helen swept around him and hurried toward the door. She had only taken two steps when a strong arm snaked around her waist. In a quick jerk, his chest burrowed into her back. The contact sent a wall of fire racing over her skin, igniting an inferno inside her belly. She stiffened, alarmed by the excitement coiling through her. Desperately she fought the desire to turn around in his arms. The memory of his earlier kiss made her crave another and another until he had quenched the thirst drenching her mouth. The wanton feelings spiked through her in the form of a shudder. How had she come to this? What manner of woman was she for being willing to surrender to him without a care or thought?

Chapter 5

Sebastian wanted to groan aloud as he prevented Helen from leaving the room. Had he lost his senses? He'd never been so out of control in his entire life. Her soft body trembled against him. Was she afraid? He didn't want her to be afraid. No, he wanted her to feel something else. His eyes closed against their will. The scent of her filled his nostrils, enticing him to bend his head to take a deep breath of the soft lavender dusting her skin.

He tried to stop himself, but his body had taken on a life of its own. His mouth sought out the sweet curve of her lovely neck. She didn't resist, but instead her head tipped to the side, giving him a delicious expanse of creamy skin to nibble on. The pounding beat of her heart whispered against his lips as he tasted her. The silkiness of her skin ignited a craving need inside him as he kept her locked against him, and it threatened to undo him.

Unable to think straight, he slid his mouth across the edge of her jaw, absorbing her small tremors into his muscles. He should release her. But he couldn't. Something compelled him to hold her close. Then he heard it. The soft music of her voice.

"Sebastian, please. Let me go."

Reluctantly, he released her. It pleased him that she did not step away quickly. Rather she moved slowly out of his arms. The scent of her drifted into nothingness. His eyes flew open and he caught her studying him with a troubled gaze. Guilt slashed through him at her expression, and he turned away from her. What was he thinking, grabbing her in such a manner? One would think him a callow youth in the first throes of an infatuation. He cleared his throat.

"I seem to be making this a habit." He knew the gruff words were far from an acceptable apology, but he was still struggling with the desire to pull her back into his embrace.

"I quite understand."

Surprised, he wheeled about to face her. "Explain that remark."

Tension tightened each of his muscles as he watched her mouth twitch with confusion at the question. God, how he wanted to taste her again. He restrained the impulse. Where the hell were his senses? Insanity had touched him. He was certain of it. And all over a woman.

"I understand that my behavior has somehow encouraged you to make advances."

Sebastian stared at her. What the devil was she saying? She'd done nothing to deserve his advances, and yet she was taking responsibility for his impulsive, rash actions. Irritated that she'd do such a thing, he stiffened. "That's utter nonsense."

The sharpness of his voice made her jump. He regretted startling her, but could think of nothing to say. Damn it, but the woman was maddening.

"You are the most exasperating man I've ever met. I must have done something to encourage you, otherwise, why else would you kiss me?"

Astounded by her response, his jaw sagged open in disbelief. Did the woman really have no idea how desirable she was? How her body curved softly in all the right places. Hers was a body made for heated nights and he wanted her more every time she stood in his presence.

What would make her think she'd encouraged his advances? She was exquisite enough to drive him to drink. Keeping her at arms length required the willpower of a saint. He'd never met a siren who had no idea of the power she held over men. It made her all the more enticing, and he struggled to keep from pulling her back into his arms.

"Have you nothing to say, my lord?"

Why the devil did she refuse to call him by his name? Only a moment ago she had used his name when she pleaded with him to release her. There had been something alluring, bewitching about the way she said his name.

"You said my name a moment ago. I want to hear it again."

He watched a flicker of fear brighten her lovely features. The emotion disappeared like a flash of lightning. Haughty disdain lit her features, but he saw confusion flare in her eyes. The tip of her tongue darted out to touch her upper lip in a quick caress. The sensual motion tightened his chest as he inhaled a ragged breath. Narrowing his eyes, he studied her, content to wait until she did as he commanded. For he knew it had been nothing more than a command.

"Sebastian. There, I've said your name, are you satisfied?" A tart apple could not have been crisper than her voice. His mouth gave a slight tug at one corner.

"Not quite. You shall continue to address me as Sebastian." The statement made her stiffen. He ignored her reaction, determined to have his way. Besides, he liked the way she said his name. "Since we will be viewed as a couple on the verge of a betrothal, it will not be considered odd for you to address me as such."

"But I ... I ... surely this is most improper."

"No more improper than your trip to London, chaperoned solely by your brother."

"That is none of your concern." Pride set her head at a regal tilt.

Studying her, he remembered the boy mentioning an uncle in the carriage. Walter, no that wasn't it, Ward, no, Warren. That was the man's name. He folded his arms as he probed.

"Would your Uncle Warren find your trip inappropriate?"

Green eyes widened in panic, and she took a step away from him. Incapable of speech, she simply shook her head. Regret scraped at him with razor-like claws.

"There's no need to be frightened, Helen. I have no intention of trying to contact your uncle. It's apparent to me you would not have left without good reason."

"Thank you." Relief erased the panic in her gaze as her body wilted with the release of her fear.

The sigh she heaved tightened his muscles. Whatever her uncle had done, it had been enough to make her fear the man or at least fear the prospect of returning to the man's home. Eager to make her feel comfortable so she might provide him greater insight to who she was, he moved to his worktable. His fingers skimmed the soft leather binding of a biography on Marcus Aurelis.

"Is this uncle of yours a tyrant?" Her quiet gasp told him he had guessed correctly. "Does he have a profession?"

When she didn't answer, he turned his head to look at her. "Is he the reason you think you somehow unwittingly encourage men to kiss you?"

Chin set with tension, her features had taken on a cool, unreadable look. "My uncle owns and manages a small estate. He is a deeply religious man who expects his family to adhere to his moral and biblical teachings."

The answer didn't surprise him. In all likelihood, the man found Helen's voluptuous beauty extremely tempting. It made it easier to blame her for his lust. It was an attitude he'd seen becoming more prevalent over the last few years. Blame the victim, not the sinner. Anger surged through him at the idea of her uncle trying to destroy a beauty only the Almighty could have possibly conceived.

"And do you believe his teachings?"

"I ... I respect my uncle's wish to cling to his beliefs."

The emotions glistening in the emerald pools staring back at him struck a resounding chord with him. How many times since his mother's death had he felt the same emotions? Fear, confusion and self-loathing were all too familiar companions. Her expression made him experience a need to comfort her, but his own pain was far too great to reveal his empathy. Unable to continue watching his own emotions reflected back at him from those beautiful green eyes, he turned away.

This woman aroused feelings he didn't want to feel. Most of all, his lust for her was becoming an uncontrollable monster. If left unchecked, it would no doubt toss him into a quagmire of trouble. He needed to regain control of his senses soon, otherwise he would be as lost as he had been the day his mother fell to her death. He uttered a vehement oath beneath his breath. With his hands clasped behind his back, he faced Helen once more. The disoriented look on her face made his jaw flex with tension.

"As long as you reside in this house, Helen, you'll be safe. I'll not let your uncle or any one else harm you or your brother."

Relief lightened the darkness in her gaze. With a look of gratitude, she nodded. "Thank you," she hesitated. "Sebastian."

The sound of his name parting her lips washed over him like sweet chords from a piano sonata. He buried the pleasure it gave him and deliberately returned his attention to the papers on his worktable. Feeling irascible, he lifted a paper to study it, while dismissing her with a wave of his opposite hand. "You'll find Louisa in the salon. Make sure you heed her well, I want my aunt completely convinced our relationship is authentic."

There was no need to look at her. The soft sound she emitted said far more than any words ever could. He did not move, instead he simply waited for the door of the library to close. It did not surprise him when it crashed shut. He sighed, struggling with the remorse enveloping him. Helen wasn't responsible for his personal torment, but seeing the reflection of his own emotions in her face had twisted his gut. He clenched his fists tightly as he struggled to keep the painful thoughts in his head at bay.

What the devil was wrong with him? Why couldn't he just brush the woman's emotions aside? Why compare them to his own feelings about his mother's death. It had been a long time since he'd allowed himself to think about that terrible night. The sudden image of his mother hurrying along the upstairs landing made him cringe. She'd been late as usual. Why had he called out to her?

Sebastian closed his eyes as the picture of his mother's smiling face filled his head. Laughter had followed her everywhere she went. Whether it was something Percy had said, a funny face Caleb had made or something his sisters had done, her amusement had been contagious. Melton house had been filled with warmth and love because of her. He missed that the most. When she'd died that night, she'd taken all of that with her.

Why hadn't she just ignored him, why did she have to stop and tell him goodnight? Tension ricocheted through his limbs. No. She wasn't to blame. That burden had never been hers. She'd still be alive if he'd only done as he'd been told. Furious with himself, his balled fist hit the table in an explosion of anger. He needed to find a release for his rage if he were ever to regain any type of control over his emotions. Not stopping to think, he strode from the library to the one haven where he could always find solace.

As the doors to the music room closed behind him, he walked toward the Broadwood grand piano in one corner of the room. The cherry wood top was smooth against his fingertips as he slid his hand over it in a tender caress. Sitting down, his hands rested lightly on the black and white keyboard for a moment before he started to play.

Slow at first, the melody soon increased in speed and ferocity. With each passionate stroke of the instrument's contrasting keys, he tried hard to drive the demons from his soul until he finished the musical work. He barely allowed the notes from one sonata to float off into silence, before his fingers raced on to the next musical composition. Gradually, his fury ebbed away, leaving only a pain he knew would always be with him.

How long he played, he wasn't certain. He had just finished the last note on a Beethoven composition, when a gentle hand touched his shoulder. Glancing up, he met Louisa's worried gaze.

"Every time I hear you play like this I know something's wrong," she said with a anxious expression on her sweet face. With a half smile, he patted his sister's hand.

"Nothing's wrong. You know I like to play when I'm frustrated."

"I see." Louisa smiled, her elfin features lit with mischief. "I suppose I can guess what, or should I say who, has frustrated you."

"You're impudent and far too meddlesome, little sister."

"Which is why you love me so much." She laughed. "Besides, who else is able to put up with your foul moods as well as I do."

Sebastian rose from the piano, ignoring the statement. "Where is your student?"

"I sent her upstairs to change. I thought I would take her to the Clarendon for lunch before our shopping trip."

"And the boy?"

"He was with Madison not too long ago. Something about learning his job."

Frowning, he grumbled, "What the devil does the boy need to learn a butler's job for?"

"I heard him tell Madison that he's responsible for Helen, and he must learn a trade." Louisa bit her lip in a worrisome fashion as she looked at him. "Sebastian, there's something I think you should know about Helen, but I'm not sure … I mean it's of a personal nature, and … well, I'm not sure I should tell you."

He studied his sister's expression of distress and folded his arms across his chest. "If it's too personal, perhaps you're correct not to tell me."

"It is most certainly personal, but I think if you knew, perhaps you wouldn't think so harshly of her."

"Who said I think harshly of her?" He looked at his younger sister in astonishment.

"Well, it's not so much what Helen said, but how she reacts when I mention your name. The poor dear bristles like a hedgehog. You've obviously made her believe you dislike her and resent her being here, and yet you were the one to bring her to Melton House."

Glaring at Louisa, he turned away and walked to one of the windows that overlooked the street. "Both of you are mistaken. I do not resent Helen's presence, but I do admit to being annoyed that my schedule is in shambles."

"Well, I'm very happy that you rescued her from such horrible circumstances, but I'm afraid there's another, darker evil we might have to rescue her from."

"What are you talking about?" He turned to study Louisa's troubled features.

"When Helen was dressing earlier this morning, I helped her do up her gown. Oh, Sebastian, it was terrible. Someone's beaten her. The wounds are only just now healing, and there were scars beneath the wounds I saw. Someone's been beating her for sometime."

Stunned, he shook his head in disbelief. What manner of person would beat a woman, and why? No sooner had he asked himself the question than he found the answer. Her uncle. Chantrel would not have damaged a potentially lucrative investment so quickly, nor would she have had time to scar Helen's body.

"Did you say anything to her?"

Louisa nodded, an incredulous expression forcing her mouth to twist with dismay. "Yes, and she told me they were of no consequence! Sebastian, they were terrible wounds, and the scars underneath showed that the beatings have occurred numerous times."

"Do you think a doctor is necessary?"

"I don't know that Helen would agree to an examination. She seemed determined to avoid the subject, and the wounds do appear to be healing. It's troubled me immensely since this morning. And then the way you've been snapping at her, well it just made me think you should know. Perhaps it might make you treat her more kindly."

"I wasn't aware I was treating her any differently than anyone else." Sebastian stiffened at the gentle rebuke.

Immediately, Louisa laughed and moved to his side. "Oh, Sebastian, you are a dear, but you don't realize how frightening and distant you can be to people who don't know you. The family knows what a kind heart you have beneath that gruff, cool exterior of yours, but Helen doesn't."

"Louisa, I'm not out to impress the woman; I simply want to foil Aunt Matilda and her matchmaking plans."

"Well if you intend to do that, you need to show Helen the man your family knows, not this cold façade you display to everyone else."

The earnest note in her voice curved his mouth in a slight smile. With a shake of his head, he leaned forward and kissed her brow. "If it makes you happy, I shall try. Hmm?"

Louisa gave him a quick hug then stepped back and arched an eyebrow at him. "Although I confess to being disappointed that you would visit a brothel. If you had a wife, you wouldn't need to do such things."

"Bloody hell, Louisa, you're the one Aunt Matilda needs to marry off. You need someone to keep you in line, since I'm obviously failing at that task."

"Balderdash," she snorted. "I'm not a child, Sebastian, and it's high time you realized that. I'm well aware that you keep the occasional mistress, I'm simply surprised that you'd visit a brothel. It seems out of character for you."

Outrage and chagrin swirled together in a chaotic storm to render him speechless as he stared at his youngest sister. He had most definitely failed in his efforts to keep Louisa sheltered from the more sordid things in life. When and where had she learned of such things? He cleared his throat.

"I think this discussion is at an end," he growled.

"Fine, although I'm still curious as to why you were at a brothel. I hope this doesn't have anything to do with Georgina missing."

"What the devil do you know about her disappearance?"

"Really, Sebastian. Caleb's my brother too. I met his Georgina at a dinner party given by the Montague's almost two months ago, and Caleb's madly in love with her, although he's been quite difficult about admitting it."

Groaning at Louisa's precocious nature, he rubbed the back of his neck in a gesture of exasperation. "What am I going to do with you?"

The Rockwood charm warmed her features as she shook her head and laughed. "Nothing. I am a hopeless case as far as you're concerned. You know full well that I've always managed to appeal to the part of you that you try so hard to keep hidden from the rest of the world."

His sister's amusement had slowly faded into an expression of deep affection. With a grunt of agreement, he wagged his finger at her. "Nonetheless, there are still matters in which I expect you to obey me implicitly. One of those is the issue of you not leaving this house without an escort. This business in Whitechapel has the mark of a madman, and there's no telling when or if the devil will strike again."

"I promise I'll do as you say," Louisa said with a nod. "Several of the servants have already mentioned how horribly that poor Nichols woman was murdered."

"Then you understand why I insist you have an escort when you go out."

"Yes, I've already asked Yancey to walk with Helen and me to Bond Street." With a quick kiss to his cheek, she walked toward the music room exit. "Remember, I expect you to be nice to Helen."

Sebastian watched in a state of bemusement as the door close behind his youngest sister. It was always puzzling to him how Louisa could manipulate him better than any politician could. He'd been correct when he'd stated she was made from the same mold as Aunt Matilda. With a glance at the piano, he frowned.

Usually, playing his favorite pieces would alleviate his dark moods, but for the first time in memory, it had failed to do so. Why? It wasn't difficult to guess the answer, but he didn't want to speak or think it. Louisa's information had also confused and troubled him. The idea of someone beating Helen enraged him. He couldn't be sure her uncle was responsible, but all the evidence lay in that direction. What manner of sin had Helen committed to deserve a beating that would leave marks such as Louisa described?

Disgruntled by the troubling thoughts, he walked away from his piano and out of the music room, which until now had been his sanctuary and salvation. As he entered the main hall, the front door flew open, and Caleb strode into the house at a furious pace, wearing a dark expression.

"I got your message." For a moment, Sebastian marveled at how much his brother sounded like him. The terse statement was a perfect replica of the abrupt assertions he often made. "I'm going to get her, Sebastian. With or without your help."

"Did I say I wouldn't help you?" He scowled at the younger Rockwood.

"You didn't, but I'm not waiting another day before I get Georgina out of Chantrel's. With that butcher in Whitechapel, I'm not taking any more chances. I can't lose her."

Out of the corner of his eye, Sebastian saw Madison conversing with a servant across the hall. Any other time it would have been a normal event, except for Edward Rivenall's presence. Avid curiosity on the boy's face, it was clear he'd been listening to their conversation. Raising his hand, he silenced his brother before jerking his head in the direction of the library. "Come in here and we'll discuss a plan in detail."

Together they headed toward the library and just as they reached the door, Edward tugged the sleeve of Sebastian's jacket. "My lord, I believe I can be of assistance to you."

"Thank you, Edward, but I believe this is a matter best left to my brother and me," he said quietly as he refused the boy's offer. "This is too dangerous for you."

"I know the inside of Chantrel's, my lord and you don't. If you're thinking about another rescue, then you need someone who can help you locate the woman you're seeking."

Sebastian shook his head. "I'm sorry, Edward, I can't allow it."

Desperation in his face, Caleb grabbed Sebastian's arm. "Why can't the boy help? It isn't going to be easy getting into Chantrel's, and I haven't a clue as to where they're keeping Georgina."

"I know where she is, my lord."

Sebastian winced at the look of hope lighting his brother's face. Caleb bent toward the boy. "Do you know who I'm talking about?"

"Yes, my lord." The boy eyed Caleb with a candid expression. The only Georgina anyone mentioned at Chantrel's has black hair and violet eyes."

Caleb came upright with a jerk. "Damn it, he's seen her, Sebastian. She's there. You must let the boy help us. The very least he can do is draw us a map of the brothel's interior."

"He's just a boy, Caleb. I won't answer to his sister by involving him in this matter." Sebastian glared at his brother. Didn't the fool see how Helen would react to their blatant use of the boy? And he was little more than a boy. Although, he'd been the same age the night he'd caused his mother-- He forced his thoughts into a wall of silence.

"Please, my lord. I owe you my life and Helen's as well. You must let me do something to repay that debt. It is the gentleman thing to do."

The boy's plea struck at the heart of him. Damn, the lad knew just what to say. He wanted to protect his sister and repay his debts. Did Edward know about his sister's beatings? Had he been powerless to prevent them and felt guilty? Sebastian understood guilt better than anyone did. He could not refuse the boy's request to recover his honor. Denying him the opportunity to repay his debt would be unconscionable, and judging from the boy's face, Edward knew Sebastian would not be able to refuse this specific plea.

With a sharp nod, he turned to Caleb. "Fine, I'll let the boy help, but he's not to put one foot into Chantrel's. Is that understood?"

Relief etched fine lines at the corner of his brother's mouth, and Caleb nodded his agreement. Edward's expression was one of resolute determination. With resignation, he heaved an inward groan. If Helen found out, there would be hell to pay. Maybe she wouldn't find out. Of course, she'd find out. He could only hope that they would be back before she discovered her brother missing. But considering his luck over the past twenty-four hours, he wasn't counting on keeping the woman in the dark.

Chapter 6

"Oh, you do look lovely, Helen," Louisa exclaimed. "As always, Madame Clarissa, your talent and eye for color is extraordinary."

Straight pins tucked between her lips, the dressmaker merely nodded at Louisa's enthusiasm as she continued marking the hem for adjustment. As Helen watched the woman work, she realized it was quite likely that in a very short time she might be employed in a similar position. Once Sebastian's aunt returned to Scotland, convinced a wedding was in the works, there would be no reason to remain at Melton House. The only other possibility was finding her grandfather, and she wasn't quite certain how to go about doing that .

Finished with her task, the seamstress rose to her feet. "Well now, Lady Louisa, I can have the two ball gowns ready for a final fitting in three weeks. This dress I can hem and send over to Melton House by the end of the week. Then, of course, there are the three-day gowns that fit Miss Rivenall quite nicely. Those you can take with you now. Does this meet with your approval?"

"It does indeed, Madame." Louisa bobbed her head and smiled. "Send the bill to my brother as always."

"As you wish," the woman said quietly. Turning to Helen, she smiled. "If you'll step back into the dressing room, Miss Rivenall, you may change into one of the gowns you're taking with you."

Without waiting for a response, the woman left the small fitting room. One finger tapping the edge of her jaw, Louisa studied her with a critical eye. Satisfaction glimmered in her gaze as she grinned. "You look exquisite. I knew Madame Clarissa would work wonders with you."

"I don't know how to thank you or your brother." Helen shook her head, at a loss for how to express her gratitude.

"Phffst, nonsense. We're delighted to do so."

"I have a feeling your brother will hardly be delighted when he receives Madame Clarissa's bill. I don't know why I need so many clothes."

"Because when Aunt Matilda arrives, you need to look every inch the suitable bride for Sebastian. Otherwise she'll know it's all a sham, and then my brother will have both our heads."

The thought of meeting Sebastian's aunt made Helen bite her lip. If the woman was as formidable as Sebastian, it would be a nerve-wracking experience. "What's she like, your Aunt Matilda?"

"She's the sweetest, most generous woman, and we all adore her," Louisa said with a smile. "I'm certain you'll like her, and I *know* she'll like you."

With a slight shrug of her shoulders, Helen sighed. "I suppose the only thing that matters is that she gives up trying to find your brother a bride."

"True, but I have a feeling Sebastian won't be all that successful in avoiding marriage." Louisa said with a mysterious smile. "Now then, if you'll change, I'll have Yancey stand watch outside, while I visit Brentworths next door and order Edward's suits."

"Shall I meet you there?" Helen asked as Louisa hurried toward the exit.

"Certainly. I'll tell Yancey to keep an eye out for you."

Left to her own devices, Helen entered the dressing room and quickly changed into one of the new gowns Louisa had helped her select. A deep, royal blue silk, the dress caressed her skin like a delicate summer breeze. Doing up the buttons of her gown, she was relieved to see that she'd been left alone to dress. Although the seamstress had refrained from mentioning the scars on her back when she'd undressed, the woman's gasp of horror had been quite loud.

From that point forward, the woman's gaze had been filled with pity every time she'd met Helen's gaze. Although she knew the woman meant well, she didn't want the woman's pity. She had no need for it. All she wanted to do was forget the pain and hatred she had found in Mayfield.

For a long time she'd tried to understand why her uncle hated her enough to find any opportunity to beat her. Her transgressions were often minor, but Uncle Warren's rage always found its way into his riding crop as it landed across her back. With the exception of one time when he'd called her by her mother's name, he'd never spoken as he whipped her.

It still puzzled her. Uncle Warren never had anything good to say about her parents. It was as if he hated them and her because she was their child. None of it made sense. If he hated her and Edward, why had he taken them in? Troubled by her thoughts, she pushed them aside as she hurried to finish dressing. The past was dead, and there was no need to continue dwelling on the matter. Somehow she would make a life for Edward and herself in a place that was free of hatred and pain.

A short time later, she stepped out onto the sidewalk of Bond Street. The bright sunlight made her shield her eyes as she paused to grow accustomed to the intense light. From her left, a familiar voice said her name. Stiffening, she turned her head to meet the penetrating gaze of Lord Templeton.

"What a fetching picture you make this morning, Miss Rivenall." While there was nothing sinister in his voice, it was impossible for Helen to relax her stiff posture as the man bowed in front of her. "I can see you've been shopping at Madame Clarissa's."

Flustered, she looked around for Louisa's footman as she swallowed the knot of trepidation in her throat. "Good morning, my lord."

"Are you faring well at Melton House?"

"The earl and his sister have been most kind," she murmured as she tried to figure out a way to excuse herself from the man's company.

"I'm delighted to hear that," he said in a sober voice. "I must confess that I would be quite distressed if Melton was anything but kind to you."

Startled by the sincerity in his voice, she focused her complete attention on the Marquess. "What an odd thing to say, my lord. We hardly know one another."

"One does not always need time to know a person, my dear Helen. Sometimes it is quite easy to know from a first meeting all there is to know about someone."

The sincerity of the man's voice tightened her nerve endings with more alarm than when he'd first greeted her. Even the intensity of his dark eyes caused her body to go rigid with tension. Uncertain how best to answer him, she averted her gaze to stare at the street scene over his shoulder.

As she focused on the busy avenue, she caught sight of a tall man vigorously questioning a shopkeeper. Dressed in black, the man presented an imposing, stern figure. In some ways he reminded her of Uncle Warren. In that split second, the man reared back his head, his profile plain to see.

The ground shifted beneath her feet as she struggled to remain standing. A strong hand caught her elbow and steadied her. "Helen, are you all right?"

Nauseated, she clutched at her stomach as she tried to keep from retching. She had to get away. If Uncle Warren saw her, he'd drag her back to Mayfield. At the very least he'd demand that Edward return with him, because the man knew she'd never abandon her brother. She swayed again, sinking into the Marquess's shoulder. Despite her uneasy feelings about the man, she was grateful he was at her side to hold her steady.

"Let me take you back to Melton House, you're obviously not well." Again he surprised her as his voice echoed with a deep concern. She shook her head.

"I cannot, Louisa is at Brentworths ordering my brother a suit."

"Your brother?" Astonishment echoed in his words. Then with an authoritative wave of his hand, he motioned to someone nearby. "Well, if you won't let me take you back to Melton House, at least you can sit in my carriage until Lady Louisa is done."

The offer of sitting in the dark confines of the Marquess's carriage was a welcome one. It would make it more difficult for her uncle to see her. As the jet-black vehicle pulled up to where they were standing, Lord Templeton courteously guided her forward and into the coach. Through a haze of fear, she heard Yancey's voice at the carriage door.

"Is everything all right, Miss Rivenall?"

The Marquess turned toward the footman. "Miss Rivenall has taken ill, but she refuses to let me take her home until Lady Louisa returns. Run and fetch the woman."

Indecision clouded the footman's face, and Helen waved him on. "It's all right, Yancey, please find Lady Louisa and bring her here."

As they waited for the footman to return with Louisa in tow, the Marquess remained on the sidewalk, patting her hand in a sympathetic manner.

Despite the way her stomach was still churning, it was impossible not to note that the man's kindness. Perhaps Sebastian had misjudged the Marquess. With a nod of her head, she leaned back into the dark shadows of the carriage, her muscles tense with fear. If Uncle Warren were to find her here ... She swallowed the mounting alarm that threatened to smother her.

Moments later, Louisa's worried features appeared in the open doorway of the carriage. "Good heavens, you look like you've seen a ghost."

"I have in a manner of speaking," she whispered. "Would you mind terribly if we returned to the house?"

"Of course not. Come along, we'll go home straight away."

"If I may be so bold, Lady Louisa, I would be honored to drive you and Miss Rivenall home. From the look of things, I'd say Miss Rivenall could benefit from the ride."

Louisa hesitated, her troubled gaze meeting Helen's. It was clear she didn't want to accept the Marquess' offer. Aware of her friend's quandary, Helen leaned forward. "I suppose I could--"

"No." Louisa said firmly as she turned her head toward Lord Templeton. "My lord, we will accept your generous offer. Clearly Helen is not up to walking."

"Thank you for your trust in me, Lady Louisa." There was a note of gratitude in his voice. As she accepted the Marquess's hand to enter the carriage, Louisa bobbed her head toward the servant standing just behind her.

"If you don't mind, may my footman come with us? I gave my brother my word we would not to go any where unescorted."

"Certainly." Lord Templeton gestured to his driver. "John, make room for the man."

With the Marquess seated opposite them, the carriage lurched forward. As the vehicle was set into motion, Helen glanced out the window and saw her uncle staring at the coach. Immediately, she pressed her body back into the cushions trying desperately to remain hidden in the dark recesses of the carriage. The chill skimming over her body made her shiver. Her gaze met Lord Templeton's as she pressed her body back into the seat.

There was a gleam of curiosity and calculating assessment in his dark eyes. Suppressing the fear that assailed her, she reminded herself that the Marquess knew nothing about her uncle. And it was unlikely her uncle had seen her in the shadows of the carriage. Nonetheless, the look in Lord Templeton's eyes alarmed her. It was as if he knew exactly what frightened her, and he was trying to find a way to use that to his advantage.

* * * *

Helen crossed the foyer of Melton House, the soles of her shoes clicking against the marble floor as she headed toward the main salon. Despite her reluctance to rest after the Marquess had seen them safely home, she had yielded to Louisa's insistent coaxing. Although it had not eliminated her fear completely, the nap had eased her feelings of panic. The memory of Sebastian's promise to keep her and Edward safe had also relieved her anxiety.

Something deep inside her convinced her Sebastian would keep that promise. She could only hope it wouldn't come to that. She didn't think Uncle Warren had seen her, but it was the Marquess that worried her. Despite the man's kind behavior, she found it impossible to forget how he had bid on her at Madame Chantrel's. And as the carriage left Bond Street, there had been an expression in his eyes that said he knew what had frightened her. The man couldn't possibly know about her uncle. It was illogical to think that he might, but it was a thought that refused to go away.

Grimacing, she chose to concentrate on something else, and her eye caught the high arch of the foyer ceiling. Despite the height of the ceiling, the warm neutral shades of the walls shooting skyward offered a sensation of warmth and comfort. The entire house looked as if it belonged in a different era. Unlike Mayfield's dark, dismal interior, there was not an inch of dark wood or heavy ornamentation anywhere in this luxurious mansion. In fact, Melton House gave off a warm lighthearted air, completely unlike its owner.

Sebastian was a paradox to her. The kindness he had shown her and Edward, mixed with his brusque manner, perplexed her. She glanced in the direction of the library, remembering how he'd pulled her back against his broad, sturdy chest. His touch had stirred sensations in her unlike any she'd ever experienced. Not even her first kiss that day so long ago in the meadow with William had prepared her for the delicious heat that warmed and tingled its way through her every time Sebastian touched her. The warmth had coiled its way through her until she was wet between her thighs. Wet for him. Craving his touch there, his fingers teasing that sensitive spot she knew would pleasure her. No man had ever touched her that way, but she wanted Sebastian too. She wanted it badly. Even now the thought of it made heat rush from her belly into her nether regions until she was damp again with need.

She paused in front of the foyer's large mirror to stare at her reflection. The face staring back at her revealed none of the wild and wanton thoughts racing through her mind. Uncle Warren had always said such ideas would be the ruin of her. The unwelcome memory of her uncle standing on Bond Street made her breathe in a sharp breath. She was being irrational. She had nothing to fear.

Reverting to a childhood habit, she stuck her tongue out at the mirror. Uncle Warren wasn't here, and wouldn't find her. For the first time since her parent's death, she and Edward were free. Free of the harsh confines of Mayfield and free of Uncle Warren's tyranny.

Now she simply had to find her grandfather. She could only pray that when her search ended, he would be willing to take her and Edward into his care. But most of all, she hoped she would find him before she found herself in Lord Melton's arms again.

As she resumed her journey toward the salon, Louisa emerged from the room with the family butler close behind her. "Now Madison, I want you to be very explicit in the instructions you give the messengers. They are to wait until they receive an answer to my letters."

"Yes, Lady Louisa."

Seeing her, Louisa smiled then stopped the man from leaving with a touch of her hand. "Oh, and one more thing Madison. I want to help Miss Helen review her table etiquette, so you'll need to have the breakfast nook set with full place settings as if it were a supper party."

Madison stepped away with a brief nod and disappeared toward the rear of the house. Helen smiled as Louisa stepped forward to take her hands.

"Let me look at you." Louisa tipped her head to one side, then smiled. "Excellent, you look wonderfully refreshed."

"Thank you. The idea wasn't very appealing, but I do feel much better."

"I must admit you gave me quite a scare. Normally, I would have refused Lord Templeton, but you looked far too ill for me to refuse his offer to bring us home."

The curiosity in Louisa's voice was difficult to ignore, and Helen bit her lip as she averted her gaze. There was no reason not to explain about Uncle Warren, but to do so would only bring back the horror she'd felt in that instant when she'd seen him on the street. That was a sensation she had no wish to experience again.

"I'm not sure what came over me. It seems I should have listened to your advice about not skipping breakfast."

For a second, Louisa stared at her with a skeptical gleam in her hazel eyes before she shook her head and laughed. "But you emerged unscathed from both your encounters with Sebastian today. All of which I might add you did on an empty stomach."

The teasing note in Louisa's voice made Helen laugh. Her friend was correct. She had faced the lion in his den. But the lion and his touch had a mesmerizing effect on her. Each time Sebastian came near her, wanton urges sped through her body until every inch of her cried out for his touch. Never had she ever been willing to have a man touch her the way she wanted Sebastian to touch her. It was an intense craving that even now had her nipples hard with desire. She wanted him to touch her like he had before. To kiss her--

"Well, you're miles away. Have you heard a word of what I said?" Louisa's amused tone pierced her thoughts.

Heat flushed her cheeks as she shook her head. "I'm sorry, you were saying?"

"I was saying that unlike you, your brother has a considerable appetite." Louisa linked arms with her and pulled her toward the salon. "I understand from Madison that Edward polished off a plate of eggs, a large helping of kippers and several pieces of toast this morning."

"*All* of that?" Helen exclaimed. "He never ate like that at our uncle's house."

"It's nothing to be concerned about. Mrs. Haversham is thrilled that she has another boy to feed. She used to indulge my brothers all the time when they were growing up."

Helen glanced over her shoulder, half-expecting to see her brother sneaking up on her in an effort to scare her for the fun of it. Young and irrepressible, it was hard for her brother not to make himself heard, and it suddenly occurred to her that Edward was being more quiet than usual. She looked at Louisa.

"Speaking of my brother, have you seen him recently?"

"The last I saw he was hot on Sebastian's heels as they went into the library with Caleb. When we returned from our shopping trip, I asked whether Sebastian was home, and Madison indicated he'd gone out after we left. He repeated some cryptic remark Sebastian had made about playing knight errant."

Puzzled, Helen pondered the information for a moment. "But then where is--"

Helen's words died on her lips as she came to an abrupt halt. Knight errant. They'd gone to rescue the young woman she'd seen. She knew it. Sebastian had gone back to Chantrel's, and the man had taken Edward with him. No doubt, he thought having someone who knew where things were inside the brothel would be useful to him.

He'd used her brother for his own ends. He'd risked Edward's life. She sucked in a sharp breath of fury. She'd known he wasn't to be trusted. Clenching her fists, she fought to keep from screaming her rage. What sort of a man would drag her brother back to that hellish place?

"Helen, are you all right?" Louisa's hand on her arm made her jumped.

"*No*. If I'm right, your brother--"

The front door of Melton House crashed open, interrupting her in mid-sentence. The first person through the door was a younger version of Sebastian, only his hair was dark blond. In his arms, he carried the woman Helen had seen at Chantrel's. The sight of the other woman filled her with relief. At least they had rescued the girl. The young woman lay unconscious in her rescuer's arms and she immediately stepped forward, as did Louisa, to offer assistance.

A moment later, Edward barreled through the door, followed by Sebastian. Fury scraped against her spine as she realized she'd been correct in assuming the earl had taken her brother back to Chantrel's. The voice of the young man carrying the dark-haired woman was a roar similar to his brother's. "Madison! Come quick, man."

Louisa stretched out a hand to the unconscious woman. "Is she hurt, Caleb?"

"No, but she's been drugged." The man gave an impatient toss of his head. "Damn it, where the devil is that man? Madison!"

Realizing she could do nothing to help the rescued woman, Helen skirted Caleb as she headed toward her brother and the earl. Edward saw her first and grimaced with dismay. Before he could speak, she eyed him coldly. "Upstairs, young man. I shall deal with you later."

"But Helen--"

"*Now*, Edward." Despite her authoritative command, he glanced back for the approval of the tall man behind him.

The look incensed her all the more. Glaring at Sebastian, she watched him nod at Edward to obey. Watching her brother hurry away at the man's approval, her fingernails bit into her palm. If there were something close at hand to break, she would be hard pressed not to send the object crashing onto the floor. How dare this man act as her brother's keeper? She was responsible for Edward not him. Scowling up at him, she noted the pinched look to his mouth. Resignation at the chastisement to come, no doubt, had tightened his lips into a firm line. For a split second, the pallor of his skin surprised her.

"I believe you owe me an explanation, my lord."

"Now is not the time, Helen."

The terse note in his voice simply added fuel to her anger. She gave a fierce shake of her head. "I disagree. I want to know why you took my brother back to that hellish place, my lord."

Sebastian swayed toward her, his brow suddenly beaded with sweat. One large hand gripped her shoulders as his jaw grew rigid with tension. Startled, by his touch, she pushed against his arms in an attempt to break away from him. The moment she did so, a colorful oath broke past his lips. What on earth was wrong with the man? One would think he'd been injured--she jerked her gaze upward to see his strained features blanch to a grayish color as his fingers bit painfully into her shoulder.

"I'm afraid your lecture will have to wait, Helen," he muttered.

"I'm not--"

Sebastian's words died abruptly as he lost consciousness and swayed unsteadily in front of her. Without thinking, her arms quickly slid around his waist as he sank into her. Shouldering the weight of his sagging body, she struggled to keep him from collapsing on the marble floor. The weight of him pushed a small gasp of air from her lungs just as his strong head drooped onto her shoulder. Behind her, she heard Louisa cry out frantically.

"Oh dear lord, Sebastian's bleeding."

The shocking exclamation made her glance down at Sebastian's hand. A thin stream of blood dripped off his fingertips on to the floor while the weight of him pressed relentlessly into her with each passing second.

"Bloody hell! Why the devil didn't he tell me he was hit?" Caleb's voice filled with remorse and worry.

Glancing over her shoulder, she saw the younger man staring helplessly at his brother. Louisa stood next to Caleb, her face as pale as Sebastian's, if not more so. Flustered and struggling to keep from falling under his weight, Helen saw Madison and two footmen race into the foyer.

"Damn it, Louisa, sit down now before you faint as well. He's going to be fine." Caleb's sharp words sent his sister stumbling toward a stiff backed chair on one wall. "Madison, fetch Michaels to look after his lordship. Terrence. Alfred. Carry his lordship upstairs."

In a matter of seconds, two footmen were on either side of Helen, lifting Sebastian off her. Still stunned by all that was happening around her, she realized that even unconscious, the earl demanded nothing but organized precision from his staff. With the exception of Louisa, everyone acted as though it were an everyday occurrence for the master of the house to faint from a bleeding wound. Relieved of her heavy burden, she turned to see Louisa with her head buried in her lap. About to go to her side, Caleb's voice stopped her forward movement.

"Helen, is it?" She nodded at his abrupt question, but he didn't pause to hear her answer. "Good, I need your help. Louisa faints at the sight of blood, and I have to deal with Georgina. Can you assist Sebastian's valet with his wound?"

"Yes."

"Come with me then," he said in a voice hauntingly like Sebastian's. "Louisa, as soon as you can pick your stomach up off the floor, come up to the Blue Room. I'll need your assistance with Georgina.

Sebastian's younger brother strode toward the stairs without another word as Louisa lifted her head. Helen hesitated until Louisa waved her away. Satisfied that her friend was all right, she scurried toward the stairway. Ahead of her, the footmen awkwardly carried Sebastian along the upper floor landing and down the main corridor. The sight filled her with guilt as she remembered the harsh manner in which she'd greeted him. Why hadn't he told her right away he was injured? She could add stubbornness to his list of faults. Deep inside, Helen refused to acknowledge the fear that had gripped her insides the moment she'd seen blood dripping off his hand.

Reaching the second floor, she saw Sebastian carried into a room close to hers. She followed close behind the footmen, uncertain of what she would find in his personal domain. It was an austere room done in dark blues. Practical in form, the furniture gave her the impression of a military man. One used to few necessities. Tall windows overlooked a large expanse of garden at the back of the house while dark blue curtains draped the glass. A large leather chair faced the room's fireplace, while several books lay scattered across the small table next to the chair.

"Miss, if you would please?"

The quiet voice of a small man beside the earl's bed interrupted her thoughts, and she hastened toward him. As she glanced down at Sebastian, she saw that someone had removed all the clothes on his upper body. The sight of a hard, muscular chest made her swallow hard, and she fought the urge to touch him. Her eyes disobeyed her brain as her gaze skimmed over wide shoulders.

An itching settled in the tips of her fingers, as she fought not to glide her hand across his rippling chest muscles and downward to where a dark line of hair disappeared into his trousers. The overall effect on her senses left her feeling flushed and unsteady. When she lifted her gaze to look at the servant on the opposite side of the bed, a heated wave sailed over her cheeks. Embarrassed the man had seen her ogling the earl, she stiffened her spine.

"What is it you wish me to do?" She kept her voice crisp, hoping the man would not comment on her behavior. In the back of her mind, she offered up a small prayer of gratitude that Uncle Warren wasn't here. If her uncle had seen the way she'd looked at the earl, he would damn her to hell for certain.

"I need to probe the wound for any debris left in the tissue. He's going to wake up in a nasty mood. I need you to keep his good hand from interfering in my work. Can you do that, Miss?"

"I think so." Helen bit her bottom lip as she leaned over the earl in preparation to restrain him.

"Are you ready, Miss? The moment I pour this brandy into his wound, he'll react with more than just a shout, I can assure you of that."

She nodded as she gently gripped Sebastian's injured arms with both hands, the dark hairs on his forearm soft against her palm. A second later, a strong arm encircled her as the patient woke with a roar of pain. Like a wounded lion, his hand tried to reach his injury, but Helen's body blocked him from doing so. Hard fingers bit into her waist, and she yelped with distress.

Caught in the trap of his arm, his thrashing pinned the length of her against his bare chest. Warmth brushed her lips as her mouth touched the smooth skin covering strong chest muscles. The spontaneous urge to rest her mouth fully on him shocked her. For a brief moment, she savored the wild sensations singing in her blood. Lifting her head, she found herself staring into black eyes that glowed with pain and desire. Desire that made her want to forget every morality lesson Uncle Warren had ever taught her. Shaken by that revelation, she shuddered against him. At that same moment, he grunted and closed his eyes in pain.

"Damnation, Michaels. Must you enjoy your work so much?" The harsh question broke from him like a lion snarling at a member of its pride.

Still pressed against him in an intimate position, Helen gently tried to ease out of his embrace. His eyes still closed, he resisted her movement. "Are you finished with me Michaels, or does Helen need to keep me pinned to the mattress?"

She could have sworn there was a note of laughter in the deep timbre of his voice. Once more a fiery heat suffused her body. With a shove, she sat up, although his arm remained about her waist. His thigh pressed into hers, its warmth passing through her skirt and petticoats. The touch alarmed her. The man was dangerous, and she was grateful for the presence of the small valet.

"Well, my lord. I'm afraid you're going to need some sutures."

A groan rumbled in his chest, and he opened his eyes to stare up at the ceiling. "Then give me a swallow of brandy and get it over with, damn you."

The valet's lips held the barest hint of a smile as he offered the earl a shot of liquor. Looking at Helen, he arched an eyebrow. "Miss, are you handy with needle and thread?"

"I've mended many of my brother's clothes, as well as my own, sir."

"Good, because I need you to sew up this wound. My eyes aren't what they use to be, and his lordship will be far less likely to hit you than he would me."

The man's humor tugged a smile at the corner of Helen's mouth. A quick glance at Sebastian revealed his dark scowl. Hiding her amusement, she broke free of his grasp and stood up to walk around the bed. A strong hand grasped her forearm before she could take a single step.

"I would never hit you, Helen. But if you enjoy your task too much, I'll extract a suitable punishment, similar to this morning."

Her cheeks burned at the subtle reference to the first time he'd kissed her. The look on his face dared her to disobey him. For a moment, she could have sworn she saw a flicker of hope she would provoke him to punish her. It was a heady thought, and she almost smiled at the delight such punishment would be. Alarmed by the direction of her thoughts, she jerked free of his hold. In silence, she accepted the needle from Michaels then proceeded to sterilize the tiny instrument in a candle flame. Threading it quickly, she turned toward Sebastian and paused.

"Is there any brandy left?" She asked softly.

"Bloody hell, woman. I'm not about to let you pour more of that damnable stuff onto my arm."

Biting back a smile at his dark growl, she ignored him as she directed her gaze at the valet. "I want to clean my hands with the brandy. I believe it will help prevent infection."

With a nod, Michaels picked up a small water basin and held it beneath her hands as he poured brandy over her fingers. Shaking off the liquid, she took the threaded needle and turned to see Sebastian watching her with pain glazing his eyes. Instinct made her want to caress his brow, but she knew that was impossible.

Suppressing the urge to do so, she leaned over his injured limb to study his wound. It was the first time she'd sewn anything other than cloth. Gently, she squeezed the skin together and carefully slid the needle through. The stitch pulled a loud oath from Sebastian. The thought that she was hurting him made her cringe, but she didn't stop.

Each stitch drew a new oath from Sebastian's lips, but she was finding that suturing a wound did not differ all that much from normal mending with perhaps the exception of her patient's colorful oaths of pain. After a few minutes, she had neatly sealed the entry wound with several small stitches.

The exit wound proved to be more difficult to close given its location. Gently, she raised Sebastian's arm so it rested on the pillow above his head. The quiet thud of the door made her pause. Glancing up, she looked around to find that they were alone. She reassured herself that Michaels had just gone for fresh bandages. The nape of her neck suddenly tingled as Sebastian's free hand rose to deliberately graze the back of her neck. She sent him a stern look, poised to stitch up the bullet's exit wound. His dark eyes taunted her, daring her to say a word. Irritated by his cocksure expression, she failed to take extra care as she proceeded with her work. The stab of the needle made him bark with pain.

"Damn it, Helen. Take care with that weapon of yours."

His good hand dropped back down to his side. Allowing herself a slight curving of the lips, she murmured, "I'm sorry. I was preoccupied for a moment, but the distraction is gone."

About to return her attention to the task at hand, her heart skipped a beat as Sebastian raised his hand again to rub his thumb against her lower lip.

"A distraction, eh." Amusement glittered in the dark ingots probing her face. "Was it a pleasant one?"

"More like an annoying fly," she retorted with a sense of self-preservation as she turned her face away to avoid his touch. The man was far too attractive for his own good. Returning her attention to his arm, she worked as fast as she could. From time to time, Sebastian grunted with pain, but she ignored the sounds. As she knotted the last suture, she snapped the thread in two with her teeth then set aside the needle.

The moment she did so, Sebastian's good arm pulled her down onto his chest. Caught off guard, she tumbled toward him for the second time in less than an hour. This time her mouth brushed against his cheek. The beginnings of an evening shadow scraped her lips. Trembling at the fiery currents flooding her veins, she tried to break free of his hold.

"I seem to recall warning you to take care with the needle, Miss Rivenall."

An unadulterated hint of wicked amusement laced his words, and her eyes locked with his. The humor she saw in his gaze sent her pulse spinning wildly out of control. Swallowing hard, she tried to shove away from him.

"I think it best that I leave, now that I've seen to your wound," she murmured.

"Not yet." There was a shift in the tenor of his voice. She froze as he stared into her face with a longing that startled her.

The same vulnerability she'd seen in his eyes this morning had returned. Deep inside him there was a secret pain. It made him ache, and for some reason, she could see his pain. Without thinking, her hand caressed his cheek. Immediately, he turned his head to bury his lips in her open palm.

Fire singed her skin as his touch sent a wave of pleasure through her. It was a riveting sensation she didn't want to end. Anticipation made her breath hitch as his uninjured hand grasped the nape of her neck and slowly pulled her head downward. Black eyes gleamed up at her, and she wanted to drown in their depths. The closer her mouth came to his, the stronger her nose tingled from his spicy scent.

"Kiss me." The whispered command warmed her cheeks, and without hesitation or thought, she did as he ordered.

His lips were hard and firm. Brandy lingered on his mouth, and the fiery taste of him was tantalizing and all male. With a force that surprised her, molten heat exploded in her belly and spread its way throughout her limbs. It consumed her in a matter of seconds, creating an intense urge for something beyond this delicious moment. She shuddered at the heady sensation.

The kiss deepened as he crushed her into him. An instant later his tongue darted into her mouth tempting and teasing her with each stroke. With each passing second, the need to possess her grew inside him until it overpowered every other thought. Pressed against him like this, her soft curves melded with his in a perfect fit.

If he kept this behavior up, he'd be bedding her tonight. God knew it was exactly what he wanted. The things he wanted to do with her were enough to drive him mad just thinking about it. Her soft hands stroked across his shoulders as she breathed a sound of pleasure into his mouth. With his good hand, he parted the ruffles that rose from the vee of her breasts to cover her lovely throat. Eagerly, his fingers stroked their way across her silky skin before he slid one finger down between the softness of her warm breasts. God to have his cock slide in and out between these plump mounds would be incredible. Then he would replicate the action by sliding into her hot silky core.

A shudder rippled through her at his touch. It shot a bolt of triumph through him. She wanted him. His mouth left her lips to trail across her the edge of her jaw and down the side of her throat. Damn, she tasted good and there was the faint hint of her desire. Was she slick and wet for him? God, he wanted to feel her naked against him. Feel the heat of her desire as her hot folds engulfed him. Groaning, he sought her mouth once more, plundering, demanding her response.

With one hand, he undid his trousers to release his erection. Capturing her hand, he made her wrap her fingers around him. She jerked with surprise, but when his tongue swirled in her mouth, she relaxed against him, her hand gripping him snugly. Her thumb tentatively brushed over the tip of him, and he uttered a deep growl of pleasure. If he didn't take care, he was going to spill his seed in a matter of seconds. His hand slid back around the nape of her neck as he lost himself in the pleasure of her hand holding him.

The desire flaring between them grew hotter as their tongues dueled with need. Her hand still wrapped around his hard length, she released a breathy moan into his mouth. His hips moved against her hand, creating a warm friction against his erection. Hard and solid, her fingertips tingled at the hot, velvety length of him across the pads of her fingers.

She should be ashamed of her behavior, but she was past caring. He felt wonderful in her hand, and she knew it pleased him. Pleasing him was something she wanted to do. Wild, sensual images swept through her head. Images that tightened the tips of her breasts until she ached with need. It was a need that made her forget everything except the hard feel of him beneath her fingers, the delicious scent of him wafting into her nose and the tangy taste of him on her lips and now her tongue.

She wanted to melt into him, be absorbed into his body until she no longer could tell where she ended and he began. Excitement crashed through her as his kiss deepened and demanded more of her. Without hesitation, she answered his searing command. Lost in the wild throes of an emotion she'd never experienced before, it took her a moment to realize the change in him. A sudden chill passed over her skin as he broke the kiss, his mouth grazing her cheek.

"Someone's coming, sweetheart."

Her head fuzzy, she fought to regain control of her faculties. As she raised her head, she met his fiery gaze. The passion blazing in his eyes made her swallow hard. She wanted to kiss him again. Wanted him to touch her. The knowledge made her elated and fearful at the same time. How was it possible to feel such emotions with a man she hardly knew? Uncle Warren would know the answer to that question. He'd say she was a temptress. A wanton.

Mortified, she pushed away from him and scooted off the bed. Voices from the hall echoed in the room, making her quickly adjust her clothing as Sebastian deftly closed his trousers. A moment later, a knock on the door preceded Caleb's entrance into the room. "Well, brother, you look none the worse for wear, and you've even managed to secure the attentions of a lovely nurse."

Flustered, Helen fiddled with the ruffles at her gown's bodice as heat flushed her cheeks. Did Caleb realize she'd been in lying in Sebastian's arms? Mortified at the possibility, she avoided the eyes of both men as she smoothed the silk material wrapped snugly about her waist. Did she look like a wanton? A woman who'd provoked Sebastian into kissing her. No. She'd not instigated the kiss. Sebastian had. She was certain of that. But she hadn't objected to his caress. No, she'd eagerly responded to him. And God help her, she wanted more of his touch. She craved it. Desperately, she struggled to keep her composure as she swallowed the knot in her throat.

"I shall send Michaels in to bandage your arm, my lord," she said in a breathless voice as she hurried toward the door. "If you'll excuse me."

Without waiting for either man to respond, she bolted from the room as if the hounds of hell were pursuing her.

Chapter 7

"Bloody hell," Sebastian cursed softly as Helen darted out the room.

"I do believe Louisa is right. Miss Rivenall seems to have you in a dither." Caleb said as he grinned like a cat that had eaten a canary.

"Louisa is a miniature Aunt Matilda in the making." Glaring up at his brother, he grimaced. "Your Georgina. How is she?"

Caleb's face grew dark with anger. "She's going to be fine. From what the police got out of Chantrel, she simply used laudanum to keep Georgina quiet. Unlike the drug the woman used on your Miss Rivenall."

Ignoring the personalization his brother had inferred, he shifted his position in bed. The moment he did so, pain clawed its way up his arm. "Damnation," he growled. "Remind me to say no to you the next time you invite me along for one of your little adventures."

"Actually, I seem to recall you did say no at first." One corner of Caleb's mouth tipped upward in a wry twist. "But I'm grateful for your help. I'm only sorry you were hurt in the process."

"That's what brothers are for I suppose." He shrugged as he smiled. A knock on the door rocked him with tension. "Come in."

The door opened and he stifled a growl of disappointment at the sight of his valet. Flopping back against the pillows, he clenched his jaw as his brother burst into laughter.

"I'll leave you to Michaels' good care, Sebastian." Caleb said with a wide grin. "Although something tells me you'd much rather it be someone else tending to your wounds."

"Get out, Caleb."

With another laugh, his brother took a step toward the door. "Yes, I do believe Louisa is right."

"Out, *now*," he roared.

Closing his eyes, he blocked out the sight of his brother's amusement. A grimace tugged at his lips. He was the worst kind of scoundrel. He'd almost compromised a guest in his home. Where the devil was his self-control? With Helen, it was clearly non-existent. If he didn't do something drastic, and soon, Aunt Matilda wouldn't have any need for a matchmaking plot. He'd already be hooked.

"Shall I bandage that arm for you, my lord?"

The question interrupted Sebastian's rueful musings. Keeping his eyes closed, he nodded. He waited in silence as the valet proceeded to cover the wound.

"Miss Rivenall is a lovely young lady," Michaels murmured.

Glancing up at the older man, Sebastian frowned at the touch of amusement pulling at the corners of the valet's mouth. Tightening his lips, he nodded abruptly.

"She is."

"In fact, she reminds me a great deal of your mother."

The words slammed into Sebastian. *His mother*. Helen didn't look like his mother. "You're growing daft in your old age, Michaels. Miss Rivenall looks nothing like her," he exclaimed in a tight voice.

"Of course not, my lord. I was simply referring to her temperament. She possesses many of the same traits that I witnessed in your mother."

Sebastian remained silent, effectively ending the conversation. The memory of his mother and his part in her death were not welcome thoughts. Silence hung between them as Michaels finished wrapping the arm. When done, the valet straightened from his task.

"Now then, my lord. You lost quite a bit of blood, and I would suggest that you rest for the time being. I cleaned the wound as best I could, but there's still a risk of infection."

"Yes, yes." Sebastian waved him away with an impatient gesture.

"Shall I send up a tray for a light meal, my lord?"

"Very well, send up a tray. And Michaels …"

"Yes, my lord?"

"About Miss Rivenall …" Sebastian hesitated. "Would you look in on her, please? I may have upset her."

"I see."

The disapproving note in the valet's voice stung like an angry bee. Michaels had been with him for years. There was a bond between them that despite their class differences allowed the servant some latitude. The man took advantage of it now. Condemnation had been quite clear in the older man's voice, and Sebastian grimaced with renewed guilt. With another wave of his hand, he dismissed the man and turned his head away, not enjoying the look of disappointment on the man's face. Suddenly he was extremely weary. Closing his eyes once more, he heard the door shut with a soft thud. The quiet enveloped him, and he drifted off to sleep.

* * * *

Flames licked at his skin, eating away at him bit by bit. The heat scorched and burned him, leaving him raw and miserable. Through the fire, he saw his mother. She smiled at him. It was a gentle smile, and it made him cry out to her. The call went unanswered as she turned and walked away into the darkness. He tried to run after her, but the flames engulfed him, searing his flesh.

The music of a soft voice wrapped itself around him, and the heat from the fire ebbed. Replacing it was an icy chill that buried itself into his bones. He groaned as sharp icicles pricked and scraped across his skin with the vengeance of a thorn bush. The sight of his mother leaning over him filled him with remorse.

"I'm sorry, Mother ... my fault ... should never ... run after ... only... tell you ... how beautiful ... you looked."

She whispered words he that couldn't hear. He struggled to touch her face, but her features retreated into the darkness.

"No." He pushed himself up to follow her. "Mother ... stay!"

The fire surrounded him again. He moaned from the pain and heat. Something cool touched his face. Again, he heard the lyrical voice. The words were impossible to make out, but he knew they offered comfort. Twisting beneath the scorching heat of the fire, he thrashed about. He needed to go after her. A firm touch pushed him back, and he saw Helen in front of him. Tenderness and compassion glimmered in her emerald eyes. It was a look that told him everything and nothing. He reached out for her, but like his mother, she disappeared in a burst of flames. The searing pain from the heat pulled a groan from him. Coolness brushed his forehead once again, and he sighed from the relief it offered. The touch soothed and relaxed him. Sleep called his name, and he willingly answered the cry.

* * * *

Pain was the first thing to wake him. He cursed softly at the inconvenience of his injury. Sunlight illuminated his room. He'd slept through the night, although he remembered strange dreams and calling out for his mother. Pushing the thoughts aside, he inhaled the pleasant smell of coffee. He turned his head toward the aroma, expecting to see Michaels. The sight of Helen pouring a cup of the delicious-smelling brew astounded him. His treatment of her yesterday had been abysmal. Now, here she was tending to his breakfast needs. In silence, he watched her graceful movements. Her back to him, the musical sound of her voice floated over her shoulder to him.

"How do you feel this morning?"

She knew he was awake. Recovering from his surprise, he pushed himself up with his good arm until he was sitting upright in the bed. "Much better, thank you."

"Good, we were concerned your fever might hinder your recovery."

"My fever?" He watched her turn and move toward him with his coffee. Her serene expression was unreadable.

"Yes, you had a very high fever, but it broke just before dawn. Michaels and I stayed with you through the night. The poor man was exhausted, so I sent him to bed."

She handed him the cup she carried, and then proceeded to fluff the pillows behind his back. The efficient movements irritated him for some reason. Her perfunctory manner showed no outward sign of her being bothered or distracted by his presence. The idea annoyed him further. He wanted to prick her icy exterior.

"So you were never alone with me during the night?"

"Actually, Michaels and I took turns tending to you." The cool rejoinder revealed nothing.

"I see."

"You see ... what?"

Ah, he'd finally broken through. Testing the heat of his coffee with a cautious sip, he studied her over the rim of his cup. A smile tugged at the corner of his mouth as he saw her hands curled into fists.

"I see Michaels has found an apt student." Sebastian saw the tension drain from her. She relaxed her combative stance and returned to her efficient adjustment of his bed. He took another sip of his hot drink as she adjusted his blankets. Her profile was lovely, and he suppressed the urge to reach out and run his thumb over her full lower lip. Instead, he set his coffee cup on the table beside his bed.

"It appears you've quickly learned how to tend to the needs of a patient."

She immediately stopped in the middle of fiddling with his blankets. A shuttered look swept over her face as she straightened to an upright position. "I am not unacquainted with illness, my lord. I tended to my parents up to the time of their deaths."

The quiet words slashed his heart. He'd hurt her again. Blast! He wished the words unsaid, but a retraction was impossible. Quickly, he caught her hand before she could move away.

"Tell me about them."

She glanced down at the hand enclosing hers before looking at him. A haunted expression dimmed her green eyes. Lifting her gaze, she stared off into space.

"They were wonderful parents. Father was the youngest son, and as such, he had little income other than what he made as a local schoolmaster. He met mother quite by accident, or as Mama always said, it was fate." She paused for a moment, a small smile curving her lips.

"Mama came from a prominent family who disapproved of father. When she couldn't obtain her father's permission to marry, she and Father eloped. They were very happy, and any misfortune that came our way never dimmed their happiness. When a flu epidemic swept through our village, they took ill. They went rather quickly," Her voice cracked slightly as she finished her story.

"You loved them very much." At his statement, a single tear rolled down her pale cheek. She brushed it away quickly and nodded. Curiosity made him probe further. "How old were you when they died?"

"Thirteen." Helen inhaled a shuddering breath. "Edward was just a baby. I didn't want to leave our home, but I was grateful when Uncle ... Uncle Warren came to fetch us."

As if realizing she had revealed far more than she wanted to, she pulled away from him. His hand grew cold without her fingers to warm him, but he didn't try to prevent her retreat. The suffering in her eyes tore at his heart. It spoke of a similar pain he'd dealt with since his mother's death. He wanted to comfort her, but couldn't. Doing so would only break open wounds that had never truly healed. The pain of his mother's death had always lay just beneath the surface, tearing at him on a daily basis. It was a warning. A reminder that impulsive actions had deadly consequences. Offering her comfort, meant facing his own demons, and that he wasn't prepared to do. Unable to bear watching the emotions he lived with daily mirrored in her face, he looked away. Although he didn't see her move, he knew she had retreated from his side. Cool air drifted over the spot where she had stood.

"Why didn't you tell me you were hurt yesterday?" Her quiet words made him think she might have been worried about him.

Sebastian sought out her figure at the foot of his bed. She wore another of Louisa's dresses. The material reminded him of a spring sky, soft and billowy. He'd seen Louisa in the garment, but it had never looked this pleasing on his sister. His eyes met hers, and she quirked an eyebrow at him while he considered the question. The memory of her anger brought a smile to his lips. "I don't recall you giving me an opportunity to speak."

Although she had the grace to blush, she bristled at his remark. "I was angry. You put my brother in danger. It was reprehensible and reckless behavior."

"Edward never left the carriage."

"But you took him with you," she snapped.

Pushing himself into a more comfortable position, he bit back a ribald curse as the movement jarred his wound. "Bloody hell, woman! It wasn't my intent to take him with me. When he overheard my discussion with Caleb, he begged to help. The boy insisted that his honor was at stake and he needed to make restitution for your rescue as well as his own. How could I refuse a plea like that?"

"His honor! He's just a boy," Helen snapped. "What does he know of honor?"

"He knows enough to want to protect you from harm and to repay his debts when others do what he cannot. That's a rather heavy burden to put on a *boy*, isn't it? But then that's precisely what you did by fleeing from your uncle's house with Edward in tow."

A sharp gasp broke past her rosy lips. He cringed at his sharp words. When would he learn to soften the knife-like edge of his tongue? She stood stiffly before him, the guilt in her gaze poignant. Silence stretched between them for a long moment before a hot fire ignited in her gaze.

"His guilt would have been far greater if we had remained at Mayfield."

"*Why?*"

"It is of little consequence, since we are no longer under my uncle's roof."

The cold note in her voice grated on him. Why couldn't she trust him? He was only trying to help. The memory of yesterday bit into him. How could she trust a man who kissed her whenever the fancy struck him? The fact that she was even talking to him now was a miracle given his behavior yesterday. And she would flee even more quickly if she knew how he wanted nothing more than to keep her with him, exploring every silky inch of her.

The thought of such a pleasant diversion made his groin tightened. Damn, why would it be so difficult for her to explain why she left her uncle's home? Even if he hadn't been acting like a gentleman, surely he'd proven his trustworthiness by rescuing her and her brother. Couldn't she see that it was near impossible to help her if she refused to tell him anything?

"Surely any guilt on Edward's part would have been far greater if I had not happened upon your unfortunate circumstance the other night."

"Your implication that I'm neglectful of my brother is insulting." Her face reflected the image of a sainted martyr. He wasn't happy with the direction or tone of their conversation.

"Damnation! You're twisting my words. I don't think you've been delinquent in your care of Edward. I'm merely suggesting you might not have thought through your decision to come to London.

"Do not judge me, my lord," she hissed. The gold flecks of anger in her green gaze reminded him of a provoked feline.

"I am not sitting in judgment of you, Helen." His clenched fist crashed softly against the mattress.

"Aren't you?" She was a voluptuous goddess intent on chastising a mortal. Straightening to her full height, she glared at him. She awed him, enticed him. "But then I suppose it's easier to focus on the troubles of others rather than one's own dark secrets."

He went rigid at her words. Narrowing his gaze, he studied her closely. "To what shadows in my past are you referring, Helen?"

Hot color suffused the pale sheen of her cheeks. Watchful, he pinned her beneath his gaze. Had it been her sweet voice soothing him through his nightmares and not a dream last night? She shifted uncomfortably under his steady look. When she failed to answer, he arched an eyebrow. "I'm waiting, Helen."

"Forgive me, I spoke without thinking."

"No doubt, but you've piqued my curiosity. Tell me what terrible secret I'm hiding."

"I don't ... it's just ..." With a fidgeting twist of her hands, she exhaled a sigh. "You talked during your fever last night."

The words made him clench the coverlet of the bed with a slow curl of his fingers. He remained still against the pillows as she looked at every other spot in the room except where he was. Heavy and thick, the silence crept over him like a smothering blanket. How much had he revealed? He'd never shared the events of his mother's death with anyone, not even with the sibling who understood him the best, Louisa.

Forcing himself to act as though nothing inconvenient had occurred, he relaxed his grip on the bedspread. Tension tightened the sutures in his wound, and he grimaced at the pain in his arm. The next time Caleb needed to rescue a damsel in distress his brother could do it alone. With a control that came from extensive practice, he offered her a small smile.

"Your imagination is running amuck, Helen. I've no dark secrets."

Another flush of pink coursed through her cheeks. Embarrassment darkened her eyes and she swallowed hard. The sight of her discomposure made his heartbeat slow to a normal pace. Some devil in him wanted to tease her more, just to keep her cheeks rosy with the same color as her heart-shaped mouth.

He stifled the urge.

"I deeply regret my insult, my lord." The stilted tone of her voice emphasized her chagrin.

"I thought we agreed that we would not be so formal with one another." He sent her a stern look, intent on bending her to his will.

"Actually, I think it was more of a command ... Sebastian," she said in a stilted voice.

Not about to confirm her observation, he shifted his gaze to stare out the window. She was right of course. He'd practically accused her of being careless with the care of her brother. She'd had little choice but to defend herself by reminding him of his own foibles.

"Perhaps you were justified in reprimanding me. I was quite persistent in my questioning." He frowned at the statement then shifted his gaze to her face. Watching her closely, he saw her green eyes widen. Did she really think him such an ogre? Sighing, he shook his head. "I must be mindful of your temper. It is a keen instrument when giving me the tongue lashing I deserve."

Helen's lips curved slightly with amusement. The image of covering her lovely mouth with his brought his blood to a low boil. Damnation, if he didn't secure a mistress soon, he'd be caught like a fly in an ointment. He winced at the thought.

"Are you in pain?" She hurried to his side. Warm fingers brushed over his bare bicep as she bent to examine his bandage. The scent of lavender filled his nostrils, and his groin ached with need. A need he suddenly realized a mistress would not be able to quell. Remembering the reason Helen was in his home, he struggled to keep from trailing his fingertips down the side of her neck. Where she was concerned, he would keep his distance. The peaceful existence he'd created would be completely shattered if he allowed himself to trifle with her. A brief dalliance would be enough for him, but he knew Helen would expect more. And more he could not give.

"My injury is troublesome, nothing more." He kept his voice low and deliberate. "Actually, I'm tired."

"Of course," she murmured. "I'll leave so you can rest."

Despite his resolve, he could not resist touching her. His good hand stretched out to capture hers. Holding her in place with gentle pressure, he studied her soberly. "Thank you, Helen."

Hesitation forced her tongue out to flick over her dry lips. The sight nearly undid his decision of less than a moment ago. God in heaven, the woman had no idea how sensual that motion was. But his body knew. He was hard. Harder than an iron hitching post.

"You're welcome," she said softly.

He released her arm, and fell back against the pillows, his groin sending a pulsating ache through him. Closing his eyes, he heard Helen's soft tread across the floor as she left the room. The door thudded quietly behind her departure.

Alone, he tried to ignore the demand for satisfaction his body was craving. God, he wished she were still here. Her warm curves burrowing into his. The thought of her silky skin sliding against his made him swallow hard. Damnation, the thought of the woman made him harder than any mistress he'd ever had. The memory of her hand on him made him suck in a ragged breath.

He ached for her touch. His body throbbed at the idea of Helen's hand encircling him as she had done yesterday, sliding up and down over his hardened flesh. His breathing hissed between his lips as his hand imitated the fantasy in his mind. What would it like to have those luscious red lips of hers wrapped around his cock, sucking on him, licking at him, bringing him close to a release? If they'd had more time yesterday, he would have taught her how to please him with her mouth.

The thought of her hot mouth burning his flesh with hot friction tantalized and excited him. In his daydream, her tongue flicked across the sensitive spot just below the tip of him before moving to swirl around the head of his cock. He bucked against the image, and his hand gripped his cock harder as he imitated the act he wanted her to perform on him.

Images of her doing so flowed fast and furious until a muffled cry escape his lips. He groaned as the picture of Helen and her sweet tongue vanished from his mind. Sweet Jesus, he wanted the real event. Not this illusion. He wanted Helen. He wanted her here, in his bed. This physical relief had temporarily eased the craving of his body for her, but it lacked completion. He needed to bed the woman to rid himself of this desire. And that he couldn't do. The devil take it. The sooner Aunt Matilda came and went, the sooner he could find a suitable position for Helen. Unfortunately, the only position he could think of for her was in his bed.

* * * *

By late afternoon, Sebastian's patience had reached its limit when it came to everyone treating him like an invalid. Visits from his siblings, along with Michaels' constant hovering, simply heightened the awareness of Helen's absence. He suppressed the urge to ask about her, despite his growing need to hear her voice or glimpse sight of her. Each time a knock sounded on his bedroom door, he could not prevent the anticipating skip his heart took at the thought it might be her. This time the light rap preyed upon his senses like a piece of chalk squeaking across a slate board he often used as a child.

"Sebastian?" The feminine voice whispered through the room. "Are you awake?"

Shoulders sagging with disappointment, he recognized Louisa's voice. It wasn't Helen. He closed his eyes in disgust. Why the devil did he care whether or not the woman came to check on him? Louisa drew near the side of his bed, and he forced himself to look at his sister, offering her a smile.

"It's rather difficult to sleep, given the parade of visitors I've had today."

A moue of dismay twisted Louisa's mouth. "Oh, dear, we've been smothering you with attention, haven't we? I'll come back later."

With a quick flick of his wrist, he captured her hand to hold her at his side. "I'm being a boorish patient."

Louisa sank down onto the mattress and grinned. "I doubt you're any more ill-refined than normal."

The cheerful slight brought a chuckle to his lips. "It can never be said you have not acquired the Rockwood penchant for blunt observation."

"I can honestly say that my best tutor has been my eldest brother," she said with a grin. "How are you feeling?"

Stretching his wounded arm slightly, he winced. "It could be much worse. I need to make note never to let Caleb involve me in any future adventures he undertakes."

"That I don't think you need fear at all." A look of satisfaction settled on Louisa's face. "I've a feeling his adventures as a bachelor are over. Rather, our brother will be busy keeping his beloved Georgina out of mischief once he's officially off the marriage mart."

"He's that serious then?" The news didn't surprise him, but the idea of his brother having found a wife created a sense of envy. He cringed inwardly at the sensation. The last thing he needed was a wife to keep track of, let alone being at her beck and call.

"Serious," Louisa scoffed. "Having grown up trailing after both of you, I despaired of any female capturing either of your hearts. But Georgina has turned our brother inside out. If they're not wed in a fortnight, it won't be for lack of trying on Caleb's part."

"Do you like her?"

"Yes. She's very different from Helen, and yet alike in some ways." A look of sadness flitted across her features. "Michaels' says they both remind him of Mama. Do you think Helen is like Mama?"

Unable to meet his sister's eyes, he turned his head to study the low fire burning in the hearth. "Perhaps."

"Helen says you asked for Mama last night during your fever."

Sebastian went rigid. He jerked his gaze back to Louisa. "Like most women, Helen is incapable of holding her tongue."

"That is most unfair of you, Sebastian. She did not part with the information easily. In fact, it took a great deal of coaxing to convince her to share what troubled her so."

"She was troubled?" The pleasure and surprise in his voice did not escape him or his sister. She arched her brow as she directed a mischievous smile in his direction.

"Indeed, she is quite sensitive where you're concerned."

Forcing his features to freeze into an immobile mask of indifference, he shrugged. "As usual, your proclivity for exaggeration is prevalent when you're up to mischief."

"No," she shook her head solemnly. "Not mischief this time, Sebastian. But, Helen's observations did raise some questions in my mind."

Tension whipped through him. "What questions?"

"I know Papa drank himself into the grave while grieving over Mama's death, but no one has ever really told me much about how she died."

"I'm not sure what you're asking, Louisa. Mama died from a fall down the main stairs."

"Please, Sebastian. I know there's something troubling you about Mama's death. Did you see something? Did Mama … was she unhappy because of me? I know babies can be troublesome … did she …"

The direction of Louisa's thoughts appalled him. Grasping her hand, he squeezed it hard. "Listen to me, Louisa. Mama did not take her own life. And she most certainly was not depressed because of your arrival. She cherished you as much as she did the rest of us."

"Then why do I feel like you've always hidden something from me about her death? Why can't you tell me what happened?"

"There's nothing to tell."

Hazel eyes glowing with anger, Louisa dislodged her hand from his. "If there's nothing to tell, then why do you torture yourself over her death?"

The fierce question cut through his heart with the precision of a scalpel. His gaze darted away from hers. "You've acquired a taste for the melodramatic, Louisa."

"No, I'm merely pointing out that you never talk about Mama.

Almost everything I've ever learned about her has come from Percy and Caleb. They're the only ones, beside yourself, old enough to have any vivid memories of Mama."

"What is it you want me to tell you, Louisa?" Wincing as he closed his eyes, Sebastian found himself drifting back to that horrible evening so many years ago. The gentle touch of his sister's hand made him stiffen in the middle of the memory.

"I want you to tell me the truth. I want to know what happened that day. All my life I've seen you hide behind an emotionless mask every time someone mentions Mama's name. You wear it even in front of your family. Oh sometimes you let if fall, but even then, you still hold back. I'm no longer the little girl who worships you so much she won't question you. I adore you, but I want to help you. It's terrible to see someone you love in pain."

The heartfelt words tumbled over him, tossing his emotions on a wild sea of sadness and pain. Her plea reminded him that she was no longer a child, and perhaps it was time to destroy her illusions about her oldest brother. He heaved a sigh.

"It was my fault Mama fell down the stairs."

"Blast you, Sebastian! I asked for the truth, not a bedtime story." Louisa sprang to her feet and glared down at him.

"It's not a story, little one," he said in a weary voice. With his good hand, he patted the spot on the bed, which she'd vacated. "Come, sit down and I'll tell you what I've never told anyone else, not even Father."

Louisa hesitated before sitting beside him once more. Squeezing her hand as she sat down, he turned his head away. He had no desire to witness the disgust in her eyes when he revealed his secret. As if in a dream, the images of that fateful day swallowed him whole.

Twelve years old again, he was impatient and eager to see his mother. She'd promised him earlier in the day she would say goodnight before she left. Waiting had become as unbearable as the torturous mathematical lessons he endured on a daily basis. He'd found a baby bird earlier and with Michaels help he'd been taking care of it. He wanted to tell her about it before going to bed. The wait grew longer until his patience was exhausted.

Without another thought, he bolted out of his room with Nanny ordering him to stop.

"I'll be back, Nanny. I just want to kiss Mama goodnight."

No need to pay her any mind. Mama would be happy to see him. The chastisement he'd receive from Nanny would be worth the pleasure of seeing his mother dressed as a fairy princess. He raced down the hall, eager to see her. She always looked so beautiful when she and Papa went out. The third floor steps leading down to the second story hallway yawned open in front of him. He stumbled in his haste. Catching himself on the railing, he slid to a stop at the foot of the stairs. Heart pounding from the frightening plunge he'd narrowly avoided, he sucked in a deep breath of relief. In the distance, he heard the rustle of his mother's gown on the floor. He could tell she was in a hurry by the furious crackle of her crinoline as she moved away from him toward the main staircase. She had forgotten him. Rejection growled inside his heart with the ferocity of an injured animal. How could she have forgotten? No. She must be late. Mama was always late. That's why she hadn't come to say goodnight.

Sprinting forward, he raced after her. A goodnight hug was all he wanted, nothing more. Ahead of him, he saw her disappear from the hallway to descend the staircase. He could not let her leave just yet.

"Wait, Mama! I just want to tell you--"

At a full run, he wheeled around the corner of the corridor. She had turned at his cry. The smile on her face welcomed him, but it changed as he plowed into her. Horror twisted her smile into a hideous mask as she violently pushed him away from her and back to safety.

Her scream pierced him with an anguish that possessed the same intensity as her sharp cry. As he staggered backward, he collapsed at the top of the stairs. His eyes never left her. With a loud crack, her body crashed against the banister. She stayed poised there for a moment. Relief brightened her face before the snapping sound of the balustrade echoed through the air, and her features grew dark with fear. He scrambled forward, his hands outstretched, but her fingers slipped through his. She screamed again as the railing gave way and she plummeted to the marble floor below.

The abrupt end to his mother's cry of terror made him scramble forward to peer down through the second landing's spindled banister. On the marble floor below, his mother lay still, her body twisted at an awkward angle. Nausea swirled in his stomach at the sight. It was his fault she lay there devoid of life. Footsteps raced out of the library, and he saw his father collapse in a crumpled heap beside his mother's still form. Grief howled its way up from the foyer. The blackness of the cry draped his skin with guilt, while the sorrowful roar rang in his head with the force of an immense bell from St. Peter's cathedral. Hands planted over his ears to block out his father's cries of despair, he scrambled to his feet. Blinded by the tears, he stumbled back the way he had come. The pain numbed him, holding him prisoner as the house exploded with cries of horror, shock and suffering.

He shuddered. Agony wrapped its icy claw about him with the same vengeance it had shown all those years ago. Fire stabbed at his eyes and he jumped at the touch of a soft hand on his.

"Sebastian." Louisa's soft voice broke through his sorrow.

Swallowing hard, he struggled out of the horrifying past. His gaze slowly focused on his sister as he prepared himself for her condemnation. As her features came into view, he quickly glanced away. He couldn't bear to see her censure and hatred of him.

"Sebastian, it's all right. It wasn't your fault. It was an accident."

The absolution was impossible to accept. He shook his head. "No. If I hadn't been running, I wouldn't have knocked her over."

"You were a child. Children run all the time. How could you have known she would turn to greet you?"

The conversation had drained him. Exhaustion burrowed into his limbs. Limp from the emotional assault, he closed his eyes. "You asked for the truth, Louisa, and I gave it to you. Now go away."

"It wasn't your fault. You must see that."

"God damn it, Louisa. Leave me be." He sent her his most intimidating glare. Not daunted in the least, she stood up.

"As you wish, but only for the time being." Without another word, she swept from the room, the door closing quietly behind her.

Chapter 8

Helen studied the complex place setting in front of her, but her thoughts were elsewhere. Earlier, she'd entered the breakfast nook to find Madison arranging the place setting for her. The thought of her grandfather had been preying on her mind, and in a sudden flight of inspiration, she'd realized that the butler might have some knowledge of her maternal grandparent.

"Madison, may I ask you a question?"

"Certainly, Miss." Madison smiled pleasantly as he looked up from the table setting. "If I can answer, I'll be happy to do so."

"Actually, I'm not sure how to ask the question."

"Why not simply ask it, Miss Helen." A twinkle lit Madison's brown eyes. Nodding her head at his encouragement, she swallowed her fear.

"I'm looking for someone in the peerage, but I'm not sure how to go about finding him. I know the family name, but not the gentleman's title."

"What is the family name, Miss?"

"Worthington."

Madison frowned as he pondered the name for a moment, then shook his head. "I'm sorry, Miss Helen, the name is not familiar, but that doesn't mean someone else might not recognize it."

"Thank you," she said quietly as he resumed setting the table.

How was she going to find her grandfather without knowing his title? It was an almost impossible task, but she couldn't give up. She couldn't stop searching. Her gaze refocused on the complex place setting in front of her.

Uncle Warren had never believed in more than one fork or spoon for any meal. Now, faced with an assortment of forks, spoons and different sized plates, frustration forced its way past her lips in a lusty sigh. How did one possibly remember what the purpose of each utensil was? A balled fist hit the edge of the table with restrained exasperation.

"Careful, you might break something, and Louisa is quite fond of this china. It belonged to our mother."

Sebastian's deep voice breathed over her skin like a hot breeze. Startled, she jumped to her feet and whirled to face him. It had been three days since she'd seen him. An even longer eternity since she'd held him, caressed him so intimately. The memory of the moment warmed her skin as her gaze met his. She should be ashamed of her behavior, but there had been something so natural and right about touching him the way she had.

Framed in the doorway of the breakfast nook, he radiated the dangerous air of a handsome rake. An aura that was nearly impossible to resist. Dressed unconventionally, he wore dark trousers and his white shirt splayed open at the base of his throat. Across the narrow distance between them, she could smell the spicy aroma of him. A scent that was becoming all too familiar.

"Good morning, my lor-- Sebastian." The low and even keel of her voice pleased her. It revealed none of the disturbing sensations barreling through her.

He stepped deeper into the room, his tall figure drawing near. She stiffened, but refused to retreat. To do so would be a sign of weakness. With Sebastian, one could never show weakness or all was lost. His injured arm in a sling, he reached out with his free hand and ran his forefinger down her cheek.

"Why haven't you been to visit me?"

There was almost a petulant sound to the question. Her mouth curled slightly at the remark. For all his masterful behavior, he sometimes reminded her of a young boy. "I wasn't aware you lacked for visitors."

Black eyes glowed with cunning as he narrowed his gaze on her. "So you kept a record of my visitors."

She laughed. "No, I didn't have too. Louisa kept me fully apprised of your progress."

"I see. So you were at least interested in my well being."

The keen expression of satisfaction on his face made her laugh again. "Yes, I was concerned for your welfare."

"Ah, so you did not completely forget about me."

"That would be hard to do given the roars of discontent that echoed through the house."

He glowered at her open amusement. "Still, you didn't come to visit me."

"I didn't think it appropriate to do so." No, visiting him would have been far too tempting. She shook her head. "Besides, you had your brothers and Louisa to fuss over you."

"Louisa is the only one who fussed over me. Caleb's been preoccupied with his Georgina, and Percy was far from sympathetic to my plight."

She laughed at his irritated tone. "Lord Percy seemed genuinely concerned for you. I can't imagine him being anything but solicitous where your health is concerned."

"You met Percy?" He narrowed his eyes as he studied her with a piercing gaze. The look unsettled her somewhat as she nodded.

"Louisa introduced us. He was quite charming."

"He's not for you," he bit out sharply. Startled by his response, she stared at him with surprise.

"I beg your pardon."

"You're to stay away from Percy."

For a moment, all she could was stare at him in amazement. The abrasive command had the same judgmental tone her Uncle Warren used with her on a daily basis. The similarity between her uncle and Sebastian made her stiffen. Did the man think her behavior with him was one she willingly repeated with other men? She stiffened at the thought.

"I can assure you, my lord," she said coldly. "I am well aware of my purpose in your household, and I have no intention of venturing outside of that role."

"What the hell is that supposed to mean?"

"It simply means that I'm grateful for your rescue of me and Edward, and in return, I am helping you to avoid any matchmaking efforts on the part of your aunt."

His gaze narrowed at her, and he closed the distance between them until mere inches separated them. The level of heat in the room had suddenly risen to a feverish pitch. His nearness made her swallow the knot that expanded in her throat. Dear Lord, the closeness of him scorched her like a blazing fire.

"I wasn't aware that I had designated you a place in my household."

"Perhaps not, but I'm well aware of my role here. I'm here to help you convince your aunt that you've found a suitable prospect for marriage. And to do that I'm required to learn these ridiculous rules the Marlborough Set enforces on people." She half turned and swept her hand out in the direction of the dinner service that she'd been memorizing.

"I have no doubt of your ability to master the rules," he murmured as he bent his head toward her. "And I'm more than confident you'll convince my aunt that you're quite suitable for me."

"You are far more confident than I am, but I will not deny being eager to dispense with this business. Edward and I must not trespass on your kindness any longer than necessary."

His eyes darkened with an unreadable emotion. Once again, his touch burned her as his long fingers stroked across the layer of gauze covering her throat and breasts. She quivered at the light caress, and a liquid fire sang through her veins. Suddenly feeling short of breath, her breasts rose and fell as though she'd been running.

"So you are determined to leave once my aunt has come and gone."

"I must find a suitable position to support Edward and me."

"Are you so eager to leave me then?" The sensuous nature of his voice skimmed across her body until the frisson of it made each of her nerve endings scream out for his touch.

"I don't understand," she said breathlessly.

"Do you deny that my touch disturbs you?" The words whispered across her skin, sending a river of fire racing through her body. Transfixed by his gaze she tried to avoid his penetrating look, but failed.

"I do not ... do not recall having said any such thing." She swallowed hard at his look of disbelief.

"So if I were never to touch you again--like this." His thumb traced the fullness of her mouth in a sensuous stroke. "You would not miss it in the least?"

The devilish amusement in his black eyes aroused a sultry heat inside her. She trembled beneath the pressure of his thumb. A wicked thrust of delight pierced her belly. "No ... I would ... not miss it."

"And if I were never to kiss you again?" His head descended toward her. Frozen, she waited for the flames of desire to engulf her. The kiss he planted on her lips was gentle. Sweet. It heightened her awareness, but it did not seek to incite her desire.

He straightened. "I have no intention of letting you go so soon, Helen."

With a ragged inhalation, she shook her head. "Once your aunt has returned to Scotland, there will be no reason for me to stay."

"Then I must think of one that will convince you to remain," he murmured in a seductive tone.

The glitter in his black gaze simmered with a heat she recognized. It smoldered inside her as well. He was her rescuer, her protector and if she did not take care, he would be her lover. The notion caused a shiver of excitement to spark its way down her spine. It was a disorienting reaction. She desperately wanted to give way to the lethargic heat melting through her. The image of Uncle Warren railing against her for such wanton thoughts made her flinch. No doubt, the man would condemn her to hell. Worst of all, she knew that even if she gave in to temptation, when Sebastian was done with her, she would exist in a hell of her own making.

But wouldn't the pleasure of a few moments with him be worth that hell? Stark need barreled through, alarming her at the intensity of the emotion. Swallowing her desire, she darted past him and hurried out of the room. In her head, she could hear the condemning vocalizations of her uncle. The judgmental thoughts shouted, threatened and harassed her.

Behind her, the sound of Sebastian's deliberate footsteps

followed her. He was the hunter and she the prey. As she sprinted along the corridor to the foyer, she realized that once again she was running. Only it wasn't Uncle Warren chasing her. It was the earl of Melton, and the terrifying fact was that she didn't want to run from him. She wanted to run to him.

The marble tiled floor of the main entryway echoed with the tap of her leather soles. A boisterous waltz floated out of the music room into the foyer. It was time for her dance lessons. With a quick glance over her shoulder, she saw Sebastian emerge from the shadowed side hall.

He halted and leaned against the wall with his good shoulder, his gaze watchful. Every inch a peer of the realm, he exuded a confidence she could never feel. Irritation settled in the pit of her stomach. Why did the man seek to intimidate her with his piercing stare? Lifting her chin in defiance, she scowled at him before moving toward the music room.

She would learn the skills necessary to deceive his aunt, and then she would run as fast as she could from Melton house. Here only the devil resided. A demon of her own making, it would soon be out of control, driving her into the arms of the man standing behind her. The result of which would be her undoing.

* * * *

"There. That one I think." Louisa grabbed Helen's arm and pointed at a deep rose hat displayed on the milliner's sales shelf. "It's perfect for your new dress."

"It's far too flamboyant, Louisa. I wouldn't feel comfortable in such a hat."

"Don't be ridiculous."

With a tug on her arm, Louisa pulled her toward the shelf. Like her older brother, the girl was an unstoppable force when it came to getting her own way. In less than a minute, Louisa had placed the hat on Helen's head. With an impish grin, the younger girl whirled Helen around to face the mirror on the shop's wall.

"See, I was right! It's just the thing for your new gown. Now, we need to order a number of accessories to go with those dresses Madame Clarissa just delivered to the house."

"Oh, but we've spent too much all ready. Surely your brother--"

"Pshaw! Sebastian coerced you into this deception with Aunt Matilda, so he must be prepared to pay the price."

"But it seems so excessive to buy a hat simply to match one dress."

"Nonsense." Louisa sniffed in disagreement. "Besides, Sebastian has been too distracted of late to question any of the bills from our shopping sprees.

"Distracted? I can tell time by your brother's daily routine," she said with a laugh.

And it was true. Sebastian's punctuality and consistent habits, made it fairly easy to know exactly where the man was at any given time during the day. It had been one of the reasons why she'd been so successful in avoiding him for the past three weeks.

"Oh, he's not abandoned his schedule, but ever since he was injured in that outing with Caleb, he's definitely been preoccupied about something." Louisa said in a thoughtful tone as she looked at Helen. "I don't suppose you know what's troubling him?"

"*Me*? What makes you think I might know something?"

"Well, the man was extremely irritable that you didn't visit him in his sickbed, and when he was well enough to go out, he didn't leave the house. In fact, he's been underfoot for the last three weeks."

"I'd hardly say he's been underfoot." Helen smiled at her friend's exaggeration.

"Perhaps not, but then you don't give him the chance to be, do you?" Louisa's slyly worded question took her by surprise.

"What on earth are you talking about?" The moment she asked the question, she realized exactly what the youngest Rockwood was suggesting. Averting her gaze, her cheeks grew hot.

"I think you know exactly what I'm talking about Helen Rivenall. You've been avoiding my brother like the plague, and I'm certain it's the reason why he's been so grumpy of late."

All too aware of the quicksand she was wading through Helen simply shook her head slightly and turned back to the mirror as if the topic was of no concern to her at all. Despite her refusal to speak, Louisa's mischievous expression didn't disappear, and it was a relief when the young woman excused herself to talk with the shopkeeper.

Helen turned back to study herself in the mirror. A giddy pleasure spread a delicious tingle through her as she admired the deep rose gown she wore. An image of her mother's sweet face entered her head. It would have pleased her mother very much to see her in such fine clothes. Her mother's features were suddenly replaced with the strong, angular planes of Sebastian's face. Was he pleased with what his money had paid for?

Wrinkling her nose at her reflection, she refused to consider answering the question. Sebastian's likes or dislikes were not for her to worry about. Louisa appeared at her side once more.

"Well now, Miss Rivenall. Are you going spend all day admiring yourself in the mirror?"

The words prompted one hand to touch a burning cheek. Dear lord, had she been taking too much pleasure in her appearance? In her head, she heard her uncle reminding her that vanity was a vice.

"Helen, I was teasing you." Louisa grasped her by the shoulders and shook her slightly. "You goose. There's not a thing wrong with liking what you see in the mirror."

"Yes ... of course. I was just imaging how much my mother would have enjoyed seeing me in such a lovely dress."

"At least you remember your mother." There was a wistful note in Louisa's voice, but it vanished quickly. "Come we have several more purchases to make before we can go home. If Sebastian finds that we've been out too long, he's apt to send Yancey reinforcements, although I suppose he has good reason."

Helen shivered at Louisa's words as she remembered the morning paper's headline. *Murder Maniac Sacrifices More Women To His Thirst For Blood*. The two women murdered had brought the overall number of victims to four. Reading the paper this morning, she'd found the news article far more vivid than she'd expected and had set the paper aside. If the papers were to be believed, the women died quickly before being horribly mutilated. The entire city was engulfed in terror thanks to the horrible and terrifying actions of a madman. Wincing at the memories of the lurid story, she shook her head.

"Those poor women. It's no wonder everyone seems on edge. I noticed it at Madame Clarissa's. I overheard one girl telling another that she lives near Whitechapel and is terrified to go home each night after work." The girl's plight troubled Helen as she tried to imagine being forced to walk into such a fearful area.

"I confess it has me a bit nervous as well," Louisa said quietly. "Did you see the paper this morning? They received a letter from the monster. He calls himself Jack the Ripper."

"It's a vile name. I don't understand why Scotland Yard is finding it so difficult to catch this monster." Helen shivered. "Surely they've interviewed someone who saw something."

With a nod of her head, Louisa frowned. "According to the accounts I've read, the fiend has an educated voice, which makes me think he's not a local. Heaven forbid he's a member of society."

"I think that unlikely. He slides in and out of Whitechapel's shadows as if he lives there."

"Well, it certainly doesn't help matters with all these conflicting descriptions of the man either. It's almost as if the witnesses were describing two different men." At her friend's observation, Helen frowned. Had Louisa stumbled onto a possible explanation for how the Ripper was able to murder and mutilate his victims while easily avoiding capture?

"Do you think that's possible? That it could be two men working together?"

"Dear lord," Louisa gasped. "It that's true, it would explain why so many witnesses have given different descriptions."

Horrified by her friend's suggestion, fear skittered through her. That one man could commit such heinous atrocities was terrifying enough, but two? What would she have done if Sebastian had not rescued her and Edward from Madame Chantrel's? Her stomach lurched violently as an icy chill layered her skin. Jack the Ripper had only murdered prostitutes, and without Sebastian's rescue, she would have been forced into that profession. She could have easily been one of the monster's victims.

"Good heavens, Helen." Louisa grasped her hand. "Whatever is the matter? You're as white as a ghost."

"I...if your brother hadn't..." She shook her head, unable to finish the sentence.

"But he did," her friend said quietly. "Sebastian saved you, and that's the important thing."

Helen met her friend's steady gaze and sighed softly. Louisa was right. Sebastian had saved her. As horrible as the murders in Whitechapel were, there was nothing she could do about it. Seeing Louisa shudder, she pushed aside her fear. Entwining her arm through her friend's, Helen assumed a no nonsense air.

"Come, enough talk about this horrid business. The papers are doing far too good a job at stirring up people's fears. We cannot change the fate of those poor women."

As Louisa nodded her head, they moved toward the shop's exit, but came to an abrupt halt a second later. "Oh look, Helen, isn't that the most adorable hat in the window? How on earth did I miss seeing it?"

"I've no idea," she said with a relieved laugh. For once she was grateful for Louisa's predilection for shopping. The change in subject was a welcomed one. "However, I believe your brother will have an apoplectic fit when he receives the bill for all these accessories you're so insistent on buying."

"Well, personally, I think Sebastian needs to be shaken out of that cool, restrained manner of his. Outspending my monthly allowance manages to do that occasionally, but of late, I've noted that he's become a little less rigid in his behavior." The sly note in Louisa's voice was back again as she examined the hat with an innocent air.

In the short time she'd known Louisa, it was easy to recognize when her friend was gently probing for information. Helen shook her head. "I haven't noticed any change in your brother's behavior."

"Of course, you wouldn't," Louisa said with a laugh. "But your presence in the house has definitely made an impression on him."

"I sincerely doubt that." Helen blushed as she remembered how many times she'd avoided Sebastian's presence over the past three weeks.

"Nonsense, Sebastian is rough around the edges, but all he needs is a little bit of coaxing to make him a prince among men."

Uncertain how to respond, Helen remained silent. The last thing she could imagine was Sebastian ever agreeing to be coaxed into doing something he didn't want to do. The man was far too comfortable giving commands, not receiving them. As Louisa continued to admire the hat she'd found, Helen lifted her head and stared directly into the eyes of Marquess of Templeton.

A pleasant smile curved the man's thin lips, as he tipped his hat in her direction. Unwilling to dismiss the man outright, given his courteous behavior several weeks ago, she forced a smile and nodded a greeting. The memory of the auction and how he'd bid on her with such avid zeal still made her heart flutter with trepidation despite his kindness toward her.

A light touch at her elbow, made Helen jump and she turned away from the window. Concern furrowed Louisa's brow. "Are you all right?"

"Actually, I'm feeling quite fatigued. Would you mind if we went back to Melton House?"

"Of course, I should have realized you're not used to all this commotion. Let me settle our bill."

Nodding her head, Helen glanced over her shoulder. Templeton no longer stood outside the shop's window front. The relief she experienced relaxed the tension in her muscles. Seconds later, she jerked at the light touch of Louisa's hand.

"My word, you're as nervous as a cat. I think this Jack fellow has ruffled that cool reserve of yours."

"No, I'm simply tired."

"Well, let's collect poor Yancey outside and summon the carriage."

Together they stepped out onto the bustling sidewalk. The moment they appeared, Yancey was immediately in their shadow, his hand motioning the carriage forward at Louisa's request. As the vehicle moved toward them, Helen sensed someone close by.

"Good afternoon, Miss Rivenall, Lady Louisa. What a

delightful pleasure seeing the two of you again."

Templeton's voice scraped across her nerve endings with razor-like tension. Slowly she turned to face him, quelling the uneasy feeling flooding through her. Once more, the memory of Madame Chantrel's auction returned to make her heart lurch with repugnance. If that event had never happened, would she still find the man's presence unnerving? Other than bidding on her at Chantrel's, the man had been nothing but polite and considerate towards her.

Even that thought failed to ease the uncomfortable feelings he aroused in her. For a moment, she studied his features in silence, her hands tightening on the handle of the bandbox she carried.

"Lord Templeton," she murmured. Beside her Louisa murmured a soft greeting before turning toward the carriage that had stopped at the curb.

"I trust you've recovered from your recent illness."

"Yes, quite. I am deeply grateful for your assistance that day," she said sincerely. "I would have found it extremely difficult to walk home."

"I did call to see how you had improved, but unfortunately, my card was refused."

Puzzled, she glanced over her shoulder at Louisa whose expression was a mixture of reluctant confusion and regret. Turning back to the Marquess, she shook her head. "I'm sorry, my lord, I didn't realize you had called. It was most kind of you to do so."

"It's not important," the man shrugged. "I understand why Melton refused to accept me calling on you."

"I beg your pardon." Tension shot through her as she realized Sebastian had arbitrarily decided to control whom she could or couldn't see.

"Melton indicated that you had no wish to speak with me. I found it most disappointing that I was prevented from ensuring your health was much improved."

Fierce anger blazed through her at the notion that Sebastian thought he could control her. She'd told him once that she was not his property, and yet he continuously acted as though she were.

"My apologies, my lord. I was unaware that you had called. I would have welcomed the opportunity to thank you for your help that day."

"Thank you, Miss Rivenall. I have admired you for some time now, and I'd hoped we might be friends."

Despite her outrage at Sebastian's behavior, the marquess's words still managed to spiral trepidation through her.

"Your offer of friendship is quite generous, my lord, but I'm not certain I am worthy of the honor."

He placed his hand over his heart in a dramatic gesture. "You cut me to the quick, my dear. Surely, you understand the nature of your appeal. Why, I'm convinced you're about to take the Marlborough Set by storm. I have no doubt that the Prince will find you most charming."

"You're too kind, my lord."

"Nonsense. Why I'm even certain you'll make a magnificent match within the next month or so."

"A magnificent match?"

"But of course, my dear. All the men in London will soon be at your feet," he whispered in a conspiratorial tone. "Including me."

Her grip on the bandbox tightened as embarrassment singed her cheeks. She didn't want Lord Templeton or any other man at her feet. Least of all finding someone to marry. It was a preposterous idea.

"I have no intention of marrying, my lord. I have no wish to see myself subjugated under the yoke of marriage," she snapped. "Why would I want to place myself under the heel of any member of your sex, given the self-centered tendencies each of you displays?"

The man's thin lips parted in soft laughter. His amusement enraged her further. Still laughing, his steely gaze narrowed on her.

"That's an image I cannot envision, my dear. You're far too spirited to let any man dominate you in such a manner. In fact, I'm certain the man you marry will soon find himself eagerly answering your beck and call."

Before she could snap a reply, another deep voice joined the conversation.

"I suggest you return to the hole you slithered out of, Templeton."

Helen turned her head sharply to meet Sebastian's glittering gaze. The fury in his eyes reminded her of the dark depths hiding below his surface. Once again, he had place himself in the role of her protector, only this time she had no need of his services. She scowled at him before she turned back to address the marquess.

"My lord, thank you again for your recent assistance. I'm most grateful. Good day."

Turning away from the Marquess, she saw Louisa already seated in the carriage. Eager to escape the presence of both men, she stepped forward to join her friend. A firm hand grasped her elbow as she started to climb into the carriage.

The familiar charge of energy speeding through her told her it was Sebastian's touch. Angry at the way he'd charged to her rescue, she jerked her elbow out of his grasp. Obviously he thought her incapable of handling Lord Templeton herself. The notion infuriated her. Ever since he had rescued her, he'd taken to handling her as though she were unable to take care of herself. Infuriated and resentful, she glared up into his dark eyes as resentment bubbled up inside her.

"I have no need of your assistance, Lord Melton."

"Helen--"

"Do not patronize me, my lord. I am fully aware of my debt to you, but it does not authorize you to act as my guardian."

Not waiting for a reply, she climbed into the coach and closed the door behind her with a loud thud. Louisa quickly tapped on the door as a signal for the driver to depart. Glancing out the window, Helen saw the thunderous expression on Sebastian's face. It was a warning of the retribution to come. Beside her, Louisa gave her hand a gentle pat.

"Are you all right, Helen?"

"I'll be fine as soon as your brother realizes he cannot dictate what I may or may not do. I can't believe I wasn't at least afforded the opportunity to thank the man."

"Actually, it was Percy who refused to let Lord Templeton see you."

"What?" Helen shook her head in surprise. "Why didn't you say that in the first place?"

"Well, because Percy was simply acting on Sebastian's orders. Apparently he told Percy and Caleb that the Marquess might try to see you and that the man was to be turned away."

"He has no right to decide who I may or may not see."

"Sebastian was only looking out for your welfare, Helen. Although I admit that the Marquess seemed quite pleasant that day on Bond Street and just a few minutes ago, I've heard enough gossip to know that it's best to avoid the man."

"But he had no right," she said with a disheartened sigh. Leaning back against the seat cushions, she stared out the window. She'd told Sebastian that she wasn't his property to do with as he saw fit, and yet his actions clearly indicated he thought otherwise. It was frustrating, but more over, there seemed little she could do to change the fact.

Chapter 9

Anger surged through him as Sebastian watched the coach roll away. Damn the woman. He'd merely been trying to protect her. A cold laugh echoed behind him. Turning about he met Templeton's malicious glare.

"It appears Miss Rivenall is quite fiery beneath that cool, queenly appearance."

"She's none of your concern, Templeton. As long as Miss Rivenall is a guest in my home, she's under my protection." Burying his fury deep inside, he sent the man an icy glare.

"Come now, Melton. I wish the woman no harm. Like you, I find her most enchanting. In fact I'm certain she's of the nobility. She bears a remarkable resemblance to a woman I once met as a young boy."

The marquess's words made Sebastian go still. Over the past several weeks, he'd been frustrated by his inability to remember who Helen reminded him of. Now here was Templeton saying she resembled some woman from his childhood. Although it was impossible to even imagine the man as a child.

"What woman?" The sharp question arched the marquess's eyebrow in arrogant amusement.

"Fascinating. You're not known for your tolerance for the fairer sex, but it seems our Helen has captured your interest."

Templeton's mocking tone made Sebastian grit his teeth. Violence wasn't something he normally advocated, but in this case, he wanted to forget he'd ever been born a gentleman.

"This woman you mention. Is she someone you know?"

"Know of, would be a better way to phrase the question. I've made some inquiries, and so far the results have been quite promising."

"For whom?" he grounded out. "You've never done a charitable act in your life, Templeton. Don't expect me to believe you're about to start now."

"Tch, tch, you misjudge me Melton. You did the right thing, taking Helen away from Chantrel's. I confess that I would have done the same if I'd been in my right mind."

Sebastian uttered a snort of disbelief. "The day you ever do anything remotely honorable is the day hell freezes over."

A strange expression crossed the Marquess's face as he shook his head in an absent-minded fashion. "I don't expect you to believe me, but I've known from the start that Helen was special.

The truth is that I find her quite worthy of being a marchioness."

"You aspire to heights greater than the gutter you call home, Templeton."

"Ah, the infamous Melton deportment at its best. Your reputation for boorish behavior is well deserved. And where Helen is concerned, she might soon be free of your yoke."

"What the devil are you referring to?"

"Well, you certainly didn't expect me to give the woman up so easily did you? As I said, since you wouldn't sell her to me, I needed to find another way to secure the young lady's affections. I believe I may have done just that. Only time will tell."

The malevolence in the marquess's smile tightened every muscle in Sebastian's body until he was as taut as a piano string. Had the man discovered Helen had an uncle? Impossible, she'd revealed next to nothing about her past, and since she'd never been alone with Templeton, the man could only be bluffing. Still, where Helen was concerned the marquess seemed obsessed, and obsession had a habit of leading men into darkness. God knows he was struggling with the emotion himself where Helen was concerned.

"If you think the lady in question has any interest in you at all, you're delusional."

"And you, Melton, should note the fact that Miss Rivenall hardly seems enamored with you." With a sneer curling his mouth, the marquess bowed then walked away.

Templeton's parting shot riddled Sebastian with frustration. As much as he hated to admit it, the marquess was right. Helen did seem to avoid him whenever possible. In the past three weeks, she'd applied herself diligently to Louisa's instruction. So diligently, in fact, that she darted out of any room he entered.

And he was tired of her avoiding him. He turned sharply to begin the walk home. Pulling his watch from his vest pocket, he snapped open the gold timepiece. The old habit nudged at him like a fishwife. With a scowl at the watch face, he closed it with a vicious clench of his fist and shoved the watch back into his pocket.

Now there was Templeton to deal with. The man was up to something, and it couldn't be good. If he could just remember who Helen reminded him of, perhaps he could thwart whatever plot Templeton was hatching. He released an angry sigh that was more of a growl.

Why was he allowing this woman, *any* woman, to disrupt his life? His stride brisk, he barely noted the people he passed on the sidewalk. One would think him ready to surrender his quiet solitude for the chaos of letting Helen into his life. The soft scent of lavender drifted beneath his nostrils. Startled, his heart skipped a beat at the thought that she was close by. The sight of an open apothecary shop door explained the aroma.

A growl of irritation rumbled in his chest. He needed to stop acting like a besotted schoolboy and concentrate on how he was going to go about convincing Aunt Matilda that with Helen in residence, it was unnecessary to present him with a bevy of potential brides. His pace increased as he headed home. The moment Aunt Matilda returned to Scotland, Helen would leave him and Melton House. Hadn't she said so, herself? Once she was gone, his life would return to normal. The peace and quiet he'd surrendered more than three weeks ago would return to him. For some reason, the thought made him feel decidedly grim.

The number of people on the sidewalk ebbed as he turned the corner onto Warwick Street. He quickened his steps. It was time Helen Rivenall and he came to an understanding. In the space of three weeks, he'd acquired responsibility for a damsel in distress along with her young brother, been shot, served as the woman's protector general against Templeton's advances and been assaulted with the bedlam that had taken over his household.

And was the woman grateful for all his efforts? No. She was acting like every other female of his acquaintance. She was behaving illogically and with a stubbornness that was more than annoying. In short, she'd turned his household upside down. Helen Rivenall had a great deal to answer for.

Reaching the steps outside Melton House, Sebastian clenched his fists. No, indeed, his beautiful protégé was finally going to take responsibility for her actions. He charged up the steps intent on victory. The front door gave way to his annoyance with a sharp swing inward. Lips tightened in a firm line, he stripped his gloves off his fingers in precise strokes. Madison stood ready to accept his hat and gloves.

"Where are my sister and Miss Rivenall?"

"They're in the library, my lord."

With a grim nod, Sebastian headed toward the reading room. Not wishing to have his quarry fly the coop, he restrained from opening the door with a loud crash. As much as he wanted to break something, he needed to control his temper. Discipline, learned over long years of practice, allowed him to enter the room soundlessly.

Louisa was laughing as she flipped open a fan and fluttered it in front of her face. He paused in the doorway to watch Helen trying to imitate his sister's motions with the fan. Biting her bottom lip, she snapped her wrist in an attempt to open the fashion accessory. Only half of the fan splayed open. With an exasperated expression, she closed the fan and tried again but failed to open the accessory to its complete fullness.

"This is hopeless, Louisa." She collapsed the half-open fan into her free hand. "Are you certain I need to know how to use this ... this ridiculous trinket?"

"Any society maid worth her salt considers the fan one of the primary weapons in her arsenal for securing the surrender of the opposition." At the sound of his voice, Helen whirled around to face him. Keeping his gaze pinned on her, he moved forward. "The fan allows a woman to communicate silently with a gentleman."

A weak smile sent the corners of Helen's mouth upward. The nervous look in her green eyes pleased him. He turned to face his sister as she burst out laughing.

"Of all the etiquette lessons Constance and I gave you, Sebastian, why am I not surprised that it is the one on silent communication that captured your ear."

He tilted his head in a slight nod. "I've always had a talent for foreign languages."

"You're an incorrigible rogue," Louisa said as she moved to his side. "Will you be a dear? I have another charity meeting to attend, so I'll rely on you to further Helen's education in the finer points of the art form."

With an impudent grin, Louisa sailed from the room, the library door closing behind her with a quiet thud. The moment the door closed, the tension between them thickened. Slowly, he turned to meet her nervous gaze. Trepidation furrowed her brow while her tongue wet the fullness of her bottom lip. Ignoring the lust tightening his groin, he folded his arms across his chest.

"There is a small matter we need to discuss."

"Why bother with a discussion, when you've so clearly dictated that I'm not free to do as I like?" Despite the apprehension in her green eyes, she defiantly stared at him without flinching. He narrowed his gaze at her.

"I am not trying to dictate to you, I'm simply of the opinion that you are being most unwise in cultivating a friendship with Templeton."

"Two conversations with the man hardly constitutes a friendship." She scowled at him. "But at least it did give me the opportunity to thank him for his assistance a few weeks ago. Something I wasn't allowed to do at the time."

"My instructions were for your protection, nothing more. Given the terror gripping the city, I think my actions were quite logical."

"Simply because an action is logical, does not mean it is justified."

"Damn it, Helen, I'll not apologize for my efforts to keep you safe."

"This conversation is pointless." She snapped. "If you'll excuse me--"

"No I will not. Not until we settle this discord between us. You've been avoiding me, and I'll know the reason why."

"I don't know what you're talking about," she said quickly. The breathless sound of her voice teased his body into a sharp awareness. In two quick strides, he towered over her.

"No? Then perhaps you'll explain to me how it is that you view Templeton in a far kinder light than you do me."

"That's ridiculous. Lord Templeton did me a great service the afternoon that you returned to Chantrel's to rescue Miss Bainbridge. I simply felt I owed him the courtesy of being polite."

"And have you forgotten that the man tried to buy you?"

"No," she exclaimed fiercely. "Nor how another man succeeded in doing so."

"And we both know what would have happened if I'd not bought you."

"Of course I know what would have occurred," she hissed at him like an angry kitten. "You've no need to point out the error of my ways, Sebastian, I live with the guilt of my mistakes every day. But they do not make me the addle-brained female you think I am."

Stunned into silence, he stared at her. Where the devil had she gotten the idea that he thought her a simpleton? Incredibly stubborn perhaps, but far from dull-witted. Until now, the only females ever to stand up to him were his sisters and Aunt Matilda. If anything, he admired her bravado in standing up to him given he was well aware that he could be quite intimidating. There was a great deal he admired about her.

He enjoyed her quick mind and wry sense of humor. She was devoted to her brother and took her responsibility for him quite seriously. Then there was her courage to flee from a place of tyranny. It explained her stubborn refusal to be dominated by him, and if he'd been less half-witted, he would have recognized that long ago. Clearly, she was a woman to be respected, but it was more than that. He simply liked being in her company. Hands clasped behind his back, he shook his head.

"You're mistaken, Helen," he said quietly, suddenly aware that his anger had abated completely. "I have never considered you an addle-brained female."

"Well you've done little to refute the impression." She sniffed in an aggrieved fashion.

"I didn't realize my opinion was valued so highly by you." He could feel the hint of a smile tugging at the corners of his mouth.

"That's not what I said."

"Ah, so you don't value my opinion." This time he smiled openly at her.

"I didn't say that either," she exclaimed, as lovely confusion parted her full lips.

"And yet you're concerned with the impression I hold of you. Could it be that you're not as unaffected by me as you would have me think?"

"Don't be absurd."

"Would it be absurd to say we're attracted to one another?"

At the quiet question, her cheeks exploded with rosy color. Fumbling with her fan, she finally managed to make it fall open into a full arc. With the fan spread open, she stirred up a soft breeze with the frippery.

"I thought Louisa charged you with the task of instructing me in the use of this ridiculous social trinket," she muttered fiercely.

Her flushed skin and rapid breathing indicated how much he'd unsettled her. She hadn't denied the question. His body tensed at the thought. In not responding to his question, she'd answered it. Lush and sensual, she made the muscles in his groin tighten with need. Struggling with the desire returning to his mid-section, Sebastian nodded his head toward her fan.

"Then perhaps our first lesson should be to improve your skill at opening a fan."

"Yes, I think that would be an excellent idea."

The look of relief crossing her face changed as he stepped closer and walked around her so her back was to him. As he pressed into her back, he tipped his head to the right of hers and curled his arm around her so his hand could guide her movements with the fan. The quiver vibrating into his chest edged its way through him. It heightened the need surging through every muscle in his body.

"Are you disturbed by something, Helen?" His mouth brushed the edge of her ear lobe and she inhaled a sharp breath.

"Yes ... I mean no."

"You seem uncertain about the fact." Again he teased the edge of her ear with his mouth as he whispered his response.

"No, I am not disturbed. Please continue." The tight note in her voice was clearly audible, but it was the way her throat convulsed that illustrated her lie.

"As you wish." Beneath his hand, her fingers trembled as he

helped her unfurl the fan with a quick flick of her wrist. "You, see? That was simple enough, now try again."

As he released her hand, he lightly trailed his fingers up the length of her arm until he grasped her shoulder. Once again, she shuddered against him. It sent blood coursing through his body until he was stiff and hard. With another flick of her wrist, she opened the fan in a single snap.

"Excellent," he murmured. "Try it again."

"If you'll step back," she said with a breathless note in her voice. "It will make it much easier for me to concentrate."

He reached out and removed the fan from her suddenly limp fingers. Tossing the accessory onto a nearby table, he lowered his head to nibble at her ear. Another of her tremors resonated its way into his chest.

"Why are you having trouble concentrating?" he murmured against her skin.

"You ... you know ... why."

"Because you find my touch pleasurable?"

"Yes ..."

His thumb slid across her plump lower lip and was rewarded with her soft moan. The small sound made his cock flex with need. Eager to feel her silky skin against his mouth, he lowered his head to slide his lips along the edge of her jaw, while his fingers brushed aside the chiffon curled against her throat. The delicious taste of her tantalized his mouth as another delicate moan escaped her lips. With a sigh, her back melted into his chest, and her head tipped back to rest on his shoulder.

His mouth went dry as he saw how the sheer chiffon ruffle edging her bodice parted narrowly to reveal the creamy expanse of her throat before it plunged downward to the shadowy valley between her breasts. God, he wanted her. His need pulled at him as if it were a taut wire stretched to its breaking point. No other woman had aroused this much desire in him before, this much lack of control or will power.

His hands kneaded her shoulder blades and drifted down toward her waist. All he wanted was to touch her, stroke every inch of her, make her his. The hard ache in his groin pressed relentlessly against his trousers. With a quick movement, he twisted her around to embrace her. The sultry glow of her green eyes made him crush her mouth beneath his. An overwhelming need to devour her raged inside him, and he struggled not to frighten her with intensity of the feelings assaulting him.

Out of control, he shuddered as her hands slid beneath his coat to caress him. The heat of her fingertips burned through the fine lawn of his shirt. He was a man in the throes of heated desire, and he knew it. Her tentative caresses stoked the fires of his desire into an inferno. To his delight, her tongue darted out to tease his lips apart. As he delved into the inner warmth of her mouth, she pressed deeper into him, her tongue dancing with his in a rhythm of insatiable need.

Parting the chiffon at her throat, he slid his fingers beneath the edge of her bodice to where her corset pushed up her breasts. With his forefinger, he gently edged a hard nipple up over the edge of her combination garment. Her cool gasp of surprise swept over his tongue.

He hesitated, his hand stilled in its exploration. When she did not pull away, his heart skipped a wild beat. She wanted him. His thumb rubbed over the hard pebble of her breast, and his mouth ached to suck on her. Bloody hell, but this was torture not being able to undress her and touch every inch of her. A groan rumbled in his chest. He wanted her to know what she'd aroused in him. Grasping her hand, he pressed her palm against his erection as he lifted his head to stare down at her.

"You feel that sweetheart?" A sultry expression darkened her green eyes as she nodded. The look made him swallowed hard. "That's what you do to me."

As he stared down into her languid expression, he realized he wanted to see that sultry passion explode into a satiated glow of ecstatic release. Gently, he guided her backwards to the wide library table. Grasping her waist, he set her onto the flat surface. A slipper fell to the floor with a quiet thump.

Glancing down at her lovely, silk-encased foot, he trailed his fingers over a perfectly shaped ankle. Desire mixed with excitement in her eyes as he slid his hand up under the layers of her dress to stroke a lush, voluptuous calve. A small moue of protest curved her mouth as his hand inched higher up her leg. Immediately, he leaned into her, kissing away her hesitation. Sighing into his mouth, she swirled her tongue around his, and he groaned with need.

Beneath his fingertips, a lush calve gave way to a luscious thigh. Then he caught the fragrance of her. The heat of her desire. Christ Jesus, she was wet for him. He shuddered at the knowledge. Pulling back from her, he marveled at the passion on her face. Eyes closed, her head had fallen back to expose the expanse of her throat. Her lips stained red from the force of his kisses, she was more beautiful than any woman he'd ever seen.

The need to touch her, plunder her secrets tightened the coils of heat in his stomach. Did she have any idea what she was doing to him? To his self-control?

"I want to touch you sweetheart. I want to feel your heat

against my hand."

At his words, her eyes flew open. The hunger in her gaze made him suck in a deep breath as she reached out to brush her finger against his lip. Nibbling at her finger, his hand slid past a swatch of fine lawn to the nest of curls that covered the apex of her thighs.

The moment his fingers parted her slick folds, a mew escaped her throat as she trembled beneath his touch. The rough pad of his thumb circled the small nub inside her nether lips and it shot a wave of pleasure through her body until she bucked against his caress. Dear lord, she was on fire. Not even her own attempts at pleasuring herself had ever created such deliciously wicked sensations.

She was risking too much by letting him caress her so intimately, but she didn't care. She didn't want him to stop. Her body ached for him. For his touch. It didn't matter that others might think their actions wrong. Nothing this wonderful could be wrong. Liquid fire slid through her veins, and as his finger slid up inside her, she uttered a soft cry of delight.

Instinct guided her as she shifted her hips against his strokes and need crashed through her as he teased her with each new caress. Sweet heaven, but her entire body tingled with a need she'd never felt before. It was as if her body was starved for his touch. She had no control over her reactions, and she was willing to do whatever he asked of her if only he continued to caress her so boldly.

As his thumb circled the small nub inside her sleek folds, she shuddered against his hand. Slowly, he increased the pace of his strokes, his finger sliding in and out of her, mimicking another act. With each gentle probe to her heated sex, her passion flowed warm and sweet between her slick folds.

Cream covered his finger as he suppressed the urge to free his cock and plunge into her wet heat. Sweet Jesus, she was ready for him now. She clung to him as he bent his head to kiss her. Her response set off a conflagration inside his loins. A small tongue darted past his teeth teasing his with unexpected passion. With one finger, he caressed the outer perimeter of her heated core coating her with her liquid passion. He wanted more.

No, not want. This was a hunger he couldn't control. He wanted her wrapped around him until the tight friction of her hot little passage made him explode. The heady thought incited him to continue creating a steady rhythm against her snug passage with his finger, while his lips drifted down the side of her neck to nip at her racing pulse.

Her hips writhed against his hand as a cry of pleasure escaped her mouth. Fully aroused, her hands clutched at the lapels of his jacket as her velvety hips arched upward against his hand. Whimpering with need, her face was radiant in the throes of passion. Beneath her cool, collected exterior was a passionate creature. She would be incredible in his bed. The wayward thought nudged at him to stop. But he couldn't. He needed to see her climax. Witness the glow of satiation on her face.

Quickly he smothered her mewls of pleasure with a hard kiss. A moment later, her slick folds erupted in a multitude of spasms. For several moments, her muscles clenched spasmodically against his finger. As he withdrew his fingers from her hot, liquid center, he feathered the edge of her jaw with kisses. She responded with a lethargy that assured him she had experienced complete gratification at his touch. He on the other hand remained rock hard and unsatisfied.

"Did I please you, my sweet?" He whispered as he kissed her again.

"Umm," she murmured.

The quiet sigh of delight sent a rush of pleasure through him. He'd been the first to touch her so intimately. Of that, he was certain. Bringing her to such an intense climax increased the pressure of his own need. If he didn't find a release soon, he would take her here and now. He rested his forehead against hers.

"I need you to touch me, my sweet. Can you do that for me?" Her eyes locked with his as he quickly released his erection from his trousers. "I want to feel your hand around me, stroking me."

"Like this?" Her voice was almost a purr as she wrapped her fingers around him.

"Tighter, sweetheart." Another groan rumbled out of his chest as her hand created a hot, tight channel for him. The tip of her thumb rubbed against the lip of his erection, and as she gripped him more snugly she slid her hand up and down the length of him with out any guidance from him. The delicious pressure of her grip pulled a deep groan from his throat as he rocked back and forth in the cavern of her hand.

She sought his mouth as she pleasured him, her tongue teasing his as she tightened her grip on him. Christ Jesus she was a natural. The way her thumb rubbed against his sensitive spot just beneath the cap of his erection. As her tongue warmed his, he groaned at the image of her mouth on him and not her hand. It made me push harder against her hand, and as if reading his mind, she increased the pace of her stroking. The heat of her touch made the sacs beneath his cock tightened in a familiar surge. Clutched in the throes of delight, he somehow found the wherewithal to pull a handkerchief from his pocket to prevent the staining of her dress as the pressure inside him built to an explosive climax.

For several moments, he shuddered in her hand, the intense pleasure beyond his wildest fantasy. The tension of his desire slowly eased, and when he pushed himself upright, he noted the pink tinge cresting her cheeks. He lifted her chin with one knuckle and planted another kiss on her mouth.

"Thank you, my sweet. I've fantasized about that for some time now." When she blushed a deeper pink, he laughed softly. "There is nothing to be ashamed of, Helen. We both experienced something incredible."

"It was lovely, wasn't it?" Her sigh of happiness wrapped itself around his heart, crushing it with trepidation.

What had he been thinking? God, he'd done nothing but toy with her. Use her for his own pleasure. Putting his own needs ahead of any possible consequences to her. He was no better than Templeton or any other rake eager to satisfy their own needs.

Stiffening slightly, he kissed her again. Her lips softened against his. The gentle touch lashed at him with the harshness of a guilty whip. It stung sharper than any pain he'd experienced in quite some time. When he drew back from her, he tried to smile. But even if her eyes had not darkened with misgiving, he would have known the attempt was a miserable one at best.

Unable to bear the uncertainty on her face, he turned and hastily adjusted his clothing. The tentative touch of her hand on his arm pitched a fiery bolt of shame throughout his body. Louisa had called him a rogue. His sister had no idea how accurate her statement had been. Hands clenched with raw tension, he swallowed the knot closing his throat.

"Helen, what we shared a moment ago was ... it was one of the most unbelievable experiences I've ever had." The gruff sound of his voice gave him the sensation of carpenter's sandpaper grating across his skin.

"I thought so too." He turned his head sharply to study her composed features. A soft smile tilted the corners of her lovely mouth.

"Still, I should not have taken advantage of you in such a fashion," he mumbled.

"I don't recall any protests on my part." There was a faint hint of amusement in her words.

"Perhaps not, but I should have known better."

"I'm sorry you regret the moment." Her words were a statement not a question. She sighed. "I don't."

She stirred the air around him as she moved toward the library door. He'd been a fool to do what he'd done. Anyone could have walked in on them, potential ruin for her and the definite tight constraints of the marriage noose about his neck. She didn't need someone like him anyway, set in his ways, a man of rigid expectations. No, she needed a man who'd consider her feelings. Someone to care for her in a way he wasn't capable.

Her back was ramrod straight as she reached the door. He couldn't let her leave thinking he regretted what had just passed between them.

"Helen ..." She looked over her shoulder at him. The expression on her face was unreadable. "I don't regret what just happened. I'm only sorry that I took liberties with you knowing that you deserve more than I'm able to give."

She studied at him for a long moment before offering him a sad smile. "I understand, Sebastian."

With that, she turned and left him standing alone in the library. Alone with the realization that he was far to close to letting chaos assume complete command of his well-ordered world.

Chapter 10

Helen crossed the foyer slowly as the grandfather clock droned out a solemn beat. Its sonorous tone reminded her of Uncle Warren's voice ordering her to take care with her wanton ways. If the man were here now, he'd be condemning her to hell for immoral behavior. She didn't care. She had no regrets. What she had shared with Sebastian had been the most wondrous experience of her life.

She'd welcomed his touch of her own free will and with no expectations of him. But the guilt on his face just now had saddened her. How could she make him understand that for the first time in her life she'd been free to make a choice? Her uncle had never given her the ability to make choices. He'd always imposed his will on her. But today, with Sebastian, it had been her choice to welcome his caresses or reject him.

As she crossed the floor to the stairs, the memory of Sebastian's touch set off a flurry of butterflies in her stomach. The images and memories of his hand touching her so intimately filled her head, and her body throbbed with the memory. No. No matter what the consequences, she would not trade that experience for anything.

Halfway up the stairs, she heard Madison answer the loud rap of the front door knocker. Her hand on the banister she did not stop her ascent until the loathsome bass of a familiar voice floated up to her.

"I'm here to claim my niece and nephew."

The harsh words wrapped around her, choking her with fear. Unable to move, her fingers dug into the banister with a deathlike grip. He'd found her. In a way it surprised her that he'd taken so long to do so. Ever since that day in Bond Street, she'd known in the deepest corners of her mind that he'd find her. Control was his motivation for everything he did, and controlling her was what had brought him here today.

The clipped sound of boots against marble thawed her limbs, and she turned to face the man crossing the foyer floor. From her position in the middle of the staircase, Helen stared down at the man who had ruled her life with cruelty for the past twelve years.

One foot on the bottom step, Warren Rivenall stared up at her with the fierce glare of a judgmental reverend. Tall and thin, his expression was one of contempt. Dense, white whiskers emphasized his sunken jowls. The miserly look of him illustrated his mean temperament.

"Well niece, aren't you the very image of a strumpet, firmly ensconced in a nobleman's home. Once you return to Mayfield, you will beg God's forgiveness for your sinful behavior."

The critical manner in which he settled judgment on her set her blood at a slow boil. For too long she'd listened to his proselytizing. If ever there was a time to break free of the man's shackles, it was now. "And if I don't uncle? If I don't beg God's forgiveness, am I to submit myself to your strap again so that you might extinguish the vile and lustful thoughts you harbor toward me?"

"You ungrateful, wicked-tongued little whore." Her uncle choked out the words as he started up the steps toward her.

"No uncle, that's how you see me. I'm none of those things, and I will not allow you control me any longer with your words or your whip."

Blood-red fury darkened his face, and with a sudden lunge, he charged up the last two steps separating them. Before she could flee, his hand lashed out and struck her cheek with a loud crack. The force of the blow jerked her head to one side, and she collapsed against the banister. The sting of the assault stole her breath. For a moment, she clung to the banister until a fury she did not believe herself capable of took root in every part of her body. Pressing one hand to her burning cheek, she glared up at her tormentor.

"You, sir, are the worst kind of reprobate in that you use God's word to further your own cause. If anyone is in danger of falling in league with the devil, it is you, Uncle, not me."

A roar of fury vibrated out of the man towering over her, making her cringe. With a brutal grip on her arm, her uncle dragged her upright. Then stepping to one side, he pushed her forward. For a moment, Helen tottered on the edge of the step. Fear clasped its grip around her heart and in that split instant, she saw Sebastian emerge into the foyer. As she tumbled downward with a cry, she heard Sebastian's anguished shout. The carpet runner on the stairs blunted the impact of her fall, and she flung her arms out in an effort to latch onto something solid to stop her treacherous descent.

The sudden shock of ramming into a sturdy chest knocked the wind out of her. When her ability to breathe returned, she dragged in a sharp breath of air. Disoriented, she heard a menacing voice rumbling out of the chest of the man holding her close. The rage in Sebastian's voice would have made her tremble had she been on the receiving end.

"You have exactly thirty seconds to leave my home, sir."

"I have no intention of remaining in this den of fornication, but I shall not leave without my nephew or this ungrateful wretch of a woman."

"Helen and her brother are not going anywhere," Sebastian said with a deadly calm. "Whether you leave this house dead or alive matters little to me, but you will leave."

Sebastian's icy words made her shiver, and she turned her head to see the color drain from her uncle's face. Despite his blatant fear, he drew himself up in his best imitation of an affronted clergyman.

"Hardly a charitable way to speak, my lord."

"Murder is far from a charitable thought, sir."

Swallowing hard, her uncle scurried down the steps. He paused as he drew even with Helen's face. Hatred gleamed in the man's eyes as he scowled at her. "This is not over, girl. I've made arrangements for you and the boy. I'll not be thwarted in this."

"*Get out!*"

The violence in Sebastian's voice sent her uncle scurrying the rest of the way across the foyer. She closed her eyes, listening for the sound of his departure. As her uncle's heavy footsteps crossed the marble floor, she heaved a sigh of relief when the front door slammed close behind him. The gentle touch of Sebastian's fingers caressing her cheek made her look up at him.

"Are you all right?" The quiet thread of agitation underlying his question puzzled her, and the haunted look in his black gaze reminded her of someone in shock.

"Yes, I think I'm more bruised than anything else."

Clinging to his forearm, she allowed him to help her stand upright. Dizzy, she swayed back into him, and a strong arm wrapped itself around her waist. Hands braced against his chest, she tested her equilibrium again. She shuddered slightly, grateful that she was unharmed.

"You're injured?"

"No, I'm just shaken."

He pulled her against him in a tight embrace. "I'm sorry."

Surprised, she tilted her head back to view his strained features. Again, he gave her the impression he'd experienced a terrible trauma. She'd seen the look on many of the villagers during the flu epidemic that had taken her parents from her.

"You're not responsible for my uncle's behavior."

"No, but I gave you my word that you would come to no harm under my roof." His lips tightened into a grim line. "However, I shall see to it the blackguard never sets foot in this house again."

"I think you've already accomplished that."

"How?"

"My uncle has no trouble bullying individuals weaker than him, but he doesn't have the courage to stand up to those who threaten him with bodily harm." A brief smile curved her lips.

Sebastian met her smile with a frown. "And how often did he bully you?"

"I ..." She caught the warning glint in his gaze and looked away. "Uncle Warren found many occasions to punish me for inappropriate behavior."

"Why do I think that means you were punished at the slightest provocation?"

"It doesn't matter now. Edward and I are free, and when we find--" Helen clamped her lips together. Involving Sebastian in the search for her grandfather would only increase her debt to him. It wasn't something she wanted. She would do this on her own, although she'd made little headway in her search. Other than asking Madison about her grandfather, or eavesdropping on conversations while she shopped with Louisa, she'd had no other opportunities to inquire about her grandfather.

Finding her grandfather would be much easier in the drawing rooms of the Marlborough Set, and she'd thought of appealing to Louisa's sense of adventure and asking for her help. Doing so would most likely ensure her success. But involving Louisa, meant the possibility of Sebastian becoming involved in the search. That was something she didn't want to happen.

If her grandfather refused to receive her or Edward, she'd have to find work and a home. She knew Sebastian would feel responsible for them, and the last thing she wanted was his pity or feelings of responsibility. She owed him too much as it was.

"Damn it Helen, why won't you let me help you find the man?" he said with frustration.

She shook her head, suddenly all too aware of his warmth invading her clothing and soaking into her body. "I will keep my own counsel, my lord."

"A few moments ago you were whispering my name with delight. Why such formality now?" he muttered. The deliberate reference to their passionate exchange drove heat into her face. She strained against his arms, eager to be free of his disturbing embrace. Edward's cry from the top of the stairs made Helen stiffen.

"Helen! What's wrong?"

"We shall finish this discussion later," Sebastian whispered as he released her.

Ignoring his emphatic warning, she turned to see Edward hurrying down the steps. She forced a smile to her lips. "I'm fine. I slipped and fell. Fortunately, his lordship was close at hand and saved me from any serious damage."

"But you've hurt your face."

The reminder of her uncle's fury forced her to raise one hand to her still burning cheek. "So it would appear. I really need to be more cautious. I'm quite all right, but I think I shall lie down for a short while."

Sebastian's hand left the small of her back as she moved away from him to continue climbing the stairs once more. Worry furrowed her brother's brow, and she paused at his side to kiss his cheek. "I'm fine, Edward. There's no need to fret."

"Well if you're certain," he said in a mature tone.

"Of course, I am. Now off with you and mind you stay out of trouble."

She continued up to the second floor and as she reached the landing, she turned to find the foyer empty except for Sebastian. He leaned against the wall, his gaze watching her with an intensity that made her shudder. The past half hour had drastically changed things between them. She could read it in his face and his body. He studied her with a possessive air, and she shivered again before quickly darting out of view.

Reaching the safety of her room, she sank down on her bed. It would no longer be possible to keep Sebastian at bay. Their intimate encounter in the library had removed all the barriers she'd erected to keep her heart free of encumbrance. The memory of his touch between her legs made her close her eyes while she grew moist in the spot he had caressed. She wanted him to touch her there again. No, not want. She craved it, craved his kiss, craved him.

She inhaled a quick breath at the disturbing thought. The memory of her uncle shouting at her made her cringe. He had tried to declare her relationship with Sebastian as being wicked and profane. But that's not what her heart told her.

With a sigh, she laid back on the bed. What were her true feelings for Sebastian? What was it about him that made her willing to cast all caution aside for the pleasure of touching him and being touched in return? She wished her mother were alive to advise her. Her parents had taught her that lovemaking was a beautiful thing between two people, but Uncle Warren had done his best to convince her otherwise.

Love was the devil's way of luring a man into a woman's trap was his favorite saying. Women were devious creatures and needed constant reminders of their inferior natures. Far too many times, he'd reminded her of his beliefs. The riding crop he used to punish her for minor transgressions had done more than inflict physical scars.

Flinching she rolled onto her side. Her uncle's constant barrage of ranting made her question her current situation. Was her uncle right? Had she committed a terrible sin by being so intimate with Sebastian? No. Uncle Warren was wrong. What she felt for Sebastian wasn't wrong. The intimacy they'd shared had been a joyful one. Nothing so beautiful could be wrong.

But it was clear Sebastian didn't feel as she did. In the library, she'd seen the troubled expression in his dark eyes. She had seen the regret in those ebony depths. He'd said she deserved more than he could give her. Did he think she would expect something from him because of their experience? She closed her eyes, tired of rationalizations and imperfect attempts at understanding her thoughts and emotions. If she slept, perhaps the answers would come more easily.

* * * *

The room was dark except for a thin stream of moonlight tracing a path across her bedroom floor. Staring up into the darkness, Helen was no closer to answers than she had been before she fell asleep. Frustration forced her into an upright position. She lit the branch of candles beside her bed. On the vanity, there was a covered tray. A quick glance at the mantel clock told her it was almost midnight. Her stomach growled as she peeked under the tray's cover. The sight of cold chicken, bread, cheese and fruit made her realize how terribly hungry she was.

A short time later, she had completely silenced the hunger in her belly. Wide-awake she knew returning to bed would only result in tossing and turning. Restless, she prowled her room. Perhaps reading a book from the library would help her fall asleep more easily.

The dim glow of the oil lamp sitting on the hall table provided just enough light for her to find her way to the top of the stairs. There was a peaceful silence hanging in the air, and as she made her way down the steps, the tension in her muscles ebbed away. Unlike Mayfield at night, she felt safe here at Melton House. At the foot of the stairs, she stopped to pick up a small branch of candles to light her way as she entered the library.

Inside the large room, she browsed the shelves for several minutes until she pulled a book of Shakespeare sonnets off the shelf. Satisfied with her selection, she retreated back out to the foyer and replaced the candle branch back on its table. As she set the silver candleholder down, poignant notes filtered out of the music room into the foyer.

The music was familiar to her, but she couldn't place the melody. Quietly she crossed the hall floor and slipped through the half open door of the music room. Sebastian sat at the Broadwood piano, his fingers racing across the keys. A single candle rested on top the instrument's lid, enlarging his shadow as it filled the wall behind him. He'd removed his coat, and his muscles flexed with power beneath the taut lines of his white shirt. The music sang out from the chords as he slowly ended the piece. He only paused a moment before continuing.

Oblivious to the world, he teased and coaxed the instrument's keys into a moving rendition of Beethoven's *Fur Elise*. Then, with barely a breath or moment's rest, he pushed on to another piece. This one she didn't recognize, but it was one of the most beautiful pieces of music she'd ever heard. She watched as his fingers danced over the keys in a frenetic articulation of passion and joy. The music rose to a fervent pitch then retreated to an expression of quiet anguish only to rise up once more in a cry of passion.

On the wall, his shadow danced against the flame's light in a powerful display. She couldn't see his face, but she could easily read his mood by the way he played. His body leaned into the piano when he caressed the softer portions of the melody from the piano, but as the sonata grew fast and furious, his shadow revealed a figure strong and defiant in its attempt to pull every ounce of emotion from the keys possible.

The notes filled the room with a soft interlude then sang forth in another forte of passionate discovery. The depth of feeling that poured out of his playing tugged at her heart. Somehow, she knew the music represented all the feelings he kept locked inside him. The music sang out with all the different facets that made him who he was. It was a language only he understood, and his fingers magically delivered a sonata that defied description. Her heart rose and fell with each impassioned note as the music enveloped and caressed her. The notes soared again to a passionate height before tumbling down to a soft languid movement that gave way to a rousing run of notes and a final crash of the keys.

As the music faded into the silence, she stood frozen, her book clutched tightly to her chest. Still unaware of her presence, Sebastian pushed himself away from the piano in a gesture of frustration. He strode to one of the ballroom windows. One hand braced against the frame the other pressed against his hip, he stared out into the dark. The starkness of his profile tore at her heart. But it was the loneliness in his posture that compelled her to reach out to him.

"Sebastian."

He whirled around at her soft whisper, peering into the darkness where she hid. "Who's there?"

Still moved by his playing, she stepped into the light of the single candle, her heart pounding with the emotion the music had stirred in her. When he saw her, a grim expression settled on his face.

"Helen," he rasped. "What are you doing down here?"

"I ... I came down to get a book. I heard you playing ... and I ... I had to come listen. It was beautiful."

"Come here."

The husky command caused her heart to skip a beat. Obediently, she moved toward him, her nerves tingling at every point beneath her skin. She came to a stop in front of him. His hand reached out to capture her chin.

"You shouldn't be here," he murmured.

"Why not?"

"Because I'm not to be trusted where you're concerned."

Slowly, he lowered his head and brushed her lips in a soft, feathery kiss. His hands cupped her face as his mouth pressed against hers more firmly. Without thought, her book slid from numb fingers and she wound her arms around his neck. Pine and leather scents tickled her nose, and the merest hint of cognac flavored his tongue as he probed the inner recesses of her mouth. Strong, sinewy arms held her close, pulling her deeper into his warmth.

The kiss intensified and she moaned softly against his lips. She wanted more. She wanted his hands on her, touching her, arousing her as he had earlier today. Sheer instinct guided her movements as she pressed her hips into his in an invitation he couldn't fail to understand. His arousal pressed into her thigh, the heat of his hard length searing its way through her robe and nightgown. Eager to touch him again, she stroked him through his trousers. With a deep groan, he thrust her from him as she murmured her protest.

"Go to your room, Helen."

"I don't understand."

"Damn it, Helen. Go to your room."

"But I--"

"*Go*," he ground out in a harsh voice.

Stunned by his rejection, she took a quick step back. When he turned sharply away, she swallowed a small gasp of pain and ran from the room. Stumbling up the stairs, she flew down the corridor to her own room. Once behind the door, she leaned against it trembling with a multitude of emotions. She wanted him. Every inch of her body cried out for him and his touch. But he'd sent her away. He didn't want her.

Pushing herself away from the door, she shook her head. No, he desired her. She'd seen it in his eyes, heard it in his voice. Why had he sent her away then? The candle in her room sputtered, distorting her shadow up on the wall. She studied it for a moment, remembering Sebastian's silhouette as he'd played with such abandon. What had he been thinking about while he played so passionately? The music had whispered a dozen different messages, but she was unable to decipher any of them.

Lost in contemplation, she sat in front of her vanity. When he'd touched her so intimately this afternoon, the feeling had been not only wonderful, but it had also seemed quite natural. The memory of how she'd pleasured him with her hand heated her cheeks.

The face staring back at her arched an eyebrow. *Well now, Helen, this is a fine mess you've gotten yourself into this time. So what are you going to do? Are you going to sit here and do nothing?*

She wanted to please him again, and she wanted him to please her. Sebastian's desire for her wasn't an illusion. She believed that with all her heart. But rejecting her because he was trying to be honorable. ... That had to be the answer. He was trying to do the honorable thing. It would explain the look of guilt on his face this afternoon and it would explain why he'd pushed her away just a few minutes ago, even though his body had clearly indicated he wanted her.

"And what am I suppose to do?" She whispered to image in the mirror.

Seduce him. She went rigid in shocked surprise, her eyes staring at her reflection in horror. With a sharp movement, she sprang to her feet. Fingertips pressed against her brow, she paced the floor. The insistent voice in her head grew louder, and she tried to drown it out by reciting the titles and ranks of society members she'd soon be meeting.

Despite her desperate concentration, the incessant voice continued to grow. It clamored and demanded that she listen. Where was the book she'd gotten in the library? Her gaze searched the room to no avail. With a groan, she remembered how she'd dropped it when Sebastian had kissed her. Well, she had no intention of listening to the wild imaginings raging in her head. She would have to go down and retrieve the book. It was highly unlikely Sebastian was still in the music room anyway.

In three quick steps she reached her bedroom door and flung it open. Standing in the middle of the hall, Sebastian's head jerked in her direction. The fiery desire in his gaze singed her skin as his eyes locked with hers, and she inhaled a sharp breath.

The voice in her head screamed at her to throw herself into his arms. To tease him. To seduce him. In his hand was the book she'd dropped in the music room. Unable to speak, she stared at him. The inside of her mouth was parched, and a shudder went through her as her body cried out for him.

A muscle in his jaw twitched, and when he didn't speak, her eyes dropped to the soft leather binding in his tense grip. Without a word, he offered her the book. Blindly, she released her clutch on the doorframe. Her fingers were so numb, the volume nearly slipped from her hand.

Tightening her grip on the book, she barely glanced at it before she returned her gaze to his face. Tension filled the air between them, and she wished he would take her into his arms. As if aware of what she wanted from him, he frowned.

"Go back to bed," he said harshly.

"No." She shook her head. Something deep inside her propelled her body forward to stand at his side. Her hand touched his wrist, and he shuddered beneath her fingers as she leaned into him.

"For God's sake, Helen," he groaned. "Go to your room before I lose what little restraint I have left."

"What if I want you to lose control?"

He started at her softly whispered question. Disbelief darkened his eyes, and his mouth tightened into a hard thin line. With a sharp movement, he pushed her away from him and strode down the hall toward his bedroom. Dismayed, she watched him walk away. How could she make him understand that this was her choice? She didn't care that her uncle and others would condemn her for being with him. There had been so little happiness in her life for so long. Why should she deny herself the joy of Sebastian's touch? The thought drove her to run after him. The moment her hand grasped his arm, he uttered a growl that at any other time might have frightened her. But tonight, it sent a shiver of excitement across her skin.

"Sebastian, please don't leave me like this."

"You don't know what you're saying," he said in a tight voice.

"Yes, I do." She shook her head at him. "You told me that what we shared this afternoon was a beautiful and natural response to our attraction for one another. Was that a lie?"

"No," he growled. "But this is different."

Something about the tension in his body had changed. It was then she knew his restraint was about to give way. She pressed her body up against the side of him, her hand caressing his tense jaw line. "Why is it different?"

"Because this time I don't intend to stop."

In an explosive movement, Sebastian lifted her up into his arms and carried her back down the hall and into her bedroom.

Chapter 11

Startled by his unexpected action, she inhaled a sharp breath as her arm instinctively wrapped around his neck. The solid feel of his sinewy arms warmed her through her thin robe, while the raw power of his strength enveloped her, reassured her. His embrace told her he would protect her. But she didn't want to be protected from him. She wanted him to touch her again. The thought sent a shiver of exhilaration skating down her spine.

As he set her down inside her room, he closed and locked the door behind him. When he turned to face her, excitement fluttered through her at the look of desire blazing across his face. Slowly she stretched out her hand to him in a silent invitation. Despite the flickering candlelight, his rugged features remained shadowed as he studied her in silence for a long, intense moment.

It was as if he were memorizing every inch of her. Taking her hand, he brushed his mouth over her fingertips. The touch sent a shiver of expectation skimming over her. An instant later, she was wrapped in his arms. The distinct aroma of brandy floated into her nostrils. He'd had more to drink since she'd left him, but his gaze was clear and steady. Mesmerized by his ebony eyes, she stared up at him.

"I want you," she whispered boldly.

A muscle twitched in his cheek as he stared at her in stunned disbelief. Had she erred in speaking her desire for him aloud? The arms around her were hard with tension as his nostrils flared with excitement. Her heart pounding, she trailed her fingers across his firm mouth in a light caress before cupping his face and pulling his head down to her.

Pine and leather mixed with the scent of brandy to create an aroma that was uniquely him. It filled her senses, tingling its way into every pore as she brushed her mouth over his in a teasing caress. Imitating the first kiss he'd ever given her, she nibbled at his lower lip with her teeth. A deep growl rumbled in his chest, and the moment he allowed it to escape her tongue swept into his mouth.

Warm hands grasped her waist and pulled her into him as she teased him with her tongue. Sweet heaven, he tasted wonderful. Molded to him, she could feel the hardness of him pressing into her thigh. She wanted to caress him again, like she had this afternoon. It had pleased him, and she loved the way he responded to her touch. Knowing that she was responsible for the look of passion on his face. Without hesitating, she traced the line of his erection with her finger. Another sound of pleasure rumbled in his chest. Her heart skipped a beat at the sound.

Impatient to touch more of him, she tugged his shirt free of his trousers, her fingers making short work of the buttons. The pressure of his mouth on hers increased as she helped him shrug out of the white shirt stretched taut over his hard muscular body. With a careless thrust of his hand, he tossed the garment aside before his fingers untied the ribbon holding her robe closed.

The touch of his warm, strong hands against her throat sent a shudder through her as he slid the robe off her shoulders and down her arms. As the robe whispered its way to the floor, his mouth blazed a trail down the side of her neck, nipping at her skin until she moaned with delight.

Sweet heaven, his caresses were even more potent than what she'd experienced earlier. Every one of her nerve endings was on fire for him and even if she'd wanted too, escaping this wild unadulterated pleasure would be impossible.

Hard and sinewy beneath her fingertips, she pressed her lips to his breastbone, enjoying the clean, spicy taste of him. Desire raced through her, and her nipples ached for his touch. Did he ache for her in the same way? Gliding her mouth across his skin, her tongue flicked out to swirl around the rough pebble on his chest.

He tensed in response to the caress and a deep groan rolled out of him. Harsh and ragged, his breathing stirred her hair as she swept her tongue across his nipple once more then gently bit down on the tip of him. The erotic sensation tightened the muscles in his groin.

Damnation. If that had been his cock her teeth had nibbled on, he would have lost his seed already. Breathing in the soft lavender scent of her, he buried his fingers in her silky, gold hair and raised her head up so he could kiss her again.

She met his mouth with an eagerness that delighted him. Even more delightful was the mewl of pleasure that parted her lips. Immediately, his tongue swept into the warm cavern of her mouth. The taste of her was tart, lemony and seductive. Desire surged through him as he stroked the inner recesses of her warm mouth. He wanted to dip his fingers in her honey again. No. He wanted to taste her honey. Taste the bite of her desire.

The touch of her hand tracing a path down his chest to his trousers made him nip at her lower lip before he raised his head. Dazed, he watched her unbutton his trousers to free his engorged length. Her fingers wrapped around him in a snug grip, before her thumb stroked the sensitive area just beneath the cap of him. It didn't surprise him when she smeared a warm bead of desire over his tip. He was ready to explode now. In several quick moves, he removed the remainder of his clothing.

Stepping back from her, he inhaled a sharp breath at the passion illuminating her face. In the candlelight, her voluptuous figure made him swell even more. Beneath her sheer gown, he could see the rosy peaks of her breasts and the dark gold thatch of hair between her thighs. He swallowed hard.

"Take off your gown," he rasped.

Without hesitation, she slowly slipped one arm out of the silk garment to reveal a creamy breast and rose-colored nipple. His mouth watered at the sight. A moment later, the silky nightgown slid across another tantalizing nipple, then down past her hips to pool at her feet. Stretching out his hand, his fingers brushed across a rigid peak. She was as exquisite as he remembered.

He wanted her. He wanted to taste her--to possess her--to make her his.

Sweeping her up into his arms, he carried her toward the bed. The softness of her skin was like silk, while her curves tantalized him. Laying her on the mattress, he trailed his finger around the hard peaks of her breasts. The sharp breath she inhaled prompted him to repeat the caress with her other breast.

Not content to simply stroke her with his finger, he leaned forward and circled a hard tip with his tongue. The ragged moan that parted her lips pleased him. He continued the slow, methodical stroke of his tongue before suckling the rosy peak. Slender fingers spiked through his hair as he alternated between sucking her nipple and flicking his tongue over the stiff bud. Another quiet cry of delight escaped her.

As she stirred beneath his tongue, his hand caressed the lower part of her thigh before sliding up to cup her damp curls. She jumped at the touch, her buttocks rising up to meet his hand. Tension coiled inside him as her body declared how eager she was for his touch.

Damn but she smelled good. She was hot and slick, and he didn't want to wait any longer to taste her. There would be time later to stretch out the pleasure, but at the moment, all he wanted was to have her on his tongue.

Sliding his mouth down across her belly, he feathered her skin with kisses. Her body responded like an instrument to him, vibrating against him with a response that astonished him. Beneath her cool, serene manner, she was more passionate than he'd ever dreamed possible. As his lips crested the top of her mons, she gasped. Raising herself up on her elbows, she looked at him in startled bemusement.

He didn't look away from her as his fingers parted her slick folds. Her eyes widened and she shook her head as if suddenly realizing what he was about to do. Not about to wait for her protest, his tongue slid into her heat and he watched as her facial expressions evolved from shocked surprise to delirious ecstasy.

The tangy taste of her cream flooded his mouth as he swirled his tongue around the hard bud inside her velvety core. A low cry escaped her, and the elemental sound of it tugged painfully at him. The mewls coming from her throat continued as he licked and swirled his tongue over the nubbin.

The rough edge of his tongue scraped over her sensitive skin as she bucked against his mouth. Dear lord, but this was the most hedonistic act she had ever imagined. Never in her wildest dreams had she ever thought a man could pleasure a woman in this way. And it *was* pleasurable. Her fingers bit into the folds of the sheets as she bit back a wild cry. She wanted to weep from the intensity of this delicious torture he was inflicting on her. It was the most delightfully wicked caress she'd ever experienced, and she wanted more. Much more.

She wanted him inside her.

"Oh God, please Sebastian. Please," she moaned.

With a nip to the inside of her thigh, he brushed his mouth across her stomach and back up to her breasts. The ache inside her was maddening, and her hands dug into his shoulders as his hard length brushed along her inner thigh. Her breaths coming in short pants, she slid a hand between them and rubbed her thumb over the tip of him. Rising up over her, his dark eyes blazed with desire as his gaze met hers.

Everything her uncle had told her was wrong. Nothing that felt this wonderful could be immoral. With every touch, every stroke, Sebastian was banishing all the shadows from her head. This was right. It was where she wanted to be. Needed to be.

A second later, the hard tip of him pushed through the outer edge of her wet folds. The ache between her thighs intensified, and she ran her hands up over his biceps in a gentle caress. Slowly, he pressed into her and then withdrew. Each time he did so, he buried himself deeper inside her, filling her, expanding her. Her body quivered with each stroke and she thrust upward to meet him each time.

Desire wrapped its tendrils tightly around him, quietly choking back the niggling of doubt threatening to force its way through. Self-control fought a desperate battle to reassert itself, but the need in his groin crushed the attempt to regain command of his senses. She wanted this as badly as he did. To deny himself the pleasure of her body wasn't within his capability. He needed her as surely as he needed air to breathe.

Increasing the tempo of his thrusts, he watched her face as he repeatedly plunged into her. Passion tugged at her mouth, parting her lips as she emitted soft cries of pleasure. Eyes closed, her back arched up to him, the tips of her breasts close to his mouth as her snug passage clutched at him with a ferocity that made him groan.

She was a silky hot vise around his hard rod. Every movement created a friction that teased and tormented him with pleasure. God, she was incredible. Never before had he been as enthralled with a woman as he was with her. Even now, he knew this moment would not be enough for him. He would want more of this. More of her.

The stiff peaks of her breasts hovered near his mouth as he rocked his hips back and forth against hers. Unable to resist temptation, he circled one rosy tip with his tongue then suckled her. Gasping, her fingertips dug into his shoulders as she clung to him. First one, and then another, tiny spasm clutched and squeezed his hard length, while her hips thrust up against his with wild abandon.

With a quiver, her body lunged upward into his as wave after wave of ripples engulfed his cock as her tight passage clutched at him with an intensity that pushed him over the edge. Releasing her nipple from his mouth, he uttered a low cry as he surged into her with one last thrust and throbbed inside her.

For several long moments, he stayed that way. Locked inside her with her body pulsating and shivering over him. A sigh of contentment broke past her lips and whispered over his shoulder. He smiled. He understood the feeling. Never had he felt so completely satiated. Reluctantly, he slowly withdrew from her, his mind protesting his action just as her soft murmur did. Lying next to her, he trailed the back of his hand across her cheek.

At his touch, she rolled over onto her side and snuggled up against him. The silence between them was more peaceful than any he'd ever experienced, and he closed his eyes to enjoy the sensation. How long he slept, he didn't know, but the seductive caress of her hand on him pulled him out of the dream world into the heat and pleasure of her touch.

She hovered over top of him, the pale gold curtain of her hair dancing across his chest. The tip of her thumb skated across the top of him, before it slowly edged its way around the rim of him. As the silky pad of her thumb rubbed over the sensitive spot on his staff, he sucked in a sharp breath.

The knowledge that suddenly darkened her eyes made him grow harder. A seductive smile curving her lips, she ran her thumb over him again in the same spot.

"Do you like that?" she whispered as she stroked him again.

"God, yes."

Soft laughter parted her lips as she grasped him snugly and pumped her hand over him, while teasing him with her thumb. Groaning, he cradled her neck in his hand and tugged her down to meet his kiss. As he teased her mouth open with his tongue, he shuddered at the stroke of her hand on him. God, she learned quickly, and he loved it. Hard as a rock, he throbbed in her hand. It wasn't enough. He wanted to fill her again.

Grasping her soft curves, he made her straddle him. Startled, she released her hold on him, her hands braced against his shoulder. The confusion on her face made him smile slightly. "I think it's time you learned something new."

With his palms on her buttocks, he lifted her up until her wiry curls brushed over the tip of him. The sensation made his erection jump with a tantalizing ache as he made her sheath him with her hot, silky core. He inhaled a breath of pleasure. Damn, she felt good. Hot and tight. Already she was slick with desire, and it heated his engorged staff as he taught her how to rock back and forth on him.

The tips of her breasts beckoned, and he reached up to cup her. She fit his hand perfectly. He brushed his thumb over a stiff nipple, and the sound of her sharp gasp excited him all the more. He could spend the rest of his life touching her like this. He stiffened at the notion, but her soft whimper of pleasure obliterated the thought.

Desire weighed down her eyelids, a languid expression of ecstasy on her face as she rocked against him. Triumph surged through him as he realized he was responsible for that look. His palm grazed across her stomach, gliding downward until his thumb slipped through dewy curls seeking the tiny nub inside.

Rapid breaths pushed past her lips in tiny puffs and when he stroked her gently, she whimpered a ragged cry of delight. He smiled at the way her mouth twisted into a tiny moue of delight at his touch. Applying more pressure to the pulsating bud beneath his thumb, he increased his strokes to the sensitive spot.

"Arch your back away from me, sweetheart. You'll find it even more pleasurable that way."

Obeying his command, pleasure escaped her lips in the form of a low moan, as she pressed her hands into his legs and rode him with a sultry intensity that made him swell inside her. Another gasp poured out of her as she increased the tempo of her rhythm against him. The hot friction of her against him was incredible, and the musky scent of her passion only served to heighten his desire to a fevered pitch.

With a tremor, she shifted her body back toward him, not once Missing a stroke. The room was silent except for the harsh labor of their breathing. Her hands rested on his shoulders, and she lowered her head and sought his mouth. It made him growl with a hunger he'd never experienced before. In the deep recesses of his mind, he knew it was a hunger that would never leave him. The touch of her small tongue on his upper lip pulled a harsh sound out of his throat while her soft mewl heated the warmth of his mouth as he deepened their kiss. The slight shift of her hips clenched his staff with a spasm as she pressed against him. The delicious, wanton manner of her movement drew a deep groan from him.

The exquisite sensations cascading over him took him into waters he'd never sailed before as the friction of her slick, honeyed core clenched at his cock. Desire flared in her eyes, her eyelids fluttering shut as he lightly caressed her nipple.

"Look at me."

Startled by the hoarse command she obeyed, and his gaze locked with hers as he held her waist in a firm grip. He wanted to drown himself in the molten heat of her look. As if she understood his need, she met his eager thrusts with a whimper of delight. The rhythm between them now was fast and furious. Her liquid warmth coated him, burned him with a demand that was swiftly reaching a frenzied pitch. She was a hot blanket around his hard length, and he surged into her over and over, the sensation pushing him into an eddy of delicious pleasure.

Passion lit her face as her velvety core clenched him like a hot, slick vise. Beneath his fingertips, her stomach rippled in a sharp spasm. Immediately, he surged up into her to meet the shudder ripping through her. In the next instant, her warm core flooded his cock with one tremor after another.

The spasms gripped him with a ferocity that drew a sharp cry of exaltation from him as he exploded inside her. White heat engulfed him, and he arched away from her as pleasure raced through his veins and into every pore of his skin. The result was a gratification he'd never experienced with any woman until now.

She trembled as she collapsed against his chest, and he kissed her shoulder through a cloud of golden hair. The light fragrance of lavender teased his nostrils, and he wrapped his arms around her to hold her tight against him. When she shivered, he reached for a blanket to cover them while he rubbed her back.

The moment he did so, he froze. Louisa had said Helen had been beaten, but were these scars? Something in the way they roughed the pads of his fingertip tightened his stomach with anger. Sitting up, he gathered her in his arms and set her on her feet beside the bed. She uttered a small protest as she stood naked before him, reaching out to trail her fingers across his chest. Her green eyes still glowed with the sultry look of a woman thoroughly satisfied. It was a look that almost made him forget what he was doing as his cock stiffened once more.

Standing up, he towered over her. She pushed her hair out of her face to eye him with a look of puzzlement. Silently, he turned her around and swept her hair off her back. The sight before him wrenched at his gut. Long lines of raised scars crisscrossed her skin, showing a consistent pattern of abuse. Louisa had obviously not seen the full extent of Helen's injuries. He reached out to trace one scar, but she darted away to scoop up her nightgown from the floor. In a flash, she covered herself before whirling around to face him.

The glow had disappeared from her face. In its place was the remote, unreadable expression he remembered from their first conversation the morning after her arrival. The silence between them stretched out for a long moment until she shifted slightly under his steady stare.

"Come here, Helen."

She immediately balked at the command, her arms folding across her chest in a defensive gesture. "I don't need your pity."

"I said, come here."

It took only a second for her to consider his terse order before she moved forward. When she stood a pace away from him, he reached out and pulled her into his embrace. Cupping her face in his hands, he planted a hard kiss on her mouth.

"The last thing I feel for you is pity, sweetheart."

She trembled in his arms. "Then why did you ... why ..."

"Because the thought of someone beating you like that is incomprehensible to me."

"My uncle is a harsh, unforgiving man."

"If I ever see him again, I'll tear out his heart," he snarled with all the protective instincts of a wolf guarding his pack.

The analogy sent a bolt of tension ricocheting through him. Fury blasted through him twisting his insides as he realized his prized self-control was almost nonexistent. He wanted to see Rivenall at his mercy and pleading for his life. Helen seemed to sense his latent hostility and she pressed her palm against his heart. Beneath her fingertips, he knew she could feel the furious beat of his pulse.

"Sebastian, he can't hurt me anymore. I won't let him." She pulled his head down to hers and laid her forehead against his. "He's to be pitied."

He captured her chin in one hand, and brushed his lips over her mouth. "You're far too generous, sweetheart."

"Must you talk so much?" The teasing note in her voice stirred his senses.

With a quick movement, he removed her nightgown once more. He stepped back to study her, enjoying the blush he saw creeping up into her cheeks. The voluptuous curve of her breasts swept down to a soft waist and pleasingly rounded hips. The mere sight of the curls at the apex of her thighs made him hard as a rock. What hold did she have over him to make him want to forget every vow of self-control he'd ever made?

Not answering the internal question, he reached out for her. She came willingly, and he swept her up into his arms. Morning would come soon enough, and there would be time to think then. For now, he simply wanted to make her his as many times as possible before dawn broke through the windows.

Chapter 12

A quiet murmur pushed through Sebastian's sleep drugged mind. He forced his eyes open and stared at the ceiling. The warm, soft body next to him snuggled closer into his side. He pulled aside a curtain of golden hair and studied Helen's sleeping profile. Rosy lips curved in a slight smile, she looked peaceful and contented.

Morning's first light peered through the window, and he knew he needed to return to his own room. Last night had been an incredible experience, but now the reality of what he'd done washed over him.

He'd lost control. Years of practiced discipline destroyed in minutes by his inability to retain a firm grip on his desire. Bloody hell, he was in a devil of a mess. Guilt whipped at him as he swallowed the knot in his throat. He'd done more than take Helen's innocence. The vow he'd made never to succumb to the Rockwood trait of irrational behavior was broken. Destroyed last night the moment he'd entered Helen's room. What the devil had provoked him to bed her?

Now, despite his resolution never to let a woman into his life, he had no other choice but to marry Helen. It was the honorable thing to do. Closing his eyes, he sighed deeply. The scars crisscrossing her spine roughed his fingers as she stirred beneath his hand. One thing was certain. In marrying him, Helen would no longer need to fear her uncle. Edward would be safe as well. Rivenall's reign of terror would no longer touch either of them.

Almost like the quiet mewl of a kitten, her yawn broke through the silence. He glanced down at her, watching her sleepy look turn to one of happiness as her eyes opened to meet his gaze. The expression made him cringe inwardly, and he looked away. He didn't want to come to care for her. Doing so opened up the possibility of too much pain. The memory of her tumbling down the stairs yesterday sent an icy finger scraping down his spine. It had brought back the terrible image of his mother falling to her death. He remembered the fear knifing through him as Helen fell toward him. No, he couldn't live with that type of fear.

Resolute in his determination never to feel such fear or pain again, he realized the only way to restore calm in his life was to set Helen up in her own house after they married. Living apart would ensure his sanity. He could visit her from time to time, and she would lack for nothing. Yes, it was the ideal solution.

The best of both worlds. There would be peace in Melton House and passionate nights in Helen's arms.

Her index finger pressed against his mouth, and he looked down to see her smiling at him. "You're looking quite serious."

"Am I?"

"Umm hmm, one would think you carried the weight of the world on your shoulders."

"In some ways I do." He untangled himself from the sheets and her limbs to slide out of bed. Despite the need to set things right between them, he delayed the matter. Searching for his clothes, he dressed quickly. As he buttoned his trousers, he turned his head toward her. She was sitting up in the bed, the sheet covering her tantalizing curves. Although the morning's dim shadows hid her expression, the tension in her still posture was evident. Blowing out a deep breath of air, he returned to the bed.

Seated on the edge of the mattress, he folded his arms and studied her quietly across the short space separating them. She smiled and reached out to him, but he pulled back.

"You realize of course that we will have to marry. I'll make arrangements today, but it will take some time to get a special license." Unable to sit still, he stood up and proceeded to pace the floor. "I'll provide you with a house, a generous allowance-- and I'll see to Edward's future. You'll both have the best of everything. Naturally, I expect you'll want to select your own house, so I'll make arrangements with my secretary to provide you with a list of suitable accommodations."

The silence in the room seemed deafening, and he turned to see her sitting stiffly in the middle of the bed. The light from outside grew brighter as the sun's rays made their first appearance. As a stream of sunshine skimmed across her face, he frowned at the fury blazing in her eyes. The lush mouth he'd taken such pleasuring in kissing the night before was set in a thin line of anger.

"Get out," she said in a low, controlled voice.

"Helen, I'm trying to do what's right here."

"You are the most arrogant, pompous, pretentious man I've ever met outside of my uncle's company." He flinched as the icy comparison sliced through him. "Your assumption that I would fall all over myself to marry you is a vain and supercilious one on your part. I have no intention of marrying you or anyone else for that matter."

"Damn it, Helen, I don't intend to argue with you about this."

"I am not arguing with you at all. I'm simply stating a fact. I will not marry you."

Infuriated by her obstinate reply, he strode toward the bed. She did not retreat. Rather she eyed him with a stare meant to freeze him in his tracks. The chilly glare brought him to a standstill. There was something about her posture that troubled him. She had closed herself off to him, surrounding herself in an icy shell of indifference. The flatness of her gaze twisted his gut as she arched an eyebrow at him.

"I believe we've said all that needs to be said, my lord. Now, I would appreciate your leaving my room before someone stumbles onto our little indiscretion. Whether the label is the earl of Melton's wife or whore, I have no aspirations for either title."

If she had slapped him, he could not have been more stunned. The steely note underlying her quiet words made them all the more sharp. A dark fury rose up and pulsated through his body. Without thinking, he reached out and pulled her toward him. She didn't resist, and her face became devoid of any expression.

"If you intend to hit me, my lord. Might I suggest you do so in a place that is hidden from view?"

The calm words horrified him. He released her immediately and watched her tumble backward onto the bed. Unable to think or speak clearly, he turned sharply on his heel. With a violent gesture, he snatched up the remainder of his clothes and strode from the bedroom. The desire to slam the door threatened to overwhelm him, but he managed to restrain himself.

In several long strides, he was at his bedroom door when he sensed someone watching him. He turned his head and met Louisa's horror-stricken gaze.

"Bloody hell," he exclaimed softly as he shrugged into his shirt and fumbled with the buttons. "Louisa, what are you doing up at this ungodly hour?"

"Sadie is about to give birth to her pups. I was on my way to see her."

The unspoken questions in her voice forced him to pinch the bridge of his nose in a dispirited gesture as he bowed his head. He expelled a harsh breath. "Well, out with it. Ask your questions."

"I have none."

The disillusioned note in her voice made him snap to attention as he watched her turn away. His sister was always full of questions, why would today be any different.

"Louisa, I know you better than that."

She stopped and sent him a sharp look of contempt. "But I'm not sure I know you. In fact, the brother I thought I knew is far removed from the man standing before me now."

The condemning words struck at him like a blunt instrument. He'd lost his sister's respect, and guilt made his body go rigid.

"I told you not too long ago that I had feet of clay, but I've always been an honorable man. I intend to marry her."

"That will please Aunt Matilda greatly. As for Helen, take care with her feelings or you'll answer to me." Louisa sent him a hard look, then turned and walked away.

Watching her retreating figure, Sebastian released a violent oath. He gave the handle on his bedroom door a vicious twist as he charged into his room. Furious with his recent blunders, he prowled the floor like a caged animal looking for a means of escape.

Helen's rejection of his proposal had not only amazed him, it had stung. She had reacted with a contempt he couldn't understand. He was nothing like her uncle, and the idea that she believed him capable of hitting her-- He uttered another epithet. Striding to the window, he slammed a fist into the scrolled frame.

As he braced both hands against the windowsill, he stared out at the garden and mews. Louisa was hurrying along the garden path, and he saw her brush at her cheek as though she was crying. Damn it to hell, he was a bastard. He'd disappointed Louisa. And Helen-- Well, somehow he'd make her understand that he wasn't a sadistic brute like her uncle.

A quiet knock announced Michaels, and the valet entered the room to stare at him in amazement. Aware he looked a sight Sebastian arched his eyebrows. "I want a bath, Michaels, and send word that I want a horse saddled and ready within the hour. Make sure its one of the stallions that hasn't been exercised this morning."

"Yes, my lord."

What he needed was a hard ride out to the country and back to clear the cobwebs from his head. For the first time in weeks, he would attack his problems with the logic and clear-headed control he'd developed over the years. When he returned, he would set things right with Louisa and convince Helen to marry him.

* * * *

It was late afternoon when Sebastian returned home. Riding into the mews, he dismounted and rubbed the neck of his horse. The animal had earned his oats today. A stable boy took the reins from him as he turned toward the house. Out of the corner of his eye, he caught sight of a coach bearing a familiar crest. Slowly he turned to stare at the lion surrounded by a belt buckle painted on the door of the vehicle. Aunt Matilda had arrived.

Wincing at the knowledge, he hurried into the house and used the back stairs to reach his room undetected. The moment the door of his room closed behind him, a deep breath of relief expanded his lungs. At least he'd be able to refresh himself before dealing with his aunt, Louisa and Helen. God in heaven. In less than a month, his calm, peaceful life had erupted into a frenzy of female activity. But did he really mind? He snorted with exasperation and strode to the washstand.

What the devil was wrong with him? Of course, he minded. Before he brought Helen to Melton House, he merely had to deal with the occasional mishaps of his sisters. Whenever they were in residence, he spent a large portion of his time at the club. It had been a pleasantly quiet existence. Helen's arrival had changed all that. The memory of seeing her for the first time in Chantrel's tightened the muscles at his groin.

Cool water splashed over his face, and with his eyes closed, it was easy to visualize her the way he'd first seen her. Long lush legs, a voluptuous thigh and a face that tempted him into securing her freedom. He'd known from the start she would be trouble, but it hadn't stopped him from rescuing her.

With each successive taste of her sweet lips, he'd been more than happy to grapple with the trouble of protecting her. Then last night, she'd given herself to him with the sweetness of a muse and the passion of a tigress. The material of his trousers stretched as he grew hard at the memory.

Why had she refused to marry him? It would be a very pleasant arrangement for both of them. Her words returned to haunt him. She wanted the title of neither wife nor whore when it came to him. Gripping the edge of the washstand tightly, he uttered an incoherent sound of frustration.

Well, he would make Miss Rivenall understand the title of wife was far superior to any other she might earn. He yanked a towel off the washstand bar and dried himself. Short, abrupt movements marked his dressing, and when he was ready to face the female army below, he strode from the room.

Downstairs, the feminine laughter echoing from the main salon slowed his pace. It was going to be difficult enough to face Helen and Louisa, but all of the women in his family? Tension wove its way through his muscles, as he debated the issue of barricading himself in the library. Grimacing at the idea, he chose to face the music and quietly entered the salon. Constance was the first one to see him. With a cry of welcome, she leapt out of her scroll back chair and raced to his side.

"Sebastian! Oh, it's wonderful to see you!" She hugged him with enthusiasm. "And we come home to find you're a knight in shining armor for someone other than us."

His sister's words made him start with surprise. Kissing her cheek, he arched a questioning eyebrow at the wicked glint of humor in her brown eyes. Patience followed close on Constance's heels to hug him tight. She accepted his kiss and pulled back to eye him with mischief.

"Well, brother, it appears you're quite the hero. Louisa has just regaled us with the story of how you rescued Miss Rivenall."

Disconcerted by their words, he searched the room for Helen. The serene expression on her features belied the frozen glare she directed at him. His gaze switched to Louisa, and he read the grim disapproval in his sibling's eye. Bloody hell. Having one woman furious with him was bad enough, but two? Moreover, exactly what story had Louisa told his aunt and sisters? There was no sign of humiliation in Helen's expression, but then her features revealed nothing at all.

"Well, nephew. Are you not going to greet me?" The soft burr in Matilda Stewart's voice eased some of his tension. His aunt's gentle accent had always had a soothing effect on him.

As his sisters stepped aside, Sebastian moved to where his aunt sat on the plush, burgundy couch. There was a distinct twinkle in the plump woman's eye as she offered him her hand. After a perfunctory kiss of her hand, he kissed her smooth, plump cheek. Straightening, he moved to stand at the fireplace.

"I didn't expect you to return to London until tomorrow."

A sly smile tilted the corners of his aunt's mouth. "Well, that was the original plan. However, your sisters were homesick, so we decided to arrive earlier than we intended. Although I confess it might not have been a wise decision, what with this madman loose on the city."

The chill whispering through the room was almost tangible, and Sebastian frowned. "Every precaution has been taken to see to the safety of the household, so there's no need to dwell on the horror in the East End."

"True, but the entire matter is a wee bit unsettling, Sebastian." With an abrupt nod of her head, his aunt ran a hand over her skirts. "But then we have other matters here to attend to don't we? Namely, how Helen came to be at Melton House."

Stiffening, Sebastian darted a look at Louisa. His youngest sister arched her eyebrow at him in a manner that was all too familiar. Whether he was deserving of her disapproval wasn't the issue, but protecting Helen was. He cleared his throat as he tried to think of a way out of his current predicament. Louisa had obviously regaled his family with some tale of heroics, but he hadn't a clue as to what that tale was.

"I think Sebastian is uncomfortable with repeating his act of heroism, Aunt Matilda." Louisa shook her head. "As I was saying before our hero arrived, Helen and her brother were attacked by robbers close to Sebastian's club. He happened on the incident and subsequently rescued them."

"Aye, it's no more than I'd expect from me nephew." The older woman shot Sebastian a look of warm approval.

"Of course, when he realized Helen and Edward had no other place to go, he offered them shelter." Louisa spread her hands in a small gesture of indulgence.

"But of course he should have brought them here," Patience exclaimed as she stood and moved to stand at his side. "Where would they have gone?"

Louisa tipped her brown head in his direction as she answered Patience's question. "Exactly. But you have to admit that it's quite unlike him, wouldn't you say?"

For a moment, the woman at his side pondered the question before she looked up at him. The brown eyes meeting his gaze reminded him of a doe's soft expression. Patience was always trying to make people feel better. "She's right, Sebastian. It seems highly out of character for you."

Gritting his teeth, he remained silent. Better to let Louisa have her fun now. She'd be much more inclined to listen to him later on. Already he could tell her fury had ebbed as she smiled at him.

"I have to admit that I was astonished by the fact that he'd brought them to Melton House," Louisa said as she pressed a hand to her throat. "We all know Sebastian and his dislike of anything halfway resembling disorder. But when he told me he was going to teach poor Helen how to behave in society, I simply had to put my foot down."

Sebastian cringed as feminine laugher filled his ears. The mockery might be well-deserved, but his sister didn't have to be quite so zealous in her enjoyment of the fact. He stole a quick glance in Helen's direction. Was she enjoying this parody of his character?

There was a stubborn tilt to her chin as she met his gaze. He suppressed a sigh at the anger thinning her full mouth. His future wife was far from happy with him, but he knew he could convince her to come to her senses. After all, she had no place to go and his proposition would ensure she was well looked after. As far as Louisa was concerned, he would be able to set matters right with her over time.

Still laughing, his aunt wagged her finger at him. "Poor Miss Rivenall. To think what might have happened to her if I'd not agreed to let Louisa come home on her own."

Forcing a smile to his mouth, he bowed in his aunt's direction. "As you said, Aunt Matilda, your timing couldn't be better. I'm sure Helen will be pleased to have as much support as possible at the Latimer affair tomorrow night. And we shall also see how good an instructor my baby sister is, for we all know a student is only as good as one's teacher."

Seated on the sofa opposite her aunt, Constance flounced the hem of her rose-colored gown with the tip of her shoe. "If anyone needs support it will be you dear brother. You've insulted more women than I can count on my fingers and toes, and most of them will be at the Latimer affair tomorrow night. I imagine it will be a unique experience for you to find yourself surrounded by those you've insulted."

Once more laughter filled the room, and ignoring his sister's teasing jibe, he turned toward his aunt in desperation. "Have you had refreshments, Aunt?"

"Yes, Louisa made certain that we were well cared for when we arrived." Amusement twinkled in the Scotswoman's eyes. Acknowledging his silent cry for help, she rose to her feet. "However, I would like to rest a bit before dinner. Our ride was a bit tiring."

"Of course." He stepped forward and politely offered his arm as his aunt stood up.

"Thank you, Sebastian," she said with more than a hint of mischief. "Naturally, I'm sure you'll indulge me before dinner with a private word in the library."

"Certainly." He suppressed a groan at the price he would have to pay.

"I look forward to it." His aunt smiled at him as she patted his arm, and then turned to Helen. "Miss Rivenall ... oh, I do hope you'll let me call you Helen."

"But of course, ma'am."

"Excellent. I think you and I should spend some time together without all this nonsensical chatter pounding our ears."

"Well!" Patience sniffed indignantly, while Constance simply laughed.

"Ach, me wee lambs, but you know my ears are quite sensitive to chatter." Matilda turned away from her offended niece and smiled at Helen. "Shall I send word to you when I've rested?"

"Yes, ma'am."

"Good, that's settled then." Her bright blue-eyed gaze rested on Louisa. "Come child, show me to my room. I've missed you, and I want to know what news of the dastardly Lord Morehouse."

Sebastian quickly turned his head toward his youngest sister to see her face crimson. God help him, surely Louisa didn't have designs on Devin. He wouldn't have it. As a friend, the man was more than amiable, but as a suitor for Louisa, he was most unacceptable. The man was a rake. As his aunt left the room with Louisa, the rest of his family expressed a desire to rest as well.

Helen stood to follow his sisters, and as Constance and Patience moved into the hall, he strode quickly to the salon doors locking Helen in the salon with him. When he turned to face her, her anger was evident by the flush of color on her cheeks and her stormy green eyes.

"Stand aside, Sebastian. I wish to go to my room."

"I want to talk to you."

"We have nothing to say to each other," she snapped as her mouth thinned with anger.

"I think we do."

"No matter what you say or do, I'll not marry you."

Irritated by her obstinate tone, he leaned back against the salon door, folding his arms across his chest as he studied her. In spite of her icy tone, he could see other emotions boiling just beneath the surface. She was struggling to contain those feelings. Her breathing was ragged and he saw her hands tremble as she clutched them in front of her.

"Actually, you have little choice open to you other than marriage to me."

"That's not true. Once your aunt returns to Scotland I'll be free to go where I please."

"And where will you go?"

She hesitated slightly. "That is no concern of yours."

"I think it is, because I'm certain you have no place to go, except back to your uncle."

"*Never.*" The bitter vehemence in her voice stretched the taut wire of tension in him that much tighter.

"You told me I'd be well rewarded for helping you convince your aunt to end her matchmaking." She lifted her head proudly. "I'll find a way to make whatever sum you offer me last ... until I find employment."

"I see, so you expect me to give you additional monies over and above what I've already spent?" He arrogantly arched his eyebrow.

"I would think last night entitled me to fair compensation," she said, her features cold as a statue.

The words ripped through him with the force of a bullet, only the pain was much greater. Inhaling a sharp breath, he moved forward and tugged her into his arms. "Fair compensation? I thought my offer of marriage was a sizable recompense."

"For whom? You?" The cold fury in her voice stung him. "No doubt, it would be too your liking, but I don't want your name or your title."

Furious that they were at odds with one another, he glared down at her. Noting the way her pulse was fluttering wildly at the side of her neck, he gently touched the spot. A barely distinguished gasp passed from her lips as she tried to push her way out of his embrace. She might not want to marry him at the moment, but she still desired him.

"But you do want me," he murmured with confidence.

"You are mistaken, my lord."

"Then prove to me that last night was just a dream. Prove to me that you can kiss me without feeling anything."

Silence chilled the air between them before she shook her head. "I refuse to play this game with you."

"Refuse all you want, Helen, but you will play." Determined to break through the barriers she'd thrown up between them, he captured her mouth in a gentle kiss.

There was a hint of nectar on her lips as he flicked his tongue out to taste her. Another gasp escaped her mouth, warming him as he crushed her against him. Already he wanted to lift her skirts and drive into her again as he had last night. He trailed his mouth across her cheek to her ear. Sucking lightly at the lobe, his hand slid across the square bodice of her dress, his fingers dipping into the valley between her soft breasts.

"Tell me you don't want this."

"No ... I don't."

"Liar," he whispered into her ear before seeking her mouth once again. This time she responded with the same enthusiasm that she'd shown last night. Triumph soared through him. It was simply a matter of time before she capitulated to his proposal. She would agree to marry him. Maybe not today, but she would soon. Very soon.

Chapter 13

Studying her reflection in the dressing table mirror, Helen sighed in frustration. For the past twenty-four hours she'd been trying to think of some way to leave Melton House. The more she tried to extricate herself from the terrible mess she was in, the tighter the web of deceit held her fast.

As she stared at the woman in the mirror, she failed to recognize the stranger she saw there. Tendrils of hair bordered her face, while the remainder of her hair was swept back and swirled up on top of her head. Elegantly simple, her emerald silk ball gown was almost devoid of any ruffles or lace. The caped sleeves hugged her shoulders as the bodice plunged downward to her breasts.

Critically, she tipped her head to one side. She would never call herself beautiful, but she was pleased with her appearance. Would Sebastian find her appearance pleasing? The unbidden thought made her flinch.

"You idiotic fool," she muttered with a glare at her reflection. "The man feels nothing for you other than desire, and yet you cling to the hope he'll be pleased with you tonight."

Tonight. She swallowed the ball of fear rising in her throat as she stood up and adjusted her skirt. She was not looking forward to this evening at all. There was so much to remember and the idea of making a mistake terrified her. There was also the unspoken fear of being recognized by one of the men who'd been at Chantrel's that night. She'd not mentioned the possibility to Louisa, but it was always there in the back of her mind. Her mouth went dry at the thought of such a thing happening. But those fears were nothing compared to the thought of Sebastian and his determination to have his way.

Yesterday, when he'd trapped her in the salon, she'd been unable to resist him. It infuriated her that she was so weak-willed where he was concerned. Why couldn't she be cold and unresponsive when he'd kissed her? And she'd been anything but indifferent to him the moment he took her in his arms. Her fingernails bit into her palms at the memory. If it hadn't been for Patience trying to enter the locked salon, she would have allowed him to make love to her then and there. Her body had been on fire for him.

Even worse, he'd known she'd been willing and eager to do whatever he asked. The knowledge had been there in his gaze as he'd opened the door for his sister. Without waiting for anyone to speak, she'd fled from the room to hide upstairs until supper. Her inability to resist him only reinforced why she could no longer remain under his roof.

But, dear lord, how badly she wanted to give in to the desire he stirred in her with such ease. Her eyes studied her image in the mirror as her fingertips pressed against her throat where he'd singed her skin with his lips. A familiar rush of heat coiled in her belly and she wheeled sharply away from the reflection.

Ironically, the bed was the first thing to come into view. Her hand caressed the tall post of the canopy as she stared at the mattress, remembering their night together. She closed her eyes. Once more, his warm hand caressed her breast, the spicy smell of his skin filled her senses and the deep, richness of his voice made her tremble. When he'd possessed her completely, the world had become sharper, clearer. Everything her uncle had ever preached to her had crumbled into ashes.

Sebastian had taught her to feel again. Taught her to hope. Hope that he might come to love her as much as she loved him. Nausea roiled through her. Oh God. She couldn't have been so dull-witted as that. She couldn't possibly have fallen in love with the man.

Clinging to the bedpost, she waited for the queasy sensation to ebb away along with the shock of her discovery. With one cheek pressed on the cool wood, she stared into space. When had she fallen in love with him? No. *How* could she have fallen in love with him?

It didn't matter. He didn't love her, and she would have no part of a loveless marriage. Only a guilty conscience would have compelled him to offer his name to her in such a cold and calculating manner. He could not have stated his contempt for her any more clearly than he'd done yesterday morning with his marriage proposal.

Even a suggestion that she be his mistress would have been far less humiliating and painful for her. At least it would have been honest. But to suggest she marry him simply so he could assuage his guilty conscience was unthinkable. No, she'd have no part of such a marriage. She wanted to love and be loved. Nothing less would do.

The sound of a knock on the door made her start violently. For moment, she hesitated. She didn't want to see anyone and the last thing she wanted was to step out into the limelight of the Set.

Another rap on the door made her close her eyes briefly as she struggled to regain her composure. The third knock was more insistent, and knowing she could not put off answering the door, she crossed the room. Opening the door, her eyes met the lively expression of Sebastian's aunt. Petite and plump, the woman reminded her of the kindly minister's wife in her childhood village, ruddy cheeks and all.

"I hope ye don't mind, dearie. But I wanted to talk to ye for a moment."

"Of course, please come in."

She stepped back to allow Lady Stewart to enter the room. Quietly, she shut the door behind the woman, before turning to face her. There was a gentle look on the older woman's face. She sat on the bed and patted the mattress beside her.

"Come sit doon fer a wee tick."

Hiding her apprehension, Helen did as requested. As she sank down onto the coverlet, Lady Stewart took her hand and squeezed it.

"Ye don't look as nervous as Louisa said ye were."

"Louisa can be overly dramatic at times," Helen said with a wry smile.

"Indeed." Lady Stewart laughed. "Still, I can see the unhappiness in yer eyes."

The words made her stiffen, and she frowned. "I'm not sure what you mean."

"Sebastian explained everything to me."

A winter pond could not have chilled her body any better, and her stomach heaved as she felt the color draining from her face. Pulling away from the woman, she stood and walked to the dresser. Her fingers fiddled with the smooth tortoiseshell brush and comb on the vanity top. "And what has your nephew told you, Lady Stewart?"

"Oh dearie, please forgive me. Ye must find this terribly humiliating."

A flame of anger ignited inside her. He'd confessed to bedding her. How could he? The wall of her chest constricted with pain and humiliation. Unable to turn around, she straightened her spine, somehow managing to keep her voice even. "It doesn't matter."

Lady Stewart stood up with a loud rustle of purple satin. "Why it most certainly does matter. Louisa's story yesterday about Sebastian's heroic rescue of ye and the boy sounded credible, if not a bit extraordinary. But when my nephew told me the truth, I was appalled. I can't believe in this modern age that there are people who still prey on the innocent. Kidnapping ye and your brother was reprehensible enough, but to auction ye off like a prized mare is unthinkable."

Relief sapped her strength, and she sagged against the vanity. He'd not reveal their indiscretion. It was still their secret. Immediately plump arms pulled her into a warm, loving embrace.

"Oh ye poor bairn. I thank God that Sebastian was able to rescue ye from that horrid place. I shudder to think what might have happened to ye if he'd not done so." The woman gently pushed her back so she could look at her. "I knew one day, my nephew would find the right woman to steal his heart."

"Oh, but--"

"It's all right, dearie, I've not mentioned this to him as I believe my nephew has yet to see the truth. Although I'm certain it won't take long, and when he does, I'm certain this house will echo with a little less precision and a great deal more chaos."

"I'm afraid you're mistaken, Lady Stewart. His lordship is far from enamored with me."

"Then why does he watch every move ye make?"

Knowing full well it was simply desire that motivated Sebastian she shook her head. "I'm certain you're mistaken, my lady."

"We shall see, dearie, we shall see." Stepping away from her, Lady Stewart looked her up and down with an intent gaze. "Aye, I do believe ye're ready to face the Marlborough Set, although they're a devilish lot. It's fortunate Sebastian informed me of the situation. To be forewarned is to be armed as Angus Stewart would say. God rest his soul."

Adjusting her clan's plaid sash, which she'd draped over her deep purple gown, Lady Stewart wrapped her arm through Helen's and drew her toward the door. "Come along, dearie. Between myself, Sebastian and his sisters, we'll see to it that the Set is completely bowled over by your charm and beauty."

Despite her heartache and fear, Lady Stewart's joviality was hard to ignore. Her personality was very much like Louisa's, and it was impossible not to like the older woman. Grateful for her support, Helen touched the woman's arm. "Thank you, my lady. I'm most grateful for your kindness."

"Nonsense. Why ye are practically family already."

The comment poured salt into the open wound in Helen's heart, the sting spreading throughout her body. Despite the knowledge that it would never be, she fervently wished it to be true.

* * * *

Helen snapped open her fan and lightly stirred the air in front of her. Flanked on either side by friends, she felt safe and comfortable. In fact, she almost thought it possible she might enjoy herself this evening. On her left, Lady Stewart whispered in her ear. "Don't look now, dearie, but I see several gentlemen who haven't been able to take their eyes off ye since we've arrived, including my nephew."

"You flatter me, my lady. However I believe it's Louisa who's causing a stir this evening."

"Well, unless that rake Morehouse appears, the lass will be difficult to live with tomorrow."

"I see." Helen sent her friend a sidelong glance. From the look on Louisa's face, the man wasn't anywhere to be seen. The girl's features revealed intense frustration. It was a sensation Helen knew all too well. Without thinking, her gaze drifted across the room in search of Sebastian. She saw him reclining against a pillar, his arms folded across his chest.

The sight of his tall, handsome figure clasped a vise around her heart. How was she going to keep her love hidden from him? The moment he discovered her feelings he wouldn't hesitate to use it to his advantage. Perhaps his aunt wouldn't stay at Melton House for long. The moment the Scotswoman left she would be free to leave. But not all of her would do so, her heart would remain forever with Sebastian.

Watching him, she could tell by his aloof expression that the last place he wanted to be was here. He would be more comfortable sitting at his piano, far away from this noisy affair. As if sensing her stare, his head turned in her direction. She quickly looked away only to meet the gaze of a handsome young man directly across the floor from her. The mischief in the man's smile made the woman beside her chuckle. Turning toward Lady Stewart she arched her eyebrow.

"As I promised, dearie, ye've captured the interest of a number of gentlemen, including the Viscount Winthrope, who is about to present himself and ask ye to dance."

"I'm sure you're wrong, my lady."

"Am I?" The woman smiled gleefully. "No, I don't think I am, but I'm certainly looking forward to seeing my nephew's expression when you're whirled out onto the floor."

"Good evening, Lady Stewart."

The deep voice made Helen turn her head toward the speaker. As the Scotswoman had predicted, Viscount Winthrope had crossed the dance floor to join them Warm hazel eyes glinted cheerfully out of the gentleman's pleasant-looking features. Bowing politely, his sandy colored hair dipped slightly across his brow.

"Winthrope. How lovely to see ye again. How is yer charming sister?" Lady Stewart extended her hand to him as she spoke.

"Happily married these past three months, my lady."

"Ah, so she accepted Billingsly after all." The Scotswoman nodded with approval.

"That she did, although my grandfather was fit to be tied with her indecision. He is a man of swift action. A trait we both share." Winthrope said with a grin. "Which leads me to a small request, might I ask you to introduce me to your lovely companion."

The viscount turned toward Helen, his open admiration a bit embarrassing, yet it gave fuel to the hope that Lady Steward was right. Would Sebastian dislike other men vying for her attention? Hope stirred inside her at the prospect as Lady Stewart laughed and quickly dispensed with introductions. Bowing, Winthrope kissed Helen's hand.

"Delighted, Miss Rivenall. Might I convince you to dance the upcoming waltz?"

She hesitated slightly, and Lady Stewart laughed. "Off with ye, dearie, ye needn't fear leaving me alone. Besides I think it will do a heart good for you to enjoy yourself."

The woman shifted her gaze ever so briefly in Sebastian's direction. With a slight shake of her head, Helen didn't follow the woman's gaze. She had no doubt Sebastian would be displeased that she was dancing with another man. But his irritation would only be because he believed her to be his possession and nothing more.

Accepting the viscount's arm, Helen allowed him to lead her out onto the floor. Seconds later the orchestra launched into a waltz. Nervous at the thought of dancing in public for the first time, she allowed the young man to pull her into his arms and swing her into a graceful arc. As they circled the floor, she slowly relaxed and allowed herself to enjoy the moment.

"You're a most unusual woman, Miss Rivenall."

Casting him a curious look, she frowned. "I'm not certain I understand, my lord."

"Well, you don't chatter like most of the other ladies do while dancing."

"I suppose that's because I have nothing of importance to say," she said with a smile.

"Ah, but neither do the other young ladies."

The wry humor in his voice made her laugh, and as he whirled her around, her eyes met Sebastian's angry gaze over the viscount's shoulder. The intimidation in his gaze irritated her, and she smiled up at the viscount as brightly as possible. Her reward was another charming grin from her companion. He studied her for a long moment as they danced.

"I hope you'll forgive me, Miss Rivenall, but I was wondering if we'd met somewhere before."

The question made her stiffen. Had he been at Chantrel's that night? Other than the faces of Lord Templeton and Sebastian, the features of all the other men that night had blurred beyond recognition. She shook her head. "No, I don't think so, my lord."

"Odd, I have the strangest feeling we've met someplace." The puzzlement on his face disappeared as the music cascaded to a halt. Walking her back to Lady Stewart's side, he bowed.

"Thank you, Miss Rivenall for a delightful dance. Might I have the pleasure of calling on you tomorrow afternoon around two?"

Helen glanced at Lady Stewart before nodding her acquiescence to the request. The viscount's happiness startled her, and as he walked away, she regretted accepting his invitation. He was a personable young man, but there was only one man she would ever want. Her gaze swung back to where Sebastian stood. Surrounded by three other men, he scowled at her before he glared at Winthrope's retreating figure.

Beside her, Louisa sniffed her indignation. "I don't understand why Sebastian insists on socializing with those three rakes."

Patience laughed softly. "You're simply irritated that Morehouse hasn't even cast an eye in your direction this evening."

"Well, I noticed you ogling Lord Westbury not more than a minute ago."

"Every woman ogles Lord Westbury."

Louisa uttered a sound of disbelief, and Helen bit back a smile at the sisterly exchange. Her amusement died an instant later at the sound of a familiar voice.

"Good evening, Lady Stewart. I hope you'll pardon this intrusion, but I was hoping I could count on you to persuade Miss Rivenall to dance with me."

As always where the marquess of Templeton was concerned, Helen found herself torn between being frightened of the man or chiding herself for doing so. Lady Stewart arched an eyebrow in a manner reminiscent of her nephew, as she looked the marquess up and down.

"I'm not certain I should allow such a thing," Lady Stewart said quietly.

"I'm well aware of my reputation, my lady." Templeton mouth twisted in a wry smile. "However, I can assure you that my intentions are nothing but honorable. If I had wanted to denounce Miss Rivenall, I would have done so already."

Hesitation flitted across the Scotswoman's face as she looked at Helen. Aware that the choice was really up to her, Helen forced a small smile to her lips. "Thank you for the invitation, my lord, shall we?"

"Thank you, Miss Rivenall."

Leading her out onto the floor, Templeton pulled her into his arms. Even though he held her circumspectly, it didn't keep her skin from tingling as if a thousand bees were crawling across her skin. After several turns around the floor, he sighed.

"Of all the women I've danced with this evening, you're the only one to remain silent, Helen."

Unable to help herself, a small smile tipped the corners of her mouth. "You are not the first person to make such an observation this evening, my lord."

"Ah, so you're reticent with others as well. I confess to being relieved since your statement implies that your silence is not necessarily indicative of the company you keep." He swung her around in a wide turn, and as they whirled past Sebastian and his friends, she saw the look of triumph on the Marquess' face. The thought of being a prize that Sebastian or the Marquess could vie for sent cold fury skimming through her veins.

"You look exceedingly pleased with yourself, my lord," she said in a tight voice.

"Of course I'm pleased. I'm dancing with you, and by your own volition I might add. I imagine Melton thinks I coerced you somehow, and it gives me great pleasure to know that's untrue. The man seems to think of you as a prize, but I've come to see that you're not."

Taken aback by the man's statement, she stared up into his gray eyes in surprise. "I'm not sure I understand, my lord."

"Your host doesn't like to think he's unable to control his life or the people in his inner circle. Somehow I think you're far from willing to let the man control you."

The astute comment made her tip her head to one side as she studied him. "Do you make it a habit to observe the behaviors of others?"

"Human nature has always fascinated me. I find it interesting how the harder people try to control their lives, the less control they actually have."

"And you do not believe that," she observed quietly.

"No. Control is an illusion. For instance, these murders in Whitechapel. The murderer appears to have an intense hatred of women, or at the very least, the profession of his murder victims. Is the man seeking to control his hatred through this violence or does he seek to control women by murdering those he considers an abomination?"

The marquess was not looking at her directly as he shook his head, a slight frown furrowing his brow. Uncertain how to respond, she remained silent as Lord Templeton seemed lost in thought. His musings were almost those of a man talking to himself.

"Ironically, it's neither. The murderer can no more control the hatred that provokes him to attack, anymore than he can control his victims. He can only silence them, but in death they scream all the more loudly, thus proving that the murderer truly has no control."

The topic itself sent ice through her veins, as she shivered with misgiving. His regret immediately evident, the marquess made a noise of regret. "Forgive me; I should never have brought up such a vile subject matter. I forgot myself. Tell me, how are you enjoying your first ball?"

"I've yet to make up my mind," she murmured, still disconcerted by the man's observations about the murders in the East End. "Given your reference to recent events, it seems somewhat frivolous in a way."

"I might have known that would be your opinion." The smile he directed at her was filled with approval. "You've been an inspiration to me from the start, my dear. In fact, you've convinced me to turn over a new leaf."

"A new leaf?"

"Most definitely, your gracious nature has convinced me that there's still hope for me." The smile he sent her was genuine and charming. Suddenly uncomfortable, she forced herself to smile back at him.

"I'd like to think there's hope for everyone to change for the better, my lord."

"Quite so, my dear. Quite so," he murmured as the song ended with a flourish and he brought them to a halt. "And with you as an inspiration, I hope to continue my transformation."

With a smile, he started to lead her back to Lady Stewart's side, but they'd only take several steps when Sebastian appeared at Helen's side.

"I'll take Helen from here, Templeton."

"Ah, Sir Lancelot to the rescue. How quaint." Amused disdain curled Lord Templeton's mouth as he sent Sebastian a look of scorn. The marquess turned back to her and bowed over her hand. "My dear, thank you for the dance, it was charming. I hope you will afford me the pleasure again in the future."

As the man walked away, Helen expelled a sigh of relief. What was it about the man that compelled her to take pity on him, and yet made her uneasy at the same time.

"What the devil were you thinking when you agreed to dance with that bastard?" The terse whisper stirred the wisps of hair that had escaped the twist at the back of her head.

"I was being polite. The man did me a kindness and to cut him simply because you or others disapprove would have been wrong. He seems eager to make amends for the past," she said quietly as she remembered the fact that the man had been in a bidding competition with Sebastian at Chantrel's. As odd as it seemed, she believed the man, but the idea filled her with confusion and trepidation.

"You're to stay away from him." Sebastian's grip on her elbow tightened as guided her across the floor. "The man's dangerous."

"He may not be of the best character, but I would hardly call him dangerous." As she scoffed at the notion, Sebastian's gaze met hers, his eyes glittered with anger.

"It doesn't matter what you believe. You're to stay away from him."

"You seem determined to believe that you have the right to order me about as you see fit. I am not your possession," she snapped in a low voice.

A muscle twitched in his cheek as he nodded at a couple passing close by them. Without looking at her, he muttered, "Think of it as a request."

Startled, she stared up at him in surprise. He didn't look at her, but she could tell by the tight line of his mouth, what the words had cost him. Sebastian wasn't accustomed to asking for things, he was used to giving orders. Loving him as she did, it was difficult to refuse his attempt at appeasing her.

"I will do as you ask," she said quietly.

Relief eased the tension in his jaw as he glanced down at her with an imperceptible flicker of emotion in his dark gaze. The strains of the next waltz interrupted their conversation, and without even asking her permission, Sebastian swept her into his arms and whirled her onto the floor. The suddenness of his action prevented her from refusing to dance, and her heart raced at the possessive way he held her closer than what she believed was circumspect. Aware of speculative eyes on them, she frowned.

"Sebastian, you're holding me far to close. People are staring."

"Let them stare."

Tension stalked the air between them, and Helen swallowed the nervous knot rising in her throat. Dear Lord, surely he wouldn't try to force her hand here. No, he would be far more subtle in his method. He would make it difficult for anyone to question his intentions toward her. Locked so tightly in he arms he was staking his claim. She could see it in the expressions of the couples they whirled past.

Unable to think clearly, she kept her gaze averted from his as she tried to keep her emotions in check. Vaguely, she noticed Lord Winthrope standing in a doorway his gaze studying her intently.

"You seemed to be enjoying yourself with Winthrope a short time ago." The disapproval in his voice made her shake her head in exasperation.

"He was a cheerful partner." Lord Winthrope came into view once more as they did another turn on the floor. Again the intensity of his gaze puzzled her.

"Do you think it wise to encourage him?" Sebastian said in a tight voice.

His disapproval darkened the expression on his handsome features as she stared up at him in surprise. The man actually thought she'd been encouraging Lord Winthrope. She was fortunate the man was so blind where she was concerned.

"I'd hardly call dancing with the man the same thing as encouraging him," she said quietly. "I found him quite pleasant and courteous."

"I know what I saw," he snarled. "The boy's already halfway in love with you."

Vexed by his outrageous statement, she shook her head in disbelief. "Don't be ridiculous. We danced one dance."

"I want you to stay away from him." His autocratic command stiffened the muscles in her arms and back. Rigid with anger, she glared at him.

"Why? Is he dangerous too?" she sniffed scornfully. "I supposed I'll find out since I agreed to let him call on me tomorrow afternoon."

"You did what?" Sebastian stared at her with furious amazement.

"I told Lord Winthrope he could call on me. In fact, your aunt encouraged it."

"The devil she did," he said through clenched teeth.

"I think your aunt is on to your little game, and she thinks to turn the tables on you. However, we both know that we're ill-suited for one another."

"I disagree, Helen. In fact, I think it will be quite easy to make you see just how well suited we are for one another."

His dark gaze bore into hers, and her breath hitched at the predatory look. As the music stopped, he released her from his embrace. Instantly, the shudder she'd restrained while in his arms whipped through her body. The look in his dark eyes said he intended to win, and fear scraped her spine at his determination. Averting her gaze, she remained silent as he escorted her back to where Lady Stewart stood with Patience.

With a brusque farewell, Sebastian left her side and disappeared through the crowd. A satisfied smile lit Lady Stewart's face as Helen stood trembling beside her.

"That, dearie, is a man ready to take a fall."

"A fall?"

"Aye, in less than two weeks, he'll be completely hooked. Mark my words."

Unable to answer, she simply shook her head. Behind her, Patience uttered a soft gasp. "Good heavens, would you look at that."

At her urging, Helen and Lady Stewart turned toward the dance floor to see Louisa in the arms of Lord Morehouse. The man had a black frown on his face, but Louisa exuded complete confidence. A happy sigh parted Lady Stewart's lips. "It would seem that the Rockwood family is going to be inundated with weddings over the next year."

Patience laughed at the comment, but Helen frowned. Despite Lady Stewart's confidence, one wedding would definitely not take place. Sebastian's distorted idea of what constituted a marriage was unacceptable to her. No, there would be no wedding between her and the earl of Melton.

Chapter 14

Sebastian leaned against the wall of the Somerset ballroom his arms folded across his chest. The sensation of gloom loitering over him was as oppressive as the damnable roses littering the room. Their cloying scent merely served to sharpen the edge of his ill temper. Across the room, he watched as Lord Dorchester guided Helen across the dance floor.

Gritting his teeth, he uttered a harsh noise of disgust. One would think him a young pup mooning after the latest sensation. He frowned at his inability to avoid watching her every move. Why in the hell didn't he just announce their engagement? It would appear perfectly reasonable, given his aunt had taken Helen under her wing. Ever since her introduction into society almost a month ago, Lady Stewart had made it clear that she was Helen's sponsor. It had stilled any rumors as to why Helen was staying in his home, but it had not changed the tension between them.

"Damn it to hell," he muttered. "I should just make an announcement."

But the memory of Helen's resistance to his proposal told him that doing so would be the same as standing on a thin layer of ice. If he tried to force her hand, the ice would break and he might lose her altogether. His chest constricted painfully at the thought. Over the past three weeks, he'd watched half of the town's male population seek to capture her attention. Hell, even Templeton seemed to be a changed man. The fellow was completely enamored with her and had offered more than one toast to her at the club.

If her intent was to dissuade her suitors by being cool and polite, it had the opposite effect. It simply incited them to seek her favor that much harder. The one thing he understood was their inability to stay away from her. She was the brightest flame in London, and the moths couldn't resist her allure.

Even amidst the terror gripping the East End and the rest of London, she was still the brightest light in the city. The memory of how one more woman had been found decapitated and limbless in the Whitechapel area made his stomach lurch. The horrendous act had made him increase the security around the house. All of the men he employed were well skilled in the use of firearms, and he knew his family was well protected. But where Helen was concerned, he had to haunt her movements simply to satisfy himself that nothing happened to her.

As he watched Winthrope guided her out onto the dance floor for the second time tonight, he stiffened. The man was becoming a problem. A constant visitor to Melton House, he was the one suitor whose company Helen actually seemed to enjoy. Every time he saw them together, she was always laughing at something the bastard had said.

"That scowl might frighten off quite a number of Miss Rivenall's suitors, but it's unlikely to deter Winthrope."

Sebastian turned his head toward Marcus Riverton, earl of Lyndhurst. "I am not scowling."

"Of course not."

The wry reply shot a bolt of irritation through him. "Blast it, Marcus, if you've something to say, say it."

"I was wondering if you might object to my calling on Miss Rivenall."

The statement sent fury coiling through him with the speed of a viper. Slowly, he turned his head toward his friend.

"What did you say?" Sebastian ground out between clenched teeth.

"Ah, so the thought of my courting the young lady doesn't sit well with you." Marcus raised his hands in a gesture of surrender. "Forgive the question. I have no designs on the young lady. I was simply testing my theory."

"What theory?" He snapped as he returned his gaze to Helen. Damnation, this was torture. Why did he insist on doing this to himself?

"My theory that your interest in the young lady is far more extensive than you would have your friends believe."

Sebastian grunted. "To hell with your theories."

"Perhaps, but I'd say Miss Rivenall is going to make an impressive match within the month, and her benefactor is none too happy about it."

"Helen won't accept any proposal."

"Care to make a wager?"

The quiet assurance behind his friend's words whipped Sebastian's anger to a furious pitch. He glared at Marcus' complacent expression, but refrained from speaking. In actuality, he knew anything he said would only confirm what his friend had deduced. Denying his displeasure at Helen's success to Marcus was one thing, but it was impossible to disavow the surge of jealous anger he experienced when he saw another man with her.

Turning away from his friend, he studied the crowd again, or more specifically, the crowd of men surrounding Helen. She looked more beautiful than he'd ever seen her. The deep blue of her gown reminded him of the evening sky just as the first star was coming into view. The color was a suitable frame for her creamy skin. Satin hugged her shoulders like the caress of a lover. The neckline glided down to a vee to where the barest hint of a shadow showed between her luscious breasts.

The memory of cupping her breasts and suckling her nipples twisted his insides with need, while he grew hard at the memory. God, how he wanted her. But what he wanted more was to hear her say she wanted him too.

When he'd kissed her the day after their night of passion, she'd responded with a desire equaling his own. Her reaction to his touch made him think it would be an easy task to convince her to marry him. He'd been wrong.

Not since the day of his aunt's arrival had he enjoyed a moment alone with her. She took care to be in his company as little as possible, and always with someone else close at hand. He'd even been desperate enough to test her door late one night, hoping to confront her, but she'd locked it to keep him out.

His hands gripped his biceps in a tight clinch at the sight of Winthrope kissing her hand. The way she smiled at the man sliced across his stomach as cleanly as a knife. Still smiling, she spoke to his aunt, then turned and made her way through the crowd toward the exit.

Predatory instinct took over as she reached the doorway. He'd had his fill of watching her from a distance. Tonight she was going to admit she was his. Pushing himself away from the wall, he took a step forward.

"Where the devil are you going in such a hurry?" Marcus asked in surprise.

"To claim what's mine."

Ignoring his friend's sagging jaw, he moved quickly toward the exit he'd seen Helen pass through. Although not as crowded as the ballroom, guests cluttered the hallway making it difficult to find her. Moments passed, and when he finally saw her emerging from what had to be the ladies retiring room, relief escaped him in a whoosh of air.

She walked toward him with her head down, her gaze intent on adjusting the fan dangling from her wrist. Hesitation stabbed at him until he stepped into her path and took her hand in his.

"Here, let me help you." The muscles in her arm stiffened at his touch, but he didn't let that sway him. She lifted her head, the color draining from her face. Instantly, he knew what he had to do.

"You look ill, Helen. Let me take you home."

With a shake of her head, she murmured, "No, I'm fine."

"You don't look fine at all. I'll take you home. I'll not have it said I'm neglectful of my guests health." The last statement he said in a loud, stern voice in order to ensure that anyone listening was aware he was deeply concerned for her well-being.

Not waiting for her to respond, he caught her elbow in his hand and guided her toward the Somerset's front door. She balked and stumbled in the process. Taking advantage of the situation, he raised his voice slightly all the while steering her relentlessly to the door. "Summon my carriage, Miss Rivenall is ill. Then send word to Lady Stewart that I've escorted Miss Rivenall back to Melton House."

"What do you think you're doing?" she exclaimed in a low voice.

"It's obvious you're unwell, and I'm taking you home."

"I'm perfectly fine and you know it."

She was like a cat, hissing in anger, but he had every intention of making her purr. He accepted her cloak from the footman and enveloped her in the lightweight material. The softness of her skin brushed his fingertips as he laid the outer garment over her shoulders. It sent a white heat streaking across his skin, and his groin flexed and tightened with need.

They moved out into the night, and down the steps toward the waiting carriage. The cool air did nothing to stifle the increasing warmth flooding his body.

"I don't want to go back to Melton House," she snapped with outrage.

The tenuous grip he held on his emotions threatened to slip at her fierce objection. A dark growl rose in his throat and he bent his head toward her. "Get in the carriage, Helen or by God I'll toss you in myself."

Anger flashed in her eyes, but she did as he ordered with a grimace. As she climbed into the vehicle, he instructed the coachman to drive until told otherwise. Following Helen into the carriage, he slammed the door shut then pulled the curtains over both windows. Beneath a glass globe, a short candle sputtered and flickered in its holder. The light it cast on Helen's features heightened the rosy anger flooding her cheeks.

Alone with her at last, he breathed a small sigh of relief. Tension racked his body due to her close proximity, but he managed to control it as he studied her in the seat across from him. Despite her composed features, her eyes blazed with anger. Something was different about her. Stiff with latent hostility, she glared at him. Then he realized what was different about her. For the first time he realized he could see her emotions in the depths of her eyes. Anger glowed there, but so did fear. Why would she fear him?

Exhaling a deep breath, he folded his arms and returned her fierce look steadily. The silence stretched between them with the taut snap of a sail at full swell. With an explosive sound of frustration she shook her head.

"What do you want, Sebastian?"

"You," he growled softly.

At the single word, her body recoiled back into the plush cushions of the carriage. "You're not making any sense."

"Oh, I think I'm making perfect sense. I want you and I mean to have you. I intend to make you want me too."

"Impossible," she sniffed.

"Difficult, but not impossible," he said with amusement.

"Your arrogance is unbelievable."

A smile curled his lips. He was going to enjoy making her hot and needy. With a quick movement, he shifted his body into the small space beside her. Delight whispered through him at the breathless gasp parting her lips. He grinned at her.

"And you, sweetheart, are going to admit that you desire me as much as I do you."

His touch light, he undid the string of her cloak tied at her neck. The material fell away to reveal her delectable shoulders, and he simply stared at her. His gaze eagerly drank in the sight of her creamy skin, pinpointing the fluttering pulse on the side of her neck.

Leaning forward, he stopped his mouth a hair's breadth away from her ear. "Do you know how beautiful your skin is? It's the color of thick cream with the palest tinge of pink."

"Your compliments are falling on deaf ears, my lord." Her breathless response broadened his grin. He disturbed her. Good. He was about to do a whole lot more than just disturb her.

"But they're such delightful ears." He gently grazed the lobe of her ear with his mouth. The action rewarded him with another gasp from her.

"I thought you were taking me back to Melton House."

Desperation lay buried beneath her words, and he pulled back from her. He didn't answer. He was content simply to watch the tops of her lovely breasts heave from her rapid breathing. Instinct guided his fingers to run a feathery caress over top the plump mounds. She sucked in a quick breath at the airy touch. Immediately, his erection jumped with tension, but he ignored its call. No, tonight he would tease and cajole her until she begged him to take her, and when she thought respite close at hand, she would find it retreating to sweep toward her again. Tonight, she would experience the joy and agony of need.

"Do you want me to take you home?" he murmured.

"Yes," she said with a firm nod.

"Afraid?"

Her gaze met his, and she eyed him warily. "I'm not afraid of you."

"Oh, but I think you are." With one finger, he lightly traced the neckline of her gown, stopping at the cleft of her breasts. He slowly slid his finger between the soft mounds then withdrew. The stroke made him think of how desperately he wanted to sink his cock into her, and he swallowed the need building inside him. A shudder ran through her, convincing him that her skill at concealing her emotions would crumble easily. "I propose a small test."

"What sort of test," she said through clenched teeth.

"Kiss me."

"*What?*" She gasped in surprise. "I most *certainly* will not."

"So you're afraid to show the passion you displayed so willingly just a few short weeks ago." Inside he winced at the words. Short was not a description he could apply to the long, agonizing nights he'd suffered since then.

"Infatuation, mixed with gratitude, is far from passion, my lord." Her cool words stung, but he restrained his temper. He knew she was struggling not to give in to him. But give in she would.

"Shall I disprove you're susceptibility by kissing you?"

"No!"

"Then kiss me and be done with it. Prove you're immune to me."

Frustration pursed her lovely rose-colored mouth, and she sniffed a noise of intense disgust. With a quick move, she brushed her mouth over his then drew back.

"Come now, I know you can do far better than that."

She glared at him at him before she dragged her gaze away. "I refuse to play this game anymore, my lord."

Leaning toward her again, he brushed his mouth along her cheek and down to her jaw line. Again, his fingertips trailed across the tops of her breast, but this time, his forefinger slid in between her nipple and corset to stroke the bud. It peaked into a hard pebble immediately. A smile of satisfaction tilted the corners of his mouth. He continued to plant feathery kisses down the side of her neck, while keeping his touch light over the tops of her breasts.

He nipped gently at the pulse beating wildly at her neck. "Do you like this?"

"Ye ... no," she moaned softly.

"No? What about this?" His lips slanted down over the base of her throat to the tops of her breasts. With his tongue, he probed the small valley between her breasts. Another small moan broke past her lips. Delighted with the quick results of his efforts, he explored her flesh beneath her stays again, his forefinger rubbing the hard nipple straining to escape the confines of her clothing.

Lifting his head, he smiled at her dazed expression. "Kiss me, and this time, do it properly."

The tip of her tongue darted out to wet lips, and a soft growl vibrated in his throat. She shook her head slightly as though to protest, and he leaned toward her until his mouth was almost touching hers. "I promise you'll enjoy it, sweetheart."

A murmur of dissent escaped her as she pressed her lips to his. Instantly, his need barreled to the forefront, and it took every ounce of will power he possessed to refrain from devouring her. Stiffening his resolve, he responded gently to her kiss. There was a hunger hidden in her caress, and when her moist tongue slid past his lips, he groaned with pleasure. Still he held back, waiting for her to entice and beguile him. It was not a long wait.

The warmth of her palms caressed his cheek as she increased the pressure of her mouth against his. She tasted of sugared lemons, tart and sweet in the same swoop of her dainty tongue, while the lavender scent of her hair reminded him of spring flowers. Instead of leaning into her kiss, he edged his way backward until she was forced to come with him or break the kiss.

Reclined against the wall of the carriage, his body throbbed with jubilant satisfaction as she followed him. Half lying on top of him, her tongue teasing him as she retreated and plunged her tongue into his mouth.

The erotic sensation made his cock strain against his trousers, anxious to perform the very act her tongue recreated in his mouth. Aware that he was fast losing control of his senses, he ran his hands up from her waist to cup both her breasts. A whimper danced across her lips. The husky moan echoing from her made him smile as he sought the side of her neck with his mouth.

Nipping at her silky skin, he slowly undid the back of her gown. "Are you enjoying yourself, sweetheart?"

A shudder shook her. "No."

The hoarse negative made him chuckle. "You don't sound too sure of that."

Her gown parted and he made quick work of her stays. When he pushed her upright to tug her gown and stays off her upper body, she willingly complied. Discarding the corset, he stared at her breasts straining against the silk chemise she wore. A surge of desire pushed through his groin and he drew in a deep breath.

Grasping her by the waist, he lifted her toward him so her breast tumbled into his mouth. He sucked at the distended nipple, his mouth wetting the garment covering her skin. A low moan of pleasure broke from her throat and she slid her fingers through his hair. Having thoroughly laved one nipple to a stiff peak, he switched his attention to her other breast.

Already he could tell she was hot and needy by the way her hips rubbed against his. His groin protested at the enticement, but he bit back the need crawling through him. Releasing her nipple, he pushed her back from him. An expression of languid desire made her eyelids droop and the green eyes meeting his glowed with a slumberous heat.

"Undress for me." The demand made her stiffen, and he smiled. The look on her face told him she was prepared to balk, and he stretched out his hand to trace circles around the tip of her areole that showed up dark against the white silk of her damp chemise. His touch pulled a gasp from her, and she arched her breasts toward him, her eyes closing.

Withdrawing his hand from her, he removed his jacket and white tie, tossing both onto the seat opposite them. Her eyes flew open, and he watched her face as he slowly unbuttoned his shirt. Her eyes widened and darkened at his movements. Full, pink lips parted slightly as her breasts rose and fell quickly. Her tongue wet her upper lip in a pensive gesture before she pushed her dress down over her hips. Just as he had his own clothes, she pushed her gown onto the opposite seat.

When she leaned toward him, he chuckled. "Tch, tch, my sweet. Undress means completely."

She bit her lip, hesitating. He reached out once more to stroke her nipples with his fingers. They hardened into rigid peaks and she released a soft sigh.

"I take it this pleases you."

"Ye ... yess." The word escaped her mouth with great difficulty, but he rejoiced in the sound. Soon, very soon, she'd beg him for her release, and he would give it too her, but not before he drove her wild with longing.

"Then let me see all of you." He pulled back his hand, enjoying the whimper of dismay she uttered. His cock pressed relentlessly against his stomach as she lifted the chemise over her head to reveal her lush, full breasts. It tightened painfully, lusting after her as he watched her trembling hands remove the remainder of her underclothing. As she shoved the garments over to the opposite seat, his mouth watered at the nest of curls between her thighs. God, but she was exquisite, and if he didn't make her climax quickly, he would lose control of his own desire before he could bury himself inside her.

She knelt trembling on the seat before him, and the image of settling his mouth over her intimate folds tightened his groin and stomach muscles with a taut, excruciating tension of the most delightful nature. He stretched out his hand, and when she placed her small one in his, he pulled her gently toward him. Sliding down further on the seat, he grasped her waist and inched her forward until she straddled his chest.

His movements deliberate, he ran his hands across her thighs, up to her stomach and then skimmed her sides to capture her breasts and swirl the pad of his thumb over her stiff nipples. The musky scent of her drifted into his nostrils, and with one hand, he sought the secrets beyond the curls between her thighs.

A damp dew drenched his thumb as he sought the nub hidden inside her slick, wet folds. The moment he reached the sensitive spot and stroked it, she uttered a small cry of delight.

"Does that please you?"

"Yes," she choked out.

"And if I stopped?"

"I ... please ..."

"Please what, my sweet?" He withdrew his hand to stroke the inside of her thigh.

"Oh God, please ... please don't ... stop."

A laugh escaped him as his thumb once again plundered her velvety folds and found the plump core of her hot sex. She bucked against his touch, and his tongue ached to taste her.

"Would you like to feel something else there?"

"You ... you know ... I do." Her words were a frantic pant as he increased the rhythm of his stroke to the hard pearl beneath his fingers.

The musk of her desire floated over him, and grasping her buttocks, he kneaded the soft flesh while urging her toward his mouth. When she settled over his lips, he flicked his tongue through her curls to lap at the cream lining her silky, hot folds. The moment he did so, she uttered a deep cry of delight.

With long strokes of his tongue, he laved the heated velvet of her before surging upward to swirl around her sex. In and out, he teased, nipped and licked her to a frenzied state. A husky cry sailed from her throat and she stiffened over his mouth before tremors rocked through her.

Blinded by the need pounding its way through her, she trembled violently as he drank from her. The primitive sensations exploding in every portion of her body were wild, wicked and deliciously sinful. With every stroke of his tongue or touch of his hand, he created a heaven on earth. It made her willing to follow him into hell if he would only continue tempting her with such sweetness.

Once more, his tongue lifted her up to an exultant summit of pleasure and she shuddered again. The touch of his hand teasing her nipple nearly drove her over the edge and she wanted to plead and beg him to ease the ache between her thighs. The exquisite torture of mouth against her took her to another fevered pitch, and she cried out again.

"Oh dear lord."

His hands gripped her waist and his strong, muscular arms settled her back onto his hips. The cloth of his trousers grazed her skin as his erection pressed into her derriere. As the hard line of his phallus pushed against her, a stark need spiraled through her. She reached behind her to rest her hand on his arousal.

Immediately he jumped against her fingers. Eyes closed she threw her head back and relished the feel of him through the cloth of his trousers. Thick and hard against her hand, she wondered if he would like her to pleasure him as he'd just pleasured her. The deliciously wanton thought teased its way through her head. Here there were no restraints, no rules, no shame, only the sheer, intense power of her desire for the man she loved.

Before he could stop her, she slid down the length of his long legs. Keeping her eyes locked with his, she reached for the buttons of his trousers. At his sharp intake of breath, she smiled. In seconds she'd freed his hard length, and she lightly ran her forefinger from the bottom of his staff up to the tip.

Without a word, she bent her head and drew him in to her mouth. His response was immediate and intense as his body jerked and his palms hit the leather cushions of the seat with a loud crack.

"Christ Jesus," he hissed.

The raspy sound of his breathing echoed over her head as she slowly eased him into her mouth. Swirling her tongue around the cap of his hard length, she kept her gaze on his face. She wanted to know how much she was pleasuring him. Eyes closed, his face told her everything she wanted to know. Tightening her lips on him, she saw his expression change from pleasure to hot passion in one brief instant.

He tasted hot and salty on her tongue as she took more of him into her mouth. The low groan he released made her relax her mouth until just the tip of him was in her mouth. With another raw groan pouring from his chest, his hips shifted beneath her as if he were in agony.

"God no, don't stop sweetheart," he ground out in a hoarse voice. "Take all of it. Take all of me into your mouth."

Obeying him, she slid her mouth down the hard, velvet length of him. The warm male scent of him filled her senses as she tightened her lips around him and stroked him with her tongue and mouth. The rapid movement of her mouth on him imitated the intimate act they'd shared weeks ago. Another raspy sigh forced its way past his lips.

She was incredible. Without even asking, she'd sought to pleasure him in a way few women dared. The way she was sucking on him blinded him to anything but the sexual need surging through him with a force he'd only experienced one other time. And that time had been when he was with her. Only with her had he ever enjoyed the delirious delight of ultimate pleasure.

The touch of her fingers on his ballocks made him stiffen and he knew he needed to stop her if he was going to give both of them satisfaction tonight. God knew he wanted to come in her mouth, but that could wait for another time.

Right now, he wanted to sink into that hot, buttery core of hers and hear her cry out his name with the same raw, sexual pleasure she had that night he'd spent in her bed. With a groan, he shifted his body so that she was forced to release him from her mouth. She sat up to stare at him in puzzlement, her voluptuous body filling him with a raging need.

"Don't look at me like that, sweetheart. That was incredible, but tonight isn't about pleasuring me."

Sitting up, he sat on the seat as he would normally, and pulled her onto his lap. The warmth of her soft buttocks heated his thighs as he nibbled at the side of her neck. With a gentle touch, he slid his hands between her thighs and parted her slick nether lips with his fingers. She squirmed slightly beneath his touch, her eyes darkening with need as he studied her features.

"Tell me what you want, sweetheart." The command was a gentle caress, and she sighed with pleasure.

"I want you."

"Tell me how much you want me." His deep voice wrapped its silky web around her, making her sigh with delight as he brushed her nipple with his tongue.

"Very much."

A low, triumphant laugh brushed across the skin as he slid her off his hard thighs and turned her to face him. Hands braced against his solid shoulders she hovered over him, the heat of his body warming her in the coolness of the moving vehicle.

"Tell me exactly what you want."

"I want …"

"Yes?" His fingers found the sensitive nub between her legs and fire exploded in her body, obliterating all thought except the need to possess and be possessed by him.

"I want you inside me," she said in a voice she didn't recognize as her own. It was like a sultry purr of need, and his eyes flashed at the sound as she stared down into his eyes. "I need to feel you throbbing inside me, making me yours."

The look of passion on his face took her breath away as his fingers dug into her buttocks and pulled her forward until her knees were touching the seat. With a sudden pull, he seated her fully on top of his hard length. She gasped at the hedonistic delight that suddenly heated every pore of her body.

With his full length of him embedded inside her, she choked back a sob of pleasure. Sweet lord, but he felt wonderful between her legs. Nothing in her life would ever be able to compare with the joy of being joined with him like this.

His hips bucked against her thighs as he silently urged her to slide up and down his engorged staff. The sensation created a hot friction between them, and it increased the intense pleasure pulling at every part of her body. With one hand on his chest, she dragged her fingers down across his stomach to their joined flesh. Her finger rubbed across the base of his shaft, and he groaned deeply.

"Ahh, sweet Jesus, yes."

The need in his voice and his hands urged her to meet the frenetic pace of his thrusts, and with each burning slide of flesh against flesh, her own need pitched and rolled inside her. Her body shuddered, gripping him, tightening around his phallus. His face twisted with passion as another groan of desire escaped him. The quick pace he coaxed from her was encouraged by his own pumping upward with his hips. A moment later, he stiffened before exploding inside her, his body igniting another flood of tremors within her.

The sound of his hoarse cry of satisfaction sent a rush of pleasure soaring through her as her own body drowned in a delirious whirlpool of heat and colors. The sensations blurred her vision as she soared into a heated mist of passion and love, before sinking forward to rest her head against his chest.

For a long moment, the inside of the carriage echoed only the silence of their panting breaths mixing with the hoof beats of the light traffic outside. Against her cheek, his heartbeat slowly ebbed from a frantic rhythm to one of quiet serenity. His chest reverberated with a deep sigh of satisfaction.

"That was a heavenly experience, my sweet. I look forward to many more such moments after we're married."

The words caused her to stiffen against the sleek muscles of his chest. He'd seduced her simply to achieve his own goals. The knowledge pulled the breath from her like a lion tearing at her flesh.

Chapter 15

How had she come to this? Why had she given in to her impulses? Because she loved him. But without his love in return-- Hastily, she scrambled off him. In the low light, she pulled her chemise over her head, ignoring the warm, sticky heat between her thighs.

She dressed in silence. How could she have been so blind as to think his feelings had developed into something deeper in such a short time? A quick peek in his direction revealed a dark frown furrowing his brow. Glancing away, she reached for her stays and wrapped the garment around her body. Unable to do up the laces on her own, she turned her back to him.

"I need help with my corset," she whispered.

He sat up and pulled her into his chest, his head bending so his lips could nip at her shoulder. "And I need you."

"Please, Sebastian."

"When you ask so sweetly, how can I refuse you anything?" His mouth pressed a heated kiss to her neck before he leaned back to lace up her stays. The smile in his voice was easy to hear, and the sound wrapped a tight vise around her chest. If only his affection extended to something deeper. No doubt, he took her surrender tonight as a sign that she would willingly submit her life to him. But she wouldn't. Without love, the desire he felt would eventually fade. Better to suffer a broken heart now than devastation when she no longer pleased him.

The moment he finished lacing her corset, she reached for her dress and struggled to get into it. Warm hands tenderly stroked one of the scars on her back, and she jumped at the touch.

"Please don't."

"Do they hurt?" There was concern and puzzlement in his voice.

She shook her head and reached behind to fidget with the buttons of her gown. Tapered fingers brushed hers aside as he fastened the dress for her. When he finished, he turned her to face him. He had dressed as well, but his shirt splayed opened at the throat to reveal part of his beautiful chest. She trembled at the way need immediately raced through her. It enticed her to reach out and stroke him. Burying the treacherous impulse, she smoothed the skirts of her gown and settled into the seat opposite him.

The frown she'd seen on his face a moment ago had returned,

and she swallowed the knot in her throat. She'd given her heart and body to him, but she refused to give him her soul.

"I'd like to go back to Melton House, Sebastian."

He stared at her for a moment then knocked twice on the roof of the carriage. Reaching for his tie, he quickly knotted it around his neck and shrugged into his jacket. When finished, he reclined back against the seat cushions and studied her with narrowed eyes.

"Tell me what's wrong, Helen."

"Nothing," she said with a slight shake of her head, avoiding his gaze. "I'm simply tired."

"I don't believe you. The moment I mentioned marriage you retreated into that touch-me-not shell of yours."

"Believe what you like, but I'm telling you the truth. I'm tired." She was tired. Tired of the ache torturing her body every time she came into close proximity to him. The desire she'd experienced had eased some of her longing, but it was certain to return tenfold in a short time. With each moment spent in his company, she loosened the tenuous grasp of her resolve not to give in to her love and desire. Not to give in to his demands for a marriage that simply the legally disguised agreement between a man and his mistress.

"Too tired to discuss our impending nuptials?" The angry growl challenged her, and tension tightened her muscles with rigid inflexibility.

"I've told you before, Sebastian, I won't marry you." She kept her voice low and calm, but it didn't protect her from his fury.

With the speed of a hawk plunging toward its prey, he lunged forward. His hands gripped her arms tightly as he pulled her across the carriage and into his arms.

"And I'll know the reason why." The determined glint in his black eyes warned her that she was swimming in treacherous waters.

"I don't answer to you," she bit out in an angry retort. "But if you must know I'm considering Lord Winthrope's suit."

The moment the lie passed her lips, she knew it was a mistake. Sebastian's eyes narrowed to thin slits of anger, and his mouth curled in a brutal farce of a smile.

"Then consider this, Miss Rivenall. If you think I'm going to let another man have what's mine, you're mistaken."

The carriage rocked to a halt, and she tried to pull free of his hold. His arms were bands of steel binding her to his chest. "Let me go."

"You're mine, Helen, and what's mine, I keep. Never forget that."

His mouth took possession of hers in a savage kiss, and despite his anger, her body reacted to his touch with lightning speed. A moment later, he thrust her from him with a growl of disgust. There was not another opportunity to speak as the carriage door opened, and the footman stood ready to assist Helen from the vehicle.

* * * *

Exhausted emotionally and physically, Helen did not wake until almost the noon hour the next day. Staring up at the gauze canopy, she remembered Sebastian's anger and his adamant declaration of possession. She knew that if she didn't leave Melton House soon, she'd be lost. Sebastian would find a way to make her marry him, and her life would eventually descend into a hellish existence when he tired of her.

She had to escape, but where could she and Edward go. Since that first night when she'd entered the world of the Marlborough Set, she'd listened closely for any word of someone named Worthington. She'd even discreetly inquired about the name to the one or two acquaintances she'd made in the past two weeks. But no one knew of any Worthingtons in London.

Trapped by circumstances and her actions, she knew Sebastian was right. She really had no place to go. Perhaps Lady Stewart or Louisa could help her find a situation as a governess. As long as Edward could remain with her, she would not protest earning a living. The idea rolled around in her head as she dressed, and when she was ready to go downstairs, she had made up her mind. She would ask Louisa's help in finding a suitable position.

Downstairs, she found Lady Stewart in the salon. Sebastian was also present, and as she entered the room, he glared at her before turning away to stare down into the small fire burning in the hearth. Lady Stewart set her teacup on its saucer and smiled cheerfully.

"Well now, so ye decided to rise and greet the day, did ye? Are ye feeling any better?"

"Yes, thank you." She struggled to return the smile and nodded.

"I was a bit surprised last night to get the message ye'd taken ill and Sebastian had taken ye home."

She averted her gaze from the woman's curious expression. Seating herself across from Lady Stewart, she filled a cup with tea.

"It came upon me quite suddenly."

The Scotswoman smiled and simply nodded her head before changing the subject. "Sebastian tells me you're considering an offer from Lord Winthrope."

The statement startled her, and the teacup she held rattled against its saucer. Instantly, her gaze darted in Sebastian's direction. The implacable expression on his face belied the blazing anger in his black eyes. She glanced away, her eyes drawn back to Lady Stewart's expression of curiosity.

"Actually, my words were that I was considering his suit."

"Ahh, I see, and what have you decided, dearie?"

"I've decided nothing."

Sebastian walked to the salon window and folding his arms across his chest, he leaned one shoulder against the window frame. Watching her from where he stood, his fiery gaze burned through her. The love swelling in her heart tightened every muscle in her body. Should she risk the excruciating pain of his rejection later for a piece of heaven now? The question sent a shudder rippling through her, and Lady Stewart's sharp eyes caught the tremor.

"Are ye all right, dearie? Ye look a wee peaked."

"I'm fine, thank you, my lady."

"If Lord Winthrope does make an offer what will you do?"

The woman's question startled her, and her gaze flew to study Sebastian's face. A grim look darkened his features, and he arched an eyebrow at her. She frowned at his expression. He'd deliberately told Lady Stewart about Lord Winthrope. Why? Did he think he could enlist his aunt's assistance in some plan he was hatching? She returned her gaze to the lady opposite her and shook her head before she took a sip of her tea.

"I don't know. I find his company pleasant enough, and he's a kind man." It was true. Lord Winthrope was a kind man. She'd witnessed it two nights ago at the Sherringham ball. While dancing with Lord Dorchester, she'd seen an elderly gentleman on his way out of the room almost fall, and Winthrope had immediately gone to the man's aid.

Sebastian gave a snort of disgust prompting Lady Stewart to turn and look at him. The inquisitive expression on her face made him glower at his aunt before he glanced away. The Scotswoman twisted back to face Helen.

"Well, dearie, as husband material he's eminently suitable, unlike others."

An explosive oath of anger parted Sebastian's lips. With a sharp movement, he lunged away from the window and strode from the room. The door slammed shut behind him. Lady Stewart chuckled softly.

"Ach, but that one is stubborn. Angry too. A true Stewart, he is."

Remaining silent, she averted her eyes from the woman's

curious gaze. She had no wish to be questioned or offer any insight as to the reason for Sebastian's anger. She knew all to well why he was angry. His parting kiss last night had stamped his mark of possession on her, and today his mood seemed no less harsh.

When she didn't speak, Lady Stewart took a sip of her tea before continuing with her reflections. "The mon never does admit to his feelings. After his mother died, we thought he would go mad with grief. Wrapped himself up so no one could reach the hurt inside. To this day, he still finds it difficult to open himself up to anyone."

Helen sighed inwardly. She could understand Sebastian's desire to insulate himself from the rest of the world. She'd been doing it for a long time herself. In silence, she sipped her tea and remembered the night she'd cared for Sebastian and the feverish dreams he'd had. Her heart had gone out to him at the agony in his voice as he'd tossed and turned. Whatever had happened the night his mother died, he believed himself responsible.

Lifting her teacup to her lips, she took another drink of the tepid liquid. Across from her, Lady Stewart set down her cup and saucer and folded her hands in her lap. "Isn't it time ye tell me where my nephew took ye last night?"

In the middle of a swallow, Helen choked on the cooling tea. Coughing, she took another quick drink to sooth her throat. When she'd recovered, she met the older woman's direct gaze. "I'm not sure what you mean."

"I was worried about ye, so I came home shortly after ye left Somerset House. Ye can imagine my surprise when ye weren't home yet."

Helen felt the color draining from her face and she set down her teacup with trembling hands. Unable to think of a response, she stared at the woman in horrified silence for a long minute. "I...Lord Melton wished to speak with me about a private matter. He arranged for us to drive around in his carriage."

"I see." She paused for a moment then continued. "What in heaven's name was the daft mon thinking? He knows better than to put ye in a compromising situation."

She stiffened at the words and rushed to forestall any unwelcome resolution. "I'm certain Lord Melton did not mean to do so."

"Well, it would seem no harm has been done. I'll see to it that he doesn't act so recklessly again."

Lady Stewart's observation brought a soft sigh of relief to Helen's lips. No harm done. Inside, a small voice mocked her with the memory of how she'd responded to Sebastian in the carriage last night. His hands and mouth had pulled from her a wanton display of need and passion. Stroking her into a delirious rapture, he'd made her plead for relief. And he had satisfied her in the most intimate manner. Heat flushed through her as she recalled the way he'd kissed her so intimately.

"Helen, did ye hear what Madison said"

The question broke through her reverie, and she stared blankly at the woman for a moment. "What?"

"Lord Winthrope is in the hall."

"Oh." Helen turned her head to see Madison departing the salon. "Oh my, I completely forgot he asked to take me for a drive this afternoon if the weather was nice."

Just as she finished speaking the man in question entered the room. Striding toward them, Helen acknowledged he was a handsome man. Sandy colored hair hung carelessly over his brow, and his physique declared he didn't indulge to excess. The cut of his dark blue coat emphasized broad shoulders, and his entire appearance was one to set any number of heads to turn. He would make some woman very happy, but not her. Her heart belonged to another.

"Good day, Lady Stewart." His blond head bent over the older woman's hand as he greeted her. He then straightened to take Helen's hand.

"How are you feeling, Miss Rivenall. I was disappointed not to bid you goodbye last night." A curious expression crossed his face as he studied her.

"It was nothing. I felt a bit ill, and Lord Melton was kind enough to bring me home."

"Are you feeling up to the drive you promised me?"

Anxious to forget the night before, she nodded. "Yes, I feel much better after a good night's sleep."

"Excellent, it's a wonderful day for a drive. I thought perhaps you might join us Lady Stewart, as my grandfather expressed a wish to come as well."

The plump matron smiled with pleasure at the invitation, her burgundy dress rustling as she rose to her feet. "Why that is a lovely thought, my lord. I would be delighted to do so."

"Well then, shall we be off?" Stepping back to one side, Lord Winthrope swept his hand toward the exit.

Lady Stewart and Helen quickly retrieved their gloves and hats then walked out onto the front steps. Sunshine lit the façade of Melton House as they emerged out into the crisp fall air. Beside her, Lord Winthrope gestured toward the open landau. As Lady Stewart entered the carriage, Lord Winthrope bent toward Helen's ear.

"I'm pleased Lady Stewart agreed to accompany us. Although I did think I might encounter some resistance to my invitation from other quarters." He sent a pointed look toward the front of Melton House. Glancing over her shoulder, she saw Sebastian watching them from the music room's large window before he turned and disappear from view.

"You worry yourself unduly, my lord."

"Do I? I wonder," he said with a grin. "But I imagine your suitors find it rather difficult."

The cheerful quip made her laugh. "I have no suitors, my lord."

"Ah, I think you're wrong there, my dear. I think you have far more admirers than you can even imagine. All of us are more than eager for you to even acknowledge our existence."

"You, my lord, are a born flatterer." She laughed again as he handed her into the carriage. Climbing into the landau, she seated herself across from Lady Stewart and an elderly man. The sharp, piercing gaze the man directed at her made her smile fade slightly. Distinguished looking, it was clear he'd once been an extremely handsome man. Although he'd lost his youth, he still cut a fine picture. Hair the color of snow matched the eyebrows framing his green eyes, which were sharp and bright. He studied her with an intensity that unsettled her. Even though he sat stiff and unmoving against the soft cushions of the carriage, she could tell he was tall. The walking stick he held in one hand bore an ivory horse's head and his hand slid up to stroke the cane top with long, elegant fingers.

As Lord Winthrope sat beside her, he leaned toward Lady Stewart. "My lady, I'm not certain if you and my grandfather have met."

The introductions complete between Lady Stewart and the earl, Lord Winthrope turned to Helen. "Miss Rivenall, may I present my Grandfather, the earl of Kettering. Grandfather this is Miss Helen Rivenall, the young lady I mentioned to you."

"Miss Rivenall." The earl nodded his head abruptly, his gaze never leaving her face.

"Lord Kettering." She shifted her eyes away from the earl's penetrating look.

The carriage jerked forward and rolled down the street. Beside her, Lord Winthrope chuckled. "Don't let Grandfather unnerve you. He enjoys disconcerting people, don't you Grandfather?"

"It passes the time." Helen thought she caught a brief glimpse of amusement in the man's green eyes before he looked out at the scenery. "So where are we off to this afternoon, my boy? Another turn in Hyde Park?"

"Actually no. I thought we might enjoy this unseasonably

warm weather with a trip out to Kew Gardens." Lord Winthrope smiled at his grandfather before looking at first Lady Stewart and then Helen. "I've been speaking with Sir William Thiselton-Dyer about improvements he wants to make in the gardens, and I've been meaning to visit for a few days now. This seemed like an excellent opportunity."

Lady Stewart made a small exclamation of pleasure. "How delightful. I understand that Sir William is the son-in-law of Sir Hooker. I'm sure he'll continue to preserve and expand on his father-in-law's restoration efforts."

"Indeed, my lady, I believe he will, but I'm also certain the man will make his own mark on the place. He has some rather interesting ideas."

"Harrumph." The earl shook his head before pinning Helen with his piercing gaze. "Tell me, Miss Rivenall, where are you parents?"

The odd question startled her, and an image of her parents hugging each other popped into her head. The bittersweet memory tilted the corners of her mouth with a sad smile. "My brother and I lost our parents more than twelve years ago, my lord."

The earl gripped his cane top tightly, and his mouth tightened into a thin line. He didn't respond for a moment, and when he did, his voice was gruff. "I'm sorry for your loss, Miss Rivenall."

"Thank you, my lord. I Miss them very much."

Puzzled by his odd behavior, Helen saw him swallow hard before he looked away. Lady Stewart met her gaze with a perplexed smile. Brushing off the earl's abrupt manner, she turned toward Lord Winthrope. A deep frown of worry furrowed his brow, but it disappeared when he caught her eyes on him.

"Well now, Miss Rivenall," he said with a smile. "You must tell me everything about yourself. Where you grew up, what you like to do. I want to hear all of it."

Laughing, she shook her head. "I fear I'd bore you, my lord."

"Nonsense." He grinned and turned to Lady Stewart. "My lady, you must convince her to speak freely here."

"Ach, Helen is one to know her own mind. I fear I'm unable to coerce her for ye, my lord."

"Well, I shall tease her answers from her." A cheerful smile on his features, he turned back to Helen. "Come now, here's an easy question. Tell us what your favorite food is."

"Hmmm, I suppose gooseberry scones with lots of butter are my favorite food."

"Remarkable! You must come visit Grandfather and me at

Kettering Hall. We have a cook there who makes the best gooseberry scones in the whole of England."

"Oh, I would like that. I've not enjoyed a gooseberry scone since my mother died. She had this wonderful recipe she'd memorized. It was a family recipe, and whenever she made it, she would tell me stories about her childhood."

"And was your mother happy?" Lord Kettering asked quietly.

Surprised by this second, oddly worded, question, she and Lady Stewart turned to look at the earl. He still looked out at the passing scenery, and his face had a pinched look to it, almost as if he were in pain.

"Why yes, my lord, she and my father were very happy. I can only hope to be half as fortunate as my parents were in their marriage." She inhaled a quick breath at the thought of Sebastian and his recent proposal. No, she would never be fortunate when it came to finding a man she could love as deeply as she loved Sebastian. Marriage was not in her future at all. Bewildered, she dragged her gaze away from the earl. Looking at the woman seated next to the earl, she saw Lady Stewart lift her shoulders in a small shrug. Turning back to Lord Winthrope, she smiled.

"Well, my lord, I've given up a fact about myself, I require one from you."

"Hmm, let me think." He folded his arms and stared up at the sky for a moment, then with a snap of his fingers, laughed. "Gooseberry scones."

Laughing, she shook her head. "That's unfair. You must give up a new fact, not rely on one I've already stated."

"Very well, if you must know, I like to paint."

"How delightful, what do you paint?"

"Landscapes mostly, but Grandfather believes it's a waste of my time." Lord Winthrope shot his relative an amused look.

"Damned ridiculous to spend one's time staring at the scenery and then trying to put it on canvas."

"Oh, but I'm sure it's quite soothing for your grandson, my lord," said Lady Stewart with an impish wink at the young couple across from her.

"Indeed it is, Lady Stewart. Although I've never been able to make Grandfather see that, have I, sir."

The old man snorted his disdain for the hobby and abruptly changed the topic. "How far a drive is it to Kew Garden, boy? I want to exercise these legs of mine."

"It will take at least an hour Grandfather, but once we leave some of this traffic behind we should make excellent time."

Winthrope winked at Helen as he spoke, and she struggled to keep from laughing. Never had she seen two men from the same family at such diverse ends of the spectrum. Although the earl's abrupt manner was uncomfortable and baffling, Lord Winthrope's company was quite pleasant.

It was difficult to find fault with such a beautiful day, and the ride was proving quite delightful in spite of the earl's brusque manner. Perhaps for a short time she'd be able to forget her troubles and Sebastian.

The voice in her head mocked her again. No, the earl of Melton was not a man one could forget, even if she hadn't been in love with him. She turned her head to study the passing scenery, and met the earl of Kettering's penetrating gaze. Her mouth went dry at the look. There was something odd about the man's stern attitude, and it was most unsettling.

Chapter 16

Raking his hand through his thick hair, Sebastian walked toward the piano. His hand balled into a fist, he smashed the keys violently. The discordant sound echoed through the room, and he braced both hands against the wood of the instrument as he stared down at the black and white ivories.

He'd been so certain of success last night. Helen had denied him nothing, and her response had exceeded his wildest dreams. Never had a woman so thoroughly occupied his thoughts and life in the way she did. Her resistance to his marriage proposal was infuriating. Didn't she understand that they were meant to be together?

Angrily, he pulled out the bench in front of the piano and sat down. His fingers trailed over the keys, just as they had over her soft, creamy skin. God, but she'd been exquisite in her hot, delirious need last night. Why did she continue to resist their need for each other? Why was she willing to deny them the pleasure they'd experienced last night?

His fingers crashed against the keys in a passionate stroke, and he began to play with a fury he'd never exhibited before. One piece after another poured out of the piano in a wild, torrid display of emotion. The keys danced beneath his racing touch with a mere second's pause between each composition. He played until his arms and fingers burned from exhaustion, but it didn't erase the pain swelling through him. Helen wasn't with him. She'd rejected him for that bastard, Winthrope.

He stumbled over a set of notes at the thought, and his hands crashed against the keys with frustration. The light touch of a hand on his shoulder startled him out of his violent thoughts. Jerking his head up, he met Louisa's troubled gaze. Ashamed, he looked away from her. How could he explain why he'd not announced his engagement to Helen yet?

"Go away, Louisa."

As usual, she did as she wanted and disregarded his command. Seating herself next to him on the piano bench, she touched his arm gently. "Why are you doing this, Sebastian?"

"I don't know what you're talking about." He reached out and slammed the lid on the keyboard.

"Blast it, Sebastian. Why are you letting Winthrope court Helen, when it's obvious you're in love with her?"

The words sliced through him with the force of a brutal sword.

It wasn't possible. He'd done everything conceivable to prevent such an occurrence. True, he found her company more than pleasurable. When she laughed the room filled with music, and when she touched him, he knew a taste of heaven. But love?

Shaking his head, he pulled away from his sister to rise abruptly from the bench. "You know me well enough to know I harbor no illusions about romantic love, Louisa."

"Then why do you follow her every night from this social to the next, glowering at her suitors from a distance."

"God damn it, Louisa I don't answer to you."

With a sound of disgust, she leapt to her feet and briskly moved to his side. "Well then you should at least answer to yourself. Ask yourself why you're wearing yourself out playing the piano like a madman. Why are you in a foul temper all the time? Why can everyone see the hunger in your eyes whenever you look at Helen? You're the only one, except perhaps Helen herself, who hasn't already figured out you're in love with her."

Stunned by his sister's vehement speech, he slowly turned toward her. A compassionate look on her lovely face, Louisa heaved a sigh. "Oh, Sebastian, you're so stubborn. Open yourself up and look into your heart."

He stared at her, his heart pounding at the idea she might be right. One hand rubbed the back of his neck as he shifted his gaze to the floor. Could it be true? Could he really be in love with Helen? A shudder coursed its way through him at the answer. The simplicity of it shocked him. He loved her. He had from almost the first moment he'd seen her. Most assuredly, from the moment he first kissed her. He loved her, and God help him, he'd driven her straight into Winthrope's arms.

The pain lashing its way into every pore of his body left a bloody trail as he acknowledged the folly of his ways. The physical agony of it made him groan aloud. Louisa grasped his arm.

"You have to tell her, Sebastian. I'm certain she loves you."

"No," he growled harshly. "No, she doesn't. She refused me, Louisa. She doesn't want to be my wife."

"What?" She exclaimed in dismay. "When did you propose to her?"

"The morning you--the morning I left Helen's room, she'd already rejected me. I tried again last night to convince her to marry me, but she refused."

"And I don't suppose you told her you were in love with her," Louisa said with a scathing tone.

"Bloody hell! If I'd had the ability to give her the world, I would have offered it to her, but love wasn't something I'd considered."

"Well you'd better consider it now, because if you don't, Winthrope is going to steal her out from underneath your nose." She sniffed with exasperation. "Men. None of you have the brains of a peacock."

Wheeling about, she stalked away from him, leaving him alone in the music room. Tension laced the muscles of his body, and he frowned. Winthrope was not going to steal Helen from him. If he had to kidnap her and whisk her off to a minister who would marry them right away, he'd do so. Helen Rivenall was about to find out that he would not be swayed in his determination to make her the countess of Melton.

* * * *

As Lord Winthrope's carriage pulled into the Kew Gardens, it rolled to a stop in front of a small gatehouse.

"If you'll excuse me for a few moments, I'd like to arrange for a gardener to accompany us through the gardens to answer any of our questions."

"Might I join you, Lord Winthrope?" Lady Stewart leaned forward. "I have some personal requests for the gardener. I'm in the midst of redesigning my gardens at Callendar Abbey, and I'd like to see if he could show us some of the flowering plants I've in mind to use for the fall season.

"Of course," Lord Winthrope exited the carriage and offered his hand to her. As the Scotswoman descended from the carriage, she turned and smiled at Helen.

"Why don't ye stay and keep his lordship company, dearie. I'm sure we won't be long."

Hiding her reluctance to remain in Lord Kettering's company with a smile, she watched Lady Stewart and Lord Winthrope walk away. Aware that she needed at least to attempt conversation, she smoothed a wrinkle from her rose-colored skirt as she tried to think of a topic she could discuss with the elderly man. Remembering his cane, she turned toward the man.

"Do you enjoy walking, my lord?"

"Hmmm?" He jumped as if he'd been somewhere far away. His piercing gaze swiveled to meet hers. "Yes, walking is good for the body. I walk at least two miles every day. Keeps me healthy."

"You do look quite fit."

A snowy brow arched upward as he leaned forward. "For someone my age you mean."

Appalled that he had misinterpreted her remark as an insult, she gasped in horror.

"No, I'm terribly--" She came to an abrupt halt as she caught the twinkle in his eye. "I do believe you are teasing me, my lord."

"You're as quick as James said you were." For the first time he smiled at her, and it changed the very nature of his features. In his prime, the man would have broken many hearts with such a look. "Tell me, Miss Rivenall, how old is this brother you mentioned?"

"Edward is twelve."

"Edward," he whispered in a strangled voice. He closed his eyes for a moment and when he opened them again, he offered her a weak smile. "Forgive me, Miss Rivenall. I've not been feeling well, and I fear I am poor company for a beautiful young woman such as yourself."

Compassion rose in her breast, and she leaned forward to touch his arm. "Nonsense, I'm thoroughly enjoying myself this afternoon. But is there anything I can do for you? Perhaps you would like something to drink?"

With a shake of his head, he smiled gently. "No, I thank you, I'm certain I'll feel much better after our walk. I'm sure whatever family you have left must find you a great comfort."

The image of her uncle blew an icy wind over her skin, and she turned her head away from the earl. "Edward and I have not known a loving home since we lost our parents."

"And what of Lord Melton, how do you come to be in his home?" There was the faintest hint of censure in his resonant voice. Her spine went rigid and she lifted her chin.

"Lord Melton rescued Edward and me from a horrible situation. He gave us a home until we were able to locate…"

The earl rested both hands on his cane and leaned forward. "Go on, until you were able to locate who, child."

She raised a hand in protest. "Forgive me, my lord. I misspoke. I should never have thought to burden you with my troubles. The day is perfect for a walk, and we should not dim the prospect with any worrisome thoughts."

"You are not burdening me, Miss Rivenall. I can only think that you are in some type of trouble, and yet you give me the impression that you have no one to turn too."

The perceptive words forced her to clasp her hand together tightly. Something about the earl's questions and reactions were quite troubling. It seemed as though he knew more about her than he revealed, and the thought unnerved her.

"My problems are of no consequence, my lord. You mustn't trouble yourself on my account."

"Ah, but it has been a long time since I was able to worry needlessly about a beautiful young woman, Miss Rivenall." The light-hearted reply made her laugh, and he smiled broadly. "You have a lovely laugh, child. You should laugh more often."

"I often do when I am dealing with my brother. He is a mischievous imp at times."

"I should like to meet this brother of yours. I think I would like him."

The sound of voices floated over the grass toward them. Helen turned her head to see Lord Winthrope and Lady Stewart approaching with a young man dressed in gardening clothes. Reaching the landau, Lord Winthrope opened the door and extended his hand to Helen.

"Come, Miss Rivenall, Grandfather. We'll start our tour here. Mr. Stoner is to be our guide."

She placed her hand in his and stepped out of the carriage. The earl followed a moment later, batting away his grandson's offer of assistance. Together the four of them followed the gardener across the narrow road into a small copse of trees already beginning to shed their colorful leaves. As they strolled through the trees, sunlight drifted through the branches filled with gold, red and orange leaves. After a short walk, they emerged into a lush area of autumn plants and flowers. Hypericum, lavender, coxcomb and chrysanthemums were mixed together in a wild cacophony of fall color.

Lord Winthrope and Lady Stewart followed the gardener to a small flowerbed, where an animated discussion ensued. Enjoying the peace and quiet of the small glen, Helen breathed in the crisp fall air filled with the soft scent of the lavender and chrysanthemums. Eyes closed, she stood silent in the beauty of the moment. The earl's deep voice softly intruded.

"I believe your mother would have enjoyed a moment such as this."

"Yes, she would. She loved flowers, her garden--" Her eyes flew open as she realized he had spoken as if he knew her mother. There was something exceedingly strange about the earl's manner, and she didn't know what to make of it. She studied him in silence, and he grimaced.

"I can see by your expression that I puzzle you."

"I must confess, my lord, that I am greatly puzzled."

Offering her his arm, he used his stick to point toward the path that stretched out before them. "Come, I will tell you a story. One that I believe you will find quite interesting as well as sad."

She accepted his arm and matched his step as they moved forward along the gravel-lined walk. Ahead of them, Lady Stewart continued to enjoy a lively conversation with the gardener, while Lord Winthrope flanked her. He glanced over his shoulder and smiled before returning his attention to the gardener and the Scotswoman. The oddity of the situation suddenly struck her. Was the earl interviewing her as a potential bride for his grandson? She frowned at the notion. The earl chuckled.

"Yes, I remember that expression well."

"What expression, my lord."

"The furrowed brow whenever something is troubling or perplexing." He smiled, but there was a distinct sadness behind the pleasantness. "Let me tell you my story. I knew a man once who had two daughters he adored to distraction. Unfortunately, this man was an overbearing, controlling man. He gave his daughters the best of everything, and he was certain this would guarantee their happiness. But he was a blind fool, and his children desired more than the material possessions he offered them.

"The oldest daughter he married off to a wealthy peer. Fortunately, it was a good match. The daughter was very happy and her husband loved her deeply. The younger daughter however refused every offer that came her way. Annoyed that his youngest child was acting as obstinate and defiant as he had been in his own youth, the man selected a husband for her.

"She immediately refused to marry the man, and declared she had fallen in love with a penniless young man of little distinction. Naturally, the father thought to put a stop to the affair, but nothing he said could convince his daughter to change her mind. Finally, in a fit of rage, the man threw his daughter out of his home, disowning her and shouting that he'd never take her back into his house."

Helen stiffened suddenly. Her heartbeat accelerating until it was racing out of control, she trembled at the earl's last words. They were so similar to the story her own mother had told her, and she pressed her fingers to her brow.

"If this father loved his daughter so much, why would he disown her?"

"Because he was a stubborn, prideful fool. When his rage eventually left him, he refused to take the first step to find his daughter. It was nothing but pride that prevented him from seeking her out."

"I would assume this gentleman is an extremely unhappy man."

"Yes, he has paid for his rash behavior with the loss of a daughter and now his grandchildren."

"Grandchildren?" Helen stumbled slightly, and the earl came to a halt, his hand providing a surprising strong support for his age.

"Yes, my dear. You see, the man in my story is me. I disowned my youngest daughter in a fit of pride and arrogance. Eleanor and I were cut from the same mold. We were both stubborn and willful."

As her mother's name rolled off his tongue, she swayed against him. Immediately, the earl called out for his grandson. A moment later, Lady Stewart and Lord Winthrope reached them. With his arm about her waist, Winthrope guided her to a nearby bench. Over top of her head, he chastised his grandparent.

"I warned you this might happen, but you were so damned insistent on testing her. Couldn't you believe what was evident to the eyes?"

Helen sank down onto the wrought iron bench, the coolness of the metal penetrating her gloved hand as she steadied herself on the arm of the bench. Light-headed, she closed her eyes trying to assimilate what was happening.

"Dearie, do ye need my smelling salts?"

She shook her head. "No, I just simply needed to get my bearings, thank you just the same."

A warm presence filled the seat beside her, and she looked into a pair of green eyes so similar to her own. Why had she not noticed the similarity before?

"Are you feeling better, my dear?"

"Yes, thank you." She nodded and looked down at her hands clasped tightly in her lap. "My lord, might I ask … what your family name is?"

"Worthington."

The soft utterance forced her to press her hands against her stomach as a wave of emotion swept over her, threatening to drown her in a sea of chaos. The warmth of the fall air abruptly turned cold, and she shivered as goose bumps cloaked her skin. Inhaling a deep breath, the late blooming flowers were a cloying scent.

"Helen." The gentleness of the earl's voice made her look up at him. "I've been a stubborn, foolish old man, and I want to make amends for all the pain I've caused."

He paused for a long moment, his gaze sweeping out to study the lush landscape in front of them. Anguish carved lines into his features as he continued. "Eleanor is gone, and I cannot secure her forgiveness, but I pray you will let me be the grandfather I should have been to both you and your brother. Do you think it possible for you to allow me that privilege?"

"Good heavens," Lady Stewart exclaimed in a whisper.

The earl's gaze turned back to her, and she shuddered at the knowledge the man sitting next to her was her grandfather. With a quiet sob, she buried her face in her hands and wept. How many times had she dreamt of such a moment, but now that it had happened, it was overwhelming.

A gentle arm pulled her against a solid chest, and over her head, her grandfather released a deep and sorrowful sigh. "Go ahead, child. Cry. Cry for both of us, for although I am joyful to find my grandchildren, I shall never be able to see or hold my beloved Eleanor again."

For a long time, she sobbed quietly in his arms. All the pain she'd experienced at her parents death, the harsh conditions of her uncle's household, her captivity at Chantrel's, the horror of the auction, her fear of Sebastian discovering her love for him and the overwhelming relief of knowing her grandfather wanted her and Edward. Why her uncle had lied to them, she didn't know. All she could understand now was that he'd lied. Every pent up emotion she'd restrained in the past poured forth from her, rolling out of her with a force that sent shudders through her body.

After a time, Helen gulped back the last of her sobs and straightened upright. Wiping the tears from her cheeks, she gladly accepted the handkerchief her grandfather extended to her.

"Thank you," she whispered. The soft linen removed the dampness from her heated cheeks, and a soft sigh parted her lips.

Lady Stewart had moved to stand just behind the bench, and Helen felt the woman's warm hand on her shoulder. She glanced up into a sympathetic gaze, and offered a small smile in return. From a few feet away, Lord Winthrope cleared his throat.

"Well, cousin, I hope you will forgive our charade today. I did try to convince Grandfather otherwise, but--"

"He's as stubborn as mother was." Helen choked back a chuckle mixed with a sob at the memory of her mother's own stubborn nature. "But how did you know? How could you have possibly known who I was?"

Lord Winthrope smiled down at her. "If you'll recall, I asked you if we'd ever met. I knew you looked familiar, but couldn't place you. I asked Grandfather to help refresh my memory, and I must say he gave me a fright with his reaction. When he saw you at the Sherringham affair, it was as if he'd seen a ghost."

The earl captured her hand in his. "When James pointed you out to me, it was as if Eleanor had never left. You look just like her. Your cousin has seen her portrait in the study at Kettering Hall dozens of times, but obviously didn't make the connection."

Helen clasped her grandfather's hand in both of hers. "I can hardly believe this is happening. I brought Edward to London to find you. Uncle Warren said you would never accept us as family, but I couldn't believe that. And life there--"

"Do you mean to tell me your uncle didn't bring you to town?" The earl arched a snowy eyebrow.

Stiffening at the disapproval in his voice, she shook her head. "Edward and I came alone."

"Then how the devil did you end up at Melton House?" The stern note and censure in her grandfather's voice made her skin grow cold. Was he no different than her uncle? Would he condemn her just as Uncle Warren had? Fear swelled up into her throat and she shook her head. "It is complicated."

"Surely, not so complicated that you can't explain it to me." Again, the reprimanding tone resounded with the condemnation she'd always heard in her uncle's voice. She could not live in that type of environment again. She would wither and die. That left her only two options, to find a situation as governess or marry Sebastian. There was Edward to consider. Her happiness was of little consequence compared to his well-being. Resignation pulled a sigh from her mouth as she stood up.

"I think it is time I return to Melton House."

"That is out of the question now," Lord Kettering said arrogantly. "We will collect your brother, and you will come home with me."

"I will not agree to that. Edward and I will not exchange the hellish existence we had with Uncle Warren for another," she snapped.

Lady Stewart and both men stared at her in astonishment, and she cringed at their expressions. One hand pressed to her throat, she struggled to bury the flood of emotions threatening to spiral out of control inside her. A bird in a cage, she could feel the sense the cat approaching her, waiting to swipe its claws at her.

"What the devil are you talking about, child."

Lord Winthrope stepped forward and caught her hand in his. "What is it Helen? There's no need to be afraid."

Overwhelmed by the events of the last half hour, fear tensed her muscles and she jerked free of her cousin's grasp. Watching her, the earl turned his head toward Sebastian's aunt.

"Lady Stewart, do you have any explanation for why my granddaughter is determined to return to Melton House rather than come home to her family?"

"I do not, my lord, but I'm certain that Helen has an excellent reason. However, I have noticed she doesn't respond well to my nephew when he tries to order her about."

The earl stood up, and leaned on his walking stick. "Helen, I'm sorry. It is difficult for an old man to change, but I am willing to do so. What have I said that would make you refuse to come live at Kettering House?"

Her eyes met his pleading gaze, and she trembled. How could she make him understand what she and Edward had experienced at the hand of Uncle Warren? That brutal existence was in the past, but she refused to take another Misstep and place them in a situation that replicated Rivenall Hall. Hands twisting the strings of her reticule, she swallowed the knot in her throat.

"My lord, I will not enter another household where my brother and I are subjected to tyrannical behavior. Why our uncle took us in I don't know, but we would have been far better off left to our own devices than to suffer in that man's company."

"Did this man harm you or your brother in some way?" The earl's puzzled expression reminded her of her mother. "Tell me what he did to you, Helen."

She stared at him for a long moment, debating whether to reveal her secrets to her grandfather, a man she barely knew. Remembering what Lady Stewart had said earlier about Sebastian, she realized how similar they were in temperament. Like him, she'd locked up all of her pain, sadness and anger inside of her. She wanted to bare her soul, but she couldn't. It required too much trust.

"It is of little consequence how my uncle treated us. We are free of him, and I'm resolved in my determination to ensure Edward and I find a safe and comforting home."

"And you shall have it at Kettering House. You're my granddaughter, I want to take care of you, see that you're happy."

"Is that why you took umbrage at my coming to London on my own with only my brother as a chaperone? I admit that was a mistake, but it was a well-intentioned one."

"I wasn't offended, child, simply appalled that your uncle did not take better care of you."

"Please I don't wish to discuss this any further. I need time to think before I decide what's best for Edward and me. So, I'd like to return to Melton House."

The earl heaved a sigh, his white head bent as he studied the path beneath his feet. A moment later, he lifted his gaze to meet hers. "Is there nothing I can say that will convince you to come home with James and me?"

The plea in his voice was filled with a multitude of emotions, and she wanted desperately to respond positively, but she couldn't. It was all too overwhelming. Aware of how much he wanted to make amends, she sighed. "Could we not get to know each other a little better before I make my decision?"

Lord Winthrope leaned toward the earl. "Grandfather, what about Sterling House. It's been empty since Aunt Elizabeth died, perhaps that would resolve this issue. If Helen and the boy took up residence, it would give both of them time to get to know you better."

"A capital idea, boy." The earl's face took on an expression of delight as he clapped his grandson on the back with his hand. Turning to Helen, the older man smiled hesitantly. "Would that suit you, Helen? Sterling House is a small townhouse my sister owned. She left it to me when she died. I believe you would like it very much. It would allow you the freedom you wish, while affording me the pleasure of seeing you often"

Helen hesitated. She turned toward Lady Stewart and the older woman stretched out a hand to her. Accepting it, the Scots woman squeezed her fingers. "Go on, dearie, ye deserve a wee bit of happiness after all ye been through."

The thought of leaving Melton House and Sebastian tore at her heart, but she knew it was the only way to end the pain. Perhaps in time the heartache would ease. Her gaze returned to the hopeful expression on Lord Kettering's face. With a nod of her head, she agreed.

Chapter 17

Sebastian lifted his head at the sound of his aunt's voice in the foyer. The ledger book he'd been trying to read for the past hour lay forgotten. They were home. A sense of uneasiness tugged at him. Would Helen give him the opportunity to express his feelings? Would she even care?

With a grunt of displeasure at his wavering, he pushed himself away from the desk. Emerging into the foyer, he saw the front door close behind his aunt, but Helen was nowhere in sight. A chill pierced him. Where was she? He strode forward to greet his relative.

"Did you enjoy your outing, Aunt Matilda?"

Removing her gloves and hat, she flapped her hands in a gesture of disbelief. "It was delightful and extraordinary. Yer never believe what happened."

The words wrapped a band around his heart, squeezing it painfully. Winthrope had proposed. The impulse to race to the door and look for Helen surged through him, and it was with supreme effort that he fought off the urge to do so.

"Come, have a cup of tea and tell me about it. Is Helen to follow?" The nonchalance in his voice pleased him. He was worried sick as to why his aunt's charge had yet to come through the front door, but she would never have guessed it.

"Ach! That's what I've to tell ye. She's gone on to Sterling House, her grandfather is making arrangements for her to stay there as we speak." The Scotswoman turned back to the butler. "Madison, would ye please have Miss Rivenall's things packed and sent over to Sterling House right away. And pack Master Edward's things as well. I'll take him to his new home after supper."

The words slammed into him with the vicious force of a battering ram. Rooted to the spot where he stood, he watched Lady Stewart sweep into the salon as he struggled to deal with the emotions assaulting him physically. Helen's grandfather. When and where had she met her grandfather?

And she'd not even bothered to say goodbye or to thank him. God knew he didn't want her gratitude, he wanted her. Still the way she'd left stung. Did that cool, serene exterior of hers run so deep that saying goodbye, thank you or something else was unnecessary?

She'd given herself to him for God's sake. How could she just walk away? The fury inside him was an icy wave threatening to possess him and induce him into an irrational display.

If she'd asked him for help, he would have willingly searched for the man. Hadn't he offered assistance in the past? But she'd always refused him.

Anger lashed at his wounds. She hadn't wanted his help. But she'd sure as hell had gone to Winthrope. The knowledge skewered him with a sword of jealousy. Why had she refused his help, but accepted Winthrope's aid? Eyes closed against the power of the pain flowing inside him, he struggled to control it, keep it at bay.

"Damn her," he rasped beneath his breath. "Damn her to hell."

"Come along, nephew, I've much to tell ye."

Lady Stewart's voice echoed out of the salon, and Sebastian strode forward quickly. Seated on the oak trimmed couch with a dark blue print, his aunt looked befuddled. His hands behind his back he came to a halt a few feet from her. Suppressing his emotions, he waited in silence for her to speak.

"Ye would never have believed it, Sebastian. It was just like a fairy tale. The earl of Kettering is Helen's grandfather." Lady Stewart shook her head in amazement. "I'd thought it odd that young Winthrope was accompanying me and the gardener at Kew Gardens while Lord Kettering walked with Helen, but then I just assumed the earl was assessing Helen as Winthrope's potential bride."

Sebastian tried to staunch the flow of despair rushing through him. So was Winthrope really pursuing Helen? He'd thought she'd lied, but now he wasn't sure. Moving to the fireplace, he rested his elbow on the mantle, and stared down at the slate hearth, waiting for his aunt to continue her story.

"While we were walking through the gardens, Lord Kettering confessed he was Helen's grandfather. He disowned Helen's mother years ago and wants to make amends."

"How the devil did Kettering find out about her?"

"Well, Lord Winthrope, who is Helen's cousin, thought she looked familiar, and when he asked his grandfather about her, the earl knew immediately who she was. He joined us this afternoon to confirm that she was his granddaughter."

"And she just agreed to up and leave for her grandfather's house?" Aware of the note of fury in his voice, he laced his fingers together in harsh grasp, hoping to control his tension. The knowledge that she wasn't coming back today, or possibly ever, tightened his chest. What in the hell was he going to do? There had to be some way to reach her.

"Actually, it's a house her grandfather owns, but yes, she

agreed to do just that," Lady Stewart said gently. "After all, Sebastian, he is her grandfather. He's the reason she came to London."

With an explosive movement, he stalked to the window. Twilight had fallen, and the dark blue and purple sky mirrored his gloom. Action. He had to have a plan of action. He could go to Sterling House and demand to see her. No, she could easily refuse to see him. What of Lord Kettering? The old man was a legend in the House of Lords, an orator and visionary, the man might reject any proposal he made to Helen. He might already have plans for her.

Then there was Winthrope. What he wanted to do to the man wasn't feasible. Hundreds of years ago, it would have been easy to do away with a competitor for Helen's affections, but civilized times called for civilized measures. He grimaced at the base manner of his thinking. God help him if this is what love did to a man.

"Give her time, Sebastian."

The soft words of his aunt broke through his primitive thoughts. Turning around, he arched an eyebrow at his maternal aunt. "Time? For what, Aunt Matilda?"

"Do ye really think ye can fool me?"

Tension stiffened his muscles as he met her steady look. With an oath of disgust, he turned away again. How could he give Helen time when the thought of Winthrope panting at her heels filled his gut with jealousy and anger, but most of all, fear.

"Sebastian, why don't ye call on her next week? Give her time to adjust to her new surroundings and grow accustom to the fact that she's found her grandfather. The wee bairn's been through so much."

Unable to answer he nodded and continued to stare out the window. Twilight was gone. The dead of night had settled outside and over his heart as well.

* * * *

Helen sat at the secretaire in the study at Sterling House staring down at the envelope she held. Another of Sebastian's letters. She set it aside unopened. She would return it just like the others she'd received in the past three days. Why did he persist? Had she not made it clear that she wouldn't marry him? She winced at the thought. Was she a fool? Should she marry him and take what little happiness he offered? Glancing down at his strong handwriting on the front of his Missive, she sighed. No, she'd made her decision. She had to believe it was the right one.

A quiet cough made her look up to see Hopkins standing in the salon doorway.

"Yes?"

"The Marquess of Templeton, Miss."

Before she could react, the butler stepped aside to allow the marquess into the salon. Rising to her feet, she smiled politely at her guest. Over the past several weeks, the marquess had been a constant member of the group of men who always sought the right to sign her dance card. She'd found his company pleasant enough, but the memory of their first meeting would always make her uncomfortable whenever he was around.

"My lord, this is a surprise." She held out her hand as he stopped in front of her.

His touch was warm, but again she experienced the sensation of bees crawling across her skin. She shivered. As he straightened, he narrowed his eyes as a perplexed look darkened his features.

"I hope it is a pleasant one."

"Of course," she said as she forced a smile to her lips. Again she was puzzled by her conflicted feelings where this man was concerned. "May I offer you a cup of tea, my lord?"

"No, thank you, my dear. Might I? He gestured toward a loveseat patterned with a light floral print. When she nodded, he took a seat and she sat in a chair opposite the small couch.

"What brings you to Sterling House, my lord?"

"You, my dear."

"Me." The astonishment in her voice curled his lips in a charming smile. It wasn't the first time she'd seen him smile, but this time he actually struck her as handsome. She'd heard about his terrible reputation from so many sources, but she'd often wondered what had prompted him to be disreputable. What would drive a man to earn such notoriety?

"Yes. I've been trying desperately over the past several weeks to come up with a way that I could make amends to you for my behavior the first night we met." When he saw her stiffen, he raised a hand in a placating gesture. "Please, I don't wish to cause you pain by mentioning that night, but if you would simply hear me out."

Swallowing the horror that the memory of Chantrel's always brought, she nodded her head sharply.

"I'm a wealthy man, Miss Rivenall, and yet I've done nothing with my wealth except spend it on fruitless endeavors of sport and pleasure. But in considering how I could somehow prove how much I regret the night in question, I came up with an idea that I wanted to share with you."

Uncertain as to how to respond, she tilted her head in puzzlement. "An idea?"

Sincerity mixed with a look of nervous anxiety as he leaned forward, his hands tightening on the brim of his bowler hat. "Yes, a way to apologize for my depraved behavior. A way to make amends to all those I've hurt in the past. A way to make my amends to you."

The look of hesitation on his face made her feel sorry for him. "What exactly are you proposing to do, Lord Templeton?"

"I'm setting up several safe houses for women who either have no place to go when they arrive in the city, or for women who want to leave an unsavory and hedonistic lifestyle."

Astounded, she simply stared at him. What on earth was driving the man to do such a thing? "I don't know what to say, my lord."

With a nod, he suddenly rose to his feet to pace the floor. "To tell you the truth, I don't quite know what to say myself. I told you several weeks ago that I was turning over a new leaf, and this is part of that transformation. It's a transformation that you're responsible for, Helen."

"And it is a remarkable one, my lord," she said quietly as she swallowed the disbelief cycling through her. The man had to be sincere in his efforts to change. It was an amazing transformation, but to take credit for it made her uncomfortable.

"I was hoping you would do me the great honor of assuming the chair of the trust fund I'm establishing for the oversight of the homes. I believe that your compassion for these women will guide you well in caring for these unfortunate creatures."

The man's generosity and thoughtful plan made her stretch out her hand to him as he halted his pacing.

"You do me a great honor, my lord. I would be happy to help you in this worthwhile venture."

With an exuberant gesture, he grasped her hand in both of his and kissed her fingers. Raising his head, he smiled down at her. "Thank you, my dear. I cannot begin to tell you how happy it makes me to hear you say that. It's no wonder that the whole of London is at your feet given your kind and gracious manner."

A disbelieving laugh escaped her as she gently pulled her hand out of his grasp. "I'm certain that is an exaggeration, my lord."

"No, I think not. Your charm and beauty are heralded in every London club, why only yesterday, I, myself, toasted your charms for at least the third time in as many weeks at the Marlborough Club."

Flummoxed by the man's compliments, Helen shook her head in startled amazement. "I confess, my lord, I don't know what to say."

"Say you believe my sincerity."

There was just a touch of apprehension in his voice as he studied her with a piercing gaze. As she debated how to answer, she watched his gray eyes darken with something she couldn't define. It wasn't malevolent in any way, but it did make her hesitate for a fraction longer than she might have. Slowly, she nodded her head.

"I confess your earnestness is quite evident, Lord Templeton, and I'm flattered by your complimentary observations."

"Each and every one is true, my dear. My solicitor will be in touch with you soon to make arrangements for the foundation's board," he said with a smile. "Well then, with that business matter out of the way, perhaps I could persuade you to join me for a ride in Hyde Park tomorrow morning."

Confused and bewildered by the man's behavior, she shook her head. "I am sorry, my lord, but I don't ride."

"Then I shall teach you." He exclaimed. "Please say you'll come."

"It's very kind of you, Lord Templeton, but I confess I've never been comfortable around horses."

"Then a drive in the park. The weather is still quite lovely."

"Please, my lord, I'm sorry to refuse, but I must."

Straightening, he stood rigidly in front of her. "I can assure you, Miss Rivenall, my intentions are strictly honorable where you're concerned."

Helen rose to her feet and spread her hands in a motion of regret. "I don't doubt you, my lord. I'm simply not available tomorrow."

Hope immediately flashed across his face as he smiled broadly. "Ah, then you are not rejecting me outright. For that, I'm grateful. I shall call on you in a day or two and perhaps I'll be able to persuade you to go for that drive in the park. Until then, I shall leave you to your letter writing."

Alarm bells went off in her head at his words. Good Lord, was the man thinking of courting her? The idea dismayed her. No, that was a ridiculous idea. The marquess wasn't interested in wooing her. Was he?

Habit made her extend a hand to him, and he barely brushed his mouth over her hand in a polite and genteel display.

"Good day, my lord."

"Thank you again, my dear. I look forward to seeing you again quite soon."

With another slight bow, he left her standing in the middle of the study completely baffled by his extraordinary behavior. Never in a thousand years would she have thought the Marquess of Templeton would ever think to open up a haven for prostitutes, let alone ask her to sit on a board to oversee the administration of such a venture. Although the man still unnerved her, his sincerity was obviously genuine, and she was hard pressed to be churlish toward him.

Shaking her head in bewilderment, she gathered her wits and returned to the secretaire. Templeton was quickly forgotten as her fingers trailed over the envelope emblazoned with Sebastian's handwriting. God, how she missed him. Would she always feel this way every time she thought of him? So lost, so empty inside.

"Enough of this maudlin behavior, Helen Rivenall. The past is dead, and you must move on," she whispered in a fierce tone. With a vicious movement, she snatched up the envelope and delivered it to Hopkins for a prompt return.

Later that evening, she was still struggling to rid herself of her low spirits as she entered the Barstow residence for their annual ball. At her side, James gently tapped her elbow.

"Whatever is the matter with you, cousin? You look as though you've lost your best friend."

"I'm fine, just a bit tired from all the social activities. I'm still not accustomed to this whirl of parties."

"Do you wish to return home? If you're not feeling well, we don't need to stay."

She smiled up at him. "No, I'll be fine for the evening, but I think I'll forego any further commitments this week. Some peaceful evenings in front of the fire will go a long way to soothing my spirits."

"Careful you don't pick up *all* of Grandfather's habits." James laughed as he guided her into the main ballroom. They joined a small group of her cousin's friends, and as she stood there listening with a half-hearted ear, a sudden frisson rippled down her spine. Without turning, she knew Sebastian was present. Unable to resist, she peeked over her shoulder and saw him standing against the far wall, his eyes pinned on her.

At the sound of the orchestra striking up a waltz, James turned to her with a smile. "Come, I'll spin you around the room before I'm forced to give you up to your admirers."

Happy for the diversion, she accepted his arm and allowed him to guide her onto the dance floor. To her dismay, the tension she felt didn't evaporate. It was as if Sebastian's hands were caressing the back of her neck instead of simply his gaze. They had barely completed a single turn about the room, when she saw him at the edge of the dance floor. As James spun her around in a fluid movement, Sebastian stepped forward and tapped her cousin on the shoulder.

The arrogance in his expression brokered no rejection, and with a frown, James reluctantly stepped back. The moment Sebastian drew her into his arms she came alive. Everything around her took on a sharper, clearer image. The scent of bergamot on his skin drifted into her nose, and she trembled at the possessive way he held her. Her palms were damp inside her gloves, and the beat of her heart was a loud drum in her ears. Silence hung between them as they danced, and in a quick whirl, he suddenly danced her out onto a small terrace that extended beyond the well-lit dance floor.

Surprised, she stiffened in his arms as he pulled her into a dark corner of the brick patio. "What on earth are you doing?"

"The only thing I can do it seems, when it comes to getting your attention."

With that, he bent his head and sought her mouth in a heated kiss. The sensuous touch of his lips against hers sent her heart slamming against her ribcage, and she shuddered in his arms. She knew it was folly not to offer up any resistance, but it was impossible not to succumb to the pleasure of being in his arms. Giving herself up to the delicious river of desire streaming through her, she parted her lips as his tongue slid across her teeth to tease the inner warmth of her mouth.

The plunging thrust of his kiss reminded her of other intimate moments, and a whimper of need trembled in her throat. The heat of him sank into her limbs, as desire edged its way across her skin like a wildfire. Unable to resist his temptation, she wrapped her arms around his neck and pressed her body into his. As his mouth left hers to caress her cheek, she slanted her mouth across his dark jaw. A low groan rumbled from his throat as he slid his mouth down the side of her neck to nip at her bared shoulder.

"I've missed you. The house is like a tomb without you in it." His words made her heart pound that much harder, and she gasped as his hand brushed over her breast.

"Sebastian, please! You mustn't ... someone might come out."

A growl parted his lips, but to her surprise, he heeded her wish. His hands cupped her face and he gave her a quick kiss. "Why haven't you responded to any of my letters?"

"I ... there's ... little point in doing so."

"For God's sake, Helen, you didn't even read them." There was a note of desperation in his voice that surprised her, and she pressed her fingertips to his mouth.

"I didn't have to. I already knew what was in them," she said quietly. "It wouldn't change anything between us."

At her words, he went rigid. "I see. And yet you melt in my

arms like a woman ready to be bedded. Is this how you act for Dorchester or others in your vast league of admirers?"

"I never denied that I desired you, I simply said I wouldn't marry you."

"Shall I take you for another carriage ride and guarantee you're compromised this time?"

"You wouldn't dare," she snapped. The arrogance of the man. Thinking he could force her into marrying him.

"I admit the thought has crossed my mind on more than one occasion since you left Melton House, but, I prefer to have your grandfather like his future grandson-in-law."

Pushing her way out of his arms, she put some distance between them. "You arrogant bastard. What makes you think my grandfather will even let you plead your case. *Not* that it matters."

"If I'm arrogant for believing what we have is special, then so be it," he bit out through clenched teeth. "But I'll be damned if I let you throw it away over some ridiculous notion that we're not meant for one another when our bodies say something different."

Her insides constricted tightly with anger. Nothing had changed. Desire was all that drove him to possess her. His heart would never be hers. The knowledge slashed through her chest making it difficult to breathe, while she balled her fists in a desperate attempt not to burst into tears. She had to end this now--otherwise she would be lost.

"Desire is a finite emotion, my lord, and where you're concerned, I find the emotion overrated and a poor substitute for another man's embrace."

The raw fury emanating from him was almost tangible. It washed over her like a wave, and even in the darkness, his anger was visible in the tight line of his mouth. There could be no doubt her words had struck deeply at his ego, and she flinched as he stepped toward her in one furious stride.

Whatever he was about to say died in his throat as James stepped out onto the terrace. Relief surged through her veins and she took a quick step in her cousin's direction. "Were you looking for me, James?"

"Yes, it seems Albertson is frantic that he might miss a dance with you," James said with a smile as she stepped out of the darkness. Seconds later, his eyes narrowed as Sebastian emerged from the shadows as well. James glanced down at her. "Are you all right?"

"Yes, quite," she murmured in a strained voice. "His Lordship and I were merely discussing that some things in this world are finite. A concept he finds difficult to acquaint himself with."

The words brought an angry growl out of Sebastian's throat, and she tipped her head back to stare up into the flames of anger blazing in his eyes. The look he raked over her body could only be described as scathing, and it stung. Without speaking a word, he told her exactly what he thought of her.

She'd led him to believe another man held her affections, and his expression revealed a contempt that encased her heart in ice. Swallowing hard, she involuntarily stretched out her hand toward him. Contempt turned his features into a stony mask, and without a word, he brushed past her and stalked away. As his tall, broad shouldered figure disappeared through the terrace doors, Helen's breath hitched on a sob. She'd followed her head in sending him away, but her heart cried out angrily at the foolishness of her actions.

Chapter 18

"Helen, has grandfather arrived yet? He's promised to take me to Tattersalls to look at a horse for me. Can you imagine it? A horse of my own!"

Helen smiled as Edward dashed into the breakfast room at Sterling House. Over the past week, he'd adjusted more easily to the fact that they had a grandfather than she had. Grandfather, the word still seemed strange to her. Despite the earl's gentle prodding it had taken her almost a week to address him so familiarly. Even though it felt strange, she could not deny the warmth and security that came with saying it.

"You know as well as I do that if Grandfather had arrived, he'd be right here. Come, sit down and eat your breakfast. It will be a long time until the noon meal."

With a sigh of resignation, he sat down and reached for a scone and some jam. Refraining from showing any amusement, she bent her head and continued to eat her own meal. Behind her, the butler quietly interrupted her.

"Pardon, Miss, but this just came for you."

Accepting the envelope, she thanked the man. The handwriting on the front of the Missive was identical to the others she'd received. It had been almost a week since Sebastian had danced her out onto the terrace at the Barstow ball. Rejecting him had been the most difficult task she'd ever done. As he'd stalked away from her, he'd taken her heart with him.

She had thought him finished with her, as he'd not written her since that night. Now, as she studied his strong, bold and dashing handwriting she realized she should have known better. He was too methodical and patient to give up so easily. She laid the envelope aside without opening it and returned to eating her meal.

"Aren't you going to open it, Helen?" Edward's quiet question brought her head up.

"No, I'm not."

"Why ever not?" her brother asked as he bit into a scone covered in apricot jam. "I thought you liked the earl."

"And how do you know who it's from?"

"Because you go all stiff like, and you get this sad look on your face whenever you get a note from the earl." The curiosity in his gaze made her gesture toward the eggs he's not yet touched on his plate.

"I think you should eat, Grandfather will be here soon."

They both ate in silence for a short time, then Edward laid down his fork. "Helen?"

"Ummm?"

"Are you in love with the earl?"

The question made her choke on a morsel of ham, and she quickly reached for her glass of milk. When her throat was clear, she glared at her brother. "What on earth makes you ask me such a thing?"

"Well, I've seen how he looks at you, and how you look at him. It just seems to me that you should both get married."

"Edward Rivenall, this conversation is entirely inappropriate. Whom I decide to marry will be my choice and no one else's. And for your information, Lord Melton and I have nothing in common."

The moment the words were out of her mouth, she knew she was wrong. They did have something in common, they had shared a wondrous passion and her heart twisted in her breast at the knowledge she'd never know his touch again.

"Well the least you could do is answer his Lordship's notes. All you do is send them back."

"What I do with Lord Melton's notes is my business."

"Well, it just seems to me that answering his notes might make you a little happier. I mean I've heard you crying at night, and I know you Miss him."

A chill settled over her skin as she felt the color drain from her face. "You're imagining things, Edward."

Stubbornly, the boy dissented with a vigorous shake of his head. "No, I'm not. You cry yourself to sleep, and I know it's because of him."

"What? What's this?" Lord Kettering's voice echoed surprise as he entered the breakfast room.

Startled, Helen jerked her head around to see her grandfather standing in the doorway, an expression of concern on his face. Ignoring the question in his eyes, she forced a smile to her lips. "Good morning, Grandfather. Have you eaten yet?"

"Yes, thank you, Helen." He moved deeper into the room, his tall figure towering over her. "So tell me, who is this mystery man Edward is referring to?"

Before she could speak, her brother answered for her. "It's Lord Melton, Grandfather. I think Helen is in love with him."

"*Edward*," she said between clenched teeth.

Lord Kettering arched an eyebrow at her, then moved forward to tousle Edward's thick blond hair. "You young man, need to learn when it's prudent to hold your tongue. Have you finished eating?"

"Yes, my lord."

"Good, then go check with Cook to see if our lunch is ready. We need to be leaving for Tattersalls in the next few moments."

Without any argument, Edward sprang from his seat and raced from the room. Left alone with her grandfather, Helen avoided his gaze as he sat down at the table. The silence in the room stretched thin until Lord Kettering cleared his throat.

"Helen, is there any truth to what Edward said?" The straightforward manner of the question made her grow still. Slowly, she lifted her head to meet his probing gaze.

"Even if it were true, there would be little point in holding any feelings of such nature for his Lordship."

"I see, so you do not have any feelings for Melton whatsoever?"

In the short time she'd been living at Sterling House, she'd learned quickly how easily her grandfather could solicit the truth from someone, simply by asking the right questions. Questions that left no room for skirting the truth.

"My feelings are of no consequence."

"And your uncle beating you was also of *no consequence*?" Her grandfather's quick display of anger did not surprise her. When he had cajoled the truth from her about Uncle Warren, his fury had been so fierce that she worried he would suffer an apoplectic fit. He'd insisted a doctor examine her, and when apprised of the scars on her back, he'd broken down and wept, blaming himself for her suffering.

"Grandfather, my feelings for Lord Melton are precisely that-- mine. I have no wish to discuss the earl or anything else about him."

"Well the least you can do is put the poor fellow out of his misery."

"Misery?"

"Yes, misery. I've never seen a man so utterly smitten in my life. Not even James and his pining for Lady Blackburn compares to Lord Melton's abject behavior. Why just two days ago, he paid me a visit. It took him nearly fifteen minutes to come to the purpose of his call."

Her heart lurched with fear. Dear Lord, had he asked her grandfather for her hand. She remained silent, afraid her voice would betray the emotions spiraling through her. Across from her, Lord Kettering narrowed his eyes.

"Don't you want to know what his Lordship wanted, Helen? Or perhaps you already know."

For the second time this morning, she could tell the color had drained from her face. "Know what, Grandfather?"

"The man expressed his desire to court you. Court you with the goal of making you his wife."

The words drenched over her like ice water. Unable to move, her trembling fingers toyed with the knife beside her plate. He'd asked permission to court her. Why? Why not just ask for her hand? Did he think her refusal to marry him was because he hadn't courted her? She closed her eyes against the pain striking its way through her. She didn't want to be courted, she wanted to be loved. It was all she wanted, and it was the one thing he didn't know how to give.

"Helen?"

Looking at her grandfather, she shook her head at the unspoken question. "His Lordship has honored me with his request, but I do not wish to consider him as a potential husband."

"I see." Lord Kettering eyed her steadily for a moment. His brow furrowed slightly before he nodded. "If you're certain that's the answer you wish me to give him, then I shall do so. However, I will let you think on it for a day or two."

"I shall not change my mind," she said flatly.

"Perhaps, but at least think it through. Hasty decisions about someone you love often result in a lifetime of pain."

Her gaze flew back to his face. Anguish blanched his face, the pinched expression and lifeless look in his green eyes painfully wrenching her heart with sadness. Springing to her feet, she hurried to his side to give him a swift hug.

"The past is finished, Grandfather, but Edward and I are here for you now. We'll not leave you."

"Thank you, child." He brushed her forehead with a quick kiss, the pain on his distinguished features ebbing away. "Now, I believe I need to go see what your brother is up too. If I'm right, he'll have persuaded Cook to pack two lunch baskets and not one."

She laughed as he rose to his feet. "And we both know you'll hardly receive a bite from either basket."

"Another reason why I should investigate his disappearance," he said with a chuckle. With a quick kiss on her cheek, he smiled. "We shouldn't be gone more than a few hours. Are you certain I can't find a nice, quiet gelding for you?"

"Good heavens, no. I wouldn't know what to do with a horse." Laughing once more, Helen pressed a kiss to his cheek, and watched him depart from the breakfast room. Alone in the room, her gaze focused on the note card beside her plate. Should she open it? No, it would only bring heartache to read his false platitudes. Irritated with herself for even considering the possibility of opening the letter, she hurried to the place setting, and scooped up the envelope. Her stride purposeful, she went into the foyer and left the note with the butler, instructing him to return it. Satisfied with her willpower in doing so, she walked into the study.

The warmth of the small room brought a sense of peace to her. Despite its size, it had become her sanctuary. Upon discovering that she enjoyed reading, her grandfather had shipped several boxes of books to Sterling House. Although he'd told her to redecorate the house as she wished, she'd refused. The simplicity of the décor suited her, and the study in particular made her feel at home.

Picking up the book she'd been reading, she curled up into the window seat overlooking the garden along the side of the house. The novel was one her grandfather had suggested. He'd expressed a secret indulgence in the works of American authors Nathanial Hawthorne and Edgar Allan Poe. She smiled as she recalled his quip that if losing the colonies meant the development of such magnificent writers, he was glad of it.

It was a pleasant discovery to find her tastes in literature ran in a similar vein to her grandfather. With the books he'd provided her, she'd willingly devoted her free time to reading. Eager to retreat into another world where her love for Sebastian didn't torment her so harshly, she tried to focus on the book in her hands. It was difficult to do, but after a long battle, the story blocked all her thoughts except for what was on the page. The time passed quickly, and a quiet knock announced the entrance of the downstairs maid.

"Begging your pardon, Miss, but there's a coach and driver waiting outside for you. The driver says there's been an accident and your grandfather wants you to come straight away."

Fear spread its way through her with the insidious strength of an ivy vine growing out of control. Trying to control the panic that dried her mouth, she scrambled out of the window seat. "Thank you, Martha. Would you fetch my hat and gloves for me? There's no time to change."

Following the maid out into the foyer, Helen accepted the accessories handed to her. The man standing in the entryway was of medium height and dressed in nondescript clothes. Something about the man tugged at her. It was a vague recollection, but she couldn't begin to place the memory. Ignoring the odd thought, she reminded herself that fear always drove one's imagination wild. Worry about her brother and grandfather spiked to a higher pitch, and she settled her hat on her head.

"Can you tell me what type of accident my grandfather was in, sir?" Her question made the man hesitate, and she immediately thought the worst. "Is my grandfather all right? My brother?"

"They're banged up right good, but your grandfather reckoned it would be best for the boy if ye came quick." The man brushed the brim of his ratty looking cap as he spoke.

"How did the accident happen? Where did it happen?"

"Don't rightly know how it happened Miss. They'd just left Paddington Station when their carriage turned over somehow."

"Oh dear lord." Helen breathed in a sharp breath at the thought of her grandfather and Edward being hurt. With a quick look at the maid, she tugged on her gloves. "Martha, hopefully his lordship and Master Edward are not too badly injured. Have Hopkins send for a doctor. Paddington Station isn't too far away, so we should be back within the hour."

Without waiting for the maid to respond, Helen followed the driver out to the black lacquered coach. The roughly dressed man was already in the driver seat, but the door of the carriage stood open. Dismissing the oddity of the man's behavior as a need to hurry, Helen entered the vehicle and closed the door behind her.

Instinct screamed danger the moment the door snapped shut. Seated in the far corner was her uncle. Before she could lean out the window and cry for help, he sprang forward with the speed of a striking snake. His white handkerchief pressed against her nose, stifling and smothering her. Clawing at him, weightless sensation sped its way through her body and her vision became blurred. As she struggled to stay awake, the last thing she saw was the hatred and disgust in her uncle's beady eyes.

* * * *

Helen shivered. Goose bumps layered her skin, and she slowly opened her eyes. Pushing herself up on her elbows, she stared around at her surroundings. The bed she was on had an expensive coverlet on it, but there were no draperies or canopy hanging from the four tall posters. A washstand stood in one corner and a desk in the opposite corner. The only light source, other than a single window, was a branch of candles on the night table. There was no other furniture in the room.

Another shiver shuddered through her. Glancing down, she understood why she was so chilled. The only thing she wore was a chemise and her underskirt. Her gown, shoes and stockings had been removed and were nowhere in sight. Sitting up, she rubbed her hands over her arms to warm them.

Fear assailed her as she wondered where her uncle had taken her and why. How was it possible for a man to hate his flesh and blood so much? She'd never understood that about her uncle.

Her bare feet hit the cool wood planks of the room's floor, and she padded her way to the door. Twisting the knob, she sighed with disgust. Of course, it would be locked. She turned and walked to the window, her hands rubbing over her arms in attempt to ward off the chilly air.

The window overlooked the small space between two town houses, and in the fading light, she could see she was at least two or three stories up. A nervous churning ripped through her stomach, and she quickly swallowed the bile rising in her throat. What did her uncle mean to do with her? Behind her, a key scraped its way into the lock, and the door opened to reveal Warren Rivenall. Entering the room, he locked the door behind him and tossed a robe in her direction.

"Cover yourself, girl."

Grateful for the covering, Helen stooped to retrieve the garment from the floor. Slipping the robe over her shoulders, she tied it securely in place before looking at the man across from her.

"Why have you brought me here, Uncle Warren?"

"Because you're a harlot, and harlots are only good for being sold to the highest bidder."

The characterization made her swallow hard, and she shook her head firmly. "I'm not a harlot."

"Then tell me you've not slept with Melton. Tell me you didn't use your feminine wiles to enslave more than a dozen men over the last month. You're every bit the strumpet your mother was."

Furious, she drew up straight. "You're a liar! My mother was a lady."

"No, girl." His lips curled back in a feral smile. "It's how she trapped that miserable brother of mine into marriage. Your wanton mother parted her legs for him, and then she had the audacity to refuse me the same pleasure."

The words of hate pouring from him made her gasp. "You were in love with her."

"No. I desired her," he snarled. "I could never love a harlot."

"And because I look like her, you punished me."

"I only punished you for your sins, never for anything else. The Good Lord knows you're evil and so do I. Tempting men, teasing them, you'll rot in hell for it, but before that, you'll at least have some semblance of respectability. I've seen to that."

"What are you talking about?" Another sliver of fear spiked its way beneath her skin.

"I've made arrangements for your marriage. Something I should have done a long time ago."

"What arrangements?" She tried not to let her fear show, but her voice quavered nonetheless.

"Given your Cyprian behavior, I've made you a spectacular match. What man would want soiled goods such as you is beyond me, but then I suppose the Marquess is an unusual man."

"The ... Marquess?"

Helen watched her uncle's face twist into an evil smile. Horror raced its icy hand over her skin, and she couldn't hide the tremor that shook through her.

"Yes, niece. Lord Templeton has offered a substantial settlement in exchange for your hand in marriage. I couldn't pass up such an opportunity for you. It's likely the only offer you'll ever have once news of your harlotry circulates this den of sinners called London."

Nausea swirled in her stomach, and she pressed her hand to her stomach in an attempt to calm the churning inside her. Staring at her uncle, she saw the pleasure he took in tormenting her. He enjoyed seeing her misery. He fed off it. Anger, hatred and pain welled up inside her, alleviating her queasiness. Defiant she straightened to her full height and narrowed her eyes.

"I won't marry him."

The quiet firmness in her voice made her uncle's head jerk back as if she'd slapped him. Fury flared in his gaze as his hand swung out to hit her. Without thought, she blocked his swing with one hand. A purplish hue rose beneath his cheeks.

"By God, girl, you'll pay for that."

"If you think I'll cower before you, think again. You hit me because it makes you feel strong and mighty. But you're not. You're a coward, uncle. A man without honor who flays the innocent because of some twisted notion of unrequited love."

The hatred and anger in his face made Helen flinch, but she stood her ground as he took a step toward her. Something in her face made him pause, and with a snort of fury, he stormed from the room. Relief cascaded through her in the form of violent tremors. Turning, she clutched at the bed poster and rested her forehead against the cool wood. Dear God, she'd known all along he hated her, but had never known the reason until now.

He'd been in love with her mother, and her mother's rejection had twisted his heart. He was a monster. A sound behind her made her turn her head, and she saw her uncle storming toward her with his riding crop. Before she could move, he'd ripped her robe offer her shoulders and the leather tip lashed through her thin chemise. The pain jerked a scream from her lips as the crop fell upon her back a second time. She tried to run, but she tripped over the robe tangling her arms and legs. Sprawled on the floor, she screamed again as he whipped her a third time.

Whimpering, she scrambled across the floor trying to escape the lash of his crop. The sound of a door flying open and bouncing off the wall reverberated in the room.

"God damn it, Rivenall, you'll kill her."

The whip came down on her back once more. "She's my charge. She's defied me and now she'll pay."

"No." Lord Templeton's steely shout barely registered with Helen as she waited for the leather thong to hit her again. A sickening thud hit the floor close to her, and through her tears, she saw her uncle rubbing his jaw as he sat up. The look of hate in his gaze sickened her, and she grasped the bedpost to pull herself up from the floor. A gentle touch to her elbow made her jerk, and she looked up to see Lord Templeton at her side.

"I'm sorry, Helen. I would have spared you this had I known the man meant you harm."

Without answering him, she jerked free of his touch. Why was he doing this? He'd led her to believe he'd reformed. How could he be a part of this? Even more horrifying was the knowledge that he was actually dismayed at the way her uncle had beat her. She watched him stoop to pick up her robe and she snatched it from his hand as he offered it to her. As quickly as her stinging back would allow her, she covered herself with the garment.

"Forgive me if I question your sincerity, my lord."

The man frowned then turned to Helen's uncle who had scrambled to his feet. "You've received your money, Rivenall. Now get the hell out of my house."

Her uncle glared at them both. "You've bought yourself nothing but a harlot, Templeton. Why you insist on marrying the whore--"

The soft click of a pistol halted her uncle's speech. Helen froze in horror as the marquess pointed the weapon directly at the other man's forehead. His mouth twitched wildly as the Marquess glared at the other man.

"If I ever hear you speak about Helen like that again, I'll kill you." The softly spoken words carried a deadly intent that was all the more insidious due to the quiet, even tone of Templeton's voice. "Now get out."

She watched her uncle swallow convulsively, before he sent her a final scowl of hatred and strode from the room. Trembling, she took a step back as Lord Templeton turned toward her. He uncocked the small pistol and placed it back in the inside pocket of his jacket.

"I'm truly sorry about all this, Helen. I'll send for the doctor."

"No." She stood straight and tall as she sent him a contemptuous look. "Let me go home so that someone can tend to me there."

He frowned, his head bent in contemplation. A long moment later, he raised his head to look at her. "I can't do that Helen. I intend to marry you."

"And if I refuse."

A cold look swept over his features that made her shiver in spite of her determination to stand up to him. "You won't refuse me, Helen. Accept the fact that we're to be married."

"I will not marry you," she snapped.

"Would you marry me if I were to tell you I love you?"

The question astonished and appalled her in the same instance. Her hand flew to her throat, clutching the material of her robe at the neck. "You jest, my lord."

"I wish to God that I did, Helen, but even the wicked occasionally fall victim to the tangled web of love."

"I'm sorry … I … I've never said or done anything to make you think I might care for you, my lord."

The bitter laugh escaping his thin lips made her flinch. "Of course you didn't, and that's precisely why I fell in love with you. I told myself it was just my need to best Melton. That day on Bond Street, I even told Melton you'd make a wonderful marchioness. You've been nothing but gracious and ladylike whenever you've spoken to me, even in spite of how we first met. I think I knew then that I loved you and wanted you for my wife."

"Please don't say that."

"What? That I love you?" He scowled at her. "Why? Are you afraid Melton might suddenly despise you because of my love?"

"No, I … please … you must understand I don't love you."

"Perhaps not now, but in time--" He paused as he stared into space for a moment. "In time you'll come to care for me. You'll want for nothing, and I'll even take care of your brother as well. I only ask that you try to love me."

"I'm sorry, I can't do that."

His face grew dark with a surge of angry color. "Why? Because you still hold out hope for Melton to declare his undying love for you? If so, you'll be waiting a very long time. The man's not capable of the emotion."

"That's not true. He's simply afraid to love. I …." Her voice trailed off at the fury on the marquess' face.

"So what they say is true. You're in love with the man."

Horrified he'd discovered her secret, she shook her head vehemently. "No, I don't--"

"Don't lie to me," he snarled. "Do you take me for a fool simply because I've told you I love you?"

"No, I'm sorry."

He stared at her for a long moment. "I don't expect you to develop feelings for me overnight, Helen. But I will be a good husband to you. I promise you that."

Without waiting for her to answer, he turned and left the room. As the door closed behind him, she heard the key turn in the lock. Collapsing onto the bed, Helen pushed back the urge to burst into tears. The idea of Lord Templeton saying he loved her had shocked her to the point of incoherent thought.

What was she going to do? She pressed the palm of one hand to her forehead. Glancing toward the window, she saw the sun had faded until night had swallowed up the day. Would her grandfather be able to find her? Would anyone tell Sebastian she was Missing? Would he even care? Would he come looking for her? Would he think to visit Templeton?

She was a fool to even think the man would come. Sebastian wasn't in love with her anymore than the marquess was. Both men lusted after her, but neither of them knew what true love was. They both wanted to possess her, not love her.

Hunching her shoulders in a gesture of defeat, she gasped as the muscles pulled on the wounds over her back. She'd endured worse beatings than this, but the sting was a brutal reminder of her uncle's hatred. A hopeless feeling sank into her bones, and she crawled up toward the pillow. Pressing her face into the goose feather headrest, she wept with an intensity she'd not done since the death of her parents.

Chapter 19

Sebastian sat at his worktable in the library. The mantle clock chimed the dinner hour, but the thought of food turned his stomach. In front of him spread out on the mahogany surface were his letters to Helen. He took a swig of Scotch, grimacing at the taste. Alcohol had never been a pleasurable pastime for him, but tonight he intended to drink himself into a stupor. Perhaps then he might find some peace from the torment wracking his body.

His gaze returned to the envelopes spread before him. She hadn't even opened them. Not one. Each letter he sent her had been confessions of his soul and his love for her. They'd been difficult enough to write, but to have them returned unopened-- what was he going to do? How could he reach her if she refused even to let him beg her forgiveness? With a groan, he rested his head in his hands. He'd been a fool. Misery overtook him, pounding at him with the persistent beat of a hammer.

The sudden sound of male voices outside the study pierced his suffering. Lifting his head, he watched the study door fly open with a vicious crack. The sight of Lord Winthrop striding into the room pulled him out of his chair with a whip like movement. What the hell was this bastard doing here?

"What the hell do you want, Winthrope." The snarl in his voice made the other man frown darkly.

"Your help."

At Winthrope's statement, a bitter laugh parted Sebastian's mouth. The man had stolen Helen from him, and now he wanted his help? The man could rot in hell for all he cared. He shook his head.

"My help? Not bloody well likely."

"Then perhaps you'll consider my request, Melton." The Earl of Kettering followed closely on the heels of his grandson as both men invaded Sebastian's private hell. As the older man crossed the floor to face him, his green eyes pinned Sebastian with a sharp stare. The remarkable similarity to Helen's gaze made him flinch. He turned away and took another drink of whiskey.

"And what could you possibly want from me, Kettering?"

"Before I tell you, I need to ask you a question. Do you love my granddaughter?"

A bullet could not have caused more shock or pain to lance

through his body. Stiffening, he paused for a long moment. Without turning around, he shrugged. "It's hardly relevant given that your granddaughter doesn't want anything to do with me."

"Damn it, man! Answer the bloody question."

Wheeling about, Sebastian glared at the earl. For the first time, he noted the strain and worry on the earl's face. Instinctively he knew something was terribly wrong. The desperation in Kettering's eyes made him swallow the expanding knot of fear in his throat.

"Yes, I love her." he growled through clenched teeth.

Kettering nodded and leaned heavily against his walking stick, his air one of age and weariness. "Then prepare yourself, my boy, my news is far from good. Helen is missing."

The world spun around him, and Sebastian clutched at the tabletop to steady himself. Winthrope came to his side, but Sebastian righted himself and brushed the man's offer of assistance aside in a brusque gesture. One hand still gripping the edge of the furniture, he steadied himself and met the earl's worried look.

"When? How?"

"Early this afternoon, while Edward and I were at Tattersalls."

"This afternoon," Sebastian's explosive tone echoed around the room.

"I didn't find out about it until I returned a short time ago. As soon as I discovered her Missing, I sent for James, and we came here straightaway. I had thought ..." The elderly man shook his head. Somehow, he was certain the earl had hoped to find Helen at Melton House.

"Tell me what you know," Sebastian said in a tight voice.

The earl nodded his head toward the decanter of Scotch on Sebastian's worktable. "Pour me a drink then, and let me sit down. This entire affair has been a devastating blow."

Filling another glass with the liquor, Sebastian offered the man the drink. In silence, he glanced at Winthrope and arched his eyebrow before sending a pointed glance toward the decanter. The younger man shook his head, the tension between them only slightly diluted. Kettering sank down into one the chairs facing the worktable, and took a deep draught of the Scotch. When finished, he lifted his head.

"A carriage called for Helen about mid-morning, and according to the household staff, the driver indicated Edward and I had been in an accident outside of Paddington Station. The driver said I had sent the carriage to bring Helen to me. She didn't hesitate, why should she? I'd promised her that her uncle would never be able to touch her again."

"Are you sure it's Rivenall behind this? Did anyone see the man?"

"No, the person the servants saw was the driver. But who else could it be?" Winthrope exclaimed with a note of bitterness.

"Templeton."

"*Templeton.*" Grandfather and grandson spoke at the same time.

"How much has Helen told you about how we met?" Sebastian asked softly.

The men both shook their heads, and Kettering frowned. "She's been more tight-lipped about it than a bull terrier. Not even her mother was ever so elusive to pin down."

Sebastian bent his head, uncertain how to proceed. Returning to the worktable, his fingers caressed the letters on his desk. "The night I met Helen, Morehouse and I were investigating the possibility of young women being kidnapped and sold at private brothel auctions."

"What the hell does any of this have to do with my cousin?"

Directing Winthrope a scathing look, he continued without pause. A quick glance at the earl revealed that the man's face had gone gray. Unable to spare the man, he looked away.

"When we arrived, Chantrel invited us in to a private auction. Helen was the woman up for sale that night. Morehouse and I were thoroughly disgusted. Then when the bidding started and Templeton bid a thousand pounds--"

"Sweet Jesus," Winthrope choked out the exclamation.

"I knew I couldn't let her go to Templeton, so I outbid the man for her."

"*What?*"

He ignored Winthrope's cry of outrage. The memory of the moment washed over him once more, the disgust he'd felt at the event, his astonishment at his own bid, the censure of his friend and his own lustful feelings for a woman he'd only laid eyes on less than a few minutes before.

"And you think Templeton might be the one behind her disappearance?" Kettering asked quietly.

Sebastian frowned. "What reason would Rivenall have for kidnapping Helen? Templeton has everything to gain, Rivenall nothing."

"Then we need to go to Templeton's home this very moment."

"He'll be expecting that." Sebastian shook his head at Winthrope's impulsive exclamation. "No, if he's responsible for Helen's disappearance, he'll be careful to remain above suspicion."

"Well, we bloody well can't just stand around here twiddling our thumbs," Winthrope snapped.

"And if Templeton does have her, we can't endanger her by charging in without a plan."

His hands balled into fists, he eyed the viscount coldly. Holding back his fury, he strode to the window overlooking the back of the house. With one hand, he gripped the window sash. Think. He had to think. If he were Templeton, where would he take Helen? Fear gagged him. He didn't have an answer or a plan. The knowledge frightened and horrified him more than the night his mother had died. He knew now her death had been an accident, something he'd had no control over.

Surprisingly, it occurred to him that he'd never been in control of anything in his life. Until Helen had entered his life, he'd been emotionally dead. His ability to command every situation's outcome had been an illusion. The only thing he could count on now was his ability to think, plan and organize. And God help him if he failed to find her.

* * * *

Sebastian sank down into the leather chair facing the fireplace. Elbows on his knees he leaned forward and rested his hands on the back of his head. Two days. She'd been gone two days. He'd had private detectives scouring the city for any word on Rivenall's and Templeton's activities, but neither man had been seen. Where had the bastard taken her? He'd had men go to Paddington Station and retraced every possible path back to Sterling House, questioning people along the way. He'd Missed something. Somewhere he'd overlooked a clue.

It was as if she'd disappeared into thin air. One of the detectives standing watch over Templeton House, and had managed to become friendly with one of the stable hands. While the stable hand hadn't been on duty the night Helen was kidnapped, he hoped the man would at least prove valuable if Templeton suddenly left town. Heavy boots thundered against the floor behind him.

Turning his head, he watched Winthrope charging into the library with Lord Morehouse at his side. The horror on their faces made him leap to his feet.

"What?"

The men looked at each other before Morehouse swallowed hard. "The Ripper's killed another woman in Whitechapel."

"What the hell does that have to do with Helen?" Sebastian frowned. Winthrope blanched at his question and looked at Morehouse. Frustrated by their hesitation, he glared at them both. "Out with it. What does it have to do with Helen?"

"The woman was so brutally mutilated, they've not been able

to identify the body …" Morehouse hesitated.

"Out with it Devin. What are you getting at with all this?"

"The victim had hair the same color as Helen."

Morehouse's reply slashed through him with a furious dull roar as he stumbled backward and sank into his seat. Immediately, his friend hurried to his side. "It's not her, Sebastian, I'm certain it's not, but we wanted to tell you before one of the detectives mentioned it. You know how they are. Believing they have to give you every last gory detail."

"But what if I'm wrong. What if Rivenall was the one who took her and not Templeton. It would be like Rivenall to take her to Whitechapel … try to sell her to someone …" Sebastian shuddered at the terrible direction his mind was taking him.

Helen's uncle was more than capable of doing just that. Selling her into prostitution. It would suit the man's twisted sense of righteousness. No, he couldn't think that way. If Rivenall was involved in any of this, it had to be because of Templeton. He wouldn't let himself consider any other possibilities.

She was alive, and she was with Templeton. And by God, he was going to find her. But how? Rising to his feet, he moved to the fireplace and gripped the mantle. The small flames licking at the wood in the hearth appeared to be fighting a losing battle with the thick log. The futility of the flames efforts reflected his own sense of overwhelming desperation.

A soft rustle of silk and taffeta made him stiffen as he heard his aunt enter the room. His entire family was concerned, but his aunt and Louisa were feeling the strain more deeply. Kettering had already succumbed to the stress of the search, and was now under a doctor's care. Edward had wanted to assist in the search for his sister, but Sebastian had convinced him to remain with his grandfather. Straightening, he clasped his hands behind his back and turned to face his aunt.

Fear lined her face, and the concern gave her the appearance of having aged years in just the past two days. Grimly, he shook his head at her unspoken question. The stalwart Scotswoman heaved a sigh of worry as Morehouse cleared his throat.

"Where do you want us to look next, Sebastian?"

"I don't know." Even he could hear the desolation in his voice.

"Perhaps we should send someone to the Rivenall's home to wait for his return," Morehouse murmured.

"No, if he's not returned by now, he won't show until whatever Templeton has planned comes to pass."

Sebastian stared at Helen's letters strewn about on the worktable. He was out of ideas, and he didn't know where to turn. He stared at the floor, as if doing so would spark some plan in his head.

"Damn it! We can't just stand around and do nothing." Winthrope's explosion caused Sebastian's head to jerk upward.

"What do you suggest, Winthrope? Storm Templeton's mansion? If she's there, he's bloody well not going to let you just walk in and take her. I've not called in the police simply because they'll pay the man a visit, and if she is inside, he'll deny it. But he'll know we're on to him and God knows what he'll do to her then."

Winthrope paled at the icy condemnation. "You're right, Melton. I know you're doing everything you can."

"He's simply worried, Sebastian. We all are," Lady Stewart said softly. Her Scottish burr more pronounced from lack of sleep.

With an abrupt nod of his head, Sebastian turned away. His hands curled into fists, he wanted to hit something, strike out against the pain and frustration assaulting every inch of him. Out in the foyer, the marble echoed with the sound of running feet as Louisa flew into the library, her hands tugging her hat off her head.

"Sebastian! I know what Templeton is planning to do!" Morehouse glared at her as she plowed past him. With a triumphant smile, she hastened across the floor to her brother's side.

"I know how much you despise paying my clothing bills, but they've finally paid off. I visited Bond Street to see if any of the modistes had received any special orders lately." Louisa inhaled a deep breath as she plunged forward. "Orders for new gowns from unusual sources. Gowns for special occasions."

Sebastian stared at his sister. If Templeton did have Helen, he would need clean clothes for her. Why the devil hadn't he thought of that. Then as her last comment sank into his weary brain he froze. Damnation, Templeton had told him that Helen would make an excellent marchioness. As his gaze met Louisa's she nodded as if able to read his thoughts.

"Madame Fontaine received a wedding gown order for the future marchioness of Templeton a week ago. It's to be delivered to Templeton Manor this afternoon. Madame Fontaine told me she's delivering the gown herself. If the gown needs alterations, she'll do them there as the wedding is to take place tonight."

"Like hell it will," he exclaimed with renewed energy. He reached out and pulled Louisa into a tight hug. "Remind me never again to lecture you about overages on your clothing allowance, little one."

"Go to her, Sebastian," Louisa whispered in his ear as she

hugged him back. "Bring her home where she belongs."
 Releasing his sister, he strode toward his Morehouse and Helen's cousin. "We'll take two carriages. Devin, I want you and Winthrope to take the unmarked coach to the mews behind Templeton's. If anyone tries to leave, stop them. I'm going to pay a long overdue visit to the marquess."
 "Sebastian, are ye sure that's wise. The mon might be dangerous. What's to prevent him for hurting ye?"
 The concern in his aunt's voice made him cross the room to take her hand. He squeezed her fingers with silent reassurance. "Send word to Kettering that we've found her. And send for the doctor, we might have need of him."
 Lady Stewart nodded her head, eyes glistening with tears. With a quick spin of his heel, he turned and strode quickly from the room with an air of determination.

* * * *

Helen paced the floor of her prison, the wood cold against her bare feet. It had been two days since her uncle had brought her to Templeton's. Her captivity had been filled with visits from the marquess, which left her uncomfortable and fearing for her future. He seemed determined to marry her whether she wished it or not. But would there be a reverend willing to marry them if she was unwilling?
 Time had passed slowly with her only visitor, aside from the marquess, being the maid who brought her meals and bathwater. It had given her plenty of time to try and develop an escape plan, but with little success. There weren't enough bed covers to tie together for a makeshift rope, and there was nothing to use to pick the lock. And even if she were to get out of the room, getting out of the house would no doubt be just as difficult. She'd even thought about hitting the maid over the head with the candle branch, but she couldn't bring herself to do it. The poor woman looked just as terrified as she felt.
 The familiar sound of the key in the lock broke the silence, and she turned toward the door. Her only clothing still consisted of her chemise and the robe, and she clutched the collar of the robe closed. The marquess entered the room, his expression one of supreme satisfaction.
 "Good afternoon, my dear. You must forgive me for not visiting you this morning. I was seeing to last minute preparations."
 "Preparations?" The word caught in her throat to emerge in a whisper.
 "Our wedding, my dear Helen. I've settled all the arrangements, and we'll be husband and wife tonight. The

dressmaker will be here shortly to fit your wedding gown."

"I won't marry you."

"We shall see, my dear. All brides are nervous, but there is no need for you to be. I've seen to everything, and we're going to be quite happy."

The marquess strode toward her, the back of his hand caressing her cheek with a gentle stroke as he stopped in front of her. The gentleness of his touch revolted her, and she struggled to hide her distaste.

"Don't touch me." She stepped back from him.

Anger tightened his mouth into a paper-thin line at her rejection. His hand snapped out to capture her neck in a cruel grip. "That will be the last time you ever say that to me, Helen. As your husband, you'll not deny me my rights."

His head bent and he took her mouth in a harsh kiss. Stunned, she froze. It was the first physical advance he'd made toward her during her captivity, and it horrified her. Bile churned its way up into her closed throat, choking her. A second later, she was free. Fear guided her instincts, and she turned away so he couldn't see her revulsion. She had no idea what would happen if he saw how much he sickened her.

"I'll leave you to contemplate our wedding night, my dear. It will be one of many loving nights in our future."

She didn't turn or look up until she heard the key locking the door. Swaying slightly she wiped her mouth with the back of her hand as if she could remove his vile touch. There had to be some way she could escape. No one knew where she was, and she had only herself to rely on as always. With a noise of frustration, she hit the wooden bedpost with her fist. Had she Missed something?

Moving to the window, she threw up the sash and leaned out. Even if there was something she could tie the bed sheets to, she didn't have enough to reach halfway down the side of the house. Glancing to either side of the window, she noticed a small ledge lining the house just below the windowsill. No, it was anything but a ledge, it was more like a ridge not even as wide as her biggest toe. Above the short window span, another decorative stone casement protruded from the wall, offering the semblance of a handhold. She looked down and swallowed the fear threatening to freeze her muscles.

The wind blew in a small amount of the drizzle that fell from the gray sky above as she looked at the two ridges again. Slowly, her gaze followed the inch-wide footing to where it ended at the back of the house. The low roof of what looked to be stables jutted out toward the house. If she could reach the end of the ledge, it would only be a short drop down onto the stable rooftop. From there it would be a longer drop to the ground, but it would be worth the risk.

The granite looked slick from the light rain, and she hesitated. The odds were against her making it to the roof of the low-lying building, but she couldn't remain here. She wouldn't marry Templeton. She had to do something. Her mind made up, she removed her robe.

Grabbing the window frame, she pulled herself up onto the sill and crouched there for a moment. Slowly, she turned her body and slid one foot out onto the tiny ridge of stone. Her fingers dug into the wooden slats of the shutter bordering the window. Blood tasted salty in her mouth as she bit her lower lip in concentration. With careful precision, she straightened until her body was balanced partly on the stone ridge and the windowsill, while her fingertips sought a firm grip along the ridge above her head.

The rain had soaked through her chemise already and she suppressed a shiver. She wished she could borrow some of Sebastian's steely control at the moment. She wasn't just wet and cold, she was frightened. Any unplanned movement would send her falling three stories to the ground, and the thought wasn't a pleasant one. Gradually and painstakingly, she moved forward. As she gained ground inch by inch, she found that sliding her feet lengthwise along the ridge was the best way to achieve a stable position.

With her chest pressed against the granite façade, the rough exterior pricked at her chemise. Her senses attuned to everything, the rain splattered against her face in flat plops while she breathed in the damp smell of granite. Carefully, she inched one foot forward along the almost nonexistent foothold, before sliding her fingertips along the ridge she clung to with such tenacity. She then repeated the process with her other foot and hand.

Her hair lay plastered against her neck, while her chemise molded against her figure like a slick, second skin. Although the cold rain eased the sting, the rough surface of the ridge beneath her feet tore at the tender skin of her soles. Already the nerve endings were telling her to stop moving, but she ignored the pain. It would be difficult to walk if she reached the ground, but if she could at least make it to the street, she could find help. No not if, when. She was going to do this. It wasn't that much further.

As she continued her perilous journey along the wall, she began to question the wisdom of her present course of action. Sebastian had been right. She never thought things through. From leaving her uncle's home to trusting Madame Chantrel to giving herself to Sebastian, everything she'd done in the last two months had smacked of irrational thinking. Now here she was clinging to a wall several stories above the ground. Hysterical laughter threatened to break from her.

Her concentration lost for a brief moment, her foot slipped off its narrow foothold. Terror surged through her veins as she bit off her cry, her teeth sinking into her lip.

* * * *

Sebastian ordered the carriage to halt several houses down from Templeton's place. He would walk the rest of the way. Surprise would serve him well if there was nothing to announce who he was.

Emerging from the vehicle, the cool rain dripped off his coat collar to dampen his neck. He ignored the discomfort as he walked toward the marquess' home. His insides jerked with spasms of dread. Had Templeton forced himself on Helen? The idea horrified him. He should have paid closer attention to the man's activities. Templeton House loomed before him, and he came to a halt.

He didn't have a plan.

The thought floored him. With typical Rockwood style, he'd charged out of the house intent only on saving the woman he loved. No plan, no idea of what he was doing. What the devil was he going to say to the marquess? How was he going to get to Helen?

Once more, his mind lumbered to a halt. He couldn't think. Over the sound of the rain and light traffic, his senses detected something out of place. The hair on the back of his neck rose with the sensation when he heard a soft cry of fear, followed by the light reverberation of crumbling rock.

He glanced around, his nerves tingling and alert. Nothing seemed out of order, as he peered down the gloomy expanse of space between Templeton's home and the house next door. Instinct forced his gaze upward, and his mouth went dry with fear as he saw Helen struggling to regain a foothold against the side of Templeton's house.

Frozen, he watched in horror as her foot fought to reclaim its precarious position on an invisible ledge. Seconds later, her body regained its tenuous hold against the wall. The moment she steadied herself against the side of the house, the paralysis fled his body. In one giant stride, he leapt for the wrought iron gate blocking off the narrow stretch of grass between the houses.

Panic clutched his heart as he watched her continue to creep forward along the perilous path. If she were to fall--with quiet stealth so as not to startle her, he raced to stand just beneath her.

Watching her clinging to the wall, his heart thudded painfully against his chest. How had she gotten so far along the wall without falling? From the height of her position, a fall would be fatal without someone standing below to catch her as she fell.

"Helen." He spoke her name softly, terrified his voice might disturb her concentration and cause her to slip. There was only a slight hesitation in her movement, as if she'd heard him but discounted the sound. "*Helen.*"

This time she paused more noticeably. His gaze never left her rain-soaked figure as she dropped her head to look down. The moment her eyes met his, relief swept across her features. She closed her eyes, then opened them again as if to confirm she wasn't hallucinating.

"You're not dreaming, Helen. I'm here, my love."

She pressed her cheek against the side of the building. From where he stood, he could her shudder. His heart beating with the fury of a mad bull, he called out to her again.

"Helen, I want you to jump. I'll catch you."

"No, I can't."

The hysteria in her voice ripped at his insides. Her terror had her frozen against the wall, her precarious hold fragile at best. He stretched out his arms, his hands encouraging her down.

"Yes you can, sweetheart. I won't let anything happen to you."

She shook her head. Fear locked her in place. The drizzle falling from the sky had changed to an icy rain, and the sting of the drops pricked at her skin. Below her, she heard Sebastian's voice urging her to let go. She closed her eyes to let his calm voice soothe her. Glancing down once more, she saw him urging her to fall into his arms. The idea filled her with terror. She was almost at the end of the wall, if she jumped now, she risked injuring not only herself, but Sebastian as well.

Ignoring his voice, she moved forward. One step forward, then two, she inched her way toward the end of the wall. Her foot, raw with small cuts, slid over the rough ridge. A sharp protrusion of stone on the ledge bit into her sole, and she uttered a cry of pain. Instinct forced the foot off the tiny ledge and she struggled to retain her grip on the thin strip of rock above her head.

"For the love of God, Helen, trust me." The note of anguish in his voice tore at her heart.

Trust him. She pulled herself back into place against the wall and pressed her body against the roughly chiseled stone. The rough surface scraped every part of her body it found, and she closed her eyes against the tears. He wanted her to trust him.

How could she? When she'd offered him her heart, he'd refused it, wanting only to possess her physically. Below her, his voice broke through the turmoil twisting her heart and mind.

"Helen, please, darling, you have to trust me. I won't let anything happen to you, my love."

For the first time she heard the loving endearment. He'd never used the word love with her before. Could he have changed? She'd not opened his letters, and her grandfather had described him as a man lost. Clinging so tightly to the slender lifeline of the stone façade, she flinched at the rain pelting her cheeks. Chilled to the bone, her fingers were cramping from the tension of her perilous exercise.

"Helen, for God's sake, you have to jump."

Desperation echoed in his voice, and she tried to quell the shudder spiraling through her. She looked down once more, and her gaze locked with a pair of black eyes dark with fear.

A sudden roar of anger sounded behind her as Templeton's fury skimmed across her back like a hot iron. She turned her head back toward the window and in the process slipped again. This time both her feet left the thin ridge of stone, and her fingers dug as deep as possible into the rock façade. Her grasp loosened with each passing second, and she knew she wouldn't be able to hold on.

Templeton leaned out the window, his face twisted into a mask of fury and fear. The crazed expression in his eyes frightening her. Below, Sebastian's strong voice sounded the only note of reason in the terror streaking through her.

"It's all right, Helen. Let go, my love. I'll catch you. Don't be afraid. I'm here."

The soothing calm of his voice washed over her, and she realized she needed to trust him. She needed to let go of the wall and trust that he'd catch her. Swallowing her fear, she twisted her body to its side and flung herself outward, away from the wall.

The air and Templeton's wild cry of fury whistled around her ears as she fell. In the blink of an eye, she hit a solid wall of muscle. The air whooshed out of Sebastian in a loud grunt as he stumbled backward. Together they fell to the wet ground. Beneath them, the remnants of a lush summer lawn cushioned their fall.

Stunned, Helen didn't move. Beneath her hand, the steady beat of his heart reassured her. A strong hand cupped her cheek and warm lips pressed against her bruised forehead. Another wild roar of anger echoed above them.

"Damn you, Melton! I'll kill you for this."

The sound of the marquess cocking his pistol pulled a cry of fear from Helen's lips. In a split second, Sebastian rolled the two of them into the cover of a small clump of bushes. Gunfire ricocheted off the walls of the houses, and Helen shuddered at the sight of a bullet burying itself into the ground close to them.

"Can you run, sweetheart?" He saw her nod, then cautiously parted the branches of the bushes and looked up. Templeton no longer hovered in the window, and Sebastian knew the marquess was on his way downstairs. Scrambling to his feet, he pulled Helen upright. His hand gripping hers tightly, he raced toward the rear of the house with her in tow. They reached the stables in just a few strides, and he ignored the amazed stares of the stable hands. Shouts of anger echoed from the side of the house and he knew Templeton was too close for comfort. The faces of the stable hands took on a look of suspicion, but he didn't hesitate another second. Pulling Helen toward the rear of the stables, they raced into the mews.

Desperation turned to triumph as he saw the carriage near the end of the mews. He glanced down at Helen stunned by the pain glazing her features. His gaze swept down to the ground to see the light trail of blood she'd left behind.

"Sweet Jesus." Scooping her up into his arms, he ran toward the carriage. "Devin. Open the door, man. *Now.*"

The door swung open and he saw Devin leap down to the ground. Behind him, Templeton screamed with rage as Sebastian set Helen inside the coach and followed her. A moment later Devin was seated opposite them and the vehicle rocked forward as they made their escape.

Chapter 20

Sebastian held Helen close, his eyes drinking in the sweet shape of her face. Scratches covered her forehead and cheek, but she was more beautiful to him than when he'd first seen her at Chantrel's. Wrapped in his coat, he noted a tinge of pink beginning to fill her pale cheeks again. She'd fallen asleep in the carriage, and her eyes fluttered opened briefly, before they closed again.

As he climbed the steps to Melton House, he remembered the first time he'd brought her home. This time he'd see to it that she remained. Somehow, he'd convince her never to leave him. As he reached the front door, it opened and he strode into the foyer. For a split second, he surveyed the small crowd before his gaze settled on his aunt's worried features.

"Is the doctor here?"

"He's waiting in Helen's room." Lady Stewart's eyes took in Helen's white features as she answered.

"Good." With this abrupt response, he headed for the stairs. Behind him, vehement protests echoed through the foyer.

"Damn it Melton, the least you could do is tell me what's wrong with my granddaughter."

"I agree, nephew," Lady Stewart exclaimed. "The wee bairn's white as a ghost. And dear heaven, those scratches."

"She's exhausted, but she'll be fine." He didn't bother to look at them as he snapped out his reply. Reaching the second floor, he glanced behind him to find his family and Kettering following in his wake.

"I said I'd see to Helen's care," he growled. "When the doctor's finished his examination, I'll send the man down so he can give you a report."

"Sebastian?" The soft voice floated up to him, and he jerked his gaze down at Helen. Her weary expression eased his anger.

"It's all right, my love. You're home now."

"Home," she sighed before her eyes closed again. Pressing his lips to her brow, he carried her down the hall.

Inside her room, he paced the floor as the doctor tended to his charge. Once or twice Helen murmured a protest despite the dose of laudanum the doctor had forced down her throat. As the man finished his examination, Sebastian came to a halt at the foot of the bed.

"Well?"

"As you stated earlier, my lord, her injuries are primarily superficial and the wounds will heal nicely. If there is anything to be worried about it is her mental state."

"Her mental state?"

"She's obviously endured a frightening and traumatic experience. It's been a shock to her system, and she may experience irrational fears, nightmares or other manifestations related to her captivity."

"Thank you."

"I'll send someone to sit with her until morning. She should be fairly well rested by then."

"No. I'll stay with her."

"But, my lord, if she should wake during the night--"

"I'll stay with her." He glared at the older man. "And when you give your report to the masses downstairs. Ask Lord Morehouse to come up here."

"As you wish, my lord," the doctor said with a shrug of defeat.

Moments later, Sebastian breathed a sigh of relief as the doctor left the room. He moved to stand at the bedside, staring down at Helen's still features. She slept deeply. His hand resting on the headboard, he leaned over and brushed her brow with his lips. What would he have done if he'd lost her? Life would have no meaning. It would have been a pointless existence. It might still become meaningless if he wasn't able to convince her how much he loved her.

The hard rap on the door made him cross the room. Devin stood in the hallway, his face filled with concern as he bobbed his head in Helen's direction. "The doctor said she's doing well, but my question is, are you?"

"She's safe," Sebastian murmured as he glanced at her. "And that's all that matters to me at the moment. But there's some unfinished business--"

Devin raised his hand to interrupt him. "I've already taken care of everything. The moment we returned, I sent one of the men to fetch the Constable. The man's already been and gone. He's dispatching a group of officers to Templeton's house to arrest the man."

Grateful for his friend's actions, the news made the ache in his muscles ease as the tension holding his body rigid slowly dissipated. With a sharp nod, he glanced over his shoulder at Helen. "He was willing to kill her today to get to me, and I don't think the man's going to wait quietly for the police to pay him a visit."

"I agree. Winthrope and I have already discussed remaining here until Templeton's in custody." Devin said quietly. "I suggest that--"

"Sebastian, you need to come to the library," Louisa's cry echoed softly down the hall as she hurried toward them. "Constable McBride has returned. He insists on seeing you."

A wave of indecision engulfed him as he glanced back into the room at Helen's still figure. Louisa's gentle hand touched his arm as she showed him the small pistol she held. "I'll keep her safe until you return. The doctor said he's given her a great deal of laudanum, so she's not likely to wake for some time."

With one more look at the woman he loved, Sebastian nodded and with Devin on his heels, he hurried downstairs. As he entered the library, his gaze swept over Constable McBride for the first time. A short, stocky man with a piercing gaze, the constable was clearly disturbed by something. It was evident in the grim set of his mouth and by the way he rocked back and forth on his heels. Winthrope stood near the man, his brow furrowed in a look of deep concern.

"I take it you're Constable McBride." Sebastian offered his hand in greeting to the police officer as he stopped in front of the man.

"I am, my lord." The man gave him a sober nod as they shook hands. "I'm afraid I have some bad news. Miss Rivenall's uncle is dead."

Relief was the first thing he felt at the officer's words. Then as the man cleared his throat he realized there was something about Rivenall's death that had upset the constable.

"Where did you find him?"

"Templeton House, my lord. But it's not where so much that bothers me, but as to how the poor devil was murdered. He'd been eviscerated and his tongue cut out." The constable swallowed hard as he spoke, his hands gripping the brim of his bowler hat until his knuckles turned white from the pressure.

"Good God," Devin exclaimed as Winthrope uttered a similar phrase of shock.

Trying to take in the full significance of the man's words, Sebastian sent the man a fierce look. "And Templeton? Did you find Templeton?"

"No, my lord. The man was nowhere to be found in the house, and none of the staff know where he went." There was a distinct thread of alarm in the man's voice.

Eyeing the Constable carefully, the man's sickly pallor shot a bolt of fear through Sebastian. Something about the way Rivenall had been murdered made the officer afraid. The similarity of this murder compared to the ones in Whitechapel wasn't lost on him. McBride had to be thinking what he was thinking.

"Is it possible, Templeton and Jack the Ripper are the same man?" Sebastian's quiet question made the police officer blanch a pasty color. Swallowing hard, he shook his head.

"I don't know, my lord. There are similarities, but there are distinct differences as well. What I do know is that the carnage I saw tonight was the same as what was inflicted on the Kelley woman in Whitechapel."

"Christ Jesus," Sebastian muttered as his stomach roiled at the knowledge that Helen had been held prisoner by that monster.

Shoving his hand through his hair, he remembered the horror that had gripped him when Devin had described the woman murdered last night. That was nothing compared to what he was feeling now. Templeton had gone over the edge. Something had snapped in the man this afternoon when Helen had escaped him. The man was desperate, and desperate men were dangerous men. Piercing his thoughts was the sound of the constable's voice.

"My lord, I've made arrangements for two officers to patrol outside the house in the event the man tries to come here."

"Good," Sebastian said with a brusque nod. I'll let my staff know they're to cooperate fully with your men."

Not waiting for the man's reply he turned and strode to a cabinet on the library wall. "Madison."

His shout reverberated through the room as he threw open the solid doors to pull out a pistol and loaded it. As he did so, the butler hurried through the library doorway.

"Yes, my lord."

"Lord Templeton is Missing and possibly responsible for a man's death. Notify the staff that two police officers will be posted outside the house. They're to receive full cooperation. Daylight's almost gone, which makes it easier for the man to move about unseen, but if the marquess tries to enter this house, I want him stopped at all costs. Is that clear."

"I'll see to it at once, my lord." Even as he spoke, Madison was leaving the room.

"I'll be on my way then, Lord Melton." Across the room Constable McBride slapped his hat onto his head as he moved to follow the butler out of the room. "We'll catch him. I can promise you that."

With those last words, the police officer hurried from the room. Suddenly realizing that Lord Kettering wasn't in the room, Sebastian turned to Winthrope. "Where's your grandfather?"

"Lady Stewart and I convinced him to go home to rest, thank God," Winthrope said quietly as he crossed the floor to where Sebastian stood at the gun cabinet and extended his hand. "I'm a better shot than he is anyway."

Not hesitating, he offered Winthrope the loaded weapon then turned back to the cabinet. As he retrieved another pistol it was smoothly taken from his hand by Devin.

"Ah, I was wondering when you were going to return this to me. As I recall, I lost this in a wager to you."

A reluctant smile tugged the corner of Sebastian's mouth at his friend's attempt to lighten a dark moment. His hand reached out to squeeze the other man's shoulder. "Thank you, Devin."

"Wouldn't Miss it. Now I suggest you get back upstairs to your future Countess. Winthrope and I will handle things down here. And for God sakes, tell that sister of yours to stay out of the way."

"Louisa?"

"Yes, *Louisa*. I've never met a more willful or stubborn woman, perhaps with the exception of my mother. I can see why you've had trouble with her over the past year."

Sebastian eyed his friend carefully, but could only read annoyance in Devin's gaze. When they'd resolved the situation with Templeton, he'd have to take a keener interest in his sister's affairs. The sudden sound of a loud crash of glass filled the library.

"What the hell--" exclaimed Sebastian as he recognized the sound of crunching shards of glass echoing from the music room. Cursing beneath his breath, he raced out into the foyer to see Templeton emerge from the shadows of the music room. Without a second thought, he cocked and aimed his pistol at the man.

Blood dripped from the man's arms, chest and hands as Sebastian met the man's eyes. There was a wild, primitive look on the marquess's face as the two of them faced each other. As he took in the man's appearance, he noted the gun held tightly in Templeton's hand. Mad desperation glittered in the marquess' eyes, and he looked capable of anything. Holding his hand steady as he kept his weapon trained on the man, Sebastian stared into Templeton's bitter expression.

"You're far too impatient, Templeton, I would have opened the door for you," he said with sarcasm. "But now that you're here, I'm afraid you'll have to surrender your weapon."

Shaking off glass debris from his jacket, the marquess sent him a look of blazing hatred. "I've come for my bride, Melton."

"Bride? I wasn't aware you were the marrying sort, Templeton."

"I wasn't until I met Helen. She changed me."

"*Changed* you?" Sebastian scoffed. "You haven't changed.

You're still the same twisted, libertine you've always been. What you couldn't achieve by honorable means you want to take by force and murder. I find you contemptible."

"When Helen's my wife, I'll be the most honorable man you'll ever meet."

He could only stare at the marquess. The man was mad. How could he even think Helen would be willing to marry him? Had the bastard forgotten her desperate attempt to flee his prison? With a slow shake of his head, Sebastian kept his tone even.

"I'm sorry to disappoint you, but Helen isn't going to marry you. Now put the gun down and have a seat," Sebastian said as he gestured to a nearby chair against the foyer wall.

"She's mine. She would have been mine a long time ago, if you'd not interfered that night at Chantrel's." The marquess's voice climbed a notch, his eyes wild with hate as the gun in his hand slapped erratically against his leg.

"I did what was necessary to keep her out of your bed," Sebastian said coldly.

"And yet you had no problem taking her into your own bed, did you?"

The truth struck home, and Sebastian tightened his lips. "You know nothing about my relationship with Helen. Now drop the damn gun."

Templeton's eyes narrowed as he ignored the order for a third time. Glaring at Sebastian, the tic in the marquess's cheek jumped with increasing agitation. "Perhaps I know more than you think, Melton. Ask yourself this--does she love you? I seem to recall asking you that question once before. As I remember it, the lady in question effectively cut you off at the knees."

"Helen's feelings for me are none of your concern."

The question aroused a deep fear inside Sebastian. What if Templeton was right? What if Helen didn't love him? What would he do? Desperately, he struggled to hide the effect the marquess' words had on him. The deranged expression of triumph on the man's face told Sebastian he'd failed to do so.

"You're terrified I'm right, aren't you Melton." Bitter laughter poured out of the marquess. "You think you can hide that kind of fear? I can see it in your eyes. You're not sure of her."

"And I can see desperation in your eyes, or is it perhaps the realization that you've lost."

"Oh, I've not lost yet, Melton. Far from it."

"Perhaps you've not noticed, but believe I have the advantage here."

"Advantage?" Templeton cackled with cold laughter. "Do you really think you're in control? If so you're about to be disappointed given what I have in store for you."

"I'm tired of playing your games, Templeton. Put the gun down now and take a seat."

"What? And Miss all the fun? I'm quite certain John is just getting started with his little diversion." The marquess's grin was a mixture of malevolence and madness.

"Who the hell is John?" he snapped, frustrated by the marquess's twisted games.

"My driver," the Marquess said with a feral grin. "He's quite talented actually."

"I'm sure he is, but I don't care about your driver."

"Tch, tch, come now, Melton. I'm certain you're bound to be interested in the man." Templeton laughed. "Did I forget to mention his nickname is Jack?"

For a moment, Sebastian simply stared at the man as if the marquess had two heads. What was the man's purpose in discussing his driver? And exactly what was this John fellow's special talent. "Damn it, Templeton. Put the gun down, and--"

"Surely you're going to let me pay my respects to the dearly departed."

The words chilled Sebastian down to the bone as his brain instantly collected all the facts, but the conclusion was too staggering to fully comprehend in a brief instant. Rivenall was dead, killed in a manner similar to the Whitechapel murders, Templeton's driver went by the nickname of Jack and now the marquess was asking to pay his--

"Ah, at last the blind man can see." A maniacal laugh parted the marquess' lips. "If I can't have her, you won't either. Jack is quite handy with a knife as Rivenall found out."

"*Bloody hell.*" Sebastian didn't stop to think, he simply wheeled about to race from the room. Behind him, Templeton's wild laugh drifted toward him.

"Watch your back, Melton." Winthrope cried. A moment later, the other man slammed a hard shoulder into Sebastian's side, pushing him out of the way. Behind him, a pistol went off and Sebastian straightened to see Templeton crumple to the floor. With barely time to send Winthrope a quick look of gratitude, he pounded toward the stairs, his footsteps crashing against the foyer floor. From the stairs, he heard Louisa scream and another shot rent the air.

With a speed he didn't know he possessed, he took the steps two at a time with Devin right behind him. Reaching the landing, he charged toward Helen's room. Knuckles white as his hand gripped the doorframe, he whipped his body through the opening. Louisa was standing in the middle of the room, holding a small pistol. At her feet a man lay sprawled out on the floor, blood pouring out of the hole in his forehead and a long, knife still bright with blood. His heart in his mouth, he crossed the floor in two long strides to where Helen lay still sleeping under the heavy dose of laudanum. The soft sound of her breathing made him dig his fingers into the bed post as tension forced its way out of his body in a loud whoosh of air.

Louisa turned toward him, her face ashen with fear as Devin gently pulled the weapon she held out of her fingers. White-faced, her eyes met Sebastian's.

"I didn't let him near her, Sebastian. He …" Her voice died away as she shuddered at the memory and tears streamed down her face.

Immediately moving to her side, Sebastian engulfed her in a tight hug.

Having ensured the assailant was dead, Devin looked up at Louisa with a strange expression in his gaze. Quickly rising to his feet, he nodded at Louisa. "I'll see to her, and notify the police. You stay here with Helen."

As Devin guided Louisa out of the room with a gentle touch, Sebastian's eyes gaze flitted over the dead man on the floor. A guttural sound poured out of him, and he strode to the bed and gathered Helen up in his arms. Holding her close, he carried her out of the room and across the hall to his bed chamber.

Tenderness and love flowed through him as he tucked her beneath the covers of his bed. He'd come so close to losing the most important person in his life. Sinking down onto the mattress beside her, he lifted her cool hand to his mouth. He'd been a fool.

Why hadn't he realized how much he loved her? To think he might have lost her to Templeton and the madman Louisa had shot. Fear slithered down his spine. He might still lose her. The memory of the marquess taunting him with the possibility that Helen didn't care for him made him flinch. The sound of a knock on the open door pulled his head up with a jerk as his aunt crossed the threshold with a soft smile of relief.

"Constable McBride is downstairs and would like to take your statement," she said in a soft voice.

"Send him up here. I'm not leaving her alone any more tonight." He refused to leave her like he had earlier. If not for Louisa, she would have been dead.

Her hand patting his shoulder, Lady Stewart nodded. "Aye, I'll send the mon up."

The next hour passed in a blur as McBride took his statement along with everyone else in the household. For the first time, he learned that one of the policemen patrolling the house had been murdered by Templeton's driver, and one of his footmen had been seriously injured as the assailant had forced his way into the back of the house.

Several policemen from Whitechapel had come by as well to look at the assassin's body. Although the officers found traces of blood on the man's hands, and the knife he'd been carrying was viciously sharp, none of them were willing to state that the man was Jack the Ripper. But Sebastian didn't care about Templeton or the man who might be the monstrous Whitechapel monster. Helen was alive and that's all that mattered.

As he gave his statement to Constable McBride, his gaze continued to dart in her direction just to ensure she was still there. Still safe. Through it all, she didn't stir, the laudanum doing its work well. Silence eventually filled his room except for the soft, gentle breaths escaping her lips and his.

The last of the police officers gone, he took up residence in a chair close to the bed. From where he sat, he could watch her face for the first flicker of wakefulness on her part. He sank low in his seat and stretched out his legs for a long wait. If she'd managed to sleep through all the turmoil that had transpired in her room such a short time ago, she would no doubt sleep until sunrise.

Time seemed to pass slowly, and as he waited, he memorized every shadow and light of her face. If everyone, including the marquess, had recognized he was in love with Helen, why hadn't she realized it as well. God help him, perhaps she had. Was that why she'd returned his letters unopened? She didn't care for him? The thought stabbed at him mercilessly, twisting his insides with pain and anguish. She'd even told him that night on the terrace at the Barstow affair that she knew what was in the letters. He closed his eyes against the pain assaulting his heart. Quietly, he forced himself to shut the troubling thoughts out of his head. When Helen woke, he'd have his answer then.

* * * *

Sebastian shifted in the chair, the muscles in his back protesting as he realized he'd been asleep for some time. The soft rose of dawn drifted through the windows, and he stretched his body to shed the kinks it had acquired during his sleep. A swift glance in Helen's direction told him she still slept.

Sometime during the night, he'd shed the confinement of his jacket and tie. Now he tilted his neck from one side to the other as his shirt splayed open. His tread silent, he moved to stand at the window. One shoulder propped against the window sash, he folded his arms and stared down at the street below. Already the city was alive and moving to greet the day. But would it be a good day or would darkness take over his life for good.

"Sebastian?"

Fear held him frozen for a long moment. Slowly, he turned to see Helen sitting up in bed. She watched him with a cautious expression. Swallowing the dread threatening to overwhelm him, he put his hands behind his back. The old control returned to haunt him as he faced her.

"How are you feeling?"

"I have a slight headache, and I'm a little sore. But in truth, I feel quite rested."

"The doctor seemed to think you'd make a rapid recovery, although he did say that you should stay off your feet for a few days. It will be painful for you to walk for at least a week."

She nodded her understanding as an awkward silence fell between them. A man hanging from a gibbet could not have felt more pain than he did at this very moment.

"You--"

"I--" They both spoke at the same time and Sebastian let a small smile come to life on his lips. "You first."

Hesitation forced her to chew thoughtfully at her lip as a sigh escaped her. "You came for me."

"Did you think I wouldn't?"

"At first I … I thought you might, but when no one came, I … I decided to try and escape on my own."

"I would have come sooner, if I'd known where you were."

"You would?"

"Yes." He hesitated. "I'd do anything to protect you."

"Anything?"

The breathy, one word question punctured his steely control. Wheeling away from her, he stared out the window so he wouldn't see her pity as he bared his soul to her. "I would go to hell and back for you, Helen. From the first moment I kissed you, I knew I had to have you. At first, I thought it was lust, and I could accept that. But as time passed, I recognized that my feelings ran much deeper than I could ever imagine. I came to realize that without you life was meaningless, but I still wasn't able to put a name to it."

He paused for a moment, waiting for her to speak. When silence hung over him, he slowly turned. The pallor of her face forced him to inhale a deep breath. He was going to lose. She didn't love him. Still he had to try. He had to give up complete control and place his heart in her hands, whether she wanted him or not.

"That night in the carriage. I thought if I could make you

realize how much we needed each other, you'd come to see how much I cared for you. But I was a fool, I didn't speak the words that I felt. I failed to convince you that I wanted more from you than your body. I wanted the heart and soul of the woman I made love to that night."

"And yet you wanted us to live apart." There was a painful bitterness lying under her words. He closed his eyes for a brief moment before looking at the accusation darkening her face.

"I was an oaf. I should never have suggested such an arrangement. Then when you returned my letters, refused to see me, I …"

His courage failed him, and his voice trailed to a halt. The expression on her face seemed so unforgiving. He bent his head to avoid seeing her rejection.

"You what, Sebastian."

Hands clenched, he lifted his head and faced her with what little fortitude he still possessed. The ache in his belly surged up into his throat before receding back down to become a slow churning in his stomach.

"I gave up wanting to breathe. Every breath I take is dependant on you. It took me a long time, but I've finally come to understand that I can't control circumstances, people or events. I can only control what's in my heart, and I've given it to you. I love you, Helen. All I want is for you to be happy. Give me the chance to make you happy. I'm nothing without you."

She turned her head away from him, her profile strained and pale. He'd lost her. The expression on her face was all he needed to know that he'd lost the one woman he'd ever love. The knowledge nearly ripped his heart from his body. Wheeling back around to the window, his hands grasped the framework until his knuckles turned white. How was he going to survive without her?

"I can see by your face my proposal is unwanted," he muttered in a hoarse voice. "I'm sorry if I've made you uncomfortable, it was not my intent to do so."

Silence met his words, and he stared blindly out the window, seeing nothing beyond the barest glimmer of a reflection in the glass. Swallowing the tight knot in his throat, he knew he had to leave her, but it was the last thing he wanted to do.

"Sebastian." The musical sound of her voice called to him, but he refused to turn around. Pity wasn't something he wanted from her. "Sebastian, please look at me."

Slowly, he turned to face her, prepared for what he was certain would be her refusal to have anything more to do with him. The sight of her limping toward him propelled him forward to lift her up into his arms.

"What the devil are you doing up on your feet?" he growled as he carried her back to the bed. Laying her down on the mattress, he tried to pull back, but her arms wrapped around his neck and prevented him from rising. Hands braced on either side of her, his heart slammed into his chest as he looked into her green eyes. The embers glowing in her gaze took his breath away.

"I propose a test, my lord," she whispered.

"Test?" His voice was hoarse as he stared into her eyes, unable to look away.

"Make love to me." Dumbfounded, he stared down at her, unable to speak. He was dreaming. That sultry smile on her mouth was an illusion. Then the heat of her index finger singed its way over his mouth. "I promise you'll enjoy it, my love."

The endearment made him stiffen as he hovered above her. Had he heard her clearly? Shaking his head slightly, he watched her flick her tongue out to wet her rosy lips. The seductive gleam in her eyes told him it had been a deliberate action. With a deep growl, he lowered his head and captured her lips in a hard kiss.

Her response nearly undid him. Unprompted, her tongue teased his lips apart as she probed the inside of his mouth. Deepening the kiss, he drank in the sweet, hot taste of her, reviving himself with each dance of her provocative tongue. The mating duel they imitated with their mouths made him grow hard in an instant. God how he wanted her. He wanted to slide into the wet heat of her and have her body clenching tightly around him as he came inside her.

The erotic images flowing through his head pulled a deep groan from him as desire tugged persistently at his groin. Releasing her, he shot up into an upright position. She'd suffered so much in the past two days. How could he possibly ask her to satisfy his needs? Worst than that, it was quite possible she might not even realize what she was doing. The moment the fearful thought slashed through him, he pushed himself further away from her. Murmuring a protest, she slipped her hands through his open shirt. The tips of her fingers skimmed across his chest, before gliding downward to his trousers.

"I love you, Sebastian."

Her words whispered through air so softly he wasn't certain she'd actually said them. Dazed, he stared into her eyes. With a slight shake of his head, he closed his eyes then opened them to meet the love and desire burning in her gaze. As if aware of his doubts, her hand pressed warmly against the solid heartbeat in his chest.

"I love you, Sebastian." Husky and low, her voice caressed him like warm silk. "Please let me show you how much."

"Oh God, sweetheart," he groaned. "If you only knew how much I want to do as you ask."

Confidence and love sparkled in her eyes as she smiled. If he hadn't already been bewitched by her, he would have found her impossible to resist. He sucked in a quick breath as her hand slid down his chest before her fingers followed the line of hair that led down to his erection. With a light stroke, she rubbed her fingertips over him, before she started to undo his trousers.

A growl of frustration echoed from his throat as he rolled away from her to sit up on the edge of the bed. Hunched over, his fingers bit into the edge of the mattress as he struggled to control his desire. Damn it, she'd just been through a life and death ordeal. He couldn't just take her here and now. She need time to heal, but God, how he wanted her. From across his shoulder, the captivating sound of her voice danced in his ear.

"If you want me, then say yes." Amusement threaded through her words as she brushed her fingers across the tip of his ear as she smoothed his hair.

"You've been through so much, sweetheart. I couldn't bear to hurt you."

"I promise you, my love. I won't break."

In a tender caress, her hand slid down his arm until she reached his white knuckled grip on the bed. In silence, she gently pried one of his hands loose and raised it to her lips. Turning toward her, his eyes locked with hers and he swallowed hard.

Desire flared in the lovely green of her gaze, and he sat transfixed as she kissed the tips of each one of his fingers. Then she slowly took one finger into her mouth, her tongue swirling around it. The move drew a swift intake of air from Sebastian.

Bloody hell, she was learning far too quickly how much power she held over him. Worse yet, she seemed determined to have her own way. With a leisurely motion, she eased his finger from her mouth, dragging her tongue across his skin before licking her pink mouth in a display of erotic seduction.

"Undress for me," she said in a throaty voice that made his cock strain at his trousers.

Incapable of resisting her any longer, he slowly rose to his feet. Turning to face her, his gaze never left hers as he did as she commanded. Hunger narrowed her eyes as she watched him remove his clothing. The desire and love flaring in her gaze pleased him--excited him. She wanted him. Loved him. And he was going to make her as hot and needy as he was for her.

With deliberate movements, he slowly did as she commanded. Her gaze raked over him as he tossed aside the last of his clothing. The desire burning in her gaze was a blistering sun against his skin as he joined her on the bed. A warm hand gripped him and he jerked at the pleasure it gave him.

A seductive smile curved her mouth as her gaze met his. The awareness and knowledge he saw glowing there astonished him. She was incredible. In the next moment, she released him, and his body protested the withdrawal as one would an addictive drug. With the same deliberateness he'd just exhibited, she reached and slowly lifted her night gown.

Revealing her body with excruciating slowness, she tantalized him as she inched the fabric past her knee to a voluptuous thigh then upward until the sight of a triangular patch of wiry curls made his mouth go dry. As he stretched out his hand, he gently slid his finger through her curls to find the small button of her sex.

She was damp already, her desire heating her silky folds. Beneath his touch, she arched upward, but she didn't stop the seductive removal of her night gown. The delicate material skated ever so slowly over her stomach and up to her breasts. The moment the stiff peaks of her breasts appeared from beneath the material, he leaned forward and circled one nipple until a moan of pleasure escaped her.

The musky scent of her filled his nostrils as she writhed against his hand until he slid one finger up inside her and she exploded with hot, creamy passion. With a quick movement, she tugged the nightgown over her head. Immediately, his cock swelled and strained at the sight of her naked and supplicant before him. Throbbing with need, his body ached to plunge into her. No longer in control, desire exploded inside him. Heated passion blinded him to any other thoughts except his need for her as his mouth sought hers in a passionate kiss.

Eagerly she met his kisses, her tongue dueling with his. His hands slid over his skin, caressing, enticing and teasing her into an intense, white hot response of blinding passion. Imitating his touch, she stroked his body, her hands finding his erection. As her thumb rubbed across the tip of him, she slid her mouth across the edge of his jaw and down his throat.

"Sebastian, I want you." The sultry warmth of her voice caressed him like a hot summer breeze. "I want you inside me."

Lightly scraping her fingernail over the length of him, a warm satisfaction sailed through her as her touch tugged a low growl of delight from his throat. The ache between her thighs grew in intensity, its call demanding an answer. Strong warm fingers swirled around the nub of flesh inside her nether lips, and the familiar surge of liquid passion flowed between her thighs as she moaned again.

Dear lord, the man knew exactly what to do to make her body cry out for him with a desperation she'd never known before. She needed to feel him inside her, filling her, throbbing inside her, until they were one. The craving for him made her mouth go dry, and she uttered a soft moan of need.

"Oh God, Sebastian, please," she exclaimed with a soft, pleading cry. "Love me, love me now."

With a swift motion, he captured her lips again in a kiss that spoke of love and passion in one heady breath. She returned his caress with equal emotion. A deep groan escaped him as he rained feathery kisses across her cheek and down her throat

Sliding his hands across the soft lushness of her thighs, his cock brushed against her wiry curls. He needed her. Needed to be joined with her in a way that would bind her to him forever. He wanted to feel her clinging to him, surrounding him, clutching him as he plunged into her with loving strokes of passion.

It was at that moment, he knew she would always be his obsession. She would always hold his heart in her hands because he would never be able to leave her. Never would he give up this passion, this heat, this love. Impatient and demanding, she thrust her hips upward against his with a moan.

"For the love of God, Sebastian. Please."

Answering her plea, he plunged into her warm depths. The heat of her wrapped itself around him, burning him as he buried himself in her to the hilt. Her green eyes flashed with desire and love as he shuddered inside her. She was his. His to love. Slowly, he eased his way out of her only to slide back into her hot, creamy core. The hot friction of their joining gripped him as he increased the pace of their rhythmic dance. Desire claimed his senses as her slick, tight passage clutched at him with delicious abandon.

Lost in the most exquisite moment of passion he'd ever experienced, her spasms of need rippled over him as he plunged into her time and time again. The blissful cries mewling from her throat mixed with his cry of release he shot his seed inside her, his body exploding with an exaltation he'd never imagined. The intense pleasure of the moment had him gulping in deep breaths of air as she clenched around him in the aftershocks of her own delight.

His gaze found hers and he marveled at the love shining out of her emerald eyes. He had exposed his soul and won a lifetime of happiness. After a long moment, he rolled to one side. Rising up on his elbow, he brushed a gold curtain of hair off her shoulder and gently pressed his lips to her soft skin.

"How soon will you marry me, my love?"

A smile quirked the corners of her mouth as she lightly ran her fingertips over his face. "I suppose it had better be soon. We won't have opportunities like this again until after we're married."

"Where you concerned, sweetheart, I'll always make sure there are opportunities to show you how much you mean to me." He pulled her tight against him. A sober note filled his voice as the memories of the past three days assaulted him. "When I thought I'd lost you...."

"But you didn't." Her hand caressed his cheek as she gently kissed him.

Silence filled the room for a long time as they lay quietly in each other's arms. The world didn't exist outside of their room. All that mattered was that they were together. Snuggled against him, Helen sighed softly.

"What will happen to the marquess?" He quiet question made him tense. With a grimace he remembered she knew nothing of the previous night's events.

"He can't hurt you anymore."

A look of understanding filled her gaze. "He's dead?"

"Yes," he said tightly, then paused a moment. "And your uncle. He's dead as well."

Sadness darkened her eyes as she stared into space. "I don't suppose I'll ever understand why they did what they did."

"They were obsessed with you," he murmured as he pushed a gold curtain of hair back behind her bare shoulder. "Just like I am. I have been since the first time I saw you."

Her soft laughter broke the tension in the air. The light touch of her fingers across his chest warmed him. Love and obsession were what tied him to her. It would always be like this for him. She smiled as she kissed him gently.

"Are you certain you're obsessed with me? I thought you were simply irritated by the fact that I refused to listen to your dictates and that I turned your schedule upside down. And of course there's my, what did you call it ... ah yes, stubborn, willful behavior." The mischievous note in her voice made him laugh.

"I'll always be frustrated, madden and obsessed with you, Helen." He brushed a heated kiss against her lips then lifted his head to meet her loving gaze. "For me, you'll always be my love, my obsession."

With another deep kiss, he pulled her close, determined to prove his words in every way possible.

The End

Printed in the United States
62936LVS00004B/118-270

9 781586 088446